KU-326-950

burst from the container. She'd seen enough of them from her work as an archaeologist uncovering once-lost burial grounds within the Templo Mayor excavation site. Alma pinched the push-to-talk button between her thumb and index finger. "You mean apart from the urn I just found? Which looks to be full of someone's ashes."

The chief's laugh filtered through static and the call of crickets but didn't ease the knot of tension in her gut. "That would be Greta's husband. Last time I spoke with her at the diner, she told me they'd gotten into an argument, and she'd made him sleep outside. Kids must've picked him up. Thought it'd be fun to play hide-and-seek with her. Bring him back to the station if you can."

"Yes, sir." Was this what life was going to be like now? Nights filled with field trips into the bowels of Battle Mountain and something slimy stuck to her arm sleeve? As an archaeologist, she'd been an explorer, a truth finder. One of the best in her field. Only now, instead of uncovering ancient rituals, belongings and civilizations, she'd had to settle for—she picked up something vaguely familiar—whatever this was. Nausea churned in her gut at the smell, and she tossed the raccoon's corpse as far away as she could. Nearing gagging, Alma wiped her hand down her pants. She doubled over to clear her lungs of decomposition. "That was really gross."

There was nothing out here. Whoever had called 911 about the suspicious activity must've imagined it. She'd make one more pass. After that, she'd head back to the station with Greta's husband. Alma ran her flashlight over the bottom of the gulch.

Only this time, something reflected back.

Twenty, maybe thirty, feet away, a metallic surface brightened under her beam. A small piece of jewelry? She'd seen all kinds of stuff she wouldn't have expected, but nothing valuable. Silence descended. Thick and unknown. Her instincts warned her to run in the opposite direction—the same instincts that had braced her for her ex-husband's violence—but the logical part of her brain said the 911 call hadn't been a hoax. Someone had seen something, and she intended to find the truth.

Alma forced one foot in front of the other, her flashlight steady on… A locket? The shiny silver chain had been buried in the dirt, but the main component had been left exposed to the elements. The petite oval shape clouded under her touch. A clear stone had been set in the middle. A diamond. Wedging her thumbnail into the grooves along the side, she pried it open. To find a photo of an infant boy inside. No more than a few months old, if she had to guess. "Who do you belong to?"

She caught the small manufacturer stamp on the back, the kind that charged upward of a thousand dollars for an item like this. No. This wasn't a gift picked up from the local big-box store. It was special to the owner. So what was it doing all the way down here?

A moan pierced through the night.

Alma automatically fisted the locket to grip her flashlight harder. Straightening, she tried to swallow a familiar tendril of fear charging through her. "Battle Mountain police. Is someone out here?"

No answer. No movement.

She pocketed the locket in hopes of returning it back to its rightful owner along with Greta's missing hus-

Nichole Severn writes explosive romantic suspense with strong heroines, heroes who dare challenge them and a hell of a lot of guns. She resides with her very supportive and patient husband, as well as her demon spawn, in Utah. When she's not writing, she's constantly injuring herself running, rock climbing, practicing yoga and snowboarding. She loves hearing from readers through her website, www.nicholesevern.com, and on Facebook, @nicholesevern

Danica Winters is a multiple-award-winning, bestselling author who writes books that grip readers with their ability to drive emotion through suspense and occasionally a touch of magic. When she's not working, she can be found in the wilds of Montana, testing her patience while she tries to hone her skills at various crafts—quilting, pottery and painting are not her areas of expertise. She believes the cup is neither half-full nor half-empty, but it better be filled with wine. Visit her website at danicawinters.net

014448276 X

Also by Nichole Severn

The Line of Duty
Caught in the Crossfire
Grave Danger
Dead Giveaway
The Fugitive
The Witness
The Prosecutor
The Suspect
Rules in Blackmail
Rules in Rescue
Rules in Deceit
Rules in Defiance

Also by Danica Winters

A Loaded Question
Rescue Mission: Secret Child
A Judge's Secrets
K-9 Recovery
Lone Wolf Bounty Hunter
Hidden Truth
In His Sights
Her Assassin For Hire
Protective Operation
Ms Calculation
Mr Taken
Mr Serious

Discover more at millsandboon.co.uk

DEAD ON ARRIVAL

NICHOLE SEVERN

MONTANA WILDERNESS PURSUIT

DANICA WINTERS

MILLS & BOON

All rights reserved including the right of reproduction in whole or in part in any form. This edition is published by arrangement with Harlequin Enterprises ULC.

This is a work of fiction. Names, characters, places, locations and incidents are purely fictional and bear no relationship to any real life individuals, living or dead, or to any actual places, business establishments, locations, events or incidents. Any resemblance is entirely coincidental.

This book is sold subject to the condition that it shall not, by way of trade or otherwise, be lent, resold, hired out or otherwise circulated without the prior consent of the publisher in any form of binding or cover other than that in which it is published and without a similar condition including this condition being imposed on the subsequent purchaser.

® and ™ are trademarks owned and used by the trademark owner and/or its licensee. Trademarks marked with ® are registered with the United Kingdom Patent Office and/or the Office for Harmonisation in the Internal Market and in other countries.

First Published in Great Britain 2022
by Mills & Boon, an imprint of HarperCollins*Publishers* Ltd
1 London Bridge Street, London, SE1 9GF

www.harpercollins.co.uk

HarperCollins*Publishers*
1st Floor, Watermarque Building,
Ringsend Road, Dublin 4, Ireland

Dead on Arrival © 2022 Natascha Jaffa
Montana Wilderness Pursuit © 2022 Danica Winters

ISBN: 978-0-263-30358-2

0922

This book is produced from independently certified FSC™ paper to ensure responsible forest management.

For more information visit: www.harpercollins.co.uk/green

Printed and Bound in Spain using 100% Renewable electricity at CPI Black Print, Barcelona

DEAD ON ARRIVAL

NICHOLE SEVERN

I dedicate this book to all the readers
who let me kill them in my books.

Chapter One

This was not why she'd joined the Battle Mountain Police Department.

Reserve Officer Alma Majors leveraged her heel into the dirt, trying not to fall flat on her face down into the gulch. She clutched her flashlight in one hand and tried to balance her weight with the other extended. Dirt collapsed under her, and the world tilted on its axis.

She couldn't hold back the scream lodged in her chest. Pain ricocheted around her skull as stars blurred into white lines over and over. She hit the bottom of the gulch. Air sawed through her chest. Her official first day on the job, and she'd already made a fool out of herself. Sounded about right. "Damn it."

Aches stabbed through her joints as she fought against the weight of her Kevlar vest to sit up. Dirt coated the inside of her mouth and dove deep into her lungs. Hand over her mouth, she coughed the worst of it up. Her flashlight had ended up a few feet from her. The beam cut through the darkness and cast shadows across rocks and boulders. Craning her neck over her shoulder, she gauged she'd fallen about fifty feet down a near straight incline. She rocked onto her sore hip and stretched for the flashlight.

What the hell was she doing out here? A year ago, she'd been happily married, with dozens of stamps in her passport, dirt under her fingernails and a career on the verge of surpassing the queen of Mexican archaeology herself. Alma brushed dirt from her uniform. Now what did she have? A one-bedroom apartment, a part-time job as the world's smallest town's rookie cop and no idea what she was doing with her life. "Well, at least I got the dirt part down."

The call about suspicious activity at the gulch had come in thirty minutes before, but from as far as she could see, there was nothing down here but broken bottles—evidence humans had yet to figure out where their garbage should be disposed—and what looked like a photo album that had been stabbed through with a kitchen knife. She shoved to her feet, stretching her neck to ease the pain.

Her radio crackled from her vest. "How you doing out there, Majors? Find anything?"

Weston Ford, Battle Mountain's police chief and her boss for the foreseeable future. The sleepy town of less than a thousand residents didn't have much in the way of a police department, but the work Chief Ford had done this past year had made national news. He and his brother, the town's second reserve officer, had brought down not one but two serial killers in a span of months. When her world had ended, the former mining town had seemed like the safest place on earth. Until she'd decided to join the department.

Making her way around the boulders, she kicked into something ceramic and jarred the lid free. Dust band and unbuttoned the strap of her holster. The hairs on the back of her neck stood on end as she forced herself deeper into the gulch. Her pulse thudded hard behind her ears. "Hello?"

"Please," an unfamiliar voice said.

Alma locked onto an outstretched hand, fingernails clawed into the dirt. Every cell in her body protested as she followed the length of that hand farther up the woman's arm, to a section of red-crusted blond hair and then to hooded eyes. She collapsed beside the victim. Air crushed from her lungs as she reached for her radio. "Ma'am, my name is Officer Majors. Hang on. I'm calling for help."

She pinched the radio and opened the frequency. This wasn't an accident. This woman had been left at the bottom of the gulch to die. Why? "Chief Ford, I've got what looks like a 217. Assault with intent to murder. Please be advised, victim is conscious and speaking but in shock. I need an ambulance sent to my location. Now." Alma didn't dare move her, but the urge to comfort the woman had her setting one hand against the victim's shoulder. Blood seeped through Alma's fingers. "Ma'am, can you tell me your name?"

In a burst of desperation, the woman shot her hand out and latched strong fingers around Alma's arm. Hooded eyes widened as though she expected to see her attacker right in front of her. A lacerated lip split deeper as the woman pushed Alma back. "Run."

Alma landed on her rear, and the locket slipped from her pocket. The woman's gaze instantly homed in on the necklace, but where Alma had expected recognition, there was only peace. Acceptance even. "Ma'am, the ambulance is on its way. You're going to be okay.

Tell me about the locket. Is it yours?" She leaned forward. "Is this your baby?"

The flashlight beam registered the small tick at the corner of the woman's mouth. Smile lines softened as she rested her head to the ground, her gaze unfocused. "Tell them I'm sorry… I wasn't strong enough."

The victim's final exhale hit her as though she'd taken a punch straight to the gut. Tears burned in Alma's eyes as she stared at the colorless face of a woman she'd never met. Alma sat straighter, her heels digging into the dirt as sirens echoed through the darkness. It was too late. She'd been too late. Her first day on the job, and she'd let someone die.

A series of beeps reached Alma's ears. She checked her watch, but she hadn't set an alarm apart from the one that got her up in the mornings. The beeping wasn't coming from her. She centered her attention on the hint of a light beneath the victim's shirt. It was coming from the victim. Alma rocketed forward. She skimmed her fingers over the woman's stomach and tugged her blouse from her jeans.

Red light haloed around her as she exposed the source, and she froze. "No. No, no, no, no."

Twenty. Nineteen. The timer on the clock ticked off second by second.

The tendril of fear she'd carried all night contorted into outright fear. Alma shoved to her feet, the locket still in hand, and pumped her legs as hard as she could. Boulders and small rocks threatened to block her escape, but she couldn't stop. Cold air burned down her throat, pressure building in her chest. She'd lost count of how many seconds had passed. Too few. The urn she'd nearly tripped over mere minutes ago stood stark against the uneven landscape, and she scooped it up as fast as she could. Slamming her hand over the lid, she tried to keep Greta's husband inside as she raced up the incline.

Her boots lost grip in the loose dirt. She cascaded back down a few feet, and a sob escaped without her permission. She hadn't survived her husband to die here. Not like this. Not tonight.

The explosion reverberated through the ground a split second before the blast knocked her forward. The urn slipped from her arms as she face-planted in the dirt. Heat and pain seared along her spine, and the world caught fire.

HIS ENTIRE APARTMENT SHOOK.

Cree Gregson shot upright in bed. The nightstand lamp hit the floor as he threw back the damp sheets. Single blast of an aftershock. Not an earthquake. Sirens punctured through the hard thud of his heartbeat behind his right ear. Shoving to his feet, he collected his jeans and boots from the end of the bed and dressed as fast as his grogginess allowed. Reality chased back nightmares of fire and pain bit by bit. "That was an explosion."

He was still in Battle Mountain, a small former mining town, with nothing more to lose. A thousand residents, limited resources and charm coming out of every brick down Main Street. Cree parted the bedroom sliding glass door curtains overlooking a small patio facing Henson Street. Thick trees, family-owned businesses and pristine mountain ranges attracted all kinds of people keen on hiding from the world. It was the perfect place to escape the past…as long as it hadn't followed him from Loveland.

A Battle Mountain PD patrol car raced in front of his building, emergency strobes flaring. Hell, it was close to midnight. Something had happened, and his gut said it had to do with whatever had shaken his house. Cree grabbed his keys from the top of his dresser in the corner and charged straight through the one-bedroom apartment and down the hall until he reached the front door. He slammed it behind him in a hurry.

"Cree, is that you? What's going on?" The elderly woman in the apartment across the outdoor corridor peeked her head through the crack in her door. Confident she hadn't mistaken him for an intruder, she stepped out into the halo of her lit, front-door sconce. The frayed edges of her floral nightgown swayed under the burst of a breeze as she clutched her equally old and equally well-fed Siamese. Stark white hair kept in rollers brightened under the addition of his apartment lights. "Was that an earthquake?"

"Go back to bed, Mrs. Faris. I'll check it out. Okay?" His gaze wandered to the apartment on the other side of his, but there didn't seem to be any sign of distress from the woman he'd run into a handful of times the past few weeks. Alma. He didn't know much about her. In fact, he knew less about her than he did about Mrs. Faris in the same amount of time, but there was an old compulsion he hadn't been able to ignore that urged him to learn the source of the storm in Alma's eyes.

A compulsion he wouldn't follow.

"You be careful. Don't be sticking your nose in something dangerous, you got me?" Mrs. Faris secured her door behind her.

In seconds, his knees protested his rapid descent down the stairs to the first floor and into the parking lot. He hit the unlock button on the key fob and hauled himself behind the wheel of the pickup that had become more than a way to get from point A to point B over the past few months. He threw day-old fast-food bags into the back seat as the engine growled to life under his touch.

He wasn't law enforcement anymore. While he was still technically considered one of Larimer County's bomb techs, he'd left that life and his need to get to the truth behind when his last assignment had blown up in his face. Literally. He had no jurisdiction and no business getting involved, but here he was ripping out of the parking lot and barreling toward the sirens.

Darkness encroached along the single-lane road leading to the east side of town. Grip tight on the steering wheel, he considered any number of possibilities for an aftershock like the one he'd felt. Gas explosion, a gasoline eruption after a fatal vehicle accident, a bombing. The police would have everything under control. So why was he still racing toward the other side of town?

The answer—no matter how many times he tried to drown it—knotted tight in his gut. Because it wasn't a gas explosion. It wasn't the aftermath of a fatal car crash. Every cell in his body had become all too familiar with that kind of physical discharge, even from a distance.

A bomb.

Town stores pierced his peripheral vision and failed to hide the massive rise of cliffs just outside of the city limits. From what he'd learned from the visitors' center, Battle Mountain had once been a rising star in the world of coal and energy, but when the mining companies had bled every last resource from the mines, it had become nothing more than a dying limb. Most of the police force had become resigned to finding work elsewhere. Town residents lost jobs, lost their retirement and their dreams. All in the span of months. The only thing left going for a place like this was acting as a pit stop to better pastures on the other side of Ten Mile Range. That, and the newly constructed veteran rehabilitation center out at Whispering Pines Ranch.

A firefighter stepped in front of his truck.

Cree slammed on the brakes. The pickup slid along the curb before coming to a halt, and his heart shot into his throat. The emergency responder directed him to turn around, but he shoved the truck into Park instead. His boots hit the ground as he surveyed the controlled chaos of the scene. "Bloody hell."

Half a dozen fires burned along the edges of the gulch. A combination of firefighters and EMTs roamed through what was left of the debris littered across the desert landscape, but the focus seemed to be on one spot in particular. The point of the blast's origin? Instinct kicked him hard and had him stepping forward. "What happened here?"

"Sir, I'm going to need you to get back in your vehicle." The firefighter, dressed in full protective gear, motioned toward his truck. "This is an active crime scene and too dangerous for civilians."

"I'm not a civilian." He unpocketed his wallet and flashed the badge he'd tried to reject since turning his back on his former life, but there were just some things he couldn't escape. "Cree Gregson. Larimer County bomb squad."

"Of course. Sorry about that, Officer Gregson. We've already had residents start pushing the perimeter." The firefighter backed away. "You're looking for Chief Ford. He just arrived on scene. He's interviewing Officer Majors in the ambulance."

"No problem. I'll get the details from him. Thank you." Cree pocketed his wallet and headed for the single ambulance angled into the center of the street. Fire hoses roared over the orders and shouts coming from inside the gulch. From the look of it, the small canyon had been filled with all kinds of garbage even before whatever went off, but the perimeter of houses looked untouched other than a few shattered windows. Lucky break. In his experience, this could've been a lot worse.

The back door of the ambulance slammed shut, revealing a woman on the other side. Recognition flared, and Cree nearly missed his next step. Long, dark hair cascaded down her back, hiding a lean frame and Hispanic heritage he'd memorized the first time he'd set eyes on her. Bruises and scrapes interrupted smooth olive skin along the backs of her arms, right where the Battle Mountain PD uniform ended. His next-door neighbor was a cop. She hadn't stepped out of her apartment with curiosity after the blast because she'd been here. She swiped her brow with a white rag, coming away with blood, and Cree double-timed his approach. "Alma?"

Almond-shaped, brown eyes locked on his, then widened impossibly further. Full lips parted under a rushed exhale as she looked up at him. Tension visibly tightened along her dirt-smeared neck and shoulders.

She twisted to scan the rest of the scene as she fidgeted with the bloody rag between both hands. "Cree, what are you doing here?"

"You two know each other?" A beige, ten-gallon hat shadowed the police chief's face, but Cree had seen him around enough times to recognize Weston Ford. The man had reached legendary status in the short amount of time he'd taken over as chief, taking down two serial killers in the past few months to protect this town and its residents.

"Chief Ford, we haven't officially met. I'm Cree Gregson, Larimer County bomb squad." He extended his hand as he took position next to Alma. Visceral awareness had him memorizing the spread of injuries across her face and arms. Shallow lacerations and mostly dirt across her front torso and legs. She'd been front and center at the time of the blast, but her uniform and vest had obviously protected her against the brunt of the explosion. What the hell had she been doing here?

"A little out of your jurisdiction, aren't you, Gregson?" The chief shook his hand. "I've got Silverton sending me a team."

A humorless laugh escaped his control as he stepped back. "Yes, sir, and as I'm sure you'll learn when you call my CO, I haven't been active in about eight months, but the team you have coming from Silverton isn't here yet. I am. I'm happy to help anyway I can."

The weight of Alma's attention raised the hairs on the back of his neck, and he risked a glance in her direction. A mistake. His gut twisted hard as he followed the line of blood from her temple down the curve of her cheek, and he physically fought the urge to swipe it from her face. Seconds distorted into minutes, an hour, as the chaos around them dissipated. Until all that was left was that same storm he'd noted in her eyes the few times they'd met before.

A low jumble of words pierced through the ringing in his ears, and reality punched its way back into existence. The chief took a step into his vision. "Officer Majors has already given her statement. She responded to a disturbance call here at the bottom of the gulch where she found a woman strapped with the device. As of right now, we have no way of identifying who the victim was or what she was doing here. Do you think you'll be able to give us something to work with?"

Alma ducked her chin, effectively breaking the spell she'd cast with a single look, and the constriction in his chest eased. Her hair fell in a long waterfall over her shoulder, and he caught a glimpse of evidence still clinging to her uniform.

"I'll need to take a look at the scene before I can verify Officer Majors's statement. Until then, you said you have no way of identifying the victim." Cree closed the distance between him and Alma, drawing her attention upward. "You're wrong." Ducking into the ambulance door, he tugged a latex glove from the nearest box and snapped it into place.

"What are you doing?" She flinched as he reached for her, her hand cutting to her sidearm. Alarm filtered across her expression as she glanced at Chief Ford then back to him, and Cree hesitated.

"I'm sorry to be the one to tell you this, but you've got a bit of victim on you." He nodded at the blackened curve of calcium as he took a step back to give her the space she obviously needed. "Or rather, stuck in you. That's a piece of bone shard in your shoulder."

Chapter Two

She'd nearly drawn her weapon.

It had been an automatic reaction, the flinch, the bracing against a possible threat. She hadn't meant to reach for the gun holstered at her hip, but when Cree had broken into her personal space, she hadn't seen any other option in the moment. Chief Ford hadn't seemed to notice, but Cree had. She'd noted it in the way his gaze had lowered to her hand, how he'd increased his distance between them, and it was then she felt that bone-jarring pity that came with her truth.

Embarrassment heated Alma's neck and face as she pulled her hair up and out of the way. The physical awareness of her next-door neighbor refused to let up. Even in the middle of a crime scene, she'd noted the perfect symmetry of his facial features, the exact shade of forest green in his eyes, how he double-tied his bootlaces. Of course, she'd trained to take note of minor details, but this…this was something else. "You never mentioned you were law enforcement."

"To be fair, neither did you." Cree folded his arms across his chest, his weight leveraged against the back of the ambulance door. "How long have you been on the force?"

Alma rolled her lips between her teeth and bit down. "Tonight was my first shift."

"Hell of a way to get on-the-job experience." He straightened to his full height, somewhere around six-two, maybe six-three. Valleys and peaks of muscle flexed and receded under his every direction, and a slow burn of appreciation carved through her. "I'm glad you're okay."

Sincerity drove through her defenses and tried to pry up the armor she'd girded over the past few years, but she'd been deceived by all the right people before. She wasn't going to give anyone else the chance to get under her skin. "You said you're with the bomb squad. Shouldn't you be down there looking for pieces of the device instead of making sure this guy uses the right kind of suture for my stitches?"

"It'll take days to collect all the bits and pieces," he said. "I'd rather hear your account firsthand."

"Okay, Officer Majors. This might sting." The EMT who'd seen to her minor cuts and bruises positioned one hand against her shoulder blade and extracted the bone shard with the other. "Got it." He preserved the bone shard inside an evidence bag and handed it to her. "We'll get you cleaned up once CSU has had a chance to collect any other evidence from your clothes and hair."

"Thank you." She focused on the rounds Chief Ford made through the scene as a shot of pain arced through her shoulder, but Alma held her expression. She'd been through worse. She'd survived worse. Although she hadn't been required to thread one arm out of her top and expose her sports bra for the entire town to see while she was stitched up in the middle of what looked like a war zone. That would normally happen behind the emergency room curtain, but she had to admit the urge to hide had faded over the past few minutes. She wasn't sure why. As much as she hated to face it, Cree was involved now. "All right, Officer Gregson. What do you want to know?"

"Cree." He centered himself in front of her. The fluorescent lights from inside the ambulance accentuated the ridges between his eyebrows and the deep recesses of his biceps. In another life, he might've been handsome. Now he just looked weathered. "Tell me what you remember about the device."

"Not much. I only got a look at it for a few seconds before I ran as fast as I could." In the few times they'd met in the corridor outside of their apartments, she'd kept the upper hand. Given as little information as possible while mining for details about the people around her. Couldn't be too careful. Mrs. Faris, for example, kept to a very strict routine Monday through Friday that consisted of walking her overweight Siamese on a leash each morning, followed up by locking herself out of her apartment directly after. Within the first week of moving in, Alma had resigned to making a duplicate key and hiding it underneath the loose knocker of the elderly woman's front door.

As for Cree… Well, she'd found herself learning a lot more about him than anyone else when she wasn't required to put in face time at Whispering Pines Ranch. How he took his coffee—black, one cream, one sugar at the diner—how he tended to wear the same pair of jeans with the stain on the right shin most of the week, and how much time he dedicated to his physical fitness at six every morning. No television, from what she'd been able to hear through their thin shared wall. Which left her wondering what a man like him did in his spare time. And why he'd come to Battle Mountain in the first place.

"Anything that stood out?" he asked.

She closed her eyes to cut her curiosity about him short. She hadn't left one relationship to immediately fall into another, and she sure as hell wasn't about to forget why she'd asked Easton Ford to train her to become a reserve officer for this town. "It had a rolling countdown. It looked like some kind of computer motherboard with an LED screen attached. There were coiling wires leading from it to a brick of white clay." She opened her eyes, steeling herself against his study. "It was set to detonate a couple minutes after I got there. It looked as though the device had been sutured into her midsection. The woman… She was almost dead, left there like garbage."

"You're lucky to be alive," Cree said.

She tightened her grip around the small shard of bone safely housed in the evidence bag. The crime scene unit would ask her for her clothing as soon as they were finished with the main scene, but for the time being, she wasn't going anywhere. The victim. Air crushed from her lungs, and the images she'd tried to block out flooded back. An earthquake of emotion pounded through her, one aftershock after the other. Tremors rocked through her until the pressure behind her sternum reached its peak. The shock of what had happened had already started wearing thin. "She told me to run."

"Hey." Cree crouched in front of her, so close. Too close, but at the same time not nearly close enough to keep her from shattering right here in the middle of the scene. He clamped his hands on either side of the rig's bumper, careful not to touch her. "Alma, I need you to look at me. Take a deep breath through your nose and let it out through your mouth." He notched his chin higher to level his gaze with hers, and the world stopped trying to tilt on its axis. For now. "This is not your fault. You know that. Chief Ford knows that. You responded to a call, and there was nothing you could've done differently. You understand me?"

She tried to follow his command, but her lungs wouldn't fill. Darkness filtered into the edges of her vision. What kind of police officer was she? She should be better than this, stronger than this. Sweat built along her hairline, her skin clammy. "She was still alive. I could've—"

"No. Because if you'd tried to get her out of there, you would've been caught in that explosion, too." His words failed to unwind the knot of guilt tightening in her stomach, but his voice kept her grounded. Gave her something to focus on other than the aimlessness inside. "Your brain is processing a trauma. I know this is hard, but all of the pieces will come back to you. Is there anything else you remember that didn't end up in your statement?"

She pressed her fingers into the ambulance bumper, one after the other in a repeating pattern. An old habit she'd used in the minutes before her ex-husband had stepped through the door each night. Her hand drifted to her cargo pant pocket, and she drove it inside. The thin chain threatened to snap under her grip, but she'd never let anything happen to the keepsake she'd picked up beside the victim. "I found this a few feet from her body. It's what drew my attention to her." She tugged the item free and offered it to him.

Cree met her halfway, and she dropped the necklace into his palm. Confusion warped his handsome expression. "A locket?"

"I think it's hers." The image inside had burned itself into the recesses of her mind, and an urgency she couldn't describe took hold. One she hadn't felt in a long time. "If the shard of bone isn't enough to identify the victim, do you think this will help?"

He coiled the necklace into his palm, holding it between them as he stood. "That depends. You can turn it over to the forensics lab to see if there are any viable prints other than yours or epithelial cells between the chain links, but it's a long shot. Until then your best bet is the bone shard and checking missing person reports."

Her best bet. Not theirs.

"Battle Mountain doesn't have a forensics lab. It'll have to go to Unified Forensics in Denver, which will take at least a week to run DNA." She took back the locket, the pad of her middle finger trailing along the main crease in his palm, and her heart jerked in her chest. "You offered your help to the chief back there until the Silverton team arrives. I'm guessing that expertise will be limited to the device once techs collect all the pieces."

The low vibration of heavy tires on asphalt combined with the slam of truck doors pulled his attention down the road. Two officers hauled equipment from the back of their vehicle, both sporting BOMB SQUAD windbreakers. "Actually, it looks like that's my cue. Like he said, I'm out of my jurisdiction. I'll fill the Silverton team in on the device you described and potential starting points of component suppliers. Otherwise, I'm done here."

"Right." Alma shoved to her feet, offering her hand. Raw nerves protested the action, but if she was going to move on with her life—to get back to being the person she used to be—she had to push herself out of her comfort zone. "Well, it was nice to officially meet you, Officer—" She caught herself. "Cree. I'm sure I'll see you around the apartment complex once this investigation is concluded."

"Probably sooner if Mrs. Faris locks herself out again." Cree shook her hand, calluses catching against the skin of her torn-up palms, and the sensation wasn't…unpleasant. He pointed behind her with his free hand. "I do have one more question for you, though. Is that an urn behind you?"

IN THE WORLD of 24/7, when the sun started breaking over the horizon, Greta's on Main seemed to be the only place in town to get a decent meal.

Black-and-white tiled flooring expanded the length of the entire diner, the red pleather seats and barstools reminiscent of the old days. Ancient recruitment posters from the mining companies peeled right along with oil-spattered paint above a border of matching floor tile. In a town like Battle Mountain, it was easy to get caught up in routine. Hell, Cree bet most of the customers already taking their seats at the crack of dawn had been showing up on the regular. It wasn't a matter of what they were going to do with their days. It was more like what were they going to order at the diner.

Cree slid onto the end barstool and pointed to the steaming pot of fresh coffee behind the counter as

Greta Coburn herself closed the distance between them. He flipped the upside coffee mug in front of him straight up. "Coffee, please. Black with cream. Oh, and I've got something for you." He hauled the urn he'd taken off Alma's hands onto the Formica surface. "Officer Majors found your husband at the bottom of the gulch."

"Serves him right having to spend last night outside." Waist-length gray hair practically floated around Greta's thin shoulders as she tucked a notebook and pen into her apron and hauled the urn against her hip. "I told him what would happen if he watched our show without me, but the man never listens." Carefully manicured pink fingernails highlighted weathered hazelnut skin and offset the grunginess of the diner she'd dedicated her life to running since 1961. She set her husband's remains near the cash register, then shuffled toward the coffeepot and filled his mug. "What can I get you, boy?"

He studied the single-page, laminated menu that had seen better days. "What's good?"

"Go for the chipped beef," a familiar voice said from behind. "It's a town favorite." Alma stepped into his peripheral vision as she took the barstool beside him. The patches of blood he'd noted at the scene had been washed clean, and it looked as though she'd gotten the chance to change into something not covered in dirt and explosive residue. "I'll have the same, Greta. Coffee, too. Thank you."

Greta filled her mug, then mumbled her way back into the kitchen.

Cree stared straight ahead as he took his first sip of coffee. He should've known the risk of getting involved in a local case, but he couldn't deny the relief forging through him at seeing her stand on her own two feet. "Didn't expect you here." Whatever had happened in that gulch could've ended with two bodies instead of the one. He settled his coffee on the counter. "I already know what you're going to say. You can save your breath."

"You're giving yourself too much credit." Alma shifted herself on the barstool, resurrecting a hint of fresh soap and some kind of floral shampoo. Her hair was curlier than he remembered from the scene. Still drying from the look of it. The waves softened her features, but there wasn't anything that could take away from her overall beauty, even the nasty gash across her temple. She took a sip from her own mug and sighed distinct pleasure. "I'm just here for the chipped beef, like most of the people in this town. It's actually the only edible item on the menu. I think Greta stopped caring if people liked her food a long time ago, but it's the one thing her husband would eat at the end."

"You're a regular," he said.

"Born and raised. My parents brought me here every morning before school, all the way up through college. I can't tell you how many cups of Greta's coffee got me through my graduate program. Even after they decided to retire in warmer climates a couple years ago, I can't seem to stop myself. And after my divorce, I couldn't see myself leaving. Greta's has a way of working under your skin like that. Becomes who you are, just like this town." She nodded toward Greta and cleared a spot for her plate as the old diner owner settled what looked like a half-hearted attempt at biscuits and gravy in front of them. "Thanks, Greta."

"Whatever." Greta shuffled onto another customer.

"If I'm being honest, I think she and I are on our way to being best friends." He tried to pick out a single identifiable ingredient as he studied the mess across his plate. "What the hell am I looking at?"

Alma's laugh pierced through the confusion closing in and drove up under his rib cage. "Squares of top sirloin over white toast and mixed with gravy. It's a mixture of hot oil, flour and milk. The meat has a spicy kick that overwhelms the blandness of the gravy, but most people add salt and pepper for some taste. Go on. I promise you won't regret it."

"I'm going to trust you on that." He unwrapped his silverware from the napkin to his right and sliced through a thick slab of meat. Spearing a bite, he grated the tines of his fork between his teeth. Hell, she was right. The kick of the meat, combined with the flavorless gravy, combined to make one hell of a heavy and rich breakfast. "The toast isn't bad."

Her smile nearly shocked the life out of him as she took a bite from her plate. They ate in silence for a few minutes, switching off between spicy meat slop and coffee.

"You're divorced." He hadn't expected that, but he'd seen plenty of his colleagues' marriages crumble to ashes because of the pressures of the job. Late nights. Early mornings. Obsession with certain cases. Then again, Alma had told him last night had been her first shift. "I'm sorry to hear that."

Her shoulders stiffened, and she pressed the back of her hand against her mouth to stop the humorless laugh. In vain. "You're assuming he was the one who ended it." She kept her gaze on her own breakfast for a

series of breaths, and Cree could practically feel the ca-
maraderie they'd built at the scene icing between them.

He shook his head and sat back away from his near-
empty plate. His chest tightened. Wiping his mouth
with the napkin, he crumpled it in his hand as guilt
raged. She'd reached for her weapon when he'd pointed
out the bone shard stuck in the back of her shoulder.
She'd tried to back away. At the time, he'd justified her
actions because most people—trained or not—tended
to suffer some kind of trauma after an explosion like
that. But what if it had been something more? What
if it had been a learned reflex? "I'm sorry. I didn't
meant to pry. It's none of my business, and I shouldn't
have asked."

"It's not something I like to talk about." Long fingers coiled round her fork, and Alma seemed to focus
all of her attention on taking her next bite.

"Right. Then it's probably a good idea if I remove
my foot from my mouth elsewhere." He raised his hand
to signal Greta for the check and pulled his wallet from
his jeans.

"The Silverton bomb squad is still processing the
scene. So far they've got enough pieces to start reconstructing the device that had been strapped to that
woman." Her voice deadpanned. "Seems they're more
interested in putting it back together than finding out
who the victim was it killed."

"You're right. I can tell you from experience, they
are. As soon as they can trace the components, they'll
have a better idea of who built it." He tossed a few
bills onto the counter and stood. "You said last night
was your first shift, which means you haven't worked
a homicide investigation before. The only way you're

going to be able to identify the woman at the bottom of that gulch is working backward."

"You're saying if the bomb squad identifies where the device's components came from, they can determine who built it, then who would've wanted the victim dead," she said. "But what about the victim's family? What if it takes days, if not weeks, for the bomb squad to reassemble the device, to track each component and determine who designed it? Do they just get to suffer not knowing what happened to their mother or wife or sister?"

Frustration bled from her every pore, and Cree gripped the edge of the counter. That same desperation to do the right thing had controlled him. Right up until the clock on his last bomb defusal hit zero. An all-too-familiar flash of pain burned down his legs and across his chest, and he took his seat. Alma hadn't come to the diner out of some routine she couldn't shake. She'd come for a lead. "You've already been through the missing person reports."

Had she even taken a break since he'd left her at the scene? He'd been so caught up in the larger details of her features he hadn't noticed the traces of exhaustion in her eyes and the sluggishness in her body language.

"No one fitting her description has been reported missing in the past two months." She ducked her head, her food forgotten. "I tried pulling prints from the locket I found, but you were right. There were no usable markers to go off, and the bone shard the EMT pulled out of me will take weeks to process at the lab. Right now, I have nothing but a photo, and who knows how old it is. There's a baby out there with a missing mother, and there's nothing I can do about it until the bomb squad or the lab uncover a lead." She craned her gaze to meet his. "You have more experience with cases like this, Cree. I know this investigation is out of your jurisdiction, but I need your help. Please. Just tell me where to go from here, and I promise I won't drag you deeper than I already have."

Understanding seized his next breath. He hadn't come to Battle Mountain to get involved in a case. In fact, he'd run from Larimer County because of how his last one had ended, but his gut told him whoever had strapped that device to the victim had done so to destroy evidence of her identity. They didn't want her found, and the more Alma pushed to solve that mystery, the more danger the rookie would find herself. He leaned back on the barstool. Acceptance wedged itself in his joints despite his stern promise not to get involved with the people of this town for their own benefit. Then again, Alma wasn't just people. She was a puzzle all on her own his training urged him to solve. "Pay for your food. We're going on a field trip."

Chapter Three

Galaxy Electronics wasn't anything out of the ordinary. The narrow aisles and dusty shelves had been a reliable escape for her once upon a time. Before life had gotten so messy. Alma swung open the heavy glass door leading inside and immediately sucked in a thin veil of dry rot and dust. The bell over the door announced their arrival. "You think whoever made the bomb might've gotten the components here?"

"It's not much to go on, but most locals shop local, even when premeditating to commit a crime." Cree kept close on her heels as she scanned the disorganized masses of cables, wiring and computer parts. "Galaxy is the only electronics store in town. It's as good a place to start as any."

Her boots skidded against built-up debris across the cement floor, and Alma was nearly taken back to the long hours she'd spent in this very store reassembling a cuckoo clock for Mr. Thorp's wife. She'd always been good with her hands, and the store's owner hadn't a clue how to put the poor thing back together. As far as she'd been able to tell from research, the clock had been an original. Older than her. It was in the shadows of these dusty shelves that she'd found her penchant for the past, for digging through history, and trying to make sense of it in the modern world. "Most of the computer motherboards are in this aisle here."

The soft sound of footsteps filtered through the space, and a smile tugged at her mouth as she recognized her former employer. "Mr. Thorp. You probably don't remember me, but—"

"Dr. Alma Ortega, of course I remember you." Thin, papery skin enveloped both of her hands as he clasped her gently. The curve through his spine had gotten the best of him over the years, evidenced by how much… shorter he seemed to be than she remembered. The receding hairline she'd noted all those years ago was gone now with little evidence the seventy-year-old electrical engineer still had the ability to grow anything but white tuffs. "That damn clock is still waking me up every hour, but my wife wouldn't have it any other way."

"I'm so glad I could help her hold on to her wedding gift a bit longer," she said. "I know how much it meant to her."

His weak smile shook under his notice of the firearm at her hip and the badge clipped on the other side of her belt. "You're a police officer now?" His disbelief combined with the acid in her stomach, and she swallowed the grief charging up her throat. "What happened to archaeology like you dreamed?"

"That's a story for another day." She angled her upper body to face Cree, all too aware of him behind her. She tugged a crude drawing of the device she'd seen before detonation and unfolded the paper. "Mr. Thorp, this is a friend of mine. Cree Gregson. We're here because there was a bomb that exploded in the gulch on the east side of town last night. Unfortunately, there was a woman who was caught in the blast. I got a look at the device before it went off, and I'm hoping you might be able to remember if anyone was in here recently to buy some of the components."

She handed him the drawing.

Shock parted the old man's thin mouth and jarred the thick protrusion of skin underneath his chin. Age spots darkened in sharp contrast to Mr. Thorp's brilliant blue eyes, not just in color but lividity. He fumbled for his glasses by sweeping his hand down the front of his button-down shirt pocket, then raised them to what was left of his hair. Centering the frames over his nose, the proprietor took the paper she offered and gave it a once-over. His balance waned as he backed toward a stool positioned under his old workbench nearby. "Your drawing skills have obviously transferred with your career change. This here looks like a run-of-the-mill circuit board. You can find them anywhere. Heck, you can find two hundred in this store alone. They're everywhere. Laptops, medical devices, home appliances and such. Even those touch-screen things people are carrying around now days. I've been recycling people's old stuff for years now and breaking them up for parts. What makes you think whoever built this bought it here?"

"Yours is the only electronics store in Battle Mountain." Cree maneuvered to her side, his bare arm brushing against hers. "In my experience, bomb builders shop local. Someplace they're familiar with and know they can get what they need."

Mr. Thorp shook his head as he hauled himself off the stool. An exasperated groan followed suit. "I can pull receipts for the past couple of months, but I'm not sure it'd help. I may be getting old, but I remember every part and cable I sell. No one has purchased this size circuit board for a while."

"Is there anyone else who works here with you?" Alma offered her hand for balance as Mr. Thorp trudged to the back of the shop. "Someone you might've hired to help with the long hours or inventory?"

"Not since you up and left for graduate school, young lady." A low laugh accompanied Mr. Thorp's shuffle to the outdated Sanyo ECR-240 cash register he'd kept from the eighties. "No one in this town is interested in learning the way things work anymore. They're too impatient. When something breaks, they just buy new and move on with their lives. Don't even bother trying to figure it out themselves." He pulled a beaten shoebox that she knew still contained receipts from under the counter and offered it to her, the drawing still in hand. "You were something, kid. If you hadn't gone off to school, you'd be running this place yourself, and I'd be on a beach, as far as I could get from the damn cuckoo clock."

Alma couldn't hide her smile. The sincerity behind his words brought out a nostalgia she hadn't let herself think about in a long time. The staleness in the air worked deep under her skin and into her lungs, calling on better days. Happier days. She'd been a teenager when she'd worked here. She'd taken apart and reassembled almost every device she could get her hands on, but after a while, even she had needed to escape the small-town suffocation. The whole world had been waiting for her, and she'd taken it. For a while. In the end, though, she'd known she'd end up right back here. Where it was safe, familiar. She hefted the box higher.

"Do you mind if we borrow these for a couple of days as well as any security footage you might have?"

"No problem. The tapes are in the back. You can grab them before you go." A gruffness that hadn't been in Mr. Thorp's voice registered as he used the counter for balance. "As for the receipts, I don't have to do my taxes until the end of the year. Then it's my accountant's problem." He pointed at Cree with the drawing. "You said you had experience with this kind of thing. What is it you do?"

Cree straightened a bit taller, his eyes cutting to the dust-bunny-coated floor. He shifted his weight between both feet and set a coil of red wire back on its shelf. The same kind of wire she'd drawn from memory in that sketch? "Bomb squad. Larimer County for the past decade. Explosive Ordnance Disposal before that."

"Ah, army man. I thought so." Mr. Thorp notched his chin higher, crossing his varicose-veined arms over a broad chest. "Where abouts?"

"Camp Bondsteel. Kosovo." Cree leveled dark green eyes on her, as though he hadn't meant for that detail to slip, but there really was nothing he could hide from Mr. Thorp. The old man had the eyes of an eagle and the nose of a bloodhound when he caught on to something that interested him. It was one of the things that had made him such a great electrical engineer. The patience. "The 720th."

"Ah, cleaning up the mess left behind, were you? Hard work." Mr. Thorp nodded. "But I guess those mines weren't going to take care of themselves."

"You served?" Interest flickered in Cree's eyes, and for the briefest of moments, Alma swore that same interest had centered on her while the EMT had been removing a shard of a person from her shoulder.

"Vietnam." Mr. Thorp unbuttoned the sleeve of his shirt to show off the intricate but faded tattoo underneath. "20th Engineer Brigade."

Cree saluted, standing at full attention, and the warmth in her chest spread. "Thank you for your service, sir, and for your help with the device. If you don't mind, I'll grab those security tapes from the back."

"Straight back, son. Can't miss 'em." The ancient store owner pushed himself to his feet and slowly closed the distance between him and Alma. He offered her the drawing back as Cree disappeared into the employees-only section of the small shop. "I like him."

"He's something else, for sure. We'll have your receipts back to you in no time." She set her free hand over Mr. Thorp's wrist. "If your accountant gives you any trouble, send him my way."

He handed off the drawing. "I'll keep an eye out for any of these other components. You said you got a look at the device. You were there when it went off?"

"Yes." She swallowed remembered panic before the countdown had hit zero and pulled her shoulders back. "But I'm fine. I made out. Not everyone who was there can say the same."

"This work you do now… Are you sure about this? Because I wasn't kidding before. I die, this place is yours. You're the only one I trust to know what to do with all this crap." His smile wavered with effort and then was quickly replaced with concern. "You worked so hard to accomplish your dreams. Maliya and I never had children. You and this place were all we had. We are both so proud of you. We just want to know you're happy."

Alma forced a smile as her eyes threatened to burn with tears. The weight of her weapon demanded attention from her hip, a heavy reminder of why she'd left her life behind. "This is for the best."

Heavy footfalls penetrated the bubble she and Mr. Thorp had built apart from reality, and Alma zeroed in on Cree racing to the front of the store.

"We need to leave. Now!" He threaded his hand between her rib cage and arm and thrust her toward the entrance. Cree ducked in front of Mr. Thorp and hauled the old man over his shoulder. "Go!"

"What's going on?" She shoved through the dirt-caked glass door and out onto Main Street, Cree close on her heels. The muscles down the backs of her thighs burned as he raced ahead of her into the street and set Mr. Thorp behind a parked vehicle on the other side. She followed suit, protecting her former employer with her body as much as she could.

Cree raced around the street side of the car and swung his arms wide as he directed residents away from the building. "Get back! Get out of here! It's going to—"

Fire and heat exploded outward in a cloud of black smoke and deafening rage.

In an instant, Galaxy Electronics was gone.

THE SCARS ALONG his back burned in memory.

Only this time a device had detonated, he'd walked away without a scratch. Well, almost.

Cree held a square of gauze to his forearm as firefighters worked to keep the flames engulfing the old electronics store from spreading to the connected buildings. Echoes of screams and pain threatened to rip reality straight out from under him, and that undeniable guilt he'd tried to bury clawed up his throat.

"That's a pretty nasty gash on your arm. You going to make it?" Alma's voice penetrated through the darkness and planted him firmly back in Battle Mountain.

Relief slammed the lid on the box he'd shoved to the back of his mind. Time caught up with perception. He'd gotten Thorp and Alma out in time. This wasn't Loveland. This wasn't the case that had sent him into hiding. Dark brown eyes centered in his vision, and for a split second, he forgot about why he was here in the first place.

Cree pushed his weight from against the hood of the car. He pried the gauze from his arm, scanning the laceration spanning the underside of his forearm. The bleeding had already slowed. It might need stitches, but EMTs were already busy enough as it was. He wasn't going to keep them from their work. "Mr. Thorp told me he suffered a similar wound in the exact same spot about fifteen years ago when some punk teenager played a prank on him at the store. Something to do with a broken antenna and a lesson in velocity."

A laugh escaped that iron control she seemed to thrive on. Alma settled beside him, surveying the remains of the electronics store that had obviously played a large role in her life growing up here in town. "I remember that day. Mrs. Thorp—Maliya—made me a whole plate of brownies afterward. With walnuts, no less. She thought it was funny as hell when he told her about what had happened. She couldn't stop laughing."

She slid one hand beneath his arm and rolled his elbow. "Guess this makes me bad luck."

"I'd hate to think of whatever else I have coming for me if that's true." The pain receded under her touch, a trick of his own mind after living through the latest threat, but he'd take advantage of it anyway. The brain had a funny way of working like that, pretending it hadn't survived a trauma by focusing on something comforting. Something warm. He motioned toward the old man armed with an oxygen mask strapped over his face. Less than twelve hours ago, Alma had been in the same position. He wasn't sure what to think about that. "How's he doing?"

Alma pulled back, and his skin grew cold. She hefted herself on to the damaged car hood, her boots hitting against rusted metal. "He's in shock. And blaming himself for not noticing there was a bomb in his store. I keep telling him he's nuts, but it doesn't make a difference. His wife is on her way."

"That's a true soldier, right there. We take the blame for everything." Cree straightened. Hints of smoke and moisture drove deep into his lungs. "I'm sorry about his store, though. There aren't enough of these places around anymore. Family-owned stores and shops. Hate to see one go, but I'm glad you two got out in time."

"Thanks to you." She knocked one boot into his shin, then focused on the blackened, crumbling structure. "Insurance will pay for any damages as soon as the department releases the store as a crime scene. The Silverton bomb squad is still busy at the primary scene, but they've got a tech waiting for the fire crew to get the flames under control. I'm sure she'll want to get your statement."

Cree pressed his injured arm to his shirt. "It was the same bomber."

His pulse double-timed the longer she didn't answer, and he ripped his attention from the blast site back to her.

"You're sure?" The color had left her face, and there was an undeniable waver to her voice. Spits of hose water plastered against her face and caused the thin hairs near her ears to stick. She scrubbed one hand down her face, and he caught sight of the darkening skin around her arm. A perfect five-fingered bruise.

Hell. He'd been so focused on getting her and Thorp out of there after he'd found the device at the back of the store that he hadn't given a second thought to grabbing her. Only now he realized how hard he must've gripped her arm. "The device was built exactly as you described it, down to the placement of the same coiled, red wire leading from the circuit board to the explosive on the left side. It was C4. Two bricks. Not exactly easy to come by. By the time I saw it, there wasn't time to try to disarm it." He turned to face her as a void of fresh guilt carved through him. "Alma, about that bruise—"

"Officer Gregson, I hear we have you to thank for the lack of bodies this time." Chief Ford tipped his hat in greeting. The department head, whom Cree had pegged to be in his midthirties, was closely followed by a man that could've been Weston Ford's twin. Maybe slightly older.

A day's worth of beard growth shadowed the sharp angles of Easton Ford's jaw and chin. Two distinct lines deepened between his eyebrows as he closed one eye against the afternoon sun to survey the scene. Penetrating deep blue eyes locked on Cree, and the hairs on the back of his neck stood on end. There was something different about this Ford compared to the chief, something worn—battle-tested—and in that moment, Cree recognized a fellow military man. Only this one had obviously seen horrors Cree couldn't begin to imagine.

Chief Ford nodded to Alma. "Majors."

Alma straightened a bit taller, only the tug of her lower lip revealing the pain she must still be feeling from the first blast. She hung both thumbs from her belt. "Chief."

"Hell of a way to start your shift, Alma. Two bombings in a twelve-hour period." Easton Ford twisted, that sharp gaze following the movements of every man and woman on scene. He hiked the sleeves of his red-and-black flannel shirt higher, revealing tanned skin and white scar tissue. "Can't be a coincidence."

"Go big or go home, I suppose, sir." She held her head high, unwilling to let any of them read past her guarded expression, but Cree had dealt with enough victims and witnesses in blasts like this. She couldn't hide from him. "Cree was able to get a visual on the device before it detonated. If it weren't for him, Dr. Pascale would have a lot more bodies on her hands."

"Same design. Most likely the same bomber. There were only fifteen seconds left on the countdown by the time I came across it. Not enough time to defuse and clear the building." Cree said. "Thorp doesn't remember anyone buying the components we described and we lost his receipts somewhere in the blast, but there's no way the perp would've known we'd come here next. They chose this location for a reason, and considering the device was set at the same desk as Thorp's security surveillance system, I'm betting they realized he had footage of them buying what they needed for the attack at the gulch."

"And came back to ensure we'd never get our hands on it." Chief Ford scratched at the thickening hair down his jaw, one hand set against his hip. "This bomber obviously isn't concerned about hurting people, which makes them even more dangerous. And now that Thorp's surveillance system has been destroyed, we have no idea how many other devices our bomber planned to build." The chief rocked his weight back on one foot. "What were the two of you doing here in the first place, Majors? I sent you home to take it easy for the next few days. You know, considering you almost got blown up. Now I find you at not one but two bombing scenes. It's a miracle you're still alive."

Alma's gaze flickered to Cree's. "Yes, sir. I asked Officer Gregson to help me get a lead on the victim's identity. The lab won't be able to pull anything from the shard of bone left after the first bombing for another week, and the Silverton squad is focused on the device itself. She was all alone in that gulch. Someone out there doesn't know she's missing. I wanted to identify her for the sake of her family and friends."

Frustration contorted the chief's expression as Easton Ford laughed before turning his back on them. "Officer Gregson, please excuse us."

The urge to argue slithered up his throat, but Cree had no business telling Battle Mountain's police chief how to run his department. As much as he believed Alma had made the right choice in trying to identify the victim, she'd obviously ignored her commanding officer's orders by going after this thing herself. He noted the embarrassment in Alma's body language and extracted himself from the conversation a few yards away.

Alma's nods, the chief's soundless enquiries and Easton Ford's occasional input were all he was able to make out over the roar of the fire hoses, but it was enough to charge the defiance building in his chest. He wasn't sure what Alma had been running from all this time, but it was obvious she needed this job. He couldn't let her take the fall for what'd happened, and with his record already tarnished, absorbing the blame wouldn't change a damn thing for him. Cree strode back toward the threesome, water sprinkling across his neck and chest. "Chief, listen, I understand Officer Majors made a mistake in investigating this case on her own, but—"

"Settle down, Gregson, and keep arguing." Easton Ford secured a hand over Cree's shoulders, a little too tight. "I don't know what kind of department you work for, but that's not how we do things around here."

Keep arguing?

"I don't understand." He searched her expression, noting the slight lift at one corner of her mouth. His own brand of embarrassment clawed up his neck and into his face. He'd been played. Whatever this conversation was, it hadn't been for his benefit. But someone else's. "You're not being reprimanded, are you?"

"No, but I appreciate your gesture to interfere, all the same." Alma threaded one hand through her hair. "We're taking note of who's watching the scene. I believe the bomber attached the first device to the victim to keep us from identifying her. They didn't want any evidence to survive. By letting the Silverton bomb squad take the lead in the investigation and making it look as though I've been taken off the case, I can stay under the radar while I find out who she was. Maybe then we'll have a lead on who made the bombs and why."

He didn't have to fake the shock overwhelming his control. "She's a rookie, Ford, and you want her to run her own investigation into a bomber who's already set off two devices and killed someone? Without support of the department. Without backup."

"Not exactly," she said. "You're coming, too."

Chapter Four

They'd fooled Cree enough to make him believe she'd been removed from the case.

But had the ploy been enough for a killer?

Her training in bombs had been short but memorable. According to the study of a dozen investigations over the course of the past decade, it was common for bombers to stick around the scene of a crime to watch their handiwork unfold. Sometimes that obsession narrowed on the spread of flames as an arsonist would, or to watching a building crumble in on itself. Other times, it was to take pleasure in how many people had been hurt or killed.

If that was the case, this time the bomber would be disappointed.

Cree had pulled both her and Mr. Thorp from the small store before the explosion, and now they had a chance to get the answers they needed to find the person responsible. He settled against the stucco edging her apartment front door. "You'll have to go about your life as though nothing has changed. Stick to your routine whenever possible. Grocery shopping on Mondays, going for runs around town twice a week. No changes.

Understand? We don't want to give the bomber any reason for turning his attention to you."

He'd memorized her routine. Just as she had his. But had it been because of some deep-rooted survival or mere curiosity? Alma shoved the key to her first dead bolt into position and twisted. She wasn't sure which answer she preferred. She followed up with the next dead bolt and the third. Awareness chased down the length of her neck as Cree pushed away from the wall. Three dead bolts hadn't come standard with her lease, and he was too good a cop not to notice. She tightened her grip around the doorknob, the metal instantly warming under her skin. "Someone's been doing their homework."

"Not much else around here to do but people-watch." He backed off a foot, and another shot of shame pooled at the base of her spine. He wasn't going to ask her about the dead bolts. He wasn't going to ask her what Mr. Thorp had meant when he'd called her Dr. Ortega. He wasn't going to put her in a position to explain. Because he knew. That was why he was giving her space right now. He knew, and she couldn't take the weight of seeing one more person in her life face her with pity in their gaze. "Mr. Heinz from downstairs thinks I don't know he's the one who steals the cookies Mrs. Faris leaves for me on my doormat, but one of these days, I'm going to catch him in the act."

Nervous energy skittered down her spine as she considered whether or not she should invite him inside. On one hand, the survivor in her hated the idea of letting a practical stranger into her space, of exposing herself to him. On the other, it would look suspicious if she didn't at least try to pretend the reason they'd be spending time together was because of mutual attraction and not working together to uncover the victim's identity. Pressure built behind her sternum as he waited for her to open the door, and her mouth dried. She didn't have the strength or the patience for mind games she didn't understand how to play. Alma removed her hand from the doorknob and faced him. "I don't want to invite you inside." She hadn't meant the words to burst from her mouth, but it was too late. "Wow. That was a lot harsher than I intended."

Surprise registered across his handsome features as he slid his hands into his jeans. "I understand."

"No. I don't think you do. I just… I don't do this a lot. Talk to people, I mean. I've never had people over, and I don't visit with neighbors, but we're supposed to work together on this case, and I don't know how to… do that." She'd hit her head in the bombing. Yes, that was it. Because this version of herself didn't exist until she'd faced the possibility of him coming inside. She folded her arms across her chest, a classic defensive maneuver he'd spot a mile away. "Simply speaking."

"I don't know if you know this, but you may have chosen the wrong career. Ninety-nine percent of police duty is talking to people." His laugh bubbled past full lips she hadn't taken the time to notice the past few hours. Mainly because the threat of dying had been more of a priority, but now she noted the slight thinning at one side of his mouth compared to the other. A perfect flaw that only made him more real than the fantasy she'd constructed in her head. "Would it help if I asked why you have three dead bolts on your door when every other apartment in this complex has one, including mine?"

He had noticed. Her stomach twisted. His words filtered through her mind, tripping over one another before her heart rate settled at the base of her throat. "Actually, yes. If we're going to work together, I'd rather you talk to me directly than to assume you know me or what I've been through."

Cree ducked his chin. "Mr. Thorp called you Dr. Ortega. I'm guessing Ortega is your maiden name and that you had a completely different life before you found yourself in the middle of a blast zone last night."

"Majors is my married name." An ache settled around her arm, but she didn't have the willpower to pull her attention from the man in front of her. Seemed everywhere she looked these past few weeks, Cree had been there. In the corridor as she brought home groceries, in the diner she frequented nearly every day, at the scene last night. He'd slipped into her life as quietly as a shadow and set up residence just as quickly. "I keep it to remind me what I'm working toward. I was an archaeologist before I signed on with the department."

"Alma Ortega. Wait, *the* Alma Ortega?" Recognition flared in his expression, and where her first instinct had once been to hold her head high, a part of her now shrank at her two lives converging. "I've read your work. Your discovery of a buried Teotihuacán citadel in the middle of Maya has to be one of the biggest Mexican archaeological finds recorded in over a hundred years."

Excitement bled into his eyes, and her heart practically skipped a beat. "It was." Remnants of that day still played through her mind. Where her colleagues had been so determined to reveal Egyptian and Viking secrets, she and her team had shoved Mexico back into the light. Right where it belonged. She'd never been prouder in her life. There'd been new job offers to teach at universities across the country, television interviews, papers to collaborate on with peers she'd idolized all through her career, and funding to continue her research, but the spotlight, it seemed, had shone too brightly. At least in her case.

"I remember a lot of media coverage from around that time." The light in his gaze dulled. "You disappeared after that. The reigning theory was you'd retired." Cree's attention slipped to the dead bolts behind her. "But that's not what happened, was it?"

She cleared her throat of emotion, but Alma had known this day would come. One that would force her to confront the truth, that would strip her bare and expose her to the world as the coward she'd always known she was. "No. It's not." She rolled her lips between her teeth and bit down to keep herself in the moment, just as she'd been taught to do. Grounding, her therapist had called it. "It's not well known, but my, uh, husband— ex-husband—was also an archaeologist. We worked in the same field, but our focuses were very different. He'd gone the way of Egyptian study in hopes of uncovering the next great King Tut, and I followed my heart to Mexico. After my findings went public and I published, he wasn't thrilled with the attention."

"You mean the attention you were getting," Cree said. "He saw it as a betrayal."

A humorless laugh escaped past her control. It had taken her months to put that puzzle together, and Cree had solved it in minutes. "He changed. Practically overnight. It was so fast I didn't even see it coming. He was so…angry, and the only way he could control it was by directing it at me. By the time I realized the pain wasn't going to stop, that him taking his anger out on me wasn't just jealousy, he'd already isolated me from my colleagues. The job offers had stopped coming in, the phone wasn't ringing and my funding for future research had been allocated to other researchers. My career vanished in the blink of an eye while I was just trying to make it through most nights."

"But you did. Make it through." Cree's shoulders tipped forward as though he had the urge to close the distance between them, but she wasn't sure she could handle that. Not yet. Not with her nerves at an all-time high, and not out here in the middle of their apartment complex corridor. "You left. You walked away. You re-made your life and started again."

"Yes." Her voice deadpanned as the memories of her last night in the emergency room threatened to over-take the present. She kicked at a stray pebble under her boots, the edges catching on the underside of her heel. "Much to the disappointment of Mr. Thorp, unfortunately. He always had big dreams for me."

"You know as well as I do, just in the short amount of time I've known him, that man will never be disappointed in you." Cree nodded to her arm, and she craned her chin down. "I'm sorry about the bruise. After I saw the countdown on the timer on that device, the only thing I could think of was to get you out of there. I wasn't thinking about how tight I was hold-ing onto you."

The ache spread around her bicep as she inspected the dark five-fingered bruise. Her heart shuddered at her body's ability to take everything it had been through. This would be just another chapter of that story. Only, this time, she had the choice of how it ended. "You don't have to apologize. If it hadn't been for you, I wouldn't be worrying about anything at all."

"I guess that's true, but I'm still going to apologize." His lopsided smile drove straight past the pressure behind her chest and relieved the valve she'd sealed off what seemed like forever ago. Cree pointed toward his apartment. "I'm going to grab those cookies before Mr. Heinz gets to them first and give you some time to recover. I'll come by tomorrow so we can start looking into your victim. Around eight?"

"Eight is good." Her skin heated as though she'd just made a date with the handsome neighbor across the hall, which, really, she had.

He maneuvered past her, sure to keep his distance, then stopped. "And, Alma, whatever happens with this case, I'll have your back. I give you my word."

MORNING HADN'T COME soon enough. Not for him.

Cree balanced the recycled drink carrier containing two coffees with one hand and knocked lightly on her door with the other while clutching the research he'd printed off last night. Footsteps echoed from inside a split second before the door swung open. Hints of meat, onions and peppers hit him square in the face, and his stomach kicked into overdrive. He'd been up at the crack of dawn and had dived straight into the case. With nothing more than a shard of bone to identify their victim, they had a lot of work ahead of them. So much, in fact, he'd forgotten to eat.

"Hey. Hope I'm not early." He stretched to check his watch, nearly tipping their coffees onto the cement.

"Actually, you're right on time, but I'll be honest. I

got a bit of a head start last night after you left." She clutched the edge of the door, craning her head back into what looked like a barely furnished living room and wall-to-wall bookshelves. The same tension he'd noted in her neck and shoulders last night solidified. They'd agreed to work this case together, but the hesitation of inviting him inside hadn't lessened over the course of the past twelve hours. And, hell, after what she'd told him last night, he couldn't blame her. And he wouldn't push her.

"Why don't you wrap whatever you're cooking to go, and we can use the picnic tables in the courtyard to go over the plan," he said. "It'll play into the ruse, right? Us having breakfast together. Besides, it's nice enough we won't overheat for a couple of hours."

"Okay." Relief punctured through the hardened tendons running the length of her delicate neck. She disappeared inside, the door automatically swinging shut. Within thirty seconds, she backed out of the apartment, her hands full of paperwork and two paper plates filled with food. He shifted his load to one hand and held out the other to help, careful not to get too close. Alma glanced up at him with deep, rich brown eyes and a weak smile as she surrendered one of the plates. "Thank you. I wasn't sure if you eat breakfast, but I made Mexican rice with poached eggs."

"Smells delicious." His stomach knotted at the second hit of spices, cheese and sausage.

"Family recipe from my aunt Ramona." She locked all three dead bolts behind her before facing him. "I tend to cook when I'm stressed, and then I eat everything I've made, and I feel better."

"Stressed is an understatement. Getting caught in

the middle of a case like this your first week on the job is definitely not for the weak of heart." They moved as one down the length of the corridor and into the open stairwell. The concrete steps and steel handrails vibrated with their descent. "Most people, trained or not, would be curled up in the fetal position right now if they'd survived two explosions. Not agreeing to run a secret investigation into the identity of our victim, let alone cooking breakfast."

"If my history has taught me one thing, it's that I never was good at knowing what was best for me." Her laugh countered the apprehension growing behind his rib cage. Alma settled her plate and the file she'd put together on the old wood planks that passed for a picnic table in the center of their complex. She slid long, lean legs between the tabletop and bench. The denim jacket she'd donned guaranteed a heat overdose combined with her dark jeans and black T-shirt, but it worked as a prime example of her survival techniques. He imagined that with every bruise she'd sustained during her marriage, she'd learned to hide the truth from the people who cared about her. Friends, family, neighbors, colleagues. She just hadn't broken the habit. Alma nodded toward the file in his hand as he took his seat opposite her. "I take it I'm not the only one who got a head start on this case."

"Uh, no. You're not." He pulled a corn tortilla— handmade from scratch, from what he could tell— out of the mess of rice, meat and peppers on his plate and took a bite. Egg yolks broke across the mountain of comfort food, and he practically melted back in his seat. "Damn, this is good. Where'd you learn how to cook like this?"

"Growing up, my family always had dinner together on Sundays. Everyone would bring something different, and we'd throw it on this massive table that barely fit in our house like a buffet. We'd sit and talk and eat for hours together, sharing our lives and telling jokes." Alma severed eye contact as she focused on her own plate of food and scooped a bit into her mouth. One corner of her mouth tugged into a smile. "My *abuela* insisted I learn to cook just as my mother had. Hands-on. So every Sunday, she'd come over a couple hours early, have me pick out a recipe to cook, and she'd teach me. I was barely big enough to see over the counter, but we made it work. By the time I was six, I could make anything I set my mind to."

"That all sounds great." A twinge of envy slipped between his thoughts as he easily envisioned a smaller version of the woman in front of him surrounded by nothing but love and food and heritage. How had it all gone wrong? "And loud."

"It could be. The police might've been called whenever my uncles and *abuelo* argued about who could burp the loudest." Pure joy replaced the tempest in her eyes as she took another bite of breakfast. "Did you come from a large family, too?"

"Ah, no." He focused on counting each individual grain of rice he could see at the edge of his plate. "I was an only kid. Parents both had military careers. One or both of them would always be on tour."

"You were alone?" The sadness in his voice gutted him straight down to the bone.

"Not all the time." His fingers tingled for a distraction. Something to carve or a leaf to tear through. "If both of my parents were called to active duty, I'd spend that time with my grandfather. He had a cabin out here on the other side of the lake. At first, I hated it. We'd hike all day, fish for our meals and hunt the land to stock up for winter. There were no other kids around. The old man didn't believe in public schools. He home-schooled me even past my eighteenth birthday. Said the best thing I could do for myself and my family was get a real education. None of that 'state-approved non-sense.' After a while, I didn't mind spending time with him. He taught me how to work with my hands, gave me confidence to take care of myself even under the most dire circumstances." A heaviness cemented him in his seat. "But after he died, I just felt alone. I ended up joining the army. My parents were still committed. Figured I might as well fall into the family legacy."

"Where are they now? Your parents?" she asked.

"Major General Gregson and Colonel Gregson just hit thirty years together." Cree pushed back his plate, not able to take another bite. "They are comfortably situated in Washington, DC, advising how to avoid going to war and preparing for it at the same time."

"Wow. Legacy is right." Alma set down her torti-lla topped with sausage, rice and onions. She rubbed her hands together before turning her attention to the file she'd built overnight. "You said your grandfather has a cabin on the other side of the lake. To what do we owe the pleasure of your company here at Crescent Ridge Apartments?"

His laugh escaped before he had a chance to sec-ond-guess it. "Well, when you put it that way… Truth is, there isn't much to go back to. Once he was gone, I joined up, and the place went to hell over the years. There wasn't anybody here to take care of it. The vegetation started reclaiming the interior and working through the windows. The garden we'd planted together was picked over too many times. All of the appliances stopped functioning. There wasn't really anything left to save."

"I know that area. There aren't too many cabins out there. Both the chief and Easton have a ranch out that way. Whispering Pines. They recently started a veteran rehabilitation center on the land south of the main cabin. I've been helping on the weekends for the past few months between therapy appointments." She took a sip from her coffee, those equally dark eyes settling on his. "Is that why you're here in Battle Mountain? To clean up your grandfather's place?"

If he was being honest with himself, he hadn't even thought of going out there. The connection he'd had to this place, to his grandfather, had died with the old man. Cree wedged his thumbnail between the worn slats of the picnic table. Yet when the guilt and the shame and the weight of the past had started suffocating him from the inside, Battle Mountain was the first place he'd thought of to run to. Not out of any duty to his grandfather but because this place was the only familiarity he had left. This small mining town had created a distinct separation between his new life and the old one, and he wasn't sure he ever wanted to go back.

"I'm sorry. I didn't mean to pry. You don't… You don't have to tell me anything." Alma wrapped both of her hands around her to-go coffee cup and shook her head. The corner of her file folder scraped against the aged wood as she pulled it closer and flipped it open. "We should focus on the case."

"No. It's okay." He wanted her to know. Because

even after everything that had happened, after everything his grandfather had taken time and energy to teach him, he'd missed that connection. The one people shared. It had been the reason he'd gone into the military, that he'd tried to work his way into his parents' world. It was why he'd responded to the scene of the bomb last night, and why he'd agreed to work with Alma in the first place. It was that connection—not the isolation—that had brought him to this sleepy, nearly dead town. Cree gripped his coffee cup harder than he meant to. "I didn't come here to fix up my grandfather's place, Alma. I came to Battle Mountain to hide."

Chapter Five

"I don't understand." He'd come to hide? Apprehension settled in the deepest recesses of her joints and tightened the tendons down the length of her legs. The kind of people who'd chosen Battle Mountain to hide had brought nothing but death and terror behind them. The chief's fiancée and mother of his unborn child, Dr. Chloe Miles, had narrowly escaped a serial killer who'd tracked her here. And Genevieve Alexander, Easton Ford's significant other, had caught the attention of a violent killer determined to tear apart her life for a case she'd prosecuted years ago.

The people here didn't deserve to live in fear or wonder if they'd wake to find one of their loved ones the center of a homicide investigation. This town had been through enough. How much more were they supposed to take? Then again, she herself was a lure to a violent person if her ex ever decided to look for her. "You said you were with the Larimer County bomb squad. If that's true, what on earth would someone like you have to hide from?"

The edge of the wooden bench dug into the soft underside of her thighs until it was all she could think about through the low ringing in her ears. Her heart rate spiked. She'd trusted her instincts to bring Cree in on this investigation, to work this case beside her, but how long had she let herself stay blind to her ex-husband's darkness? Her stomach weighed heavy with breakfast that threatened to retaliate at any given moment. Alma shifted her weight across the bench as her skin heated.

"More than you know." Cree fidgeted with his coffee cup until he caught himself digging through the recycled material. "Listen, Alma, you were straight with me last night. It took a lot of guts for you to share what you'd been through, but I find it hard to trust people. Seems every time I do, someone ends up hurt."

She leaned forward in her seat, and their breakfast, the investigation, the pain in the back of her shoulder—it all disintegrated until there was only the two of them. "The only person who knows about what happened between me and my ex-husband other than you is Easton Ford." Her mouth dried. "Not the chief. Not my parents or the rest of my family. As far as they're concerned, my ex left me to make his own mark in the archaeological world."

"Why would you lie?" Surprise broke through Cree's guarded expression. "Why not tell them the truth?"

"Because I was afraid of how disappointed they'd be in me. The last time I was in the house we'd shared, I ended up in the emergency room with a shattered wrist, but I was so embarrassed about what was happening, I couldn't go to the clinic here in town. I drove three hours to Alamosa for treatment, sobbing because of the pain. At the time, it seemed worth the risk, but looking back, I wasn't thinking straight. I just wanted the pain to stop, so I went along with whatever story he'd prepared to explain the bruises and cast." Her inhale shuddered. "Easton was the one who found me. He was there with the Alamosa district attorney after they'd closed the case they were working together, but while she was in surgery, he saw me. Somehow, he knew exactly what'd happened, and he offered to help me get out."

She spread her hands out in front of her and pressed into the table to rein in the residual emotion attached to those memories. "My point is you can't get through this life alone. I know what it's like to be surrounded by people and still feel so isolated, but help can come from the most random sources. So if we're going to work this case together, if we're going to have each other's backs, we need to at least be honest. You don't have to tell me your entire history. I just need to know if working with you is going to get me or anyone else in this town hurt."

Cree ducked his head. "You're right. Whoever is setting these devices has already killed one person, and they're not afraid of killing more. We're not going to be able to stop them unless we work together."

A hot breeze mazed through the courtyard and kicked up the sweet scent of freshly cut grass and wildflowers. It combined with the hint of clean soap coming off his skin. Or had her desperation for connection only imagined that part?

"When I told Chief Ford I'm with the Larimer County bomb squad, that was the truth. I'm still technically a tech assigned to that jurisdiction, but I've been on leave for the past eight months." His voice dipped an octave, and goose pimples budded along her arms.

Something had happened eight months ago in Larimer County. He'd obviously been involved, which meant there'd been a threat of some sort. A bomb, maybe. Eight months. Why did that timeline sound so familiar? Nausea clawed up her throat, like something alive, and Alma straightened a bit taller. Regret exploded as she scanned the length of his arms and searched his face. "The bombing at that oil and gas meeting with the board of county commissioners." His gaze met hers head-on, and it was in that moment, she understood. "Loveland. You were there."

"An ecoterrorist group had gotten word about the policy changes the board of county commissioners were considering." The muscles along his jaw ticked in rhythm to the pulse pounding hard at the base of his neck. "By the time emergency crews got through the debris and rubble, three had died. Another half dozen of my team injured. All because I didn't find the device in time."

Despite her efforts to avoid media consumption after her divorce had gone public and the rumors had started breaking through the cracks into her new world, she remembered the coverage that entire week after the bomb had gone off. "You seemed to have walked away without a scratch."

"Just because you can't see them, doesn't mean they aren't there." His eyes glazed for a split second as though he'd become a victim to the past before he seemed to come back to himself. To her. Cree pushed the file he'd brought with him across the table. "As for this case, Silverton's squad will already have pulled a list of similar incidents in the area from the NCIC database. It's common for bombers to detonate practice devices and build up courage before the big event, so I reached out to a friend working for the ATF to search incident reports in this area going back six months that used the same kind of setup we saw. That way, the inquiry doesn't lead back to our investigation."

"Did your contact find anything?" She pried open the manila folder and set her hand over the papers inside to keep the wind from ripping them away.

"Colorado State Patrol responded to complaints filed by two different hikers concerning what sounded like dynamite charges being set off outside of Ouray three weeks ago." Cree tapped the file in front of her with his index finger, and it was only then she recognized a thin scar trailing from the first knuckle diagonal to the second. The kind of scar that would stay after having a finger reattached after a bombing. "According to the reports, when the troopers got to the area, they found the ground ripped open in several places and fresh evidence of scoring on nearby rocks. They don't have a suspect, but they did find this."

He dug out a page from the back of the file and set it on top of the reports. The photo revealed a corner of a familiar green motherboard component. The same kind that had been used in the bombs both she and Cree had seen with their own eyes. It wasn't impossible that another bomber had utilized this specific setup to design their creation. But what were the chances of it being so close to Battle Mountain?

"A motherboard." She threaded her fingers under the single photo, a hangnail catching on the reports underneath. "Was anyone hurt in the explosions?"

"No reported fatalities. State Patrol wasn't able to pull any prints from the components or get a description from the hikers who filed the report either." Cree folded his arms across the surface of the old table. "But if this incident is a practice run for our bomber like I think it is, they made a point to avoid Battle Mountain jurisdiction. Like they were waiting for the right time to strike."

"Or the right someone. Maybe our victim?" Alma set her face in one hand, her elbow digging into the weathered picnic table. One wrong move and a sliver would imbed in her skin, but it was almost preferable compared to the pressure to solve this case. "I've gone through the missing person reports a dozen times. There aren't any victims who fit the description of the woman I found at the bottom of that gulch, but it's possible I'll get a hit off the baby's photo in the locket."

"Good idea." Cree collected the file folder he'd shared with her. "I'm going to head down to the station to get in touch with State Patrol, try to get them to send us any evidence they collected at the scene. If we're chasing our tails, I want to know sooner rather than later." He collected his discarded paper plate then hers and deposited them in the trash set at the end of the expansive table. "Thanks for breakfast. I'll work with you to the end of time if this is the kind of food I can look forward to."

Warmth shot through her as his sincerity solidified between them. Appreciation hadn't ever been a habit of her ex's, and the effect of something so simple lightened the isolation determined to suffocate her from the inside. "You're welcome. Let me know where you get with State Patrol."

"Will do." He nodded once and then headed for the pickup parked at the back of the shared lot, the muscles down the backs of his thighs flexing beneath the denim that fit him perfectly.

Her own appreciation churned low in her belly as he waved goodbye through the passenger-side window and maneuvered free of the lot. For someone who'd come to Battle Mountain to hide, Cree Gregson had certainly made his mark on this town. And her. She wasn't sure how to explain it, but there was a sense of…safety that came with being the center of the man's attention. Not brittle or dependent as it had been with her ex. But grounding. Supportive even. She couldn't remember the last time she'd felt at home in her own skin, but there was something about Cree that gave her permission to loosen her need for control, that made it easier to breathe.

She headed back upstairs to her apartment and caught sight of a white slip of paper taped to the door. Alma checked the corridor, her hand reaching for the weapon she'd left secured in her safe in the laundry closet. The note hadn't been there before her and Cree's meeting, and she hadn't seen anyone climb the stairs while they'd been in view at the table. She tugged the torn paper free and exposed the unfamiliar handwriting inside. *"Back off, or next time you won't survive."*

CREE SLAMMED THE phone down. "Damn it."

"I take it State Patrol didn't buy your story about you being a Silverton bomb technician." Macie Barclay, Battle Mountain PD's single dispatcher, office manager and overall redheaded stepchild, set down a mug of coffee at the end of the desk.

"They did not." He threaded his fingers through the mug's handle. "I think I lost them somewhere around not being able to give them my badge number so they could put in the request."

"You've got to put some desperation into it. Like the entire town's future is weighing on your shoulders alone, and you are the only one who can save us." Macie lifted her hands in a dramatic pose as she leaned against the edge of one of many empty desks throughout the station. In an instant, the drama faded, leaving a wide smile across her face. "Oh, you're going to want to watch yourself. Chief Frasier gifted me that mug after he retired a few years ago. Said he made it with his own two hands, but I'm pretty sure he didn't know what the hell he was doing. Gets hotter the longer you wait to drink it."

"Wouldn't know." He hadn't been able to feel much after the bombing last year. His surgeon had done a damn fine job putting everything back where it was supposed to go, but nerve damage was a different beast altogether. Except when it came to Alma. For a moment while he'd helped her get settled at their impromptu breakfast this morning, he could've sworn he'd felt something. Then again, he'd sustained brain trauma during the Loveland bombing when a chunk of concrete had crashed down on top of him during his attempted escape from the building. For all he knew, he'd imagined a lot of things. Like the way she'd flushed when he'd thanked her for breakfast. "When is Chief Ford supposed to get back from his brief with Silverton's bomb squad?"

"Not until this afternoon." The dispatcher took a sip of coffee from her own mug, green eyes far too aware and curious. Straight white teeth and lipsticked lips added to her bohemian-style white dress and midcalf-length cardigan sweater. She curled brightly painted, manicured nails around her mug as full eyebrows drew inward. "Remind me why you can't just tell them who you are and ask with pretty pleases and cherries on top? Please tell me it has something to do with why Easton is covering Officer Majors's shift today."

"It's complicated." Apart from the fact he and Alma had to keep their investigation under the radar, identifying himself as the technician who failed to do his job wouldn't get him far with other agencies. He'd learned that from experience. Suspicion distracted him from laying out a plan to get a look at the evidence State Patrol had gathered at the scene outside of Ouray. Gossip had never been any interest to him. He'd done his homework when he'd come to town. Not only about Battle Mountain's history and its residents but its department. Macie Barclay had been a fixture in this sad excuse for a station long before trouble had reared its ugly head this past year. Going on ten years from what he could tell from her personnel records. He'd trained to pick apart bombers' motives and devices then reassemble them under pressure of saving lives, but his instincts said Macie's interest was purely for entertainment's sake. And hell, he didn't blame her given the quiet isolation of this place. In fact, he was surprised the dispatcher hadn't made hand puppets out of tissues and craft supplies to give her an excuse to talk to herself. He scanned the station for a set of plastic shifty eyes staring back at him. "You known Alma long?"

"First-name basis." Straw-looking sandals ground harder into the industrial carpet as Macie straightened, and an amused edge cut into her expression. "Considering Officer Majors doesn't talk to anyone unless she absolutely has to, I'd say you should be flattered."

His gut kicked hard. "You already know why I didn't tell State Patrol who I am, don't you? This was just a ploy to get me to talk."

"I'm good at reading people." Macie's mouth tugged higher at one side. "Let me give you some advice, Officer Whoever-the-Hell-You-Are."

"Gregson," he said.

Macie laughed, as though his name didn't matter. "You're new in Battle Mountain. From what I've been able to tell from your personnel records, you've only lived in and worked in large cities with the support of an entire organization behind you. Larimer County and the army. Here? We protect our own. We have to. Otherwise this town would've been wiped off the map when the mining companies went bankrupt. Do you understand?"

She'd done her homework, the same as he'd done his, and admiration coiled through him. "You're worried my interest in working with Officer Majors is about more than solving this case and that she might get hurt when the investigation is closed."

"Will she?" Macie took a calm sip of her coffee, too calm. "Because while there might be three official police officers in this department, I can guarantee you I know how to hide bodies better than the serial killers they've brought to justice."

"Is that so?" The threat burrowed under his skin. As much as he wanted to ignore the possibility of ending up as a victim at the hand of the sarcastic, redheaded dispatcher, a thread of truth burned behind her words. "In that case, I'll be sure to watch my step."

"See that you do, Officer Gregson of 7356 2nd Street, apartment 201." Relief loosened the tension in her shoulders as she shrugged. The desk phone rang, and Macie turned on her heels to answer. "Wow. It's been a while since I've threatened someone. I've missed it."

He turned back to the monitor taking up a good chunk of real estate on the old, dilapidated desk, as a shiver raced along his spine. Taking Battle Mountain PD's dispatcher at face value had been a mistake. One he wouldn't make again.

He accessed the national criminal database again and pulled up the State Patrol case. No fatalities. No sign of a suspect. The canines had detected the use of C4 during the scene processing, but there hadn't been any DNA to narrow down the identity of the bomber. Only the recovery of fresh footprints leading to what looked to be ATV tracks. His gut said this was the bomber who'd killed a woman in the bottom of the gulch two nights ago. He just needed something. The timing and the location couldn't be coincidences. From what he'd been able to see of the device in Galaxy Electronics before it detonated, the bomb's designer had built a solid means of destruction. That meant experience with explosives and patience. But where did the bomber get the explosive?

C4 was heavily regulated by the Bureau of Alcohol, Tobacco, Firearms and Explosives. Every company or citizen in possession of the explosive apart from the military or government had to register it with the ATF, but that didn't account for explosives that had been stolen. He read through the rest of the incident report. Since there hadn't been any fatalities, State Patrol hadn't pursued a criminal investigation. They did, however, cue in ATF. Cree opened the Bomb Arson Tracking System run by the bureau and sifted through local incidents from the past six months. The most recent entry detailed the theft of twenty pounds of C4 from a construction site in Ouray. The thief had broken the lock on the secure container in the middle of the night a month ago. "Bingo."

They had the source of the explosive. Now all he needed was something to identify the victim caught in the blast. The tests detonated in the desert outside of Ouray fit the timing, but why had the bomber waited so long to kill their victim? Why here in Battle Mountain? "Maybe you couldn't find her," he said to himself.

Cree recalled Alma's description of the victim. Blond hair, a thin face, Caucasian, tall. Approximately thirty-five years old. Alma had already gone through the missing person reports without any luck, but there was a chance they'd underestimated when their victim had gone missing. Clicking through to the national missing persons database, he set the parameters and extended their time frame to a year. Dozens of faces filled the screen, and his mouth dried in an instant. A dozen women smiling at the camera stared back at him from pixelated photos, most likely saved from social media accounts. He read through their names, but no one on the list jumped out. He'd have to sit Alma down to go through the possibilities. Too many.

Macie penetrated his peripheral vision. She handed him a note, her voice shaking. "That was Alma on the phone. She didn't want to call in over the radio in case the bomber you're investigating is listening. Something happened at her apartment. I think you better get back home."

His heart thudded hard against his rib cage as he took the note from her. Cree shot to his feet, nearly crumpling the slip of paper in his palm, and raced through the back of the station. He slammed against the glass back door and bolted for his truck across the parking lot. In seconds, Main Street's red brick buildings and green landscaping blurred in his vision as he battled with crossing pedestrians and calm traffic. Sweat built in his hairline and beneath his T-shirt neckline with every scenario that played across his mind. He shouldn't have left her alone. He should've been there.

Burnt rubber and the squeal of tires drowned the sound of his own breathing as he skidded to a stop in the complex's parking lot five minutes later. He ripped free of the truck, his legs burning with every rushed step as he climbed the stairs. Her door swung open as he reached the top step.

Alma flinched back into the doorframe a split second before recognition flared. "Damn it. You scared me."

Cree scanned her for injuries, noting her pressed uniform and the police-issued weapon on her right hip. She was undercover for this investigation, ironically in uniform and business as usual, but something had spooked her enough to armor herself in the time he'd been gone. "Tell me what happened."

"See for yourself." She stepped free of the door-jamb and motioned him inside, but where he'd noted defiance at the primary scene and outside of Galaxy Electronics after the second bombing, now there was uncertainty. "I came upstairs to start running missing person reports on the baby's photo from the locket after you'd gone to the station. I found a note taped to my door. When I got inside, I walked into this."

A small, circular kitchen table had been turned on its side, both chairs in pieces. Glass crunched under his boots as he surveyed the destruction. Every single item she'd possessed had been destroyed as far back as the bedroom at the end of the hall. Pressure built behind his rib cage, and a low ringing filtered through his ears. "You locked the doors before we went down to the courtyard. I watched you."

"Yeah." She studied the carnage of her life and settled her weight against the open front door. "But three dead bolts and an alarm system didn't stop whoever knows I'm working this case."

Chapter Six

A siren blipped from the complex's entrance.

She interlaced her fingers together and pressed the side of her hand into the same table she and Cree had sat at for breakfast this morning as Chief Ford and Easton went through the scene. The distraction wasn't strong enough to neutralize the void. Someone had broken into her apartment, destroyed everything she owned, including her clothes. The only thing to survive had been her gun safe and uniform, which had both been stored in the safe in the laundry closet.

Her cover was already blown.

Whoever had murdered the woman in the gulch hadn't fallen for the theater she and the chief had drummed up after the second bombing. They knew she was still working the investigation and that she'd taken it upon herself to identify the victim, but she wasn't the only one lost in this explosive puzzle.

Easton and Cree's canvass of the complex hadn't turned up anything concrete. Seemed the person who'd left the note on her door and ripped apart the few valuables she'd been able to escape her former life with had gone out of their way to avoid being seen. They'd slipped into her life and out as quickly as the sense of security she'd built here and turned her apartment into a crime scene. Now she didn't know what to do. Or where to go.

"You look like you could use one of these." Cree offered her a large disposable cup, and Alma automatically accepted. Coffee. From his own apartment, from the look of it. His mountainous shoulders she'd been all too tempted to relax into when he'd arrived at her apartment pierced through the haze closing in. He took a seat on the bench beside her, and her boots left the ground for a fraction of a second.

"In that case, I must look like death." She took her first swig and almost melted on the spot. The sharp kick to her senses rocketed her pulse higher in an instant, but along with the clearing fog came an awareness of the man beside her.

"I think it's best if I don't respond to that comment." Cree studied the scene as though trying to commit to memory every nosy neighbor and curious bystander considering jumping the perimeter tape for a closer look. Even Mrs. Faris had hooked her Siamese up to the leash to see what was going on outside her door. "I've gotten myself in trouble before."

The ease with which he joked with her nearly had her choking on the dark master that magically transformed reality with a few good sips. It was all too easy to imagine the two of them teasing like this back and forth over coffee in the mornings, maybe after a night in front of the TV with a coffee table full of Chinese leftovers. "I'll bet you have."

Despite the reprieve from the undercurrent of fear, anger and determination, her laugh died as quickly as it had surfaced. The fantasy dissipated in front of her as she caught sight of Easton and Chief Ford conversing at the base of the stairs that led to her apartment. Because that was all it was. A fantasy. The only reason she'd been targeted by the bomber they were chasing was because she'd become a cop. And the only reason she'd become a cop was to guarantee her safety.

Following whatever this was between her and Cree wasn't safe.

Her apartment wasn't safe.

She didn't feel safe, and without that basic need, there couldn't be anything between them. Her lungs evacuated what little air remained as she set her coffee on the bench.

"I guess the cat's out of the bag." He nodded toward the Ford brothers. "Someone knows you're still working this case."

"From the way those two are looking, I think the cat is dead, and the bag is on fire." Alma noted the frustration in her colleagues' body language. She'd learned to read people real fast during her marriage. It had been a survival technique, a way to prepare for the worst while hoping for the best. Right now, both Ford men were trying to avoid her attention to keep her from seeing their expressions, like she needed to be protected. Neither had any idea what she'd survived. Easton understood the mechanics, but there was a difference between seeing the outward damage inflicted on a person and acknowledging the permanent scars inside. "Did State Patrol agree to send the evidence they have from the incident outside of Ouray three weeks ago?"

"Not even a little." Cree set his elbows against his knees, accentuating bulky muscle up his arms and across his shoulders, and her gut clenched. What was it about that attractive casing and penetrating gaze that worked to erode the promise she'd made to herself to stop accepting people for what they were at face value? What was it about him? "But through some grunt work, I'm pretty sure I found the location where the C4 was stolen. A construction site in Ouray. A month ago."

"Pretty sure?" she asked.

"State Patrol never followed through with a criminal investigation, but the contractor in charge of the project reported twenty pounds of C4 went missing to the ATF around the same time those two hikers called in the incident," he said.

"You believe that's our bomber." Her skin prickled down the backs of her arms as she followed the curve of his jaw and patterned a design from the three gray hairs near his chin. He was handsome. She couldn't deny him that, and the way he'd gone out of his way to give her space, to not push her to give more of herself away, only made him more attractive.

"Makes the most sense. Stealing the explosive, testing it outside of Battle Mountain—no one would've seen this guy coming until it was too late." Cree tugged his phone from his back pocket and slid his thumb up the screen. The device unlocked, revealing a photo of two men standing in a patch of forest. A mere glimpse at the picture revealed a young Cree, likely taken before he'd gone into the military, standing with a much older man. His grandfather, if she had to guess. "There are still a lot of missing pieces, and now with you as a possible target, we have to tread more carefully." He slightly craned his head toward her. "I'm glad you're okay."

His flare of sincerity and concern tunneled through

the armor she'd donned every day since walking away from her ex, and straight into bone. The ache in her shoulder lessened the longer he studied her, and a wave of heat simmered beneath her skin. Her fight-or-flight instincts had been triggered countless times over the past year. A sound in the night, a shadow climbing along the wall, even calls from wrong numbers. But despite the threat…she'd never felt safer than she did now, with Cree. But what happened when this investigation was over and they were no longer partners? What happened if he decided to go back to Loveland and pick up the pieces of his own life? She slid one hand into her uniform pocket, running her thumb along the length of the locket's chain. "Whoever did that to my apartment wasn't looking to confront me directly. If they know where I live, they know I'm armed. I don't think they'll try again."

"And if they do?" he asked.

"Well, considering I don't even know where I'm going to sleep tonight, I don't think they'll have any luck tracking me down." She'd meant it as a joke, but reality had popped the small bubble they'd built around themselves the past few minutes. Everything she'd built over the past year was gone. "To be honest, I'm not really sure what I'm supposed to do now."

"How would you feel about crashing at my place?" Cree's voice wavered on the last word, and pure panic exploded through her. He raised his hands in surrender, palms forward, as though he understood exactly why that was such a bad idea. "That wasn't an invitation to… Damn it. I didn't mean… Let me start over." The terror etched into his expression broke through her primal defenses. "I meant you can crash in my apartment, and I'll sleep in my truck."

So this what was he was like on shaky ground. She couldn't say it wasn't amusing. Alma played through her options, each grimmer than his suggestion. "You're cute when you're nervous. I like it." She bumped her uninjured shoulder against his. "Thank you. I appreciate it, and I promise not to go through your dresser drawers or medicine cabinet."

"Well, now I'm worried you will." His laugh triggered a chain reaction starting with air stalling in her lungs and ending with a slight tingling in her toes. It was deep, rough, and engrained itself into her memory without a fight. "Just steer clear of the stuff under the bed. It'll be better for our partnership."

Partnership. That single word had only one meaning when she'd recruited him into this investigation, but now…the possibility for more warmed behind her rib cage. Over the course of two days, the connection between them had evolved from an emotionally detached plan to solve this case to the possibility of friendship. Maybe more. It was that last thought that should've terrified her. She'd been so blind to the rage inside of her ex-husband. She'd fallen victim to the romantic gestures, feigned support and the mask he'd hidden behind just for her. But something she couldn't identify promised Cree was exactly as he presented to the world. Perceptive to what she needed. Defensive against any possible threat. Capable of handling the baggage she carted behind her. She could only imagine how good it would feel to have that support all the time. "I give you my word. I will not go through the stuff under your bed."

That forest green gaze she'd come to trust lingered on her for a series of breaths. His phone vibrated with an incoming message, and it took everything she had to sever eye contact. "I had Macie forward me photos of missing women matching the description you gave me of the victim, going back a year. We've been so focused on believing the bombing was a spur-of-the-moment opportunity for our killer, but I'm starting to believe this has been a long time coming." He handed off his phone. "Any of these women look familiar?"

Alma scrolled down the entries, studying each face carefully before moving to the next. Every muscle in her body contracted as she reached the last photo in the lineup. She turned the screen to face him. "That's her."

It was a perfect match. The woman's hair was a bit longer in the photo, maybe a hint darker than Alma remembered under the circumstances, but the same almond-shaped eyes stared back at her. The same laugh lines carved from the widest part of her nose to the edges of her full mouth. The same necklace accentuated the woman's neck.

"You're sure?" Cree asked.

Alma shoved to her feet. She tugged the locket she'd recovered at the scene from her pocket and let Cree compare the one in her hand to the one around the woman's neck in the photo. There wasn't an ounce of doubt in her body. "Our victim's name is Erica Harmon."

THEY HAD A NAME.

The missing person report had been filed by Travis Foster, either a concerned friend or family member of the victim. If anyone could tell them why Erica

Harmon had come to Battle Mountain or what she'd been running from, it was him. His driver's license had popped with an Ouray address, and Cree maneuvered the truck down Red Mountain Pass toward the San Juan town as Alma reviewed the man's background information and personal records. Anything to give them a connection to their victim. "Navigation puts us about ten minutes out."

She shifted in her seat, her arm sling scratching against the truck's window controls. "Too bad. I think I might miss the numbness in my glutes." Gravity increased its hold as he took the next curve, and Alma's upper body crossed the midline of the cabin. The weight of her attention tightened the space between his shoulder blades. "All those times you've gotten yourself in trouble for saying the wrong thing... Was there someone in particular doling out the punishment?"

Sunlight cut through the windshield as he curved around the road. Steel guardrails separated jagged gray rocks and wild grass from asphalt, with dense green trees staggering up the side of the mountain. The one-lane road curved and switch-backed along the pass to drag out the quick descent into the valley, but Cree couldn't deny he'd grown comfortable with the woman in the passenger seat. Or that he was looking forward to the return trip. "Is that your way of asking me if I'm single?"

"I just noticed you haven't had a lot of visitors the past few months. Other than Mrs. Faris," she said.

"What makes you think she and I aren't an item?" He flashed her a wide smile. "She doesn't bake cookies for just anyone, you know."

"Let me guess. You fell in love on those long walks

with her cat." Her laugh punctured through the last of his hesitation. Free of external threats and influences these past two hours, Alma had lost the tension in her shoulders and her determination to hide behind that guarded expression. Instead, they'd talked about their mutual compulsion to learn new skills, read rather than watch television and stay physically fit for all situations. Even planned to take a run together one of these mornings. It had been nice. Comfortable. Despite her former life as an archaeologist, Alma was turning out to be more cop than he'd estimated. She was one of the most committed and loyal officers he'd worked with. Who else would've taken the responsibility of identifying a victim of a bombing when the entire investigation had been prioritized to stopping a bomber first and foremost? Hell, because of her he'd landed himself right back in the middle of an investigation, and he didn't hate it. He'd handled the most delicate, explosive components during his stretch as a bomb tech, but his partner came with a very different set of instructions. She set her uninjured hand on his thigh. "No, wait. I've got a better one. You fought for her when Mr. Heinz from downstairs challenged you to a duel for her hand."

"You think you're being funny, but that old guy hits harder than you might think. My jaw still clicks every time I yawn. Although our duel involved fighting for cookies and not to win over the heart of a seventy-year-old single retiree." Cree recalled all the instances he'd gone out for his morning run to find a plateful of baked goods wrapped in cellophane. "Wait. Now that I think about all the stuff she's baked for me, does Mrs. Faris really think we're dating?"

"Look at it this way," Alma said. "It'll only be for

another twenty years or so. If that, considering how much of her own baking she eats."

"She does make a mean pie." He couldn't remember the last time he'd laughed like this. Faster than he'd intended, the valley opened up in front of them through the windshield. Their laughter died at the realization, and Alma removed her hand from his thigh, leaving a solid print of heat behind. Cree cleared his throat to bring himself back into the moment, but it had been a good reprieve these past couple of hours. "We're getting close."

Ouray took pride in regarding itself as the Switzerland of America and the outdoor recreational capital of Colorado. Rugged peaks guarded the small town that had an even smaller population than Battle Mountain, and its colorful roofs brightening a grid-like layout made it a perfect choice for a holiday or a vacation postcard. From the east boundary of the town, it didn't take them long to find Travis Foster's town house, nestled between two just like it. Cree parked along the curb. Plain beige siding stretched horizontally across the building with a bright blue door, the garage sporting the same look. White trim outlined three windows at the front but failed to add any personality to the home itself. "Doesn't look like much."

Cree shouldered out of the truck at the sight of the Ouray Police Department cruiser pulling up in front of them. Alma rounded the hood to catch up. Her courtesy call to Ouray police had been met with frustration and defiance. Towns this small went out of their way to make sure they avoided stepping on one another's toes, but there hadn't been time to convince the local police chief they had a solid lead. Hell, they didn't even have a body. Cree nodded to the sergeant adjusting his hat as he climbed from the vehicle.

"Sergeant Hale, thanks for coming out." Alma stretched her hand in greeting. "Your chief told us you'd be joining us."

"Officer Majors, I presume." The six-foot officer dressed in navy blues and a bright gold shield on his chest hiked his thumbs under his belt. The ten-gallon hat cast shadows across a lean, square, middle-aged face with nondescript features. A man of few words. Cree could get along with a guy like that. Then again, the sergeant seemed to be making it a point to let them know he and Alma weren't welcome. "Chief told me you're here to talk to one of our residents in your bombing, but I'll be the one asking the questions here. Travis Foster doesn't have a criminal record and is just trying to get through most days as a single father. He's well-liked, especially considering how many jobs his company provides this town, and I won't have you accusing him of having had something to do with your investigation."

"Sergeant, we have no intention of accusing anyone." Alma dismissed the clear-cut hostility from the Ouray officer and retracted her offered hand. "We just want to ask him about the woman he filed a missing person report for."

"You're talking about Erica," Sergeant Hale said.

"You knew her?" Cree asked.

Hale diverted his attention to the town house. "I've been telling him for months she up and left because of the pressure of being a mom. My own wife went through the same thing after our second kid. Postpartum depression, the doctor said. Didn't take it seriously at first. I mean, most women do just fine after delivering their babies, but the more you think about it, the more you see the signs something isn't right."

"And Erica was showing those signs leading up to her disappearance?" Alma's gaze narrowed.

"The last time I saw her before she hightailed it out of here, she was in my station asking questions about a restraining order. I'd never seen her so…" Sergeant Hale shifted his weight into one leg. "Gaunt, paranoid even. I had half a mind to call Travis to come get her, but she ran out of there so fast I lost her before I'd even gotten to the door. When Travis came in to file the missing person report a few days later, I asked him about it. He swears everything had been fine between her and the baby, and that something else had her spooked. To be honest, after all these months she's been gone, I'm starting to believe him."

Gaunt. Paranoid. Restraining orders. Hell, it sounded as though Erica Harmon had been pushed to the edge and was trying to do whatever it took from keeping herself going off the deep end. Cree's attention slid to Alma, and his stomach dropped. Everything Hale had just described could fit postpartum depression. Or an abusive relationship. "Did Ms. Harmon tell you who she wanted to get a restraining order against?"

"No." Hale shook his head. "Seems she wasn't exactly happy with my answers, didn't like the idea a piece of paper wasn't enough to keep someone from breaking the order or that the offender could be back on the street within twelve to twenty-four hours."

Alma rolled her head forward a hair's breadth, a simple enough action, but one that spoke volumes. At least to him. She cleared her throat. "Public records didn't show any record of a marriage, but you said Erica and Travis have a child together, is that right?"

"Common-law marriage. Those kids have been together as long as I've known them, since high school. Always thought they'd make it. Guess I was wrong." Hale headed for the bright blue front door and pounded his fist against the wood. "Travis, it's Gary. Just need a couple minutes of your time."

Gravel crunched under Cree's boots as he maneuvered closer to the door, his awareness of his partner at an all-time high. Their victim had gone to a police station and started asking about a restraining order. That, coupled with the paranoia, would've triggered Alma's defenses. Not only was she trained to spot it, Alma had lived it, too, but for the life of him he couldn't read what was going on behind those brown eyes.

The door swung inward, and a version of the man they'd run a background check on centered himself in the doorway. A toddler, who Cree guessed was around a year or year and a half, squeezed chubby thighs on either side of Travis's hip and stared out at them with two fingers in his mouth. "Hey, Gary. I wasn't expecting you until tomorrow." Travis nodded a greeting before his attention targeted Alma and then Cree. Color drained from the man's face as he took in Alma's uniform, and he clutched his son tighter. "What's going on?"

"Travis, we're here about Erica." Hale removed his hat and fiddled with it between both hands. "This here is Officer Majors and Cree Gregson from Battle Mountain. They believe they may have found your wife."

Chapter Seven

Her heart had lodged in her throat. There didn't seem to be enough air out here in the great outdoors as she studied the toddler staring straight back at her. It was him, the baby from the locket. She could see the similarities in his wide eyes—the same as his mother's—in the way his nose bubbled at the edges and the shape of his mouth. The photo she'd clung to for the past three days didn't compare to the handsome boy laying his head against his father's shoulder.

Alma forced her hand to her side instead of giving in to the urge to tug the keepsake from her pocket. They'd found the victim's family, but the hollowness that had carved through her that first time she'd been on the receiving end of her ex-husband's rage warned that the person who'd killed Erica Harmon was standing right in front of them.

"What do you mean 'may have'? Either you found her, or you didn't." Travis Foster ran his palm up the length of the toddler's spine. He threw his frantic questions to Alma, and her gut seized up. "Where is she? Is she safe? Can I see her?"

Her pulse thickened behind her ears.

"Travis, let's go inside before the neighbors start

eavesdropping." Hale reached a single hand out and gripped Foster by the shoulder, maneuvering him back into the small town house.

Alma and Cree followed suit as the pressure intensified at the back of her skull.

Beige paint and tan floor-to-ceiling tile darkened the interior of the town house. Two separate cat towers took up a good amount of space as they stepped down into the sunken living room. Sunlight cut through the single window at the back of the main level and gleamed off a small, circular dining room set. Toys, clothing and stains added to the crowded feeling throughout as Foster turned to face them.

"You'll have to excuse the mess. Erica was usually the one to keep things organized." Foster bounced the toddler in his arms in front of what looked like an old, disassembled computer. No evidence of a motherboard inside. "I filed a missing person report for Erica six months ago. Where is my wife?"

Cree took up position at her right side, and the wash of anxiety that had nearly pulled her under lessened. "Mr. Foster, I'm sorry to have to be the one to tell you this, but your wife was killed during a bombing in Battle Mountain three nights ago."

Foster's skin paled, his mouth parting on a strong exhale. In a flash of a moment, the single father had gone from panicked suspect to sufficiently grieving actor. He seemed to realize he had yet to respond and turned to set the toddler in a nearby pack-and-play. Threading his hands through unkempt hair, Foster fisted two chunks and pulled. "I don't understand. You're saying she's dead? What…what was she doing in Battle Mountain?"

"That's what we're here to find out." Cree cut his attention to Alma, and her pulse ticked higher, before he turned expectantly to Sergeant Hale.

"Travis, I need you to go over what happened in the days leading up to Erica's disappearance again." Hale ducked his chin, his voice softening. "I know we've been through it before when you filed the missing person report, but now that we know what happened to her, it'll help figure out who could've done this."

A line of tears welled in the suspect's eyes, right on time. Foster released the hold on his hair and glanced down at his son. "I knew something bad had happened. I knew she wouldn't have left us if she didn't have a choice." He turned the fire building in his gaze onto Sergeant Hale. "I told you something was wrong, but you said there wasn't anything you could do. You tried to convince me she ran because of some pressure to be a good mom." Foster stretched one hand out and knocked a stack of baby books off the top of the television. The books slammed against the far wall or fell short, and battle-ready tension instantly tightened the muscles down Alma's spine. The toddler whimpered from his pack-and-play. "She loved Ethan. She never would've left him—she never would've left me—unless she had to, and now she's dead!"

Cree stepped forward, almost putting himself between her and their prime suspect, and she tugged the Taser in her belt free, but Sergeant Hale motioned for her to wait. She hadn't been an officer long, but there'd been plenty of times she'd read about domestic calls going wrong. She wouldn't let Cree become a statistic. He kept his distance, raising his palms out. "Mr. Foster, I understand what you're feeling right now. You're hurt, you're angry, you're grieving and in shock. It's an unpredictable cocktail you're not sure how to process, but I need you to remember your son is here. I know for a fact you love him. I saw it in the way you held him, how you unconsciously ran your fingers through his hair. He needs you to stay calm so no one else gets hurt. Okay? Can you do that?"

The tension intensified as Alma tried to predict the suspect's behavior. Cree wasn't on active duty anymore, but he'd stepped up to neutralize the situation all the same. He'd taken control, and the part of her she'd tried to forget, the part that had led her to becoming a Battle Mountain police officer in the first place, appreciated the effort. She had no objectivity here. The questions about restraining orders, the paranoia Hale described, the sudden disappearance of their victim—all of it had the potential to fit domestic abuse. Not to mention Travis Foster owned a construction company where the C4 used in the bomb could've originated.

"She wouldn't have left us," Foster said.

Soft sobs filled the small living room as the toddler took in every second, every movement. Foster's shoulders shook under the emotional weight, and Alma set her thumb to the side of the Taser's trigger. The worst of the storm was passing, but she'd let her guard down one too many times before. Alma licked suddenly dry lips and reached into her pants pocket. She holstered the Taser, then slowly unpocketed the shiny white gold locket and held it out, and Sergeant Hale relaxed in her peripheral vision. "Mr. Foster, do you recognize this?"

Dark eyes locked onto the trinket and widened. Shock carved deep lines in Foster's forehead as he closed the distance between them. Cree maneuvered to intercept, but Alma shook her head. Weathered hands—working hands—handled the delicate chain with respect, but Foster didn't move to take the locket from her. "Where did you get this?"

"The night of the bombing, I responded to a suspicious activity call. As I was searching the area, I found this. A few seconds later, I found your wife." An invisible blaze of rage charged up her throat, and Alma set the locket in Foster's hand. "It's Erica's, isn't it?"

He pried open the latch, letting her keep hold of the chain. A watery smile eased the shock from his expression as he studied the photo of his child secured inside. "The locket was meant to be an engagement present. We were going to get married, finally. She never took it off. Never." Inspecting the chain, he seemed on the verge of collapse and raised his gaze to hers. "Please tell me who did this to my wife."

"We're still trying to find that out. You should know I spoke to her, Mr. Foster." She studied the slightest changes in the suspect's expression, body language, weight distribution—anything to give her confirmation of what her gut was telling her was true. Acid burned up her throat as Foster's gaze leveled with hers, and the urge to rip the locket from his hand increased. She couldn't let something so precious to their victim to be left in the hands of the man who'd most likely killed her. "Did you know she was still alive when you attached the bomb to her stomach? Did you know the last thing she did was save my life by telling me to run before the explosion ripped her apart?"

"What?" Travis took a step back.

"Officer Majors, you are sorely out of line here."

Sergeant Hale stepped into her peripheral vision, a warning. Cree held one arm out to stop his approach.

"What are you talking about?" Foster's attention racquetballed between her and Hale. The mask of the grieving husband disintegrated in the blink of an eye and exposed the lying bastard beneath as he pulled back his shoulders. "That's why you're here? To accuse me of killing my wife? I never would've hurt Erica. I loved her. I have since I was sixteen years old. We have a child together, for crying out loud."

Cree brushed his arm against hers, but the contact didn't hold the same reaction as before. Where he'd settled the nervousness eating her from the inside a few moments ago, now there was only annoyance. Adrenaline spiked in her veins, and her heart rate rocketed. One in four women experienced domestic violence from their partner, and he was just going to pretend the signs weren't there? "Alma, let's get some fresh air."

"No." She shoved away from him. "I know you killed Erica, Travis. I know you're the one who strapped your wife with that bomb to destroy the evidence and any chance of us identifying her, but it didn't work. You left that note on my door after breaking into my apartment to warn me to back off, but I'm not going to stop. You're not going to get away with this."

Foster turned toward Sergeant Hale. "Are you just going to stand there and let her accuse me of killing Erica, or are you going to do your damn job?" He faced off with Alma and pointed toward the front door. "Get the hell out of my house. All of you."

"Come on." Cree threaded his hand between her ribs and arm and maneuvered her toward the front door, but she wasn't going to turn her back on a man suspected of hurting his wife. Not again.

Faster than she expected, a flood of cool air worked beneath her collar and along the back of her neck, but it failed to appease her fight-or-flight instincts. The front door slammed behind them, and it was only then she realized Sergeant Hale had stayed inside. Alma wrenched away from her partner and marched across the driveway, the locket still in hand. Every cell in her body needed distance between them, but she refused to run from her problems. Not after what she'd survived. "What the hell was that? You could've backed me up in there. He did it, Cree. Foster killed his wife, and he thinks he's going to get away with it."

"That might be the case, but we can't charge him with anything without evidence. You know that." Cree approached with caution. A combination of concern and exasperation etched into his expression and stole some of the heat from her anger. He reached for her, softly latching onto her upper arms. "You're tired, you're running on empty and you're on edge from everything that's happened the past few days. With damn good reason. Let's get back to Battle Mountain and touch base with your chief. The Silverton bomb squad might've found something we can use. Okay?"

She nodded as the anger she'd relied on to get her through the last few minutes of the interview dissipated. He was right. They didn't have enough evidence on Foster to make an arrest, but that didn't lessen her confidence Foster had been involved in his wife's death. Alma studied the front window of the town house before Cree directed her toward his pickup, recalling the computer disassembled in the living room.

Their suspect stared out at them from the other side, his toddler back on his hip, then Foster closed the curtain.

CREE HAULED THE comforter toward the ceiling and centered it across the bed.

Coming back to Battle Mountain should've brought a sense of relief, but the return trip had drained him dry. Alma hadn't said a word, only staring out the window for the entire two hours. Hell, he'd made a mess of things between them. Any progress he'd achieved in getting his partner to open up had been shattered the moment he hadn't backed her up during Travis Foster's interview.

The bathroom door clicked open, and Alma emerged clinging to her uniform, holster complete with gun and her boots to her chest. Tendrils of wet hair cascaded over the too big T-shirt he'd lent her and soaked through to her skin. The effect exaggerated the fatigue etched into her face, but the fact she was still standing after everything testified to the strength she'd developed the past few years.

"I've almost got the bed ready." Cree smoothed the lumps from the comforter with a few pointed slides of his hand, but there wasn't anything he could do in this room to make it feel less barren or more welcoming. He didn't know how to do…this. Taking others into consideration hadn't been a big focus while his grandfather was teaching him to survive in the middle of nowhere. His parents had never shown him any—still didn't—and for the first time since he'd walked away from his career, he wasn't sure how to proceed. He rubbed his hands together, a distraction from studying the long length of her legs partially hidden under the pair of boxers he'd lent her. "How…how are you feeling?"

"Better. Thank you. I think the smoke smell in my hair is finally starting to wash out." Alma scanned the space he'd claimed as his bedroom the past eight months, and embarrassment turned his insides. "I, um, wanted to talk to you about earlier."

"Okay." He straightened, mentally preparing for another assault.

"You were right about Travis Foster. We don't have enough evidence for me to make the kind of accusation I did, and I'm sorry I yelled at you for not backing me up." She smoothed her thumb over the shiny Battle Mountain Police Department badge still pinned to her uniform as though it gave her a bit of comfort. "You were just doing your job. I obviously wasn't thinking very clearly in the moment, and I let my own experiences color the situation. It won't happen again."

Cree swallowed the thickness building in his throat as his own past crept into the cracks of this investigation. He'd left the bomb squad behind, but the memories were still there. The failures, the wins, the screams and the praises—there was no running from it. No changing it. "Yes, it will."

Shock chased back the exhaustion darkening the circles under her eyes, and she clutched her uniform tighter. "If you don't think I'm fit for duty—"

"Alma." He rounded the end of the bed and reached for the mass of fabric and steel she insisted using as a protective barrier between them. Taking her uniform and weapon, he set them on the end of the bed. "Everything you've been through, all the pain, the nightmares and raw sensitivity and awareness—it's part of you now. It's what molded you into the woman standing in front of me, and as much as you want to ignore it or make it so it doesn't affect you, that's never going to happen. It's going to influence your decision-making on the job. It's going to make you question yourself twice. But ultimately, it's what's going to save the next woman in the same position you were in, and that is something you don't ever have to apologize for."

Her bottom lip parted a split second before Alma crushed her mouth to his. Stirring heat rushed under his skin as she pressed herself against him. His hands dropped to her waist, doing everything in their power to bring her closer. Lean muscle flexed and released under his palms, and the entire world threatened to tip on its axis. Mint toothpaste exploded across his tongue as she broke through the seam of his lips, and in that moment, he was lost. It didn't matter that they were partners, that having her stay in his apartment for the night was completely unprofessional or that once this case was solved they'd go their separate ways. He wanted her. Not just the pieces she'd let him see. He wanted it all. Every ounce. Every inch. Everything, and he wanted to give her every part of himself in return.

Three hard knocks at the front door pulled him back from the brink. Disorientation overwhelmed his control as he noted the flush in her face. He worked to contain his own physiological reaction and forced himself to release her. There were only two people who'd known Alma would be staying the night. Chief Ford and his counterpart, Easton. The only reason they'd make contact was because of the case. "I think that's probably for you."

"Unless Mrs. Faris is here for a date you forgot to

reschedule." She brushed her fingertips across her lips, hiding a brief smile. The same desire that had pulled him beneath the surface swam in her eyes. "I'll just… Yeah." Alma turned on her bare heels and strode down the hallway straight to the front door.

He made quick work of replaying the kiss they'd shared in his head as he straightened her uniform on the bed. He'd give her some privacy. Because, honestly, he didn't want to know BMPD's next steps in the case. He and Alma had done their job. They'd identified the victim left at the bottom of the gulch, and the logical part of him understood that landmark in the investigation concluded their partnership. Whatever the chief or Easton had to say, he was happy to stay in ignorance. At least for a little while longer.

What had started as a duty to ensure no one was hurt during the bombing had quickly turned into something more. Because of Alma. She'd burned through his determination to detach from the past and showed him there was life after pain, that no matter what happened, he was still here. He could still do good, and hell, if he didn't want more of that in his life. More of her. Not only had she trusted him to work this case beside her but she'd relied on him. Made him feel capable, confident, useful. Strong, even, and he didn't want to let that go.

"Everything okay out there?" Cree brushed his cracked fingertips over the gold shield pinned to the breast of her uniform. No answer. He moved in line with the bedroom door standing wide open. Confusion rippled down his spine as a sweet summer breeze filled the apartment. "Alma?"

He could've sworn he'd heard her say something

when she opened the door, but Cree didn't hear anything now. His fingers tingled, and he curled them into fists at his sides. Alma wouldn't have just left without telling him, especially not dressed in an extra set of his pajamas. Cree scanned the small bathroom off to his right. No movement. Nothing to suggest she was even still in the apartment. The kitchen was just as empty, and he moved into the front living room. Something wasn't right. "Are you here?"

A small piece of paper tumbled end over end before catching on the carpet past the entryway. Cree stomped on one side before it had the chance to escape. He read the handwritten scroll on one side, an exact match to the handwriting from the note left on Alma's apartment door. *You should've listened.*

Cree shoved the note in his pocket and launched out the front door. Shadows crawled up the walls of the corridor between their apartments, the outline of crime scene tape still visible across Alma's door. The bomber had known. The SOB had anticipated she'd stay in Cree's apartment and come for her when he'd least expected it.

Leaves shook under the stress of the wind in both directions and blocked any sounds that would give him an idea of which direction the bastard had taken her. Damn it. He headed for the nearest staircase, almost tripping over his own feet as he hit the landing. They couldn't have gotten far. He could still find her. He had to find her. "Alma!"

No response.

He sprinted toward his truck, digging his keys from his jeans, and wrenched open the driver's-side door. It wasn't a coincidence they'd uncovered the victim's identity only to have Alma vanish into thin air twelve hours later. He should've been on guard. He should've protected her better. His heart pounded too hard behind his ears as he shoved the key into the ignition and twisted.

The engine clicked but refused to turn over.

He tried again and pumped the accelerator. Adrenaline kept his body fine-tuned to external threats, and after the second try to start the engine logic crept in. His brain caught up. Too late. "Oh, hell."

Cree shouldered out of the truck.

Fire burned down his back and thrust him across the parking lot. He slammed into a vehicle two stalls over—Mr. Heinz's rusted Cadillac—as the explosion tore across the asphalt. Pain ricocheted around his head and down his legs, too familiar. Debris shot in every direction. The dragon raged to life as it fed off the gasoline in the truck's reservoir. His skin blistered from proximity, and Cree collapsed to the pavement.

Darkness encroached around the edges of his vision, but he couldn't stop. He couldn't stay here without putting his own life at risk. Black smoke tendrilled up into the cloudless night as distinctive shouts filled his ears. In seconds, the distant wail of a siren countered the pop and crack of the flames. Every muscle in his body begged for relief as Cree pulled himself over the curb and across the sidewalk. Warm grass worked to catch him but only managed to aggravate the burns along his arms and neck. "Alma."

Eruptions of memory contorted right in front of him as the past weaved into the present. The sirens, the groans of pain, thick smoke drilling into his lungs, the carnage—he couldn't escape. Inky spiderwebs closed in and numbed the burn of pain down his back and arms, but it wouldn't be enough to counter the guilt clawing to the surface.

He'd failed all over again.

Chapter Eight

"How long did you expect me to fall for your little charade, Officer Majors?"

Pain lanced through the side of her head and down into her injured shoulder as Alma struggled to right herself. Her wrists refused to support her upper body as she shoved against wet earth. Instead, her shoulder sunk deeper into the marshland and threatened to give way completely as she tried to bring her hands forward. The last seconds of consciousness seeped back into her memory. The knock at Cree's front door, the feel of hot summer heat spreading across her legs as she answered. Confusion when no one had been on the other side. Then agony as something fast and hot had pinched the side of her neck.

Humidity climbed deep into her lungs as she shifted her weight into her hips. The clothing Cree had lent her had soaked through. The question hanging between her and her abductor solidified as the fog cleared. Alma set her head against something spongey and closed her eyes to catalog her surroundings. Moss? "As long as it took."

Mud suctioned under the weight of heavy footsteps nearby, but her vision hadn't adjusted to the darkness yet. Before she had a chance to gauge her abductor's location, a dark outline centered above her. "You should've left well enough alone."

The voice warbled from the low ringing in her ears. But not enough to convince Alma the killer standing over her fit the original profile. According to Cree, most bombings were committed by males, but the distinct curves against the backdrop of millions of stars above suggested Erica Harmon had been murdered by a woman. Alma breathed through the damp muck permeating every fiber of her clothing and hair, but nothing discharged the savage pain in her side. "Let me guess. Because now you're going to kill me?"

"You catch on quick." The killer retreated from Alma's limited vision. "Hope you don't mind, but I removed your shoulder sling and jewelry. Can't have anyone identifying your remains before I'm ready."

"Like we did with Erica's locket. That's why you were in my apartment, wasn't it? You wanted it back." A ring of trees pulled away from the velvet of the night. She tested the plastic biting into the hypersensitized skin of her ankles. She couldn't have been unconscious long without the use of a sedative, which meant her abductor couldn't have taken her far from Battle Mountain. A few miles at most. Small details defined themselves around her as her senses caught up to adjust to her situation. Trees. Moss. Mud. The ringing in her ears subsided as she held her breath. Water lapped a few feet behind her, and Alma gritted her teeth as rocks cut into her side from the slightest shift of her weight. Not Gunnison River. Too calm. The only other body of water near town was the lake. "San Cristobal," she whispered to herself.

It would be easy enough for the bomber to dispose of her remains in a place like this. Days, months, years would go by without so much as a shard of bone to identify.

"She fought back much harder than I expected. After I'd stabbed her, she tossed the locket so I wouldn't be able to find it. Told me I'd never know what it felt like to love anyone other than myself. I couldn't waste time trying to find it in that garbage heap, but the good news is I learn from my mistakes." A punctured click of metal pierced through the hard thud of Alma's pulse behind her ears. Another squelch of mud hiked her heart rate into overdrive a split second before the shadow of Erica Harmon's killer solidified. "You're much smarter than I gave you credit for. It's too bad. I think you could've made a real difference with your new career, but you know as well as I do I can't have you getting in my way again. I mean, did you really think I wouldn't be watching the investigation into the bombing?"

The moonless night failed to highlight any of the woman's identifying features, but the low, whiskey-smooth voice etched itself into Alma's brain. She'd never forget that voice. The calmness, the confidence, the slight upturn of pitch on the victim's name. "You killed her. Erica."

A humorless laugh filtered through the slight up-tick of panic infusing along Alma's spine. "Seems my plan to destroy every piece of her in that gulch worked. You and your department—your partner from Larimer County—you don't even know who you're investigating, but I guess it doesn't matter now. Your forensic lab might be able to run DNA on the bone you recovered, but they won't have anything to compare it to. She was too careful. Managed to hide from me for the better part of a decade, but she made a mistake. She fell in love. Had a baby. You wouldn't imagine how easy it was to find her after that."

A rip of Velcro raised the hairs on the back of her neck, and Alma pressed her heels into the soggy mud holding her hostage. The bomber had done her due diligence. She'd studied the investigating officers on the case. She'd planned for every variable, and the location she'd chosen for her victims would guarantee a win. The stink of marshland soaked into Alma's pores. With the lake behind her and miles of wilderness on the other three sides, she'd never stand a chance, but she had to try. A hard edge of weight pressed into her gut and emptied her lungs. "Why?"

"Why?" the bomber asked. "Do you know how it feels to be outshone in every way? To be told to be more like someone else, that you're not good enough the way you are? No matter how hard you try, they're always going to be better. At baking, at family game night, at manners. They're always going to get the first serving of dessert and get to sit in the front seat of the car next to your parents. They're always going to be the favorite, and you…you're always going to disappoint. No matter how hard you try to prove otherwise. No matter how you try to change, they don't love you the same."

Dryness charged down Alma's throat as her ex-husband's verbal assaults superimposed over the killer's voice. There had been times in her marriage she'd believed him, that she'd felt bad for her success because it pained him so deeply. That she was the worthless one.

That she was the reason for his unhappiness. Blind-sided by that hurt, Alma curled two fingers into her palms just as Easton had taught her during their stint together in the rehab facility he'd founded on his family's land. The organization hadn't just been for soldiers suffering from PTSD like him or for his fiancée trying to relearn how to walk, but for anyone who'd needed support. Physically. Emotionally. The therapists there had taught her one mantra to get her through the flashbacks: stay in the moment. She pressed her short fingernails into the tender skin of her palms and counted off her pulse. One. Two. Three. Four. Five. Her forced breathing ripped her from one impossible situation into the most recent. Warm liquid bubbled from her palms, but the pain of drawing blood would center her. "You knew her. The woman you killed."

"My sister deserved every ounce of pain she suffered." The killer's voice dipped an octave as she secured something to Alma's midsection. "It didn't matter I exceeded their expectations and actually made something of myself while she decided to dance through life. She turned our parents against me. They applauded her for her creativity while my choice to investigate explosives and arson cases was ignored at every family dinner, every holiday. They wanted to know about my sister's rehearsals, the costumes, the locations, the other dancers and if she'd injured herself." Another bitter laugh rippled into the night. "Not one of them visited me in the hospital after I'd been shot on an undercover assignment gone wrong, Not once had anyone ever asked me about my work. Not once did they decide I was worth the effort."

A low, electrical buzz filled Alma's ears, and understanding hit. A bomb. The killer was going to stick with her MO to make Alma disappear. She had one chance to make it out of this alive and let Chief Ford, Easton and Cree know where she was. It all depended on her next move. Alma pressed her shoulders into the soft earth. The mud would make escape difficult, but she didn't have any shoes to worry about slowing her down. "You're a bomb squad tech."

"No, Officer Majors. I'm not, but if you can believe it, I've actually met Cree Gregson once before. I've been doing this job for so long that I can assemble a device with my eyes closed, which, as it turns out, is a nice skill when you're committing murder in the middle of nowhere." A flicker of red LED lights exploded from Alma's side. The square designs quickly rearranged themselves into a readable countdown. One minute. Long, gloved fingers moved a coiled wire from the front of the device to the back. The light-colored outline of C4 molded into bricks separated from the encroaching darkness.

Alma tried to sit up, but the killer slammed her back to the ground with the force of one foot. The countdown illuminated a lean frame and long dark hair but not much else. No identifying marks. Nothing Alma could use after she escaped. Because she would escape.

"Tsk, tsk, tsk. Now you're not going to make me stab you like I had to stab my sister, are you, Officer Majors?" The bomber reached behind her. The glint of metal in the red lighting reflected back into Alma's eyes. "Believe me. None of this is personal, and I wouldn't want to make you suffer any more than you have to."

"Don't worry about me. I can take care of myself."

Alma rolled out from beneath the killer's boot. Rocks pierced through the soft muscle of her arms and hips as she rolled. Twice. Three times. Agony ripped through her middle with every jar of the device strapped to her front, but she wouldn't stop. No matter how long it took to escape. No matter how far she had to run. Dizziness threatened to steal her control as she brought her zip-tied hands down and tucked her knees into her chest. The edge of the tie around her wrists caught on her heel and slowed her down, but while her abductor could assemble a bomb with her eyes closed, she couldn't follow Alma in the dark. Not after she lost the neon billboard displaying her position. She crouched hard and fast to break the ties around her ankles but collapsed to one knee as the pain in her side raged. The tie had broken, and it was only a hard swing of her arms that severed the one around her wrists. She pressed her hand over the bomb, searching for the strap securing it to her midsection.

"You're going to want to keep your eye on that clock, Officer Majors." The killer's outline dissipated into a wall of trees. A flashlight beam cut through the night from the bomber's position a split second before she tossed it toward Alma. The flashlight thudded hard against the ground.

The beam lit a soft halo around Alma's feet. She ducked her chin to read the monitor. The countdown had already begun. She didn't know anything about disarming the device. She had less than forty seconds to get as far from the blast as possible. She traced the edges of the device with both hands but failed to find a strap. It was then she noted the dark color spreading across Cree's white T-shirt from beneath the device.

Twenty seconds.

Air crushed from her lungs. Mud, even watered down, didn't spread like that. Which meant… Blood.

"No. No, no, no, no." The killer had threaded the line through the C4 and sewn it directly to Alma's torso. She gripped one end of the device and pulled. Lightning struck from the edges of her vision and charged across her midsection.

Ten seconds.

She'd escaped her abusive, narcissistic ex and survived. This wasn't how she was going to die. Not when the future had finally started looking so bright.

Five seconds.

Alma closed her eyes. She was out of time.

CREE KEPT HIS distance as fire crews extinguished the last of the blaze.

Stinging pain burned down his neck and face as the same EMT who'd seen to Alma assessed his wounds. The ointment helped, but there wasn't much else they could do for this kind of injury in the field. He'd learned from experience.

Red and blue patrol lights cut across his vision as Easton Ford shoved from the passenger side of the vehicle short of stopping. Guarded concern etched deep into his expression as he rounded the hood and stalked toward Cree. "What the hell happened, Gregson?" Easton fisted each side of Cree's jacket and shoved him against the back door of the ambulance. The former Green Beret had a reputation for a short fuse and a protective streak, especially for the women in his life. "Alma was supposed to be safe with you, damn it. You knew the bastard was targeting her, and you let her out of your sight."

"I told you everything I remember on the phone." Cree pushed back, aggravating the burns along his arms, but he couldn't fault the deputy for his misdirected anger. Hell, if anything he deserved worse. "One minute she was there, the next she was gone. I didn't see a damn thing before it was too late."

Chief Ford ripped his brother back. "Go get witness statements from the neighbors. It's possible one of them saw which direction Alma was taken. That's an order." He didn't wait for an answer. The chief directed his attention to the EMT. "Any casualties?"

"No, sir. Mr. Gregson sustained the worst of it," the EMT said.

"Good. Be somewhere else, then." Battle Mountain's first line of defense settled that unreadable gaze on Cree as the EMT gave them space. "I'm not here to issue fault, Gregson. I just need to know where my officer is. You and I both know Officer Majors is more than capable of protecting herself, but this killer is determined to hide their tracks. They've already killed one victim, attempted three more and blown up your truck for good measure. I've dealt with serial killers before, but bombers are your territory. Who the hell are we looking for and what do they want with Alma?"

Cree couldn't breathe, couldn't think. Old wounds itched with remembered pain across his shoulders and down his back, but he couldn't let the past threaten the present. Not with Alma out there. "I'm not a profiler. All I can tell you is whoever is behind this knows what they're doing. Wiring a bomb to detonate when a vehicle's engine starts is more complicated than putting together a few components from an electronics store and a set of instructions off the internet." Heat intensified the sting along his neck and face as he studied the flames. He pointed to what was left of his truck. "Think about what we have so far. The person who killed Erica Harmon didn't want to risk leaving behind evidence to identify her. That tells me this is someone who's studied forensics." He ticked off his index finger then moved onto the middle. "The bomber knew we'd trace the components of the initial explosion back to Galaxy Electronics, beat us to it and got rid of any video evidence they'd been there. That tells me they've worked investigations." He pressed his sore palm into his ring finger. "And the fact they know how to not only build a device but wire a vehicle to explode upon ignition… That tells me they were professionally trained."

Chief Ford straightened and stood a bit taller. The last of the flames sizzled under the onslaught of the fire hose and targeted attacks from the fire crew, kicking up steam behind him. "That doesn't sound like a civilian with a grudge against the victim. You're talking about an investigator."

"Yeah, I am." The pieces lined up, creating a blurry puzzle he couldn't see yet, but for the time being, it was his leading theory.

The chief removed his ten-gallon hat and pushed his hair back off his forehead. The patrol car's lights reflected off the large belt buckle at his waist and burned Cree's retinas. "Hell. I've got an APB out for Officer Majors and put Macie on the phones. If we're looking for a trained explosives investigator, it stands to reason they're being careful. Avoiding main roads and nosy neighbors. Somewhere out of town—"

A secondary explosion had Cree and the rest of the first responders ducking toward the ground. He twisted around and caught sight of a high plume of fire to the west. The nerve endings that hadn't been burned by the inferno of his truck turned to ice. "Alma." Cree scanned the parking lot as gut-wrenching nausea churned. He closed the distance between him and the chief and stretched out his hand. "I need your keys."

"That's my officer. I'm driving." Chief Ford issued an ear-splitting whistle of several notes as he rounded the hood and wrenched open the driver's-side door.

Cree collapsed into the passenger seat and slammed the door behind him. He spotted Easton Ford skipping the last few stairs of the apartment complex and sprinting toward the car. He clenched the dashboard to counter the unbalance wrecking through him at the thought of Alma caught in the latest explosion. "Did you seriously just whistle for your brother to heel?"

"Works every time." Chief Ford threw the patrol car into Reverse and stepped on the accelerator. He whipped the back end into the lot, barely missing the ambulance with the hood, and slammed on the brakes. Easton threw the back door open and climbed inside a split second before the screech of tires filled the small cabin of the vehicle. "Those flames are coming from outside town. Near the lake."

The map Cree had memorized as a teen growing up with his grandfather on the outskirts of town filtered through his mind. It had been years since he'd paid a visit. So much had already changed, and he couldn't rely on his history to comfort the anxiety clawing up his throat. "What's out there?"

"Nothing much. A few hunting cabins that only get

used a few months out of the year. Mostly marshland." Chief Ford took a hard right turn onto Highway 149, and momentum shifted Cree to the other side of the car. The chief detached the radio strapped to the dashboard and hit the push-to-talk button. "Dispatch, I need fire and rescue redirected out to San Cristobal Lake ASAP. We've got another explosion, and I don't want to take the chance of those flames spreading."

"You got it, Chief," Macie said.

The weight of Weston Ford's quick assessment lodged air in Cree's throat while pressure built between his shoulder blades thanks to the man's brother in the back seat. He could practically feel their concern and anxiety when it came to Alma. "Alma is a good officer. She knows what she's doing."

"I hope you're right." Cree gripped the handle above his head tighter than necessary, but it was the only thing keeping him grounded as seconds distorted into minutes and then into what felt like an hour. Town limits bled to flat valleys and mountainous peaks. The trees grew thicker and the darkness heavier.

Until an orange glow up ahead consumed their attention.

Cree pressed his heels into the floor as he took in the expanse of flames spreading fast.

"Holy hell." Easton threaded all ten fingers through the metal web barricading the back seat from the front.

The chief got back on the radio as heat penetrated through the windows and the vehicle's frame. "Dispatch, this fire is eating through everything in its path. Get Silverton and Ouray fire and rescue out here and issue an evacuation order now!"

Macie's voice barely pierced through the hard thud

of Cree's pulse at the base of his skull. Chief Ford brought the vehicle to a complete stop, and Cree hit the dirt. He jogged toward the first wall of flames as they licked up pines and devoured the brush across the wilderness floor.

"Gregson, you can't go in there!" Easton's voice penetrated through the roar and pop of the fire as a strong grip wrapped around his arm. "You won't make it a dozen feet before that fire eats you alive. You need to wait for fire and rescue!"

"I'm not leaving her!" Cree shoved the former soldier off. Sweat built along the sides of his face and pooled under his collar. The burns along his neck protested every second he held firm. He was the reason Alma had been taken in the first place. He wasn't going to fail her now. Peeling his jacket from his shoulders, he ducked beneath the fabric. "I need water."

Easton Ford rounded back into the patrol car and popped the trunk. Grabbing three water bottles, he handed off two to Cree and soaked his own jacket with the third.

"What are you doing?" Cree asked.

"You're not the only one who cares about what happens to Alma. We'll find her faster if we split up." Easton accepted the handheld radio his brother offered and clipped it to his belt, Cree doing the same. "Where did the fire originate?"

Cree scanned the fiery landscape. Every second they wasted with logistics was another second Alma didn't have, but they couldn't search this entire area blind, either. He pointed to the collection of trees and bushes at an angle. The blast from the explosive had knocked them off center. Water dripped from the hem of his jacket as he set it over his head and shoulders. "There. About one hundred yards northeast."

"You search there. I'll take the perimeter in case she got away," Easton said.

"I'll give you five minutes! Stay in radio contact. If it gets to be too much, back out." Chief Ford nodded to Gregson and slapped his brother on the back. He raised his voice over the roar of the draft. "Fire and rescue is on the way."

Cree dashed for the epicenter of the flames, his vision too narrow with the addition of the jacket on his head, but he couldn't risk not having the extra protection. The hairs on his forearm singed as the blaze closed in. He jumped over the downed tree just as the flames cut him off from Easton and Chief Ford. Heat burned down his throat. It was getting harder to breathe, but he wouldn't stop. Not until he found her.

"Alma!" Trees hissed and popped in response. Charred earth spread out in front of him, but there was no sign of her. She was out here. She was alive. He had to believe that. He wasn't sure how much time had passed. Didn't care about Ford's five-minute deadline. He was going to find her. The fire raged as though feeding off the desperation boiling over inside. He lifted the protection from his head and flinched from the intensity. Wavering flames reflected back to him from the lake. "Alma!"

Coughing reached his ears from the left. "Cree?"

Every cell in his body homed on his name. The last of his adrenaline burned off in his veins as he stepped over a grouping of devastated twigs and brush. He'd heard her. It wasn't his mind playing tricks on him. "Tell me where you are!"

"Here." Another round of coughing broke through the howl of the inferno. Then he saw movement. A hand stretched toward him through the surface of the murky water, and Cree lost his protection to reach her faster.

"Alma." He hauled himself through the marsh and swam out to meet her. The soles of his shoes failed against the algae rocks, and he went down. Soaked head to foot, Cree pulled her against his chest as the fire raged around them. "I've got you."

Chapter Nine

She'd run out of time.

Alma rolled her face away from the itchy hospital bed pillows and scanned one side of the room. The medical center in the middle of town wasn't much with its dated equipment and small patient rooms, but what it lacked for in modernity it more than paid off in staff. The emergency room physician had stopped the bleeding in her side, but it would take time and skin grafts to put her back together fully. The scent of antiseptic and sweat filled her lungs…with a hint of smoke. The reminder should've scared her, but there was only one reason her room would smell like that. "Didn't they make you change your clothes when you got here?"

A deep rumble of a laugh chased back a majority of the grogginess clinging to her brain and lightened the heaviness of throwing herself back in the investigation. Where bombers killed innocent women and started forest fires. Where she was alone and didn't have anyone to fight for other than herself. "They're fresh out of scrubs, and I'm not sure the hospital staff would appreciate me walking around in my boxers."

She closed her eyes against the bright fluorescent lighting, the blood pressure cuff too tight around one arm. The monitor off to one side recorded her stats, then quickly triggered the cuff to release. Blood rushed back into her fingers as a weight in her muscles urged her into unconsciousness. Alma sank deeper into the bed. "I can lend you a blanket."

"I'll keep my clothes on, for everyone's benefit. Especially yours." Movement registered from behind, then circled around the end of her bed. A gentle weight settled on her calf, but she didn't have the inclination or the energy to pull away. In fact, the contact was nice. Solid despite his light touch, grounding.

"Prude," she said.

The slide of metal against tile urged her to open her eyes, and she found Cree pulling a chair closer to the edge of the bed. "How are you feeling?"

"Like someone sewed a bomb to my stomach and left me for dead." Fatigue lifted with every inhale, and Alma noted a red hue to his skin she could've sworn hadn't been there before. Like a sunburn. Only worse. The last few memories of panicked desperation flashed across her mind. The timer on the bomb counting down. The realization the bomber had attached the device to Alma's skin. The pain as she'd ripped the bomb free. And the suffocating sensation as she'd thrown herself into the lake. Then his voice. So clear. So close. She'd convinced herself she'd imagined it until she'd seen him fight through the flames. For her. "You're hurt."

"It's nothing I haven't survived before." He made an effort to hide the back of his free hand, but Alma threaded her fingers through the bed's guard to keep him from retreating. The course hairs she'd noted before had been burned away, exposing angry skin and burn ointment. "I only wish I'd realized you'd been taken sooner."

"That wasn't your fault. Cree, none of this was your fault." It'd been so long since she'd opened herself to the possibility of touching someone else—of being touched—that her hand shook at the contact. When was the last time she'd reached out to someone for help? When had she trusted the person on the other side wouldn't hurt her? She couldn't remember. But she trusted Cree. Not only had he walked through a physical wall of flames to get to her in time, but he'd respected her need for space when it came to their partnership. He'd saved her life, and she wasn't sure she'd ever be able to repay him for that, short of trusting him completely. But as much as she didn't want to talk about what had happened out there, they were still in the middle of a murder investigation. "Were the fire crews able to get control of the blaze?"

"They're still working on it. So far the fire has burned around fourteen hundred acres, but the winds are pushing it into the mountains instead of into town. Your chief sent out the evacuation warning in case it changes direction. We got lucky." He smoothed cracked skin over the back of her hand, seemingly memorizing the pattern of moles and the difference in color between them. "Whoever killed Erica Harmon rigged my truck to explode when it started. They wanted me out of commission while they took you out of the investigation. If it hadn't been for Chief Ford and Easton, I wouldn't have gotten to you in time."

"Not they. She." Alma rolled her lips between her teeth and bit down to control the waver in her voice. "The bomber is a woman."

"Good to know. I know how difficult this is for you, Alma. I've been in your position. Your chief and fire and rescue want answers as to what happened out there, but I'll hold them off as long as I can if that's what you need." He brought her hand to his mouth and planted a soft kiss over the thin skin there before rubbing his own mark away. "You're recovering from surgery. If you feel that's all you can focus on right now, I'll find a way to come at this from another angle."

"I appreciate that, but no. The killer came after me. She was in my apartment to scare me. She abducted me because she knows I'm getting too close. I want to see this through to the end. I want to make sure she can't hurt anyone else." She needed to help. She needed to find the bomber before someone else ended up in Erica Harmon's position. Because if there'd been someone willing to help her when her marriage had gone to hell, she might not have suffered longer before she'd gotten the courage to claw her way out. "Has the forensic lab been able to confirm the victim's identity from the shard of bone we recovered?"

"And by recovered, you mean that time the EMT pulled it out of your shoulder? No. Not as far as I know." Confusion rippled across his forehead and deepened the lines between his eyebrows. "You identified Erica Harmon from her missing person report. Has something changed?"

The images she'd been fighting off since waking after surgery wouldn't stay buried. "I talked to her. The bomber. She told me her sister deserved every ounce of pain she suffered for ruining her life."

"We didn't find any next of kin for Erica Harmon."

Cree sat a bit taller in his seat. "All we had was Travis Foster's missing person report."

"That's just it. When I was out there, she told me we didn't even know who we were investigating. Like Erica Harmon was an alias." A shudder quaked through her, and she held on to Cree's hand a bit tighter. It wasn't much, but the physical contact eased her tendency to compartmentalize and never look back. She couldn't do that here. She had to see this through. "Travis filed that report under the name Erica Harmon because that was who he knew her as before they fell in love and started a family together. He filed a second report under what would be her married name, but what if Erica lied from the beginning? What if our victim isn't who she convinced everyone she was?"

His rough exhale shook through him. "We'd be back at square one and no closer to finding who wanted her dead."

"Yeah." The monitor beeped with a warning and pulled forest green eyes to the screen. She read the concern etched into his expression before the pain burned into her awareness. Her pain medication had run low, and her side hurt worse than the time she'd dropped an archaeology trowel on her toe, but she couldn't risk letting the bomber get away again. She released her hold on Cree's hand and sucked in enough air to brace herself to sit up. And froze. Hospital staff had taken the clothes she'd borrowed from Cree into evidence. The only thing standing between them was the thin gown that didn't offer much protection in the back, and she wasn't about to take this relationship to the next level. Not yet, anyway. "We need to talk to Travis Foster again, but first I'm going to need you to turn around."

"You really think he's going to want to talk to you again?" Cree shoved to his feet, then bent at the waist to haul a duffel bag into his seat. He headed for the door, pulling up short. He wasn't going to let anyone come through that door without her permission, and she appreciated the thought more than she expected.

"I think he's going to want to hear what I have to say this time." She set her bare feet on the floor and reached for the bag. Her uniform had been cleaned and pressed, her holster, gun and badge waiting for her on top. One side of her mouth tugged higher. He'd brought her a fresh change of clothes, including a clean bra and set of underwear, knowing she wouldn't sit here while a bomber tore her town apart. Alma pulled her uniform from the bag. Ripping the blood pressure cuff from around her arm, she discarded it on the bed and slowly pulled the needle from the crook of her arm. Blood bloomed around the already-bruising area, but it was nothing compared to what she'd already survived. "If I'm right, Erica—or whoever she really is—wasn't our killer's only target."

"You're sure?" he asked.

Alma hadn't realized how many muscles in her abdomen she used for simply dressing herself each day. She sat against the bed when the pain reared its ugly head. Pressing her hand against the wound in her side, she shook her head. "It was something in her voice, the way she accused Erica of going out of her way to show up her sister by falling in love and having a kid."

"You think she might try to go after Travis and his son." Cree's voice dropped an octave. His shoulders turned slightly toward her, but he kept his gaze boring straight into the hospital room door like the gentleman he was.

She managed to get both legs into her slacks and tugged them into place. Then her boots. After tucking her uniform shirt into her waistband as carefully as she could, Alma situated her holster, her armor back in place. "I don't know, but my gut says the grieving husband knows more than he's letting on."

HE'D NEARLY LOST HER.

Cree closed the hospital room door behind him as Alma finished getting dressed and nearly collided with two men waiting on the other side. "Chief." He nodded appreciation. "Easton."

"How's she doing?" Easton Ford angled toward the door as though prepared to check on his colleague himself but held himself back.

"She's shaken, and hell, I can't blame her. It's not every day you're abducted and wake up to find an active bomb sewn into your skin. Even in law enforcement." Cree read the concern etched into both men's expressions and tried to push as much assurance into his voice as he could. As much as he wanted to step in to be the one Alma relied on out of some sick sense of guilt, she had a lot of people who cared about her, and he wouldn't come between her and that support. "But she's strong. She's already dictating her statement into her phone so we can get back to the investigation. Anything from fire and rescue?"

"They found the device that started the blaze. Fire marshal says it's C4." Chief Ford unpocketed his phone and handed it off to Cree with a swipe of his thumb.

"Looks to be the same type of device Alma saw in that gulch."

Cree scanned through the photos, detailing the shattered pieces of green motherboard and a chunk of red coiling wire. "Same components as I saw in Galaxy Electronics before it exploded, too." He handed back the phone. "At least our bomber is consistent. Alma's going to want to know how Mr. Thorp is doing since he lost the store."

"He walked away with a mild concussion. His wife's helping him through some headaches and scrapes, but he's clearheaded and asking about Alma. He wants to make sure she's doesn't feel guilty for what happened." Easton folded his arms across a broad chest honed over years of consistent discipline and training. "He isn't the only one."

Cree nodded and returned the chief's phone. The rock settling in his gut grew heavier as the events of the past three days shattered the detachment he'd kept close once he hit town. Battle Mountain was supposed to be a way station—temporary—while he summoned the courage to go back to his life. But the thought of walking away from all this, on Alma, didn't sit right. Three days. That was all it'd taken for her to pull him apart, show him what really mattered and shove all those broken pieces back together. He wasn't the same man who'd crossed the town borders eight months ago. He was stronger, more sure of himself, less isolated. He felt…almost human again. Because of her, and that wasn't something he was sure he could turn his back on once this investigation concluded. "You two know her better than I do."

"We also know she trusts you. More than she might

trust either of us." Chief Ford pocketed his phone back, but the drop in the man's voice triggered Cree's defenses. "You and I both know she's not going to back off this case, even at the risk of running herself into the ground. She's got too much invested to walk away now and a hell of a lot she wants to prove. I don't know why you left Larimer County or what your plans are here in Battle Mountain, but I'm trusting you to have her back, Gregson. One officer to another. Don't let me down." The chief offered his hand.

The moment shouldn't have meant much. He'd worked this case from the beginning. He'd known exactly what he was getting into by stepping back into the field, but Cree couldn't help but let go of the shame and embarrassment that had followed him over the county line. And for the first time in months, he imagined himself taking up that shield again. Being part of something bigger, like his grandfather had always wanted. "Yes, sir."

"Silverton bomb squad's expecting us at the station. Call us if you need anything." Easton slapped him on the back and headed down the hallway, his brother on his heels. Both men rounded the corner just as the door swung open behind him.

Centering herself in the frame, Alma looked up at him with that gut-wrenching smile in place, and suddenly every cell in his body was vibrating at a higher frequency. The scrapes and bruises along one side of her face had lightened, but the sling around her arm reminded him all too quickly that she was still in danger. She leaned against the doorframe, careful of her shoulder and moving slower because of the stitches in her side. "You realize you were supposed to report back whether or not the coast was clear for me to escape, right?"

"Ran into a bit of a problem." Any other officer on the force would've taken the opportunity to recover for a few days, but none of the men or women Cree had served with had Alma's determination for justice. And damn, if that wasn't the sexiest thing he'd ever seen. "Seems you're a little too well-liked."

Her laugh filtered through a strained exhale, and Alma pressed her free hand into her side for support. Color drained from her face, but she didn't let her discomfort show, committed to seeing this through to the end. "Let me guess. Weston and Easton."

"They were worried about you." Cree banished the urge to reach for her. No matter how much he needed that physical contact to assure himself she was okay, he'd leave it to her to direct how far their relationship went. "They're not the only ones. You sure you're ready to get back out in the field?"

"You know what? I'm good. Honestly." She scanned the length of her body, still using the support of the doorframe. "It's going to take some getting used to all these stitches, but unfortunately, if I've learned anything from going through what I did with my ex-husband, it's that I've taught myself how to live in chaos and pain. I'm…comfortable there." She raised that dark gaze to his and straightened. Taking a step into him, Alma traced her thumb along his jaw. "If that changes, you'll be the first one to know. Deal?"

"Deal." He set his hand over hers, leaning into her touch. Warmth speared through the last of his reservations. Of all the things he'd expected from small-town, middle-of-nowhere living, he'd never expected her. "Ready to flee the scene?"

"It's not fleeing when I'm legally allowed to check myself out of my physician's care." She pointed toward the nurses' station and the thin man with curly dark hair dressed in a white lab coat. "All I have to do is sign the discharge papers."

"But fleeing sounds more fun, don't you think?" he asked.

A knowing smile tugged one corner of her mouth higher as she scanned the length of the corridor. The baby hairs around her temples swayed under a hit from the air conditioner above, lulling his high-strung thoughts into place. Hell, was there anything Alma couldn't do? The guarded officer he'd met the night of the first explosion took control of her expression. "All right. There are two security guards at the end of the hall. Both armed, and a network of surveillance cameras watching our every move." She motioned toward the officers with the crown of her head. "Think you can distract the guards while I make a break for it?"

"Only if you grab some of the orange Jell-O from that cart on the way out." He signaled in the opposite direction. "I'll head for the car. Rendezvous in five out the west entrance."

"Orange Jell-O? And here I thought I'd already learned about all the skeletons in your closet these past few days." Squeezing his hand, she maneuvered around him but didn't make it much farther than a couple of feet. "See you on the other side."

"With the Jell-O," he said.

"With the Jell-O." She nodded, trying to hide another smile.

Cree headed for the two guards camped out at the opposite end of the floor. Ringing phones, low conversations and announcements over the PA system kept him focused when all he wanted to do was watch Alma talk her way out of lifting orange Jell-O cups from the food cart. He waved to the officers to keep their attention on him, and not the partner he couldn't get enough of. "Hey, guys. Not sure if you know this, but I found a suspicious coin in the men's bathroom down the hall. I tried to get a closer look, but it's behind one of the urinals, and I'm just not willing to get on my hands and knees for that kind of thing. Would one of you mind taking a look for me?"

The guards looked at each other, one laughing. "A coin?"

"Yeah. I think it might be a quarter. I could really use it." Cree maneuvered around both guards to get a view of Alma, who was scrupulously checking each Jell-O color from the bottom. She stacked what looked like a collection of lime-green ones in the crook of her good arm, and the tendons in his neck tightened without permission. "Not green. I hate green." He did his best to get her attention while still appearing to be engaged in conversation with the security guards, but as Alma tossed him a smile before making her exit, the truth lay in front of him. He'd been set up. "Turns out I'm a bit of a germophobe."

"All right, buddy. Let's get you back to the psych ward on four." The smaller of the guards moved to cut off his escape, but Cree dodged the attempt.

"You know, now that I think of it, it was a button." He clicked his tongue with a strong point of his index finger while following after Alma. "Thanks for your help anyway." Jogging to catch up with her, he ignored the call of Alma's physician and a few whispered questions from visitors and nurses as he headed for the stairs. He caught sight of her long brown hair just before the door two flights down slammed shut behind her. "Now, where do you think you're going?"

Cree rushed down the stairs after her, excitement building under his skin. He exited through their agreed-upon route and hit the parking lot on the west side of the building. His lungs worked to keep up with his racing heart, but he couldn't let his guard down. Not yet. He scanned the lot and targeted the truck Easton had loaned him after they'd reached the clinic. There, leaning against the hood and peeling back the lid to a lime-green Jell-O container, stood his partner, every ounce the woman he'd started falling for. Acceptance reverberated through him. She'd won. He hiked a thumb over his shoulder as a quick laugh overwhelmed his control. Hell, it had been a long time since he'd let himself enjoy the moment. Too long. "They almost detained me."

"I would have, too," she said. "A suspicious coin?"

"I read it in an article a few years ago. The cops who responded to the call reported it was a quarter." Cree took up position against the passenger-side door as she slurped the last of her dessert. "That doesn't look orange."

She reached for the short stack of containers she'd piled on the hood of the truck, most likely slower than she would've wanted to, and tossed him one with her uninjured hand. He caught it against his chest. Orange Jell-O, the same as he'd grown up on while living off the grid with his grandfather. Alma collected the rest and moved to stand in front of him. "Thank you."

"For what?" he asked.

"Reminding me there's more to life than the chaos and pain." She rose onto her toes and pressed her mouth to his.

Chapter Ten

It was too late to haul Travis Foster into the station all the way from Ouray, and going back to her apartment wasn't an option. While the crime scene techs Chief Ford had called in to process the evidence had cleared her to move back in, she couldn't face the destruction. Not yet.

The thud of Cree's keys on the nearby table frayed her nerves. She flinched against the sensory overload as he flipped on the living room light. The pain medication from the clinic had worn thin, leaving her nerves raw and exposed. She could still distinguish his taste through the remnants of lime Jell-O at the back of her throat. A perfect combination of citrus and mint when the two shouldn't have gotten along. Their kiss had chased back the ice crystallizing in her bones and shocked her back to life in the same moment. But while she'd wanted to physically push herself to break through the chains holding her back since her divorce, other parts of her body had already started failing. He'd noticed it when she'd unwillingly swayed on her feet back in the clinic's parking lot. In what seemed like seconds, she'd gone from rebellious and playful to exhausted and beaten. Now Alma didn't know what to do, didn't know where to go from here.

"The bed is still made up. I can get you a new pair of clothes since your chief commandeered the last set as evidence." He secured the dead bolt on the front door and armed the alarm panel off to the right. Considering the last time she'd set foot in this place she'd been abducted, she imagined he wasn't willing to take any chances of her disappearing this time. "I'm not sure how much you were able to clean up at the clinic. You're welcome to take another shower if you need, and I have some leftovers in the fridge if you're hungry."

She didn't move. Couldn't. "I think I'd just like to sit down for a few minutes, if that's okay with you."

"Yeah. Sure," he said.

The tremors she'd noted in her hand on the drive back to the apartment worsened, and no amount of breath work or counting helped. Alma tried to cross her arms over her chest, but the shoulder sling stopped any attempt. The control she'd developed over this past year had started to crack, and with that realization anxiety screamed through her. Her heart rate spiked, her breath shallowing. Her body felt too light and too heavy at the same time, and nothing—not even the floor—seemed strong enough to hold her in place. She'd been through enough of these moments throughout her marriage to recognize when they got the best of her, but she'd gotten them under control. She'd risen above letting the world and everybody in it break her. "Cree, I don't seem to be able to move. Could you…"

"I've got you." Three words. The same three words he'd whispered when he'd pulled her from the lake. His strong grip grounded her as he maneuvered them toward the nearest couch. Reliable. Focused. "Sit right here. I'll get you a glass of water." His outline rounded into the kitchen, and before she had a chance to count the seconds, he was offering her a cold glass. Cree took his seat, keeping a few inches of distance between them. The couch cushion dipped under his weight, but instead of her being thrown off by the unbalance, it was reassuring having him so close. "You can be honest with me. I give you my word I won't be offended or think any less of you. Is this because of the kiss? My truck is currently a smoldering pile of metal, but I can get a hotel room for the night if you need space—"

"What? No, that's not… That's not it at all." She didn't regret the kiss, and she didn't want him to leave. Because for the first time since striking out on her own—separate from her career, her marriage, the woman she used to be—she wasn't scared. The low temperature of the glass bled into her palm and calmed her nervous system. Her humorless laugh died almost as quickly as she'd forced it free. "I guess I'm just not as unbreakable as I believed. Can't even get through one attempt on my life without having a panic attack."

Cree moved slow, slower than she wanted him to move, and set his hand on her arm. The water shook under her grip, but his hold supported her from dropping it outright. "Tell me."

"After the bombing at that conference, was there ever a moment when you told yourself that was the worst it could be? That no matter what came next, you'd survived, and you weren't going to let anything stop you from moving on?" she asked.

He removed his hand from her arm, then interlaced his fingers together between his knees. "Honestly, I tried to pretend it had never happened. I ran here, and it wasn't until recently that I even looked back." His gaze roamed over her face as though he was trying to memorize every line, every curve. Cree turned his knees into hers, his jeans brushing against her. "You? You faced your fears. You did something about it and got yourself out of an impossible situation. You're a hundred times stronger than I am for that reason alone, but I can tell from the look in your eyes you're worried you haven't recovered from what your ex-husband did."

His words settled between them, drilling straight into her core.

"I know I can't flip a switch and make everything be okay. In my head, I know that's not how trauma works. I know there will be these times throughout my life that I'll get blindsided by something that will throw me back, but it's been a year." She struggled to take a full breath. "I feel like I should've made more progress than this, that the same things shouldn't be affecting me anymore. I left him. I got help. I moved on with my life by coming home and changing careers. What else am I supposed to do?"

"I don't know if there's anything else you can do but give it time," he said.

She curled the fingers of her uninjured hand into a fist. "I can't even stop the shaking in my hands. What if the next time my anxiety gets the best of me it's during a call? What if it happens again during this investigation?" Desperation and helplessness tornadoed through her, and she didn't know how to make it stop. "I chose to become a reserve officer so I could protect myself, but I'm not even sure I can do that anymore, let alone protect the people of this town."

"Come here." Cree secured his arms around her back and tugged her into his side. His shoulders and chest rose on exaggerated inhales, and Alma realized he was doing it for her benefit, to remind her to breathe. The physical connection was enough to anchor her in the moment, but it was his constant consideration for her well-being that drained the tension from her muscles. He settled back on the couch, bringing her along with him, as she set her ear over his heart. Calloused fingers smoothed the hair back from her face in a hypnotic rhythm as they sat there.

She wasn't sure how long. Didn't care. In the span of three days he'd done more for her than anyone she'd believed cared about her, and she never wanted to go back. To her empty apartment. To her isolated existence. To the hypersensitive paranoia that surviving had scratched into her bones. Her heart rate stabilized in a matter of minutes, and Alma took her first full breath since waking up in the hospital. "Have you thought about what you'll do after this case is closed?"

"Not really." His voice echoed through his chest and burrowed under her skin. It soothed the rough edges of her thoughts and elicited a chain reaction of desire at the same time. "I'm still with Larimer's bomb squad, but my CO told me to take as much time as I needed to get my head right. I'm on indefinite leave, and I intended to take full advantage as long as I could. But working this case with you... It's helped."

Alma pushed against him, leveling her gaze with his. Her stomach twisted as her next question formed. "You want to go back?"

"My life is there. I only came back to Battle Mountain to escape it for a while. After my discharge from the army, I made something for myself, built a career on my own. I wasn't sure I was entirely ready to let it go." He squeezed her against him. "Then Chief Ford asked me to watch your back while we were at the hospital, and I went from thinking about this case to thinking about the next one. And the one after that. There's still a lot of good I could do in Loveland. There's also a lot of good I could do here."

Apprehension coiled low in her belly as she processed his meaning one word at a time. Her voice deadpanned as all those feelings of inadequacy charged through her, and Alma untangled herself from his arms. "My CO asked you to watch my back?"

"Yeah, and I'm glad he did. Because he knows you. He knows you won't stop investigating this case, even with a torn rotator cuff and a new skin graft in your side, and Battle Mountain's department is barely functioning. The chief can only stretch himself so far, and Easton is still splitting his time between the department and the rehab center." Cree slid to the edge of the couch, setting his burned hand over hers. "This town has become the epicenter of three major cases in the past year. It doesn't have the support it needs, and neither do you."

"What are you saying?" She wouldn't let herself hope. She needed him to say it. She needed him to tell her she was worth losing the life he'd built because no one else had. "You want to transfer from Larimer County's bomb squad to a smaller department? That's career suicide."

"Yeah, it is, but there's a part of me that doesn't care." Cree framed her face with one hand and leaned in to kiss her softly. "Part of me knows partnering with you on the job and off would be worth it. You'd be worth it."

HE HAD TO get himself a new couch.

Aches and pains lightninged through his joints as Cree wrenched open the glass door of the Battle Mountain Police Station and held back to let Alma through first. The place hadn't changed since he'd been here last, but the entire world had.

Four bombings. Each designed to achieve a different goal. Murder, distraction, evidence tampering. But there was a piece of this puzzle they still couldn't see: the victim's real identity. Only Travis Foster could give them that.

He stepped over the threshold and followed his partner through the too-narrow hallways leading past the break room, the cells and the chief's office. Pressing the pads of his fingers into the tendon along his neck, Cree fought to relieve the tension that came with giving Alma the bed for the night. Then again, he'd never slept better. He was tempted to believe it was just exhaustion—maybe even his endless fantasy of what it would be like to stay in Battle Mountain—that had finally given his overactive mind a break. But Cree knew the truth. His gaze flickered to Alma as she rounded into the lobby of the station. It was her, and once they closed this case and the paperwork cleared, he'd make it official. He wasn't going anywhere.

"Mr. Foster, I'm Chief Ford. I wanted to thank you for being here. You've already met Officer Majors and her partner, Officer Gregson." The chief came to a stop a few feet from the victim's husband, hand outstretched. Once he realized Foster wasn't going to shake, he motioned down the hall. "Why don't we talk in my office?"

"I told you people everything I knew when you came to my house and accused me of killing Erica." The circles under Foster's eyes had grown a bit darker, the hollowness Cree noted in the man's house deeper, as he took a seat in front of the chief's desk. The glare he settled on Alma raised protective instincts Cree didn't know he still had, but he would let her and the chief do their jobs without interference. "Not sure what else you want from me."

"Mr. Foster, we're very sorry for your loss." The chief removed his hat and set it off to the side, interlacing his fingers across the surface of the overrun, earth-tone-stained desk. "I've lost a spouse. I know the toll it can take on you not just in the moment but for years, and I don't wish it on anyone."

The fight left Foster's body language, and he settled deeper into his seat. "You brought me here for a reason. Have you made progress in Erica's case? Can I finally take her home?"

"Our investigation hasn't concluded." The chief nodded to Alma, who stepped forward. "I'm sure you've heard about the four bombs that have gone off here in Battle Mountain, one of which started that fire near San Cristobal Lake."

"Kind of hard to ignore." Another bout of defensiveness seemed to tense the man's shoulders as Foster pressed his heels into the industrial carpet. He bounced his gaze between the chief, then Alma and finally Cree. "You going to accuse me of setting those off, too?"

"No, sir. In fact, we have a pretty good idea of who designed and detonated the devices. We believe the initial explosion was meant to destroy any evidence of Erica's murder, and it did a damn good job," Chief Ford said. "Now, I know my deputies already questioned you about Erica when they paid a visit to your home a few days ago, but now I'm asking. Can you think of anyone who might have wanted to hurt your wife?"

Foster shook his head. "No. We were…happy."

"Sir, I owe you an apology. I was out of line when I implied you'd been the one to kill Erica, and I'm sorry." Determination laced Alma's voice, which sounded stronger than it had last night, and Cree couldn't do anything but admire her ability to keep moving forward, no matter the setback. "I realize the last thing you want to do at a time like this is answer more questions, but we need to know. Has there been anyone hanging around your home? Any calls at odd hours with no one on the other line? Issues at your construction site?"

"We had some C4 go missing from one of our projects about a month ago, but we reported it to the ATF. They're still investigating, but that didn't have anything to do with Erica," he said.

"Does your wife have any relatives? A sister, maybe?" Alma asked.

"No. She was an only child and her parents died while she was in high school. Some freak accident that set the whole place on fire. Erica felt guilty she was the only one who survived, even after all these years." Foster turned his attention back to the chief. "I don't understand. You said you had a good idea of who did this. Why are you wasting time with me when you could be building a case against them?"

Cree stepped into the grieving husband's peripheral vision so as to not take him by surprise. "Mr. Foster, we've run background checks, searched financials and phone records, gone through missing person reports across the country and have sent your wife's DNA to the state forensic lab for testing." He shrugged as though there were no other explanation. Because there wasn't. "Erica Harmon doesn't exist."

Color drained from Foster's face, his mouth parting slightly. "What the hell does that mean?" He shoved out of his seat, and the chair tipped backward. "Is this some sick game to you? Erica was my wife. You ask anyone in Ouray who knows us. I've known her since she was a senior in high school living out of her car. You test my baby's DNA. I'm telling you Erica…" Disbelief brought Foster's hands to his head. "No. This isn't… This isn't happening. Her name was Erica Harmon. We've been together going on ten years." He pulled his wallet from his back pocket and flipped it open to a photo taken sometime in the past few years, if Cree had to guess. "She loved me. She loved Ethan. She wouldn't leave us. She wouldn't lie to us."

"Even if it was to protect you?" Alma asked.

Silence filled the too-small room. Tears streaked down Foster's face, and Cree collected the tissue box from the chief's desk. He took the offering, still staring at the photo of him and his wife. Acceptance eased the pain in the man's gaze. "She'd never talk about her childhood. No matter how many times I asked. I wanted to do a family recipe book, you know. Something we could pass down to Ethan when he was older and ready to move out on his own. He could learn about his family and how to cook from all his ancestors. We both picked our favorite recipes, but Erica…

She wouldn't write down the stories behind them, like it was too painful to remember." Foster swept his hand under his nose. "She'd have nightmares about the fire, the one that killed her parents. Whenever I asked her about them, she'd change the subject. After a handful of times, I stopped asking." He swiped at his face, then replaced his wallet in his back pocket. "She was still having nightmares up until she disappeared. I never told her she talked in her sleep."

"What did she say?" Chief Ford asked.

"The same thing every time, a name," Foster said. "Christine."

Cree set the tissue box in front of Foster on the desk and took the opportunity to study Alma for a reaction. Her move to record the admission in her notebook was quick and efficient, a testament to the detail-oriented reserve officer he'd come to respect. "Does that name mean anything to you?"

"No. She never talked about anyone named Christine." Foster reached into another pocket, this time in the front of his jeans. "But after you'd told me what happened to Erica the other day, I mean…my wife… I started going through her things to figure out what I needed to keep to pass down to Ethan and what I could donate. I found this with a small bag of clothes under her side of the bed. I thought it was just in case of emergency, you know? Like those preppers do. If the house caught fire, and we had to make a quick escape…" He pulled a black flip phone free. "She'd packed outfits for each of us."

Chief Ford stood from behind his desk and tugged open the top drawer. Extracting a pair of latex gloves, he snapped them over his hands before taking the evidence Foster offered. "This isn't Erica's?"

"No." Foster shook his head, a habit at this point. "We both have smartphones. I don't know why she thought she needed to hide it from me. I couldn't even find a charger for it."

Cree examined the phone from beside the chief. "Old phones like this are harder to track." He pointed at the notification on the small exterior screen. "Says there's a voice mail. Did you listen to it?"

Foster scrubbed a hand down his face. "Not yet."

Chief Ford flipped the face of the device open and held down the number 1 to dial voice mail and hit the speaker button. *You have one new message.* Static filtered through the dated speakers.

"Did you think you could run from me, Danny? Did you think I wouldn't find you? I have the resources of the entire United States government at my fingers. You don't get to have your happily-ever-after with your family. It's my turn."

The call ended.

Danny? Cree raised his gaze to Alma, but from the set of her expression, she was soaking up everything she could from the call. Only the longer he studied her, the more shaking he noted in her hand. Just as he had last night.

Message received at 8:07 a.m., April fourth, the electronic voice reported.

"April fourth?" Foster's defeated expression drained as a bolt of energy lit up his eyes. "That's the day Erica disappeared."

"If she was in possession of the phone, it stands to reason the message was meant for her." Chief Ford flipped the phone closed and bagged it into evidence. "Do you know who Danny is?"

"I don't know anyone by that name," Foster said.

"Could be short for Danielle. Danny might be a nickname." Cree offered his hand to shake. "Thank you for your help, Mr. Foster. We're going to get a warrant for the phone's records. With any luck, we'll be able to trace the number the call came from and go from there."

"Just…find who did this. For my son." Foster hesitated, then took hold of Cree's hand. "Please."

"We'll call as soon as we find something. Thank you again for coming down." The chief stood, rolling his gloves from his hands, and directed Foster out the door and from the station.

Cree followed on their heels only as far as the chief's office door and closed it behind them, giving Alma a minute to collect herself. "What is it?"

"It was her. The voice mail." Alma lowered her voice and craned her head over her shoulder to get a lock on Chief Ford. She wasn't the type to keep information from her commanding officer, especially concerning an investigation, but she was the type to hide how that voice mail had rocked her. "I recognize the voice."

"You're sure?" he asked.

"It was the last thing I thought I'd hear before I die." Alma fisted her uninjured hand in front of her on a strong inhale. "I'll never forget it. I don't think our victim did, either."

Chapter Eleven

We're sorry. The number you have dialed has been disconnected. Please check—

Alma ended the call. The calls received log in the phone Travis Foster recovered from his home listed only a single number. The incoming voice mail. No saved contacts. No fingerprints to match to their victim. Nothing to give them a clue as to why Erica Harmon—or whoever she used to be—had been on the run or why she'd kept a connection to her old life. If she believed her life was in danger, why keep a separate phone at all? To use in case she and Travis Foster and the baby had to leave? Phones like this had become obsolete, but they weren't difficult to attain. Why this phone? Why hide it from her husband?

She twisted her hand and nudged at the locket sitting open on Cree's small dining table with the end of her pen. *Did you think you could run from me?* Alma closed her eyes against the last image of her abductor at the edge of the trees, seconds before the bomb strapped to her midsection was scheduled to detonate. *You're going to want to keep your eye on that clock, Officer Majors.* It was the same voice. She'd known the moment it had filtered through the speaker, and every cell in her body had screamed for her to run. She imagined she'd have the same reaction if her ex-husband decided to reenter her life. "One issue at a time, Majors."

"Any luck?" Cree stepped into the narrow hallway with a thick shower towel draped across his shoulders. Droplets of water ran along the tendons in his neck and darkened the color of his hair.

Alma pulled herself straighter and set the phone on the table. "No. Nothing. Whatever number the killer called Erica from is disconnected."

"Not surprising." He maneuvered into the kitchen and reached for one of the mugs stacked next to the coffeepot. In seconds, he'd filled two cups and crossed the short distance between them to offer one of them to her. "According to that message, whoever's behind this has the resources of the US government at their disposal, and from what I've seen and what you've said, she's well-trained. She wouldn't want something as simple as a phone number connecting back to her."

"Easton's working on who the number was registered to before it was disconnected, but even with a warrant, it's going to take time." She set her pen over the edge of her notepad, mesmerized by the single name written in the center of the page. Christine. "You know, I've been trying not to let myself think about what happened apart from what was important to put into my statement, but when I heard her voice on that voice mail, I remembered something when she mentioned her resources."

Cree took a seat opposite her, the table barely big enough to seat two adults. His knees brushed against hers for the briefest of moments, and a fraction of the spark she'd felt when he kissed her exploded through her. "I'm listening."

"She said she'd met you before." Alma memorized his expression, waiting for any change. The slight narrowing of his eyes wasn't enough to reveal the internal dialogue going on behind those forest green eyes, but she liked to think he was as transparent with her as she'd been with him.

"Did she say where? When?" he asked.

"No. She was mostly focused on making sure I didn't walk away from those woods alive." She tramped down a shudder, tracing the rim of her mug with one finger. "But if the killer is telling the truth on that voice mail—and I can't think of a reason she'd lie about having the US government behind her—then I'm inclined to believe the two of you might've crossed paths professionally."

Cree leaned back in his seat. He blew out an exaggerated breath, directing his gaze out the small bay window lighting the breakfast nook. "It's possible. She said she met me. Not that she knew me?"

"Yes." She took a sip of her coffee, willing her nerves to settle.

"She has experience with explosives. She's confident in her skills, which leads me to believes she's most likely professionally trained." He scrubbed a hand down his face. "If she's a peer, there are any number of ways we could've met. Our initial training consists of engineering, chemistry and explosives. I got mine in the army, but there are dozens of bureaus that train bomb techs. FBI, ATF, other branches of the military, law enforcement. Even if we were to narrow down who she works for, I'm required to train with other counties and stay up-to-date through continuing education courses across the country to keep my certifications. She could've been in any one of those classes."

The pick-me-up she'd hoped to get from her coffee failed. Another dead end. Her attention went back to the notes she'd taken during Travis Foster's interview and the frenzied circle around a single word. Christine. "We have a potential name. According to the victim's husband, Erica frequently had nightmares where she recalled the name Christine. If this is who she'd been running from all these years, it's possible we can narrow the search. Does it sound familiar at all?"

"No, but I still have contacts in Larimer County. I can start asking around. If there was a Christine in any one of our trainings, they'd have a record of the registration." Cree took another pull from his mug, that too intense gaze weighing on her. No judgment. No expectations. Just curiosity. "Did you get any sleep?"

"A little." A lie. Alma twisted the base of her mug into the table. Exhaustion had caught up with her for a couple of hours, but her brain was still trying to process the details of this investigation. "I was going through old arson cases most of the night."

"The fire Erica Harmon's parents supposedly died in when she was in high school." Admiration bled into his voice, and the hairs on the back of her neck stood on end. "We're not even sure of the victim's real name. Did you have any luck?"

"Not really. There are too many unknown variables. City, victim identity, when the fire took place, location. I plugged in both 'Danielle' and 'Christine', but there were no hits. As an archaeologist I trained to trace the smallest detail back to the beginning. I got really good at it, too, but this case is nothing but a bunch of dead ends." A humorless laugh punctured through the gloom in her mood. "I did, however, find something interesting when I looked under your bed."

Cree leaned back in his seat and closed his eyes. "Oh no."

"Oh yes." The tension she'd been holding on to since walking through the front door last night eased as she reached down near her feet. Alma grabbed the collection of soft yarn and metallic needles. "I'm really interested in what you're doing here." She arranged the deep green yarn on one side of the table and positioned the knitting needles in both hands. "From the look of it, you've started a...scarf? You could stand to tighten up the tension here on one end, but you've got a good start."

Buried embarrassment twitched at the corners of his mouth. Cree kept his voice even, those calloused fingers itching to rip the project out of her hands, but he held himself back. It seemed he wasn't going to let her get the best of him. Yet. "The winters here are harsher than in Loveland. I needed a scarf, and my grandfather taught me to do things myself instead of going to a store to buy what I needed. And if you must know, knitting keeps my hands strong enough to do my job."

"Your grandfather taught you to knit?" she asked.

"Crochet and sewing, too. Though every once in a while, he'd get the crochet hook caught in his beard and throw the hook across the room." A wisp of a smile softened his features. "He considered himself a Jack of all trades."

"He sounds like someone I would've liked." She meant it. Because without the dedication and love of

Cree's grandfather, Cree wouldn't be here now. And she didn't want to imagine a world without him. Not anymore. As much as she didn't trust herself to make the right decision under pressure or to look past the masks people presented to the world, she trusted him.

"He would've liked you, too," he said. "You're a lot like him. Hardworking, cautious, definitely not one to let others make decisions for herself." His laugh permeated her senses, filling her with a lightness she'd hadn't felt in years. "He was a good man, someone who gave to the community as much as he took. Tough, though. You never wanted to find yourself on the wrong end of one of his lectures. To him, everything was life and death. You did what you were told or you died."

"Sounds like he cared about you very much." Heat worked up her neck and into her face. Her parents had supported her, loved her, but she'd mostly gone through life on her own. Always looking for the next adventure, the next dig site, the next research proposal, and they'd given her that independence. When her ex had come along, they'd gotten married so quickly: Alma had considered their relationship an adventure too, and her parents had thrown their support behind her. But when she'd filed for divorce, they hadn't understood why she couldn't try to fix it, why she'd had to leave, why she was giving up. They'd meant well, she knew that, but the way Cree talked about his grandfather... She envied the kind of support that really mattered.

She ran her thumb along the three inches of unequal stitches he'd knitted and raised the project higher. The partial scarf caved under her touch, and she found herself imagining what it would feel like complete. "Can you teach me?"

"You want me to teach you to knit?" Cree asked. "Isn't that already one of those superpowers you inherited from your *abuela*?"

"Not yet, but I have a feeling you could show her a thing or two." Alma pinned the project in her uninjured hand and slid out of her seat. Setting the mass of yarn on the table in front of him, she scooted her chair closer and sat. "I'm all ears, and one hand. So go slow."

His resulting smile cut through the last of her defenses and opened an entire realm of possibilities she hadn't considered before she'd taken on this case. An entire future. "All right. First things first. You have to learn how to cast the yarn onto the needles." He stripped his work in progress free and handed over both needles. "It's going to be hard with only one hand, but as long as we work together, nothing can stop us."

THEY'D ONLY KNITTED a few rows when Alma's phone rang with an incoming call from Chief Ford. She'd excused herself to take it in his bedroom and left him to finish off what they'd started together. Despite Alma's superhuman breadth of skills, knitting hadn't been one of them. Cree gathered the yarn and needles and shoved them in the junk drawer in the kitchen. Even after he'd realized their combined efforts weren't enough to save the scarf, he'd enjoyed the few minutes they'd taken together, the partnership they'd built.

It hadn't been enough for her to show him the kind of dedication and sympathy it took to investigate a case like this, she had to go convince him this town belonged in his future. Whether that future included Alma, he wasn't sure, but he knew what he wanted. He knew what he was ready to give up to get it, too.

He unplugged his cell from the charger on the kitchen counter where he'd left it the night before. One missed call. He tapped on the notification, and his phone instantly dialed his CO's number. Two rings. Three. The line picked up.

"Wasn't sure you'd call me back." Glen May didn't make small talk. With the entire county and two other city departments to rope into cooperation under his purview, the man valued his time over everything else, and he didn't mince words. It was one of the qualities that had rocketed May from a patrol officer into the county's good graces enough for him to run for sheriff. He got the job done—no heroics, no frills—even when one of his technicians had gone off the deep end.

"Sheriff, it's been a while." Cree didn't know what else to say. May wasn't the kind to drop a line without good reason, and Cree was still on leave. Something had happened.

"Heard you been chasing a firecracker down there in Battle Mountain. Four bombs in as many days." A chair squeaked on the other side of the line, and Cree's brain automatically constructed the image of May behind his desk twirling that mustache at one corner. "That chief you got down there called me to verify you're one of my techs. Didn't really know what to say to him considering our last conversation, but I vouched for you."

Cree directed his attention down the hall, catching Alma's warped voice from the other side of the door. It had been four days since that initial explosion in the gulch—the one that had nearly killed Alma in the process—and he felt just as lost as he did then. "I've got your thank-you note right here, Glen. Just need to stop by the post office."

"We both know that's a lie." The sheriff's deep laugh resonated through the phone, and a twinge of homesickness barked up Cree's spine. While he hadn't thought much about going back to his life, there were some things he'd missed. Including the old man who made Cree imagine himself forty years from now. "Listen, I know you're working that investigation in the bomber around those parts. That Ford fellow says you've been doing some solid work, but it's time to come home, Cree."

"What do you mean?" he asked.

"I mean I've been holding your job for you for eight months while you get your head right, which I was happy to do after what happened at the county commissioners meeting, but now I hear you're investigating a bomber out of your jurisdiction." May lowered his voice. "I know you. I know you feel obligated to offer assistance given your background and the fact you're probably the only one capable of helping those people, but Battle Mountain isn't a place guys like you make a career. You're the best tech I've got. Let them sort out their own problems."

The phone protested under Cree's grip. "And if I want to see this case through?"

"The mayor's office wanted me to let you know how much they appreciate your service and what you've been through since the bombing," May said. "They know you're a man they can depend on the next time a bunch of ecoterrorists decide to take matters into their own hands, and I agreed. You're a hell of a tech with the skills to do a lot of good here, but their fuses are getting short, Cree. I can't hold them off anymore. They made their decision clear. Either you come back to the squad or your career in explosive ordnance is over."

"That's… That's not… Wow." Disbelief burned through him, almost as hot as the blisters along the backs of his hands.

"Come on, man. It's an easy choice. This is your career we're talking about. Tell me you're not actually considering giving all that up." May's desk chair protested under his weight again. "Now, I've been patient enough, and I can't make any more excuses as to why you're not here doing the work."

"I just…thought I had more time." He turned his back to the bedroom door. This wasn't why he'd called his CO back. Cree closed his eyes to regain a fraction of focus. "I don't really know what to say other than I'll have to think about it."

"Well, don't make it sound so dreary. Your life is here, son. Your team, your career, they're waiting for you to get your head back in the game." The sheriff's voice dropped into manipulative territory. "Isn't that what you want?"

Cree didn't know. On one hand he'd found a better version of himself in this small town—found Alma—and on the other, the life he'd spent years building, one where he could prove himself. "Give me twenty-four hours. Okay? Until then, I need your help. Do you remember any recruits or agents that go by the name Christine? Someone who would've interacted with our squad in the past few years."

"Does Christine have a last name?" May asked.

"If she does, I can't remember what it is or what she looks like. All I have is a first name." Cree's energy spiked from impatience.

"I have hundreds of people come through here a year who interact with the squad. Deputies, witnesses, federal agents. Bound to be a few named Christine. Does this have to do with your firecracker down there?" The sheriff's tone leveled off enough for Cree to understand the man had already gotten his answer.

"I'm not sure yet," he said. "Might be nothing."

"Let's see what we've got here." Slow typing bled through the line as Cree envisioned May balancing the phone receiver between his shoulder and bulbous jaw as he pecked at the keyboard. "The only Christine I recall is from a training seminar we hosted about two years ago. ATF agent. I've got her card around here somewhere. Feisty, redheaded thing who seemed to have a problem with everyone she talked to, including me."

"Maybe it was because you called her a feisty, redheaded thing instead of calling her by her name like a normal person." Cree pressed his phone harder against his ear as the call threatened to cut out.

"Agent Christine Freehan," May said. "According to this, she presented a seminar on HMEs about four years ago."

"Homemade explosives. I remember. We identified precursor chemicals used in homemade devices in a blind test. We had to figure out the compositions without any direction." Cree filtered through the dozens of courses he'd taken over the years but still couldn't get a visual of the agent in charge. The Alcohol, Tobacco, Firearms and Explosives Bureau didn't post their agents' photos or information for public consumption, but it was possible he could get access through his ATF contact. "Send me the agent's contact information. I'll get a hold of her myself. Thanks, Glen."

Cree disconnected before May had a chance to manipulate an answer about coming back to Loveland, and turned for the bedroom at the end of the hall. He nearly ran straight into Alma. "Hey, I might have a lead on the name Christine. Turns out there's an ATF agent who taught a continuing education course to my squad a couple years ago…" He noted the lack of color in Alma's face and the strain of her uninjured hand around her phone. He braced himself, his own grip too tight as every muscle in his body hardened with battle-ready tension. "What's going on?"

"I'm needed back at the station," she said.

"What happened?" A flood of possibilities hiked his blood pressure higher.

"That was the chief on the phone." She motioned behind her. She avoided his gaze, as though she were trying to keep herself together. "There's been another attack."

"When?" Blood drained down the length of his body. He hadn't heard the explosion, hadn't heard emergency response. No. It hadn't been a bomb. The chief wouldn't have called Alma on her cell for that. "Where?"

"In Ouray. Last night." Her voice shook, and Cree closed the distance between them.

Ouray. He tossed his cell on the couch and reached for her, but Alma's quick dodge triggered a flood of rejection and confusion. "Travis Foster."

"The unit assigned to keep an eye on Foster's home was attacked. When they came around, they realized someone had broken in. Sergeant Hale responded to the scene. When he arrived, he found the front door smashed in and the place torn apart." Her shoulder rose on a shaky inhale. "Foster was on the floor, unconscious. Someone beat him to within an inch of his life. Chief Ford is headed there now. From what he was able to get from Sergeant Hale, it looks as though Foster fought back."

"Do they think it's the same person who killed Erica Harmon? The bomber? The killer wasn't happy with the way her sister died, she had to go after Erica's family?" He wasn't sure why he expected Alma to have any of the answers. She'd been just as blindsided at this development as he was. Then a single thought iced in his mind. "What about the baby?"

The muscles in her throat worked overtime to swallow. "He's gone."

Chapter Twelve

The Amber Alert had gone out hours ago, but Alma hadn't heard any response. Travis Foster and Erica Harmon's baby was out there, and they had no idea where to even start looking.

She glazed through the latest report blurring in front of her. No matter how many cases she'd gone through, Alma couldn't find one that linked back to a couple who'd died in a fire, leaving two teenage daughters behind. Not in the past decade, at least. No mention of a Danny or Danielle. Nothing to link the ATF agent Cree suspected of having a hand in this case. Not even a recent photo of their victim other than the one Travis Foster had used to file the missing person report.

She swept her hair back away from her face and scanned the empty station. Chief Ford had gone over to Ouray to assist at the scene of the break-in, and Easton had been needed at the rehab center for his fiancée's therapy. Macie was on break for the next twenty minutes, leaving Alma to man the phones, and she wasn't sure where Cree had gone. She didn't need to keep tabs on her partner, but there'd been a distinct separation between them since learning of the break-in and abduction. Her gut tightened as she buried the urge to

overassess the phone call she'd overheard with Cree's
CO. It wasn't her business whether or not he stayed in
Battle Mountain, but for the first time since escaping
the gulch and that first explosion, she wasn't just physically alone, she felt alone.

Alma hauled herself away from her desk and pushed
her hips forward to counter the ache building in her
lower back. Her boots skimmed across the old car-
peting as she made her way into the break room, Macie's headset firmly squeezing her head on either side.
Gripping the coffeepot handle, she reached for a clean
mug and tipped the pot to one side. Empty. "Damn it."

There was still too much they didn't know. Year of
the fire, location, victims' names. Erica Harmon had
been living a lie. She'd run from whatever life she'd had
to escape the person she blamed for the house fire—
even going as far to change her name—but it hadn't
been enough. The killer had caught up to her, had made
sure no one would interrupt the sick game put into play.

She replaced the pot on the stand and cleaned out the
grounds from the filter. Within a couple of minutes, the
scent of fresh coffee chased back the apprehension set
up under her skin. Bubbling water popped from inside
the machine as she considered her next steps. Silverton's bomb squad had collected as much evidence as
they could from the primary scene and the electronics
store, but without confirmation from the shard of bone
concerning the victim's identity from the forensic lab,
she had nothing.

"Hey. Thought you might need a pick-me-up from
Caffeine and Carbs down the street." Cree leaned
against the doorframe leading into the break room
with a white paper bag in his hand, every inch the

man she'd grown comfortable with these past few days. She hadn't heard him come through the back door, having been too overwhelmed with a never-ending loop of questions in her head. "I told the guy behind the counter that I was heading over to the station, and he sent along a chocolate glazed doughnut just for you."

"Reagan is good at remembering customer favorites, but I think he keeps notes to make sure he gets it right." She wished something as simple as a doughnut could bring her out of this…emptiness that wouldn't leave. She'd been here before. After her divorce. She'd spent so long fighting to survive, to move forward, that she wasn't prepared for what happened after she'd escaped, after the charges had been filed, after the arrest had been made. She wasn't prepared for the hollowness and loneliness on the other side, even knowing she was free to do whatever she wanted with her life. This job had helped pull her from the depths, and Cree… He'd given her the strength to keep herself from falling back in. Only now his career was at stake back in Loveland, and there was nothing in this sleepy small town that could compare. "Thanks."

He moved to set the bag on the counter beside her but didn't come any closer. "Everything okay?"

"Yeah. It's just…" She shook her head to pull herself out of what-if territory. No. Now wasn't the time to ask him about his decision. The case. The bomber. Travis Foster's missing baby. That was all that mattered. Not her, not him, or any theory of the future. "The shard of bone the EMT pulled from my shoulder is the key to all of this, but without something to compare it to, we have nothing."

"Travis Foster supplied direct reference samples

from Erica's toothbrush and hairbrush, as well as a biological family member reference sample from the baby," he said.

"All that means is we've confirmed what we already knew: the woman we know as Erica Harmon died in that bombing. But who was Erica Harmon?" Alma folded her uninjured arm across her midsection. "She changed her name, went on the run. For all we know, she could've had cosmetic work to change her features. The photo used to file the missing person report might be useless, and I haven't been able to find anything on a Danny or Danielle or Christine in all those old arson case files."

"I put in a word with a buddy who went to work for ATF earlier this year. He doesn't operate out of her field office, so he's not familiar with Agent Christine Freehan personally, but he's heard her name through the grapevine. Apparently she's the kind of investigator who does whatever it takes to get an arrest. Rumors include bribes and threats, although the bureau hasn't been able to find anything solid to suspend her or investigate. She's good at her job, one of the best in her field, and she's got the confidence and the training to go with it." Cree waited for her to answer, but none of what he'd said put them a step closer. "Silverton's squad is finished processing the primary scene. They recovered more fragments of bone and some tissue. Only problem is, as individual pieces, they don't lead anywhere we haven't already been."

"Individual pieces." Alma shoved away from the counter. Her heart rate ticked up a notch as a dose of adrenaline dumped into her veins. There'd been times in the field during a dig she'd unearth a fracture of pottery or a sun stone that had been damaged over the course of thousands of years. One piece. That was all she needed to complete the puzzle. "That's it."

Cree hesitated bringing his to-go coffee cup to his mouth. "What's it?"

"Individual pieces are a good start, but until we have the whole picture, we're just going in circles." Unpocketing her cell, she rounded back into the station's lobby and sat behind Macie's two-tiered expansive desk. She rolled the desk chair from one side to the other and located the tacked contact list pinned to a homemade corkboard. She knocked over a bottle of bright nail polish as she skimmed her finger down the list and switched her phone into her uninjured hand to dial.

"Okay. And by whole picture, you're talking about the victim?" Cree asked. "You said it yourself, the victim might've had cosmetic surgery to alter her appearance. If that's the case, what will the whole picture accomplish if we don't know what she looked like in the first place?"

"Cosmetic surgery doesn't alter bone structure." Her breath shallowed as a hint of the joy she'd found in uncovering Mexico's lost heritage boiled to the surface. "The victim's skull might be in pieces, but if we can reconstruct it using tissue depth markers based on her race, sex and approximate age, we'll have something we can run a search for to give us Erica Harmon's original identity."

"Battle Mountain doesn't have a forensic artist," he said.

"No, but they do have the next best thing." Alma hit dial. "An archaeologist." Bringing the phone to her ear, she waited for the line to pick up, Cree in the wings of her peripheral vision. The line connected. "Dr. Miles, it's Officer Majors. Have you received all of the bone fragments recovered from the bombing scene yet?"

"They were just delivered. I haven't been able to do a complete examination yet, though. They're still in their evidence bags." Dr. Chloe Miles had run to Battle Mountain to hide from the killer desperate to keep her from exposing him for malpractice in the death of a patient and straight into Chief Ford's protection. The thirty-something coroner's background lay in cardiothoracic surgery and saving lives, but with her past behind her, the mother-to-be had reinvented herself as a key asset of the town. Without her, the department wouldn't have been able to bring down not one but two serial killers focused on tearing Battle Mountain apart. Now Alma needed her help. "Why?"

"Great. I need you to start separating the bones of the victim's skull from the rest of the fragments." She raised her gaze to Cree. "It's going to take some time, but I think I have a way to identify her."

"I hope that's true." Dr. Miles's doubt bled through the line and set up residence in Alma's bones. "But if anyone can help me put her back together, it's you. Meet me at my office as soon as you can, and we can get started."

The line disconnected.

She pocketed her phone and stood, all too aware of Cree's proximity. There'd been a shift between them in the time he'd ended his call with his CO and now. She didn't blame him for wanting to give in to the temptation to leave. Given the choice, she never would've walked away from the career she'd loved, and he deserved to be happy, even if it meant him leaving. She could already feel herself pulling away in the time that had passed between that call and now. Which didn't make sense. He hadn't told her he wanted to go back to Loveland, but her instinct to detach, to protect herself from losing anything more, had already taken hold. "I need to get over there. The sooner Dr. Miles and I can start reconstructing the skull, the sooner we'll have a fresh face to search for. With any luck, we'll get a hit."

"I'll grab my stuff," he said.

"That's okay. You stay." Her voice hiked an octave, giving away the emotional tsunami pummeling her control from every direction. "Macie's not back from her break yet. Someone needs to cover the phones in case the Amber Alert pays off." She headed for the front door. "I'll call you with any updates."

"Alma, wait." He reached for her, but thought better of making contact, which she appreciated. "Did something happen? You've barely said a word since we left the apartment, and when you do... Did I do something to upset you?"

Her heart threatened to shatter right there in the middle of the station. Alma gripped her backpack strap to give herself a distraction, a reason not to commit to the moment, as she'd done so many times before. "No, Cree. You didn't do anything. I just..." She deflated. "I overheard your phone call with your CO. I know your job with Larimer County's bomb squad is at risk, and I think you should go back."

HE DIDN'T KNOW what to say to that, what to think. Cree fought to keep his breathing even as he replayed her words over in his mind, but there was no point in denying the truth. He tossed his empty coffee cup and slid his hands into his pockets. "The mayor got word I'm involved in the investigation here. Seems they don't like the idea of me working a case out of my jurisdiction when I'm supposed to be on medical leave."

"So your CO gave you an ultimatum. Come back or lose your career." The mask Alma had slowly surrendered over the past few days had set back in place, and suddenly Cree didn't recognize the woman standing in front of him. She peeled the dispatcher headset from her head and set it on the desk. "Sounds like an easy decision to me."

Pressure built behind his sternum as he studied her. The warmth he'd grown to rely on over the course of this investigation was gone. What he now saw was the detached deputy he'd met at the primary scene, the one who'd taken on the weight of the world and shut down any possibility of letting someone close. "Is it?"

"Cree, I've walked away from a career. Something I'd spent my entire life training for, something I loved with all my heart, and I let someone take it from me. I don't want to be the person you resent because you felt like you had no other choice." She shifted her weight from one leg to the other. Antsy. Anxious. Nothing like the woman he'd gotten to know while they'd worked together to knit a scarf or pretended to escape the hospital. "I know you said you could see yourself giving up the life you built back in Loveland, but we both know Battle Mountain's department isn't going to keep you happy. I mean, look at this place." She diverted her attention to the stained beige walls. "We're barely functioning as it is. There are no days off because we're so short-staffed. There's no pension. There's nowhere to go here."

"Did you consider none of that mattered to me?" Cree had respected her need for space all this time, but it hadn't done either of them a damn bit of good. She wanted him gone? Fine. He could deal with that, but hiding behind their insecurities wasn't going to satisfy the pain carving through him. "Did you ever consider this town has become more than an escape for me? That I might want to stay because I've gotten to know the people? That my feelings for my partner outweighed any reason I had to leave?"

She didn't answer. Didn't even seem to breathe. There was no crack in the armor she'd donned because she'd gotten too good at living life behind it. What had happened with her ex-husband, the crumbling of her marriage, had served only one purpose: to protect her from having to feel anything ever again.

"You don't really want me to go back, Alma. I think you're scared. I think you have feelings for me, too. I saw it when you let me hold you on my couch and when you trusted I would find you in those woods. You're afraid to get hurt again. Like your husband hurt you. You're terrified of someone else getting close, someone who could potentially hurt you, and that kind of risk just isn't worth taking." Anger charged through his veins, and with it rejection, pain and worthlessness. The fight drained from his shoulders and face. "This isn't about whether or not I try to salvage my life in Loveland. It's that I'm not worth the risk, am I?"

A line of tears glistened in her eyes, but from the look of how tight she'd clamped her teeth, Alma wouldn't let them fall. "No. You're not."

Her words hit him as solidly as a sucker punch to the gut, but there wouldn't be any taking them back.

It hadn't been enough to give her space or a safe place to hide during the investigation, to earn her trust and make her laugh. Cree wouldn't ever be capable of getting through that hardened exterior. Not as long as Alma fell victim to the fear of her past. The realization punctured through his chest and stole the air from his lungs. He'd been willing to leave his old life behind, to start something new with her, but it hadn't been enough. He wasn't sure it ever would be. "You don't deserve to live like this, Alma. There are people here who care about you, who would do anything to make you feel safe and put your happiness before theirs. I like to think I could've been one of them."

"But that's the thing. None of them have survived what I have. None of them could understand I have to do this on my own." Alma swept the back of her hand across her face. "What we had these past few days... It was always going to end like this. I'm just cutting the root before it strangles us both."

His gut twisted. She was a domestic abuse survivor. He knew she was planning ten steps ahead to survive multiple possibilities, but this wasn't the way he'd imagined their partnership dissolving. If anything, he'd been testing himself to ensure he was enough for her when she needed him. Truth was, he wasn't, just as he hadn't been enough to save those people who'd died in the conference bombing eight months ago, and he would have to live with that weight for the rest of his life. "Understood, Officer Majors."

She flinched at his use of her title and last name, but the forced detachment did nothing for him.

"For what it's worth, I thought we made a good team." He pointed to the front desk. "I'll cover the phones until Macie gets back from her break. Good luck with your reconstruction of the skull. I hope you find what you're looking for."

Her rough exhale filled his ears a split second before she turned her back on him and headed out the front doors.

Skimming his fingers across Macie's desk, he took up the dispatcher headset and fit it into place before taking his seat. Tension lined his jaw, but no amount of control released the pressure building in the space beneath his ears. A headache bloomed behind both eyes, and the text on the computer monitor blurred. The past four days had thrown him from one end of the emotional spectrum to the other, leaving him unbalanced and high-strung. The grief from having to walk away from not only this case or this town but the first person he'd felt closest to since his grandfather had passed drilled through his chest. The coffee he'd slugged raged in revenge. Where the hell was Macie?

The station line rang in his ear.

The square yellow indicator on the nineties-era phone flickered, and Cree hit the button. "911, what's your emergency?"

"That baby, the one from the Amber Alert on my phone, I think I just saw him." The distressed voice on the other line didn't sound familiar, but Cree's attention hung on every word. "Please. You have to send someone."

"Okay, ma'am. Can you tell me where you are and if the child is with someone?" He reached for the pen cup near the dispatch monitor and pulled a hot pink glitter pen from the collection of the rainbow assortment. Biting the cap off, he waited for an answer. "Ma'am?"

The call disconnected one second short of the system logging name and location details.

Confusion arced through him. The computer automatically logged the recent call and recorded the call back number. Dropping the pen, he hit the number to reopen the line. It rang twice. Three times. Voice mail picked up on the other end after the fourth, but the automated message failed to identify the caller. It did however give the computer time to narrow the phone's GPS. Cree surveyed the map on the screen. Dispatching software was able to narrow down a caller's location to within fifty feet, but this… "That can't be right."

The call had originated right outside the station doors.

Another indicator on the screen filled in the caller's name, and a flood of clarity washed through him.

Erica Harmon.

It hadn't been a concerned citizen on the other end of the line.

It had been the killer.

Cree reached for the radio on the other side of the desk and pressed the push-to-talk button. He shoved to his feet and headed straight back to the chief's office. In a matter of seconds, he'd located Chief Ford's backup weapon secure in the bottom drawer of the man's desk, then headed for the front of the station. "All units, be advised, 10-33 in immediate need of assistance. Battle Mountain Police Station. Bomber is in the vicinity—"

The glow of a red LED light beneath the chief's desk bled onto his boots, and he froze. His finger slipped from the push-to-talk button.

"Ford to dispatch, I missed that last part. Repeat."

Chief Ford's voice echoed as though Cree were somewhere else, like static on the television set his parents
used to own. Just out of reach.

Cree's knees popped as he crouched beneath the
desk. His gaze instantly went to the countdown tick-
ing silently from the four-stack of C4 duct-taped underneath the thick wood. His exhale slid up his throat.

"Dispatch, do you copy? Cree, what's going on over
there?" Easton's voice threatened to distract him. The
uneven tone suggested the deputy had gotten the hint
and was hauling ass back to the station. "Officer Majors, do you copy? 10-33."

He peeled the tape free, one strand at a time, and
cradled the device. C4 in and of itself was very stable.
It needed that extra spark to ignite, but there was no
telling how far the bomber had gone to ensure no one
left the station alive this time. The same red wire coiled
from the motherboard into the center of the C4. The
caller had wanted to make sure someone was in the
building. It hadn't been good enough to target Alma.
She wanted to take out the entire department closing
in. Fingers shaking, he registered the last minute and
a half of the countdown as he tugged the coiling wire
free from the explosive.

The clock stopped.

Nervous energy skittered across his shoulders as
he set the entire thing on top of the desk. This was the
only surviving explosive the bomber had left behind.
He pulled an evidence bag from the chief's desk and
wrapped the device as carefully as possible. No sudden movements.

The back door of the station swung open, heels

clicking on the floor a few seconds after. "Honey, I'm home."

Macie.

"Back here." Cree slumped in the chair, his head pounding. The call outside the station had been a diversion. He ripped off the dispatch headset and tossed it on the desk as Macie rounded the corner, grip still tight around the handheld radio.

The bomber had been watching. Waiting.

"You really should treat other people's property with more respect." She moved into the office and reached for the headset. She knocked into the evidence bag and tilted it at an angle.

Cree wrapped his hand around hers, holding her completely still. A red glow bled into her already red hair from above, and he raised his gaze up. To the air vent directly above them. "Get out."

Macie pulled on her arm. "I don't know who the hell you think you are, Cree Gregson, but you don't get to talk to me that way—"

"Get out now!" He shoved out of the chair and pulled her along with him. A soft click registered just as they escaped the office.

And then there was fire.

Chapter Thirteen

The aftershock jarred the victim's skull fragments across the table.

Alma locked onto the edges to keep herself upright as fluorescent lights flickered overhead. Air stalled in her chest as she raised her gaze to Dr. Miles opposite. She'd felt an echo of that same punctured vibration the night she'd found this very victim at the bottom of the gulch. Releasing her grip on the table, she stripped out of the latex gloves and tossed them in the hazardous materials bin.

"What was that?" Dr. Miles fought to right herself.

"An explosion." Alma collected her utility belt and weapon from the counter and tightened them around her waist. They hadn't gotten far reassembling the victim's skull, but given enough time, there was a chance they could uncover exactly who'd died in that gulch. And who'd wanted her dead. She scanned the remains. The bomber had gone to extreme lengths to ensure Battle Mountain PD never properly identified this victim. No body, no crime. No way to connect the pieces back to the device or the person who had killed her. Alma unholstered her weapon as screams and frantic curiosity filtered through the steel door separating the medical examination room from the rest of the funeral home. She twisted the power knob on her radio, not realizing she hadn't turned it back on when she'd left the station and delegated her dispatch duties to Cree.

"Gregson, what the hell is going on? Answer me, damn it!" Chief Ford's voice panicked. "Officer Majors, 10-33, BMPD station. No response from dispatch. Please respond. Someone get on this damn radio!"

The station. Her gut filled in the blanks as the lights flickered again. Alma raised the radio to her mouth. "Majors responding. Possible 10-80." Explosion. She turned to the coroner. "All of these buildings on Main Street are connected. It's only a matter of time before the entire block goes up in flames. I need you to get everyone out."

"What about the evidence?" Dr. Miles moved around the end of the table. "We can't just leave her here to burn. We might never get an ID."

The overhead lights flickered again, and Alma backed toward the door. "Gather as much as you can. Just hurry!" She wrenched the door open and nearly crashed into the terrified funeral home director and his son. "Everyone outside. Go, go, go!"

Her heart rate shot into dangerous territory as Alma headed in the opposite direction of safety. She had to make sure there was no one left behind. The sales floor was clear, as was the break room and the small chapel. She charged to the front of the funeral home and out into the street. Dozens of open-mouthed citizens pointed to the raging fire consuming the building at the end of the street.

The station.

"Cree." A hard push from one of the townspeople

knocked her injured shoulder back, and Alma doubled over to brace through the pain. Air hissed between her teeth. She forced herself to straighten. No on-scene support from her department. No sign of fire and rescue. All units had been sent up the mountain to battle the blaze. Even now, smoke threatened to black out the sky. She had to do this alone.

She grabbed a larger man's collar and pulled him into her chest. She couldn't remember his name in the moment, but she'd seen him several times along Main Street the past few months. Maybe one of Hopper's employees over at the hardware store. "I need you to get these people back away from the flames. Set up a perimeter, and do whatever it takes to make sure they don't cross it. Preferably on the other side of the street. Can you do that?"

The panicked, baby-faced man nodded before rushing to get the job done.

She scanned the crowd, echoes of gasps and cries filling her ears, and targeted a group nearby. "You three." The young men turned horrified expressions toward her. "That fire is going to spread to the connecting buildings. I need you to help me get everyone out. We need to evacuate."

They followed her direction. "Two of you check that building next door, one of you with me. Move!" She wrenched open the front door to Caffeine and Carbs and crossed the checkered tile matching Greta's on Main. Illuminated pastry cases brightened the space. "Battle Mountain PD! Is anyone here?"

No answer.

Smoke tendrilled through the air-conditioning vents and set off the smoke detectors overhead. It lodged in her throat and revitalized the burn along the soft tissues of her mouth while the pierce worked to make her deaf. The fire was closing in, and they were running out of time. She motioned to the man with her. "Let's check the back."

"I can't... I can't do this. I'm sorry." He backed toward the door and triggered the bell over the frame.

"No, wait!" She took a single step after him, but it was no use. "Damn it." The smoke was growing thicker, the air hotter. Alma pressed the back of her wrist to her mouth and narrowed her gaze to see through the oncoming darkness. She moved around the display cases and down the hall leading to the back. "Is anyone here?"

A groan sounded from nearby, and she froze.

"Reagan?" She pumped her legs hard, scanning between each row of pan racks. A pair of legs materialized from beneath a large baking oven on wheels, dozens of small pies scattered across the floor. Instant recognition flared from the bright Hawaiian shirt pattern, and she collapsed to his side. "Reagan! Are you okay?" She set her hand in his to get a feel for a pulse.

"Alma...oven fell...blast...you gotta go...whole building..." The hippie-age baker mumbled through the rest of his warning. He most likely had a concussion, maybe some internal bleeding from the impact. Where the hell was fire and rescue? How far out were Chief Ford and Easton?

"You didn't even need your notes to remember my name." It didn't matter where everyone else was. She was here now. She had to be the one to help him. She released Reagan's hand and took position near his head to lift the oven. "Come on. I'm going to get you out of here. Push as hard as you can. I've got you."

Alma braced one shoulder against the oven, but it wouldn't move. The injury through her rotator cuff screamed in protest as she tried a second time. Still, it wouldn't move. Her eyes burned from the smoke curling through the bakery. Sweat pooled at the base of her spine and along her hairline, but she couldn't stop. "Reagan, we're going to have to work together here."

He didn't answer. The baker had lost consciousness, trapped beneath the behemoth he relied on to run his business. The temperature suddenly felt as though it'd gone up fifty degrees. She noted the paint bubbling from the opposite wall. Soon, the fire would break through and demolish everything in the bakery. Including her and Reagan. Alma swiped her hand across her face. She was the only chance he had of getting out of here alive. She wasn't going to leave him. She stripped the sling from her shoulder and tossed it aside. "We can do this. We can do this."

A scream clawed up her throat as she put everything she had into lifting the oven. Every muscle in her body burned with exertion. One centimeter at a time, the oven rose, but another weight piled on. The one she'd shouldered since her divorce.

Her grip faltered, and she struggled to reposition her hands for a better hold. It didn't matter how hard she'd committed herself to breaking free of the past, it had engrained itself into the fibers of her being, become part of her as Cree had said. The hurt she carried had given her an exit strategy out of getting too close, out of exposing herself again, and where had it left her? Here, in Caffeine and Carbs, trying to haul a burning

hot oven off a victim of the most recent bombing. With
no support, no backup, and no one but herself to blame.
Because Cree had been right. She'd known it the moment he'd said the words. There were people here who
cared about her, and she'd pushed them all away. Including him. The anxiety and loneliness she'd hoped to
thwart by becoming part of a team had stayed buried
for a long time, but now she realized it had been a ploy
all along. A Band-Aid to the betrayal etched into her
bones. Another scream tore from her. Her head ached
with the tightness in her jaw. "Reagan, wake up! I need
your help. I need…"

Cree.

His name settled at the tip of her tongue and intertwined with the fear taking hold. Fear she wasn't good
enough for this work. Fear she'd die here. Fear she'd
screwed up the connection between her and the only
man who'd put her safety, needs and comfort above
his own. Without complaint or resentment. Cree had
punctured the bubble she'd created to separate herself
from the rest of the world while making her stronger in the same breath. He'd tested her, pushed her
to confront the pain she wanted to deny residence in
her head, and been there on the other side when she
couldn't do it alone. He'd given her all of him while
expecting nothing in return, and she'd fallen in love
with him because of it.

She loved him.

And it had scared her.

There wasn't any other explanation for why she'd
severed their partnership. The mere thought of losing
him had sent her into survival mode, and she'd run.
Not physically. But emotionally, mentally. Because if

she didn't have anything to lose, if she accepted she'd be alone, he couldn't hurt her. But she did have something to lose. Him. And she wasn't alone.

Cree had been in the station mere minutes before the explosion. Had he made it out alive? Had Macie come back from break? Sweat dripped from her chin as sizzling broke through the low ringing in her ears. A deep groan registered from above. The building was compromised. They had to get out of there. Alma dug her heels into the tiled floor.

"I can do this." She was getting Reagan out of here. She steadied her breathing and closed her eyes. Feeling for the balance between the oven and her momentum, she moved her hands closer into her chest, at risk of dropping the mammoth oven on Reagan all over again. But it didn't drop. She held strong, and with her mind clearer than it had been in days, she focused all of her energy into pushing it back. The wheels squeaked as they took the weight of the oven, and within seconds, Reagan was free. Alma could've collapsed right there, but the lick of flames breaking through the opposite wall said they'd run out of time.

She wrapped her fingers around Reagan's wrists and pulled him to the front of the bakery. She rammed her backside into the front door. "Help! Somebody! He needs an ambulance!"

"Mario. The refrigerator…he's in the refrigerator." Reagan's plea barely reached her ears, and she realized the baker wasn't talking about the cat she'd noticed prowling through the store. His assistant, Mario, wasn't staring back from the ocean of faces pushing the perimeter.

He was still inside.

A pair of residents ran to assist, and she handed Reagan off. A glance down the length of Main Street revealed the total loss of every shop south of the station. The entire complex was going to collapse. "Tell Chief Ford I'm headed back inside when he gets here. There's someone else in there." She wrenched the front door open on its hinges and ran straight toward the encroaching flames. Smoke interrupted her steady breathing, and her lungs spasmed in response. Covering her mouth and nose with her collar, she located the refrigerator. She swung the heavy metal door outward.

Empty.

"Don't worry, Officer Majors, Mario is safe," a voice said from behind. "You, on the other hand…"

Pain exploded through her skull and rocketed her forward. Alma hit the floor, her collar slipping from her mouth. Her vision blurred around the edges, but not enough to hide her attacker's identity as the woman relieved her of her weapon. Alma reached for her shield and unpinned it from her uniform, intent to use it as a weapon if needed. "You."

"Yeah." The bomber stepped on either side of Alma and clenched her collar in one hand. Arcing her hand back, she swung her gun a second time. "Me."

A HIGH-PITCHED RINGING pierced through what little consciousness he held on to.

Cree groaned under the weight of something solid and heavy on his chest, but the sound barely registered. He tried to haul his head away from whatever he'd landed on. In vain. Explosions of white light seared across his vision as he mentally scanned the length of his body. His toes had gone numb on his left foot.

He stretched his jaw to get his ears to pop, but there wasn't any relief. Scrubbing a hand down his face, he spotted blood trickling from a laceration along the side of his hand.

Seconds distorted into confusing minutes. Flames licked the edges of what used to be the station's second floor straight above him. The call from outside the police station. The device he'd found in Chief Ford's office. Macie coming through the back door—each memory intertwined with the next until it was nothing but a mashup of fire, blood and pain. Cree kicked debris from his legs and set his hands beneath the beam to get out from under it. The second device. He hadn't found it until it'd been too late. And Macie… She'd been right next to him.

"Macie… Oh, hell." Cree wrapped one arm around his midsection in an attempt to keep his ribs from breaking completely. If they hadn't already. Ash rained from the floor above and mixed with the blood running into the crease of his elbow. The same ringing in his ears wouldn't let up as he hauled the beam off his chest with everything he had left. The wood protested before angling to his right. He swallowed the buildup of dryness in his mouth. The same terror he'd barely survived threatened to undo him all over again, but he couldn't hide this time. No matter how great the temptation, he couldn't run from this. Not again. "Macie, can you hear me?"

"I'm here." Movement honed his attention to a section of splintered wood and drywall ten feet away. Red hair coated in dust matted to a color-stricken and bloody face. "I'm okay. I think."

"We can't stay here." Pain sharpened his senses, and

the ringing in his ear ceased. The building groaned above them. Water rushed from a broken pipe above but did nothing to douse the flames. "The bomb damaged the building's supports. It won't stay standing much longer."

"We should call 911." Macie swiped ash as she scanned the war zone they hadn't been fast enough to escape. Her hands shook. "But I'm not sure who would answer right now."

"Fire and rescue is still battling the forest fire." Cree dragged one arm behind him, his leg almost as useless, as he hobbled to stand. Dislocated shoulder, if he had to guess. "I'll get you out." He maneuvered through broken chunks of cement, drywall and tile and reached to help her to her feet.

"You owe me a new headset." Her words slurred there slightly at the end. The tremors quaking up her arms and into her neck signaled shock. She needed medical attention. Fast.

"Let's just focus on getting you out of here first." He secured a hand around her lower back to keep her upright and pulled her toward the only sliver of light visible in the whole damn place. From the layout of the building, he guessed the lobby door, but there were any number of things that could be messing with his sense of direction. Smoke thickened around them, but crawling through the debris for oxygen wasn't an option. They'd never make it out. "Lean on me."

"You're the one who can barely walk." Macie fisted her hands in his jacket. "Don't you mean you need to lean on me?"

The dispatcher's words were meant as sarcasm, but the sequence tunneled through the hollowness he'd lost himself in these past eight months. He'd run from Battle Mountain to hide, out of shame, out of guilt, out of embarrassment. As a highly trained bomb tech, he'd convinced himself he should've known the second device had been planted in the vent above the chief's office, just as he'd convinced himself he should've been able to disarm the bomb planted at that conference. The emptiness that had taken hold threatened to drag him beneath the surface as long as he lived, but while he'd believed he deserved it, he'd forgotten a key piece of the formula along the way. The same formula Macie wanted him to see now.

He didn't have to do this alone.

It had been easy enough to tell Alma to trust him, but the truth was, he'd only trusted himself all this time. Hell. How did he expect her to move on when he couldn't summon the courage to do it himself? The bombing in Larimer County hadn't been his fault. His team had swept that building. They'd done their job, but the ecoterrorists responsible had been cleverer than he'd estimated. Yet he'd taken on the responsibility for those lives lost when it should've been on those bombers all along.

His determination to live on autopilot, to grit through whatever came his way and isolate himself, had been his way of compartmentalizing, but he didn't want to spend the rest of his life holding on to his own dysfunctional conditioning. He didn't have to do this alone. He didn't want to, and as Macie and Cree progressed through the maze of catastrophe, he realized his life back in Larimer County didn't exist anymore. Because he wasn't the same person he'd been then. Battle Mountain—and the town's highly defensive, most recent recruit for the police department—was his future. And he wasn't going to give up on them. Ever. "Yeah. It's probably a better idea for me to lean on you."

"Gregson! Macie!" Easton Ford's distorted voice filtered through the pops of embers and flames. "Majors! Can anybody hear me?"

Cree dodged a bare nail sticking up from one of the structural beams. His lungs protested against the influx of smoke, and he buried his mouth and nose into his elbow. "In here!"

"Over here!" Macie yelled.

A flashlight beam cut through the smoke and swept across their faces. Pain lightninged through Cree's head at the onslaught, but it gave them a direction through the chaos. In seconds, Easton Ford was tightening an oxygen mask over each of their faces and leading them through the rubble with two firefighters at his back. The building groaned right before the ceiling caved in directly over where they'd been standing. Within a few steps, sunlight swarmed around them. A fire engine skidded to a stop nearby, and a mess of fighters hit the ground. Orders were given and followed, hoses unpacked and emergency personnel in place. Both Macie and Cree were led to a waiting ambulance at the edge of the perimeter, and he couldn't help but scan the officers and rescue trying to get the blaze under control. The entire length of Main Street shops had caught fire, and his stomach pitted. He pulled the mask below his chin. "Where's Alma?"

Easton Ford leveraged his hand against the back of the rig and took a long pull from his own oxygen mask. Confusion rippled across his stoic expression, and the deputy straightened. "She wasn't with you?"

Fear charged through him as Cree memorized every bystander and emergency officer. He shoved off the blanket that had been wrapped around his shoulders and tossed the oxygen mask. Clamping a hand on his dislocated shoulder, he targeted Dr. Chloe Miles speaking with Chief Ford twenty feet away. Alma had left the station to meet with the coroner. If they weren't together... He jogged to catch up to them as the couple parted. "Doc, have you seen Officer Majors? She said she was meeting up with you to reconstruct the victim's skull."

The coroner's eyes widened. "After the explosion, she told me to grab the evidence and get everyone out of the funeral home. I haven't seen her since. She wanted me to keep piecing the skull back together to get an accurate ID on the victim. It's not much, but I was able to scan the portion Alma reassembled."

"You got an ID?" Chief Ford asked.

"It's not a hundred percent match, but it's close. Alma did most of the work going through every piece of bone until a face emerged." She handed off her phone. "Danielle Sawyer. Thirty-four years old, Caucasian female. That's all I've been able to find so far."

Danny. The recipient of the voice mail they recovered from the phone Travis Foster found under his wife's side of the mattress. They had a name, but he couldn't think about that right now. Alma was out here, alone. She needed help.

"Alma wouldn't have just left." He studied the length of shops already threatening to collapse. The killer had called from right outside. If she'd gotten hold of Alma... What blood he had left in his face drained.

"She would've… She wouldn't tried to get all these people to safety because no one else was here."

"Chief Ford!" One of the townspeople waved from behind the perimeter tape. Cree wasn't sure of his name or if he'd seen him around town before today. It didn't matter. "That deputy, Officer Majors, she went back into Caffeine and Carbs after pulling Reagan out. I haven't seen her since."

"Damn it." Chief Ford pulled the radio from his belt. "All units, Officer Majors is inside the bakery. I need an EMT and firefighters to help me search the building."

"I'm going with you." Cree stepped into Dr. Miles's personal space. "I need you to reset my shoulder."

"Officer Gregson, you've been through a terrifying trauma." She shook her head. "I think it's best if you—"

"Just do it." He braced for the pain, and Dr. Miles accepted he wasn't going to change his mind. The resulting pop sickened his stomach, and he almost blacked out. Instant relief coiled through him. "Thank you." He took a single step toward the building.

A window exploded from the second story of Caffeine and Carbs, and everybody on the street ducked to protect themselves. Straightening, Cree stared up at what was left of the building just before the supports gave out. Screw his shoulder. He rushed toward the failing structure, but it was too late.

"Cree, no!" Chief Ford latched a hand around his uninjured arm and pulled him back.

The insides of the building gave out first, the outer walls folding soon after. Cree protected his face as ash, fire and brick kicked into the air. Barely able to take a full breath, he waited for the dust to settle. Too long. Squinting through the wall of debris, he nearly tripped over a structural beam. "Alma!"

No. No, no, no, no. Firefighters raced to douse the flames snaking through the rubble, and Cree hauled himself into the pile. Pulling hot bricks and rolling chunks of cement free, he searched every nook and cranny he had access to. "Don't just stand there! Help me!"

Easton Ford, the chief and Dr. Miles each started working through the pile of cement, drywall and framing. The burns along his hands ignited as he tossed another load of bricks over his shoulder. Desperation clawed through him, alive and screaming. They were going to find her. There was no other option. Not for him. "I'm coming, Alma. Just hang on."

Cree hauled the next chunk of rubble free, and a piece of metal glimmered beneath a layer of dust and ash. A police shield. Battle Mountain Police Department. It wouldn't have come detached from her uniform by accident, which meant, Alma had taken it off. Why? The answer solidified in his gut. "She's not here."

Chapter Fourteen

Incessant crying brought her out of darkness.

An infant?

Exhaustion threatened to hold her under, but Alma was stronger. She wiggled her toes in her shoes, then her fingers, bringing herself around limb by limb. Only she couldn't do much more than that. The killer had learned from her mistake this time. Instead of zip ties, ropes encircled Alma's wrists behind her back and her ankles.

"There, there. Mommy's got you. It's going to be okay." That voice. The killer's voice. It drove past the haze of unconsciousness and triggered the mind-numbing fear she never wanted to feel again. A flash of red hair blazed on the other side of the room as her abductor picked up the crying child from a pack-and-play. Recognition flared as Agent Christine Freehan kissed the boy's soft cheek. Travis Foster's son. Pressing her cheek to his, the bomber bounced him in her arms. "She'll be gone soon. I promise. Then it'll just be me and you. Like we wanted from the start."

The side of her face pulsed with her racing heart as Alma took in her surroundings. Old wood creaked as she craned her head back. The small cabin-like home didn't offer much in terms of space. A kitchenette took up one side of the room where she'd been deposited, with a single sofa and the pack-and-play on the other. Bare wood stairs connected the second level to the first, which Alma assumed contained a single bedroom and bathroom.

"Look who's awake." Footsteps reverberated through the floor as Agent Freehan closed in. Pin-straight red hair swayed under the woman's movements. Bangs covered perfectly arched eyebrows and accentuated a long thin nose, and for a fraction of a minute, Alma thought she was staring into the face of the victim she'd found at the base of the gulch. Identical twins. The only difference apart from their hair? The ice in Agent Freehan's gaze. "Just in time."

"You attacked Travis Foster. You kidnapped the baby." Alma didn't understand. The bomber had set out to destroy her sister's identity, tracked her down over years in order to kill her. All so she could have her baby? "Why?"

"I told you why at the lake, Officer Majors." Agent Freehan retraced her steps back to the temporary crib and set the child inside. Crossing into the kitchenette, she wrenched open the refrigerator and pulled a bottle from within. Milk. In as few steps, she handed it off to the boy and soothed his hair as Alma imagined his mother would have. "My sister was the constant favorite while we were growing up. It didn't matter that we were twins, that we shared the same birthday or likes. I was always expendable to our parents. I was always expected to give in to her childish meltdowns to keep the peace or surrender to her every whim."

"Danny." Alma didn't have more than a voice mail

as a resource, but based off the stiffness running through the killer's neck and jaw, she'd hit a mark.

Agent Freehan left the boy to feed and straightened. "You really are a fine investigator, Officer Majors. It's a shame no one but this pathetic town will ever have the chance to benefit from all that insight."

They were still in Battle Mountain. Although, from the little Alma noted through the single window on the other side of the room, she wasn't sure where or how far out from the city limits they were. "What is this place?"

The bomber exposed her neck as she surveyed the cabin. Shadows lined the tendons running the length of her neck as she slid her hands into her cargo pockets. Her leather jacket and bright red T-shirt didn't fit the ATF agent profile at all like she'd imagined, but from what Alma understood, this particular agent didn't really play by the rules. "This place? A safe house of sorts. Well, not a very good one as you can imagine. It didn't work for my sister very long. Danny came across it right after she left her husband and baby in Ouray. You'd think after so many years on the run, she would've gotten as far from them as possible. Funny thing is, I already knew where she was. I already knew about her husband and the baby. I knew she'd grabbed Mom's cell phone before the fire to call 911. She was smart enough to keep it turned off so I couldn't track her, but a few days ago I got a hit. She'd turned it on. I think now she wanted me to find her. I think she wanted to stop running. So I came to grant her wish."

One step. Two. Agent Freehan refocused on Alma and crouched in front of her. Fingers interlaced, she parted them for a moment, then pressed them back together. "To be honest, she didn't seem all that surprised when she opened the door. More like acceptance. I think she knew then."

Alma worked a broken fingernail against the rope at her back and slowly picked the strands apart. It would take time to get through the whole thing—time she didn't have—but it was worth a shot. Agent Freehan had kidnapped a child to get revenge on her deceased sister. Alma would get him out of here and back home to his father. "Knew what?"

"That I was going to finally get what was owed me." The bomber twisted to check on the baby, still happily plugging away on his bottle. "I worked my entire life to make something of myself, to make our parents proud, and got nothing out of it in return. She glided through life as though everyone owed her. She didn't work for anything, and she didn't deserve what she had."

"The fire that killed your parents all those years ago… You started it." Dryness caught in Alma's throat as she considered the amount of hatred and rage it would've taken to murder the very people who'd raised you.

"Once I got to be in high school, I realized I wasn't ever going to make a difference in how my parents saw me." Agent Freehan shoved to her feet, unholstering the weapon she'd taken from Alma. She hit the magazine release and caught the heavy metal before it dropped to the floor. Thumbing each bullet free, she let the rounds scatter around her boots. "I wasted years trying to impress them. Straight A's all through middle school and high school, sports, early college courses. None of it mattered, and when I asked my mother why she loved Danny more than she loved me? She told me I didn't need the attention, that I could take care of myself.

Turns out, she was right. So I did exactly that. I took care of myself, and I haven't looked back."

"You killed them because they favored your sister over you?" One of the bullets rolled against Alma's shoe, and she set her boot over it as slowly as possible so as not to draw attention. "And what about the bombing at Galaxy Electronics or the police station? Did you do those because your parents didn't love you enough?"

"I couldn't very well have you tracing the devices back to me through the components I stole from that dilapidated store, now, could I? The government trained me better than that." Agent Freehan cocked her head to one side. "As for the police station, I needed to make sure the evidence Silverton's bomb squad collected from the scene was destroyed. Can't have anything threatening my job with the ATF. How else will I support this little one myself?"

A smile partnered with Alma's humorless laugh. All this time, she'd convinced herself the killer they were after had been one step ahead. Turned out, she was just as human as the rest of them. "Well, there was your first mistake."

Amusement bled from Agent Freehan's expression, and the bomber peeled her hands from inside her pockets. "What was that?"

"The coroner took custody of your sister's remains from the gulch." Alma slid the bullet under her shoe another inch closer to her hands.

"I realize this might be your first homicide investigation, Officer Majors, but believe it or not, that's protocol," Freehan said. "That's exactly what I was counting on."

"But you haven't done your homework." She felt

the tip of the bullet brush against her fingers, and she pinned it between both hands. The bullet itself wouldn't do a damn bit of good without her weapon, but once she unscrewed the tip from the casing, the edge might be sharp enough to cut through the rope. "You see, after the mining companies pulled out of town and took all their money with them, there wasn't enough resources to establish a medical examiner's office. The closest ME we have is over in Grand Junction." She twisted the tip of the bullet free, catching it before it hit the floor and gave away her plan. "That said, Chief Ford could appoint a coroner. Dr. Miles is great at her job and is able to conduct autopsies, but she doesn't have a lab. And her office isn't anywhere near the police station."

Seconds distorted into a minute, into what felt like an hour.

"I know what you're trying to do, Officer Majors. If I hadn't already checked you for a wire, I'd seriously question why you're dragging this out. But from the way you've been hiding your hands from me, I'm guessing you're working on your binds." Agent Freehan tossed Alma's weapon to the far side of the room. "Maybe it's time to end this once and for all."

The rope strands unwound, and faster than she expected, Alma's hands broke free. "I think you're right." Hauling her feet forward, she swept the killer's legs out from under her.

Agent Freehan hit the ground. Her head snapped back, and the killer's eyes widened slightly.

Alma didn't wait for her to recover. She slapped one hand over the agent's ankle and pulled the blade holstered beneath her cargo pants. In a clean swipe, she severed the ropes around her ankles and shoved to stand. She lunged toward the pack-and-play to grab the baby. Too slow. The pain in her shoulder flared as the bomber dug strong fingers into the hole the victim's bone had left behind. A scream escaped her control, and Alma doubled over to grit through it.

"Let me make one thing clear, Officer Majors." Agent Freehand circled into Alma's vision and gripped her by the back of the neck. "You don't get to touch my son."

The stitches in her side stretched with each overexaggerated inhale. "He's not your son. He never will be, and I'm going to take him home." Alma kicked out as hard as she could. Her heel connected with Agent Freehan's knee, but not enough to shatter bone. The killer launched a fist straight into Alma's temple, and Alma staggered back into a faux plant beside the kitchenette.

"He is home." Agent Freehan charged.

CREE SWIPED FIRE hose water from his face.

The edges of Alma's shield cut into his palm as he took in what was left of the shops along Main Street, including the station. He pressed his free hand into his ribs. One broken. Maybe two. He'd been lucky the damn injury hadn't punctured his lungs. Considering the circumstances, he and Macie were both lucky to walk out of that station alive.

The town wasn't lucky enough.

Tears, sobs and disbelief filtered through the crowds pressing against the perimeter. Easton had gone through for statements as fire and rescue fought to get the blaze from spreading to any other buildings. No one had seen Alma after she'd gone back into the bakery for another bystander. But there had been reports of a midsize sedan leaving the scene a few minutes before EMTs found the baker's assistant behind the building with minor smoke inhalation. No one had been in a calm enough state to catch a plate number while their town burned around them, but Cree's gut told him Alma had been in that car. Now all he had to do was find her.

Rock and wood sizzled under the influence of hose water. While the flames had retreated for the time being, fire and rescue would ensure the blaze was completely neutralized before letting anyone close. He didn't need to get close. He needed a lead. Rivers of water and ash squished under his feet. He could still feel the heat emanating from what was left of Caffeine and Carbs. The burn lanced across the damage already done to his hands and neck from the bomb rigged to his truck. The dragon had done its job here, consuming some of these people's livelihoods along with it. He wiped a trail of sweat from the back of his neck as he studied every inch of the ground behind the line of shops. And stopped.

Tire tracks. Headed east. Too close together to belong to an SUV or pickup. The sedan that witnesses had noticed fleeing the scene? Cree shoved to his feet.

"You got something?" Chief Ford swept dark eyes along the backside of the row of shops.

"A few people behind the tape described a late-model sedan driving away from the scene. These are a match for size." He nodded to the tracks giving way under the onslaught of fire hose water. "You're going to want to get a cast of these as soon as possible. No telling how much longer fire and rescue is going to soak this area." Cree walked along the treads left behind in the dirt. His truck had been totaled with that third bomb. He needed a vehicle. "I'm going after Alma."

"Gregson." Ford tossed him a set of keys just as Cree turned to face him. "Bring her back home alive. You got me? Whatever it takes."

"I give you my word, Chief." Cree nodded. Curling his fingers around the keys, he slipped through the break between buildings and headed for the pickup truck parked across the street in front of Hopper's Hardware.

The truck started with the easiest of provocation from the ignition, and the mobile data terminal mounted between the front seats flickered to life. He planted Alma's badge on the dashboard. Lucky for him, the department's central computer wasn't located inside the station. Instead, the system connected wirelessly to Colorado's Bureau of Investigation. He twisted to type the victim's name and hit enter. Danielle Sawyer. Her photo filled the screen, a perfect match to the missing person report Travis Foster had filed for his wife. Dr. Miles had been right. Alma had found the victim's identity.

The computer ticked as it processed his request for Agent Christine Freehan's background information. Another photo filled the screen, almost identical to the first. Same birthday listed as for Danielle. Twins?

He searched for properties in Danielle Sawyer's name but came up empty.

No. She wouldn't have used her own name on a home deed. Not if she'd gone to such lengths to change her identity on the run. She would've used what was available. No connection to Danielle Sawyer. If she'd listened to that voice mail from her sister, it would've triggered her flight instinct. Maybe enough for her to consider leaving her family behind to keep them safe from her past. "In that case..."

Cree searched for foreclosed or abandoned properties. Danielle Sawyer had been killed here in Battle Mountain. Stood to reason she'd been hiding here when the bomber had finally caught up with her. The MDT spat out a list. He ran through it, one by one. The victim had been on the run since high school. She'd known what she was doing. Problem was, whoever had hunted her all these years was better. Nothing too close to town. Would've made it hard for Danielle Sawyer to stay under the radar, but not too far, either. She would've wanted access to a vehicle if she'd needed to ditch hers and groceries if she intended to stay a while. "Where did your sister find you?"

A cabin crept up the screen, and Cree stopped scrolling. Familiarity lanced through him. He pressed back into the leather seat. His grandfather's cabin. It had been years since the old man had passed away, and Cree hadn't ever intended to go back. Hadn't hired anyone to take care of it while he was on tour or working the bomb squad up in Larimer County.

It was the perfect safe house.

Not too far.

Not too close.

And nowhere near any nosy neighbors.

"Gotcha." Cree shut the terminal lid and put the truck into gear. Tires protested as he hit the accelerator and pulled away from the curb. The steering wheel caught on the blisters under his fingers. Sunlight reflected off the ash-covered badge he'd set on the dashboard, keeping him in the moment. Trees thickened the faster he raced along one of two roads out of town until he couldn't see Battle Mountain in the rearview mirror at all.

His sense of direction and the fact his grandfather had forced him to memorize a map of the area had him pulling off the main road earlier than what would get him to the cabin fastest. The truck's hood dipped and rose along the dirt and gravel road, and he slowed to a near crawl so as not to kick up dust. If the bomber had ambushed her sister at the cabin and then gone to extreme lengths to hide her involvement, she might not have had time to get the lay of the land. He cut the truck's automatic daytime lights and pulled in head-first beneath an overgrown tree Cree had used for target practice all those years ago. "Here we go."

Eyes on the cabin higher up the mountain, he reached for the glove box and found another of the chief's backup weapons. He shouldered out of the truck and closed the driver's-side door behind him as quietly as possible. After checking the magazine, he loaded a round into the chamber and wedged it between his lower back and waistband. He rounded the hood of the truck. Hatchet scars scored the thin bark along the tree's trunk, and at the base, covered in pine needles, he found the hatchet his grandfather had gifted him for his eighteenth birthday, the last time they'd been together before the old man had passed. Cree smoothed his thumb along the handle, then gripped it hard.

He kept low and moved fast through the trees, making sure he was never in sight of the cabin's west window positioned in the living room. His heart thudded steadily behind his ears. A late-model gray sedan demanded attention from the gravel driveway, and confirmation pulsed through him. Crouching low behind the vehicle, he slid his fingers the length of the tire treads. Same pattern he'd discovered behind the bakery where Alma had last been seen. This was it. His partner was in there, and he wasn't going back to town without her.

The muscles along the backs of his legs burned as he maneuvered around the rear of the vehicle. Distraction. Agent Freehan had trained with the best of the best over the years. She knew her way around explosive devices. No telling how many she'd planted in case someone got too close.

There. The stockpile of wood had grown since the time he'd left this place behind. Whether it'd been seen to by Danielle Sawyer or her sister in recent months, it didn't matter. What did matter was the white bricks of C4 hidden inside. Travis Foster's construction manager had reported twenty pounds of the explosive missing from their worksite. The bomber had already gone through at least ten between the gulch, Galaxy Electronics, Cree's truck, the lake, and the station, leaving ten pounds unaccounted for. Agent Freehan had mostly likely positioned similar devices around the perimeter here.

Cree gripped the hatchet before embedding it into a nearby log. Crossing beneath the west window, he crouched in front of the stockpile and pulled the device free. No countdown. This one had been set up to detonate with a remote trigger. A cell phone in this case. Clever. One press of a button and the entire cabin and the surrounding property would go up in flames. Carefully detaching the cell phone from the device, he scanned through the call log. Only one number in the history. Memorizing it, he reattached the phone and worked his way back to the vehicle in the driveway. He slid under the frame and used the pliability of the C4 to attach the homemade device to the undercarriage. "Let's see what you do with a taste of your own medicine, Freehan."

In seconds, he left the safety of the vehicle and retreated into the woods, finding five more devices like the one he'd discovered positioned strategically at the cabin's structural walls. Taking position at the clearing's edge, he unpocketed his own phone and dialed the number from the trigger's call history. The line rang once. Twice.

"Agent Freehan." The same voice he'd heard over Danielle Sawyer's voice mail grated along his nerves, out of breath, and Cree's body tightened in response. The screams of a kid staticked through the line, and his insides constricted.

"Let my partner walk out of there on her own two feet with the boy, and I'll let you do the same," he said.

"Officer Gregson, how nice of you to join us. I'm curious, though. How did you get this number? Couldn't have been from the friend you had looking into me at the ATF. You and I both know I've been doing this too long to make a simple mistake like using my work phone for personal calls." Freehan's outline crossed in front of the east window as she searched the perimeter. She wanted him to know she knew he'd sent someone to look into her, throw him off guard, maybe make him rethink his approach, but it wouldn't work. Red hair swept over her shoulders as she leaned into the glass, and he backed into the tree line. She moved onto the next window, making it easy to track her movements. "You took apart my security system, didn't you?"

"Not all of it. Just enough to ensure whatever you had planned won't work." Cree kept to the trees as he rounded the property. "Where are Alma and the boy?"

"Right here, of course," Freehan said. "Although I can't guarantee your partner will be here much longer."

"We'll see about that." He ended the call, then dialed a second number. Cree crossed the overgrown space between the tree line and the south wall of the cabin. He hit the green button to connect.

The explosion ripped through the sedan.

Chapter Fifteen

The boy's screams kept her conscious, almost willing her to stay in the fight.

Then an explosion rocked through one side of the cabin.

The quake rolled beneath her and threatened to bring down the entire structure. The window above the kitchenette shattered. Glass rained down around her. Alma rolled to her bleeding side. Her stitches hadn't been enough to keep her wound together during the fight, but she couldn't give in. Not yet. Blood escaped from between her clenched teeth. She spat to clear her mouth and her senses as Agent Freehan rocked back on her heels.

Now was her chance.

Alma wiped the blood from her mouth and lunged.

Shoving the bomber over the countertop, she gripped the back of Freehan's head and rocketed it into the counter. One of the drawers shook from the impact. Alma fisted a handful of the agent's long hair but had to let go at the swift swipe of a knife from the butcher block. She fell back against the floor as Agent Freehan advanced.

"Nobody is taking him from me." The baby's cries

intensified as if on cue. Both hands wrapped around the knife's handle, the bomber held it over her head. Ready to plunge it in Alma's chest.

Alma rolled as fast as she could just as the tip of the blade imbedded into the floor, and she got to her feet. Spanning her arms wide, she searched for a weapon—anything that would counter a kitchen knife—and brushed against a set of dusty curtains. She ripped one panel free just as Agent Freehan attacked, knife first.

Alma wrapped the fabric around the bomber's wrist and twisted as hard as she could. The pop of a fractured bone barely registered through the toddler's screams. She pinned her attacker's arm against her injured side and tightened her hold on the curtain panel. "Your sister didn't deserve to die in that gulch. All she wanted was to escape the past, but you wouldn't let her. You were so determined to make her pay for something she wasn't responsible for that you wasted your entire life instead of trying to move on."

An echo of that pain reverberated through Alma as she considered how many months she'd wasted following the same path. Hurt, determined to be alone, using the past as a crutch to keep herself from moving forward. But Cree had brought hope and light into her life. He'd given her the strength to face down the shadows that had become so deeply ingrained she hadn't seen a way out of the darkness. That strength, she realized, had been there all along. It had just taken someone like him to prove she was more than a victim, more than a trauma survivor. That she wasn't alone. "You're going to spend the rest of your life behind bars because you wouldn't take responsibility for your own happiness."

Agent Freehan launched her free arm for another

strike, but Alma was faster. With both hands pinned, the killer raged to gain some semblance of control. "You have no idea what she took from me."

"She didn't take anything." Alma hauled her boot into the side of the bomber's knee, and the agent collapsed to the floor. Tightening her hold around the curtain panel, she forced Agent Freehan to drop the knife. Metal met wood with a hard thud. "You were never a victim. No matter how many times you've tried to convince yourself otherwise, you don't get to have your happily-ever-after." The bomber's own words from the voice mail she'd left her sister echoed through Alma's head. "It's over."

"No." Agent Freehan struggled against the pressure on her broken wrist, a fire Alma had seen all too often during her marriage in the killer's eyes. "This isn't over. This isn't how it ends for me."

The boy quieted down, watching in angst, but still clenching small fists, his bottle forgotten. The cabin's front door crashed inward, and Alma's fight instincts automatically responded. Until recognition flared. "Cree."

Her partner stood in the doorframe, what looked like a hatchet in one hand and his phone in the other. He scanned the room and took in her hold on Agent Freehan. Cree had come for her. "Looks like I missed one hell of a party. Agent Freehan, nice to meet you face-to-face."

The bomber didn't answer, didn't even seem to breathe as she seethed.

A wave of dizziness crowded Alma's head as the entire investigation over the past four days led to this. She released her numb grip from the curtain panel and slumped back against the wall. She forced her finger-nails into the palms of her hands to keep herself from mentally detaching. The boy's cries filtered in and out through the pulse thudding hard at the back of her skull, and she crossed the room. Red stains of distress across the baby's face paled as she reached into the pack-and-play and hefted him to her chest. "You're safe now. I'm going to get you to your daddy at the hospital. Okay? He's worried about you, but you'll be together soon enough. You're safe." She automatically bounced him on her hip, pressing a hand into his back. The cries quieted, and she set her temple against his warm cheek.

"Any sudden movements, Agent Freehan, and your car will be the least of your worries." Cree wrenched the killer's hands behind her back, ignoring the groan of pain from her broken wrist, and produced a set of cuffs from his back pocket.

Sirens echoed off the cliffs, and Alma stepped near the window in time to see a Battle Mountain patrol cruiser dipping and climbing up the dirt road. Flames charred stretches of gravel as she took in the aftermath but didn't shift toward the cabin.

It was over.

She soothed small circles into the boy's back as Cree led Agent Freehan toward the front door. Then froze. The curtain panel stretched the length of the floor where she'd left it. But where was the knife she'd forced the killer to drop? Alma turned after Cree. Too late. "Watch out!"

Agent Freehan wrenched free of Cree's hold and dropped to the floor. Faster than Alma thought possi-ble, the bomber rolled, maneuvering her cuffed wrists under her boots, just as Alma had at the lake. Freehan

pulled the knife from beneath her leather jacket and
focused her wrath at Alma.

One second. Two.

"No!" Alma spun to protect the boy and braced for
the striking pain of the blade.

Only it never came.

A rough exhale reached her ears. She twisted
around, her hold tight on the boy. And found Cree
standing between her and Agent Freehand. Too close.
The woman's expression warped from surprise into
satisfaction, and Alma's heart shot into her throat. Just
as the front door burst open. "Cree?"

He didn't answer.

"Battle Mountain PD! On the ground! Now!" Easton
Ford raised his weapon and targeted Agent Freehan.

The killer raised both hands still bound by the cuffs
and backed away from Cree, the knife no longer in
her grip. She followed instructions and got down on
one knee, then the other, before laying face-first on
the floor. Cold eyes found Alma, and Agent Freehan
smirked. "You took something of mine. I take something of yours."

Cree collapsed, drawing a panicked scream from
her throat.

"No!" Tightening her hold on the toddler, Alma
dropped to her knees as the pain in her shoulder
screamed for relief. It took more effort than she'd imagined to turn him onto his back. A line of blood escaped
the corner of his mouth. "Hang on. Help is already on
the way. Just hang on."

Forest green eyes found hers—slowly—and Cree
intertwined his hand with hers. The wound spat blood
around the blade still protruding from his rib cage. Too

deep, but she couldn't risk removing it. He might bleed internally before the EMTs had a chance. "Your...theory worked. The skull. You...found her."

"Shh. Try not to talk right now." In an instant, she was back in that gulch, watching an innocent life drain in front of her eyes, and there hadn't been anything she could do. "Save your energy."

"Danielle Sawyer." A rough cough clenched every muscle in his body, and Alma strengthened her grip in his hand. "You found her."

Tears burned in her eyes. Tears for the pain he suffered, for the time she'd wasted trying to hide from the world, for the potential loss between them. Tears for the victim and the pain she must've endured to protect her son. The boy set his head against her shoulder. Her side protested from the added weight of his small body, but she wasn't going to let him go. "We found her. Together."

Easton dragged Agent Freehan outside.

Cree's eyelids fell as he sucked in a ragged breath. His grip on her hand lightened, but Alma would hold on longer for the both of them if that was what she was required to do. "I was never...going to go back."

"I know." Distant sirens bounced off the cliff walls and pierced through the pops of the smoldering vehicle outside. Her knees went numb pressed against the floor, but she wouldn't leave him. Ever. Cree had saved her. In more ways than one.

Without his knowledge of explosives and all the packages they came in, Agent Freehan would've gotten her way days ago. And without his compassion and ability to see past the mask she wore for the people of this town, she wouldn't have developed the strength to rise above her hurt. Therapy, a groundbreaking book, a new mind set on life and recovery—none of it had compared to his willingness to help her to be seen again instead of hiding behind the pain. She wasn't a lone survivor. He'd made her story part of his story, and she loved him for it. Alma soothed circles into his hand just as he'd done for her back at his apartment. She had to keep him talking. She had to keep him alive. "Cree, look at me."

The seconds ticked off one by one, and the pressure behind her rib cage intensified the longer he lay there, unmoving.

His eyelids strained to open, and a hint of a smile tugged at one corner of his mouth. The sirens were growing closer, but Cree was fighting a losing battle. They wouldn't make it in time. "Hey, partner."

She shifted on her knees, centering herself and the toddler in his limited vision. Her tears dropped to his T-shirt. "I love you."

"YOU CERTAINLY KNOW how to party down here in the middle of nowhere," a deep voice said.

A sense of familiarity punctuated through the weight of painkillers and gravity cementing Cree in place. He knew that voice. Although it had been a couple days since he'd heard it last. Prying his eyes open, he took in the whitewashed walls he'd hoped never to see again. Same monitors, too. He took in the sterile tile and scratchy bedding. Battle Mountain's emergency clinic.

Movement registered off to his left from the side of the bed, and the outline of well-built strength consumed his attention. Kendric Hudson locked mishap-pen brown eyes on him, and the past rushed to meet the present. The ATF's newest bomb squad technician instructor Cree had pulled from the ecoterrorist attack had sustained permanent scarring along one side of his face. The same scarring carved down Cree's back.

"You look as bad as I feel." His voice scraped along his throat as Cree attempted to sit higher in the bed. A dull ache ignited across his midsection. Two broken ribs were nothing compared to cold metal slicing through body parts never meant to see the light of day. A groan escaped his control, and he set his head back against the pillows stacked behind him. "The sheriff called in a favor, didn't he? He sent you to convince me to come back."

It wasn't a question. While the ATF had to absorb the consequences of letting one of their investigators off her leash and had most likely sent a few of their own to run damage control, Kendric hadn't gone back into the field since the bombing in Loveland. He trained the new recruits to save their own lives after barely escaping the bombing that had given him those scars.

His former teammate scratched at one corner of his mouth. "I think my face is supposed to be some kind of guilt trip, a reminder of all the good you've done in the past. Then again, I'm pretty sure your own scars do the trick." The tech's leather vest folded in on itself as soft as poured chocolate as Kendric took a seat. He motioned to something across the room, and Cree caught sight of Alma curled up on her side on the window seat, asleep. "Was it worth it?"

Cree tried to clear the emotion from his throat. She was safe, alive. Thirty seconds. If he'd been thirty seconds later, he would've lost her all over again. Snippets of their last conversation broke through his exhaustion and ignited the pain in his side. Even after she'd severed ties between them, he hadn't had a choice. Putting himself between Agent Freehan and Alma had been instinct, a last-ditch effort to prove their partnership had changed him, that they worked better as a team. Although he could've done without the blade shoved in his gut to make his point. "How… How long has she been here?"

"Since you landed your sorry butt here in the first place." Kendric's voice softened as though he were trying to keep himself from waking the reserve officer Cree had fallen head over heels for. "From what I hear, you're a damn hero. You made it possible for her and that baby to walk out of there and exposed a corrupt ATF agent in the process. The sheriff and the mayor's office are already taking credit, claiming they're the ones who sent you down here undercover to find the truth. Bastards."

Cree studied the slow rise and fall of Alma's shoulders, lost in her instead of what Kendric had said. He'd escaped Loveland to hide from the pain of failing the innocent lives he'd tried to save before the attack, and now, one of the men caught in the blast was here. Two separate lives in the same room. One before he'd come to Battle Mountain. One after. In reality, they weren't separate at all. Mere pieces of a whole. Just as the time he'd grown up living off the land his grandfather owned and his service in the military. Each life had built on the next, leading to this one, preparing him for her. Alma. "Thanks for your help on this case." He rolled his head into the pillows to face his teammate. "I owe you."

"More than tackling me to the ground when that bomb went off and taking the brunt of the blast?" Kendric shook his head. "You still don't get it, do you, man? I know why you left, same as you know why I applied to the ATF. You've been blaming yourself for what happened, but I don't show off these scars because you couldn't get me free of that blast. I show them off because I'm alive to do it." His teammate stood as Alma swept her uninjured forearm over her eyes in the window seat. "Now get over yourself and get back to living your life. Wherever you need to do it." Kendric headed for the door. "I'll tell the sheriff to go jump off a bridge for you."

A laugh rumbled through Cree's chest, and he wrapped both arms around his midsection, short of breath. "My answer is yes, by the way," Cree said. "To your question before. It was worth it."

Kendric paused at the door, his gaze on Alma. "Then, by all means, don't let me or anyone else stand in your way."

"You should stick around." Cree held his breath as his partner stirred. "This town has a way of making sure those wounds we like to pretend don't exist won't scar."

"Maybe I will." Kendric opened the door to make his escape. "See you around, Gregson."

The door clicked closed behind him.

Alma sighed from the window seat, slowly pushing herself upright. Sweeping her hair out of her face, she squinted into the fluorescent lights overhead. "Oh, sorry about that. I just meant to close my eyes for a few minutes. Was that Agent Hudson I heard?"

"You two know each other?" Warmth that had noth-

ing to do with the painkillers flooded through him as
he memorized her voice all over again.

"We talked a little in the hall when I ran out to fill
your water mug." She pressed her palm into the hollow
of her eye and stifled a yawn. "He's been coordinating
with ATF to transfer Agent Freehan back to Washington, DC. They're going to prosecute her in federal court
for using bureau resources for personal use, attempted
murder on law enforcement officials, kidnapping, and
the murder of her sister. All in all, she's looking at a
life sentence."

"Wow." Cree tipped his head back, brushing the
pillows. "What else did I miss? What happened with
the baby?"

"He's good. We got him checked out as soon the
EMTs got you to the hospital. Completely healthy.
Seems Agent Freehan hadn't abducted him to get back
at her sister as we thought. I think she just wanted a
piece of that happiness Danielle Sawyer found inside
her own little family. Even knowing that boy could
never really be hers." Alma brought one arm up to
fold against her midsection but thought better of it.
"Last I checked, Travis Foster was downstairs waiting
for the on-call doctor to discharge them. After everything that happened, Ouray Police now believe Erica
was asking for a restraining order to protect Travis and
the baby. Not get away from them. With Agent Freehan under arrest, they're safe. They can go home and
grieve. Thanks to you."

"And you?" He motioned to her side where she
seemed to be holding herself unconsciously. "How's
the side?"

"I may have torn a few stitches during the fight.

Nothing that couldn't be restitched." She sucked in a deep breath. "Overall, I'm glad it's over. For my first response call, I'd give it a two out of five stars."

"Just two?" he asked. "Come on. There were explosions, high-speed chases, a rogue agent, an abducted child and romance. Any action movie fan would've at least given it three stars."

"Romance?" She narrowed her gaze, amusement tugging at her mouth. "And where in this investigation was there time for a romance?"

Cree reached out, walking his fingers along her lower back, and pulled her closer to the bed. "Right now." He smiled as she leaned in to press her mouth to his, and the pain through his side dwindled to a dull awareness. The power she held over him hadn't forced him to make careless decisions or act against his instincts. No. Instead, she'd showed him the real meaning of strength by standing as an example of dedication, justice and forgiveness.

She pulled back and motioned to his side. "How's the wound?"

"Medium-rare. Thanks for asking." He shifted in the bed. Didn't help.

"Macie told me what happened at the police station." She directed her gaze to his hand as she interlaced her fingers with his, just as she had in the cabin. "I was so mad with myself after our last conversation, I'd turned off my radio. I'm sorry I wasn't there. I'm sorry I—"

"You don't need to apologize to me, Alma. Not for looking out for yourself." He soothed small circles in the space between her index finger and thumb. "You've been through a lot these past few years. Something no one should ever have to face. You and I both know the longer we take to confront the pain, the harder it will be to move on."

"I thought I had," she said. "Moved on. I came home to Battle Mountain. I signed on as a reserve officer. I didn't even have the bruises anymore. I thought I was free from having to feel that pain ever again." Her shoulders shook as she tried to hold back the sorrow building in her voice. "Then you pulled me out of the lake after Agent Freehan tried to kill me, and I got scared. I started having these feelings for you, just as I'd had feelings for my ex all those years ago, and I didn't want to… I didn't want to let down my guard again when I didn't know what was on the other side. That's why I told you to go back to Loveland."

Cree didn't know what to say to that, what to think.

"I've lived with this empty space in my chest since the divorce was final, like a part of me stayed behind." She squeezed his hand. "But when I saw the aftermath of the bombing at the police station, and I realized it'd been filled. By you. I didn't want to lose that. I didn't feel alone anymore, and I didn't want you to try to salvage your former life." Her shoulders deflated as though she'd finally let go of the weight of the world. "I don't know what the future holds or what your plans are, but for the first time, I think I'm okay with that. As long as we're together, there isn't anything that will scare me more than knowing I almost lost you. Because I love you."

"I love you, too." Pure excitement lanced through him as Cree strained to pull her in for another kiss. She met him halfway, and the guilt, the shame and embarrassment—none of it had changed a damn thing. It had never served him other than to keep him from letting it all go. There wasn't any room left for the past to come between them. What that meant in regards to his career, he didn't know. But his life would be here. In Battle Mountain. With Alma. For however long she'd tolerate him. "It's going to be harder to escape the clinic this time, but I'll give it my best shot, Officer Majors."

She hit him with that gut-wrenching smile. "I'll grab the Jell-O."

Epilogue

Battle Mountain was on fire.

Kendric Hudson surveyed the destruction overtaking the small town's Main Street as he drove through. Fire and rescue had smothered the flames, but the slushy, acrid scent of smoke and the devastation in the residents' expressions couldn't be washed clean. The people here had lost everything.

He knew the feeling.

A pair of firefighters hauled cinder blocks from the rubble and tossed them into a backhoe a few feet away. The hard thunk of rock meeting metal rang loud despite the cocoon created by the cab of his truck. It would take months for crews to get through this mess, and what were the people of this town supposed to do until then? Not only had they lost part of their town to one of the very agents they'd trusted to do right by her duty, but they'd nearly lost their homes to the fire Agent Christine Freehan had set west of city limits.

Battle Mountain PD didn't have the resources or the manpower to assure the stricken faces catching his eye. They barely had enough reserve officers to keep their heads above water.

A panicked holler breached through the driver's-side window a split second before the walls of one of the burned-out buildings crumbled. A firefighter standing nearby twisted around, staring up at the oncoming debris. Only he wasn't fast enough. The wall buried him faster than it had taken Kendric to slam on the brakes. He threw the truck in Park, then pumped his legs as fast as they would carry him to help. Two more emergency personnel closed in on either side of them. "Over here!"

Wood disintegrated in his hands as he chucked rock, damaged beams and cement to the side. In minutes, he caught sight of a single hand reaching toward the surface. Clasping the man's grip to let the firefighter know they were there, Kendric worked with one hand to dislodge him from the debris. Soon, they'd moved enough rubble to get him to the surface. Blood streaked down the man's face beneath the cracked shield of his gear. "We've got you, buddy. It's going to be okay."

He handed the firefighter off to his crew. EMTs ran to meet them, but Kendric couldn't move. Swiping the sweat from his forehead with the back of his ash-covered hand, he fell back into the rubble to catch his breath. Hell. He hadn't had this much excitement since a wall of flames had consumed Cree Gregson's body during their last assignment together.

His former teammate's words echoed through his head. *This town has a way of making sure those wounds we like to pretend don't exist won't scar.* He had no idea what the hell that meant or what wounds Cree thought he was pretending didn't exist.

But maybe he could stick around long enough to find out.

* * * * *

MONTANA
WILDERNESS
PURSUIT

DANICA WINTERS

To my readers—I hope you have found an escape in this world of secrets.

Chapter One

Unlike people, bears weren't hard to understand. All a bear cared about was getting its next meal and not being screwed with—and maybe that was what Sergeant Amber Daniels loved most about the creatures. If asked, she would have been forced to admit—against her inner voice, which told her that to confess anything was to provide an enemy with ammunition—that she and bears were like kindred spirits.

Best part about a bear? They didn't have to take crap from anyone. For all intents and purposes, they were the top of the food chain and they didn't need to do a damn thing to prove their place. They were unquestionably the masters of their worlds.

It was a bear's power and natural brutality that kept people up at night. When it came to facing the truth that all humans were fragile in comparison to the masters of the forest—regardless of who identified themselves as lambs or as wolves—this weakness turned to fear. And fear, well, *fear* turned into a need to control.

It was that fear and need for people to control that brought Amber to the field today. Trapping and moving bears was a major part of her role as a game warden in the state of Montana, but it always made her gut ache.

With her affinity for bears, it was as if in trapping the regal animals, she was also trapping herself.

As much as she recognized the need to shake the thought and the weird attachment she felt to the animals, she constantly found herself thinking about certain bears she had trapped and moved in the past. Two weeks ago, she had been called to trap and tranquilize a nuisance black-bear boar who had taken up residence at a local apple orchard. The big boy had filled up on what was probably hundreds of pounds of apples before she had arrived, but all it took was the smoky scent of bacon to lure him into the steel trap laden with a bed of hay.

Black bears were entirely different beasts from the native grizzlies that roamed in Montana. A grizzly was unpredictable—docile one day and cantankerous and lethal the next. As much as she appreciated black bears, she equally feared the griz. The last time she'd run into one, it had bent the three-inch steel bars at the entrance of the bear trap she'd used to capture it. While trying to get the bear tranquilized in order for her and the biologist to do research on him, the big boar had reached through the bars and torn open her leg.

She ran the top of her foot over the still-healing lumps. If only she had moved faster.

The entire incident had cost her vacation time and, though she logically knew she shouldn't be, she had come away from the experience fearing the grizzly even more than ever before. Just seeing a picture of one made her heart race. No matter how much she attempted to talk herself down, a cold sweat would start to bead on her forehead. Luckily, in the two months since the accident, she hadn't been near another.

After the incident, she'd been forced to make statement after statement, as well as file a report with her superiors letting them know that she had, in essence, learned her lesson.

As for the trap, it had been so badly bent that her team at Fish, Wildlife and Parks, or FWP, had decided to no longer use gated steel bars and instead they were in the process of rebuilding their bear traps to have full-slide doors. The last thing any of them needed when they were unable to get cell-phone service and hours from civilization was to have a bear who had a leg up when it came to escaping a trap, or hurting one of the people tasked with working with them.

She made her way up to the front door of the Widow Maker Ranch. The place had grown immensely since the last time she had been here, but that had to have been at least ten years ago, when it still belonged to native Montanans.

She had done a little research, but hadn't heard much about the new owners beside the fact they mostly kept to themselves for the couple of years they had been there. In that way, they fit into the Montana culture even if they were transplants. Yet, it annoyed her that the first time she was meeting them, they were having a problem with the native wildlife. Why did people move to a state known for its feral tendencies and then want to get rid of the wild things the moment they were deemed inconvenient?

She tried to check her annoyance as she tapped on the front door. They hadn't called her here for her opinions. She just needed to do her job and get things set up to keep the bear safe. Hopefully it was nothing more than a black bear. If it wasn't…well, she wasn't sure if she was ready to deal with a grizzly. Yet, there was no

one else to take the call even if it was a griz. She was
one of only a handful of wardens in the state and they
all had their hands full.

She could hear footsteps coming toward the front
door. Hopefully these people weren't too talkative. She
didn't want to play the ask-and-answer game that really
only boiled down to the fact that they wanted the threat
the bear posed eradicated.

There was the click of a lock opening, and she was
surprised to find a thirtysomething man with a dimple
in his chin answering the door. He looked her up and
down, then glanced over her shoulder toward her dark
silver forest-service truck with the Fish, Wildlife and
Parks emblem on the door. If the guy knew anything
about Montana, he would know who she was immediately based just on the color of her pickup. It was a spe-
cialty color designated just for people like her—people
who never wanted to be noticed yet constantly were.

"You must be the game warden?" He sounded at odds
with his assumption, as though he didn't think a woman
could do the job. She disliked him already—that might
have just about been a land speed record.

"Yeah, the name is Sergeant Daniels. I'm here with
Montana Fish, Wildlife and Parks. Someone called us
about a nuisance bear?" Thankfully she was on her
game, or she was sure that she would've given away
her true feelings with a poorly timed eye roll by now.

The guy leaned against the doorframe as she noticed a collection of dirty boots and shoes just inside.
There must have been at least thirty pairs. Clearly he
wasn't the only one living here, but then she should have
known that already. A ranch wasn't a place that could
be controlled and managed by one person. To be an ef-

ficient and profitable ranch, which it appeared to be, people had to have entire teams to help with animals and the day-to-day operations.

She had grown up on a wheat farm on the east side of the state; and at some points of the year, her family had dozens of different people employed just to help with harvests. Often, she didn't even know all of their employees' names. Sometimes she missed those days.

"I was thinking I would take you out to where the bear's been seen quite a few times. It's close to the edge of our property. We're thinking he has plans on denning up there for the winter. With everything we have going on in the property, we think it's best if he just hits the road, you know?" The guy gave her a smile she was sure most women adored.

She found the action irritating, but she also couldn't help but wonder who was the other half of his "we." He was probably married—he was too handsome and charming to be single.

Though she was more than aware she was better off not speaking her mind, she couldn't help herself. "You know, sir, it is the policy of Fish, Wildlife and Parks to only remove animals that pose a significant risk to people and/or livestock. A bear who is merely being a bear, well…that's actually one of those things that should be expected. He hasn't been in your garbage or killed any livestock, has he?"

The man's smile rapidly disappeared. "Not exactly."

She should've kept her mouth shut. In cases like this, where she was called out to ranches with "nuisance bears" that were really doing nothing more than annoying the landowners, if she didn't act and remove the bears, the majestic creatures were often later found dead. Or they merely disappeared. There was an old rancher saying that went "shoot, shovel and shut up" in the state of Montana, and she was sure it happened more often than not when it came to these kinds of situations.

If she wanted to save the bear, this was her chance.

At least this man didn't know the old idiom, or she probably would've never gotten the phone call. She just had to remind herself that she was removing a good bear from nuisance people. If she looked at it any other way, she wouldn't be able to keep doing this kind of work.

She forced herself to smile. "Yeah, why don't you show me where you've run into this bear? Let's see what we can get done here."

The man grabbed his jacket from a coatrack so full that its base had grown loose, making it list to the left, and the top was pressed against the wall. It made her wonder if it ever just gave up. The people who lived here were destroying everything they touched, even the things that were there to bring ease to their lives.

The coatrack teetered slightly as the man stepped by her, not even realizing the effects of his presence on the world around him and the potential for disaster that he so nonchalantly wielded. Not waiting for the rack to fall, she walked outside toward her truck. Her footfalls crunched louder than they had seemed to when she had made her way up to the house, but she wasn't sure whether it was her imagination, or if it had grown icier since she'd knocked on the door.

"You said your name was Amber, right?" he asked.

"I believe I said Sergeant Daniels." She sent him a sideways glance. The man must have been doing a little research on her before she had stepped foot onto this property. It made a strange sense of foreboding fill her. "But, yes, my name is Amber."

"I'm AJ Spade."

"What do you do for a living, AJ?" she asked, motioning for him to get into the passenger side of her pickup. She sidled on around to the driver's side and got it started while she waited for him to get buckled in.

He stayed silent, like he was trying to decide what lie he was going to tell her.

"Obviously, and from what I've managed to pull about you, you are part of a club or something?" she asked, thinking about what limited information she had been able to glean from OnX maps and what little she had found on NCIC, the National Crime Information Center.

He smirked, but the little motion disappeared as quickly as it had arrived. "Yes, I'm part of a club. Actually, I'm the head of my group. We are kind of a subsidiary of the main club."

"What club is it?" she asked, more than curious thanks to the strange inflection in his tone.

He chewed on the inside of his cheek. "You are going to need to take the left turn up here, where the road forks. The bear has been crossing the river near the US Forest Service land back there," he added, pointing toward the mountain that abutted the back of the ranch.

She had asked him to point the way, but she had seen the maps and was familiar with the land and the river, but she let him treat her like she hadn't done her due diligence. Maybe he was used to working with people who walked into situations blind, but as a woman who worked in rural areas where people usually carried guns, she didn't take her safety or planning for granted.

"Do you have fruit trees back there?" It was a little late in the year for fruit, now that it had started to freeze, but if they had apples they could have gone to rot and brought in a bear that was getting ready for hibernation.

Usually, it was this time of year, right before bears went to den, they received most of their calls for bear removal as they would move into populated lands to find easy meals. Bears were at the peak time of hyperphagia—when they were trying to put on weight in preparation for hibernation. "We are pretty careful. Don't take our garbage out—in fact we burn it on site. Haven't seen the bear in that area. As far as fruit trees, I don't think we have anything besides just the normal hawthorns that grow throughout here. Haven't seen any berries for a while." He shrugged. "I mean, we have tried to be careful not to draw any unwanted attention—from bears and the public."

Her intuition kicked into high gear. This man was hiding something from her, but as much as she wanted to press and get answers from him, it didn't matter. He could just go on hiding whatever it was that he wanted to hide. All she had to do was worry about saving a bear.

"How often have you seen the bear?"

He seemed to relax into his seat a bit more as she took the fork leading to the location he'd indicated. "It's been almost daily. The other night the dude even tried to break into one of the cabins tucked back into the woods. No one was living in it, and there wasn't any food, so we were pretty surprised."

"Bears have a damned good sense of smell—if he was going for a cabin there has to be something he wants in there." She shrugged, not wanting to start an argument while also making it clear that she didn't think any healthy bear was going to just randomly start attacking outbuildings.

"You're probably right," he said with a sigh. "We didn't have time to poke around the place a whole lot. We've been keeping pretty busy. For all I know, there could be a cache of food or something."

She was glad he was willing to come her way at least a little bit. Maybe there was hope that they could actually work together in a positive way. It would make things easier if they could, but in the end, she would get the job done with or without his support and that thought brought her comfort. Validation was only welcome when it was used to pay for parking; the rest of the time she was good on her own.

"There is the place we have been seeing him." AJ pointed to the left of the truck toward the timber, where there was a small glen covered in a blanket of snow.

There were tracks all over, deer and elk from what she could make out from here, but she had no doubt that if she looked more closely, she would see the bear's. About a quarter a mile away and tucked back into the woods was a small cabin. It looked like an old miner's cabin. The logs that made up its walls were stained nearly black from years of harsh weather and the horsehair moss chinking someone had stuffed between the logs was slipping out from the cracks, giving the place what looked like brown dreadlocks.

"Was this the place he tried to get into?" she asked.

AJ nodded. "I'd be happy to show you the claw marks."

"You know if it was a grizzly or a black bear?"

If it was a black bear, it would be easy enough to trap

or to bring in the bear hazing team and run it off from the property, but if it was a griz...well, they were far more temperamental. If it was one, she would be better off setting one of their large traps and getting up close and personal with the one thing she feared the most.

"It was brown." He shrugged. "I don't think I could actually tell you which one it was, for sure."

She pulled over and parked the truck between the cabin and the small little glen. "That's okay, most people can't, but I'll be able to tell by the prints." She waved her hand vaguely in the direction of where the tracks were. "If you want to wait in the truck, you're welcome to. I'm going to go take a look around." She made sure to give him an out if he wanted it. Most people were understandably not keen on the idea of rolling up on a bear hot spot with or without a game warden.

She got out, but took a quick glance in his direction. He seemed to be weighing his options, but after a moment he unclicked his seat belt. She checked her smile as she closed the door behind herself and made her way toward the glen. There was definitely a large bull elk and a handful of deer that had moved through the area, but from the age of the tracks the last one had been through probably a week ago. Walking the edge of the snowy meadow, near the timberline, she found her first bear print.

The edges of the print were indistinct where the snow had melted and refrozen, but there was no denying it, thanks to the enormous spread and the claw marks— they were dealing with a demon with teeth, and she would soon have to face her fears.

Chapter Two

The woman who had been sent here to help him get rid of the damn bear definitely didn't like him, but he didn't blame her for her immediate disdain. He had found as a military contractor that most people didn't like him upon first meeting. They should have been glad—it meant that he wasn't sitting on the working end of a rifle scope that could have been pointing at them instead.

Sometimes the only separation between paradise and perdition was a little perspective—not that he would be anywhere close enough to this woman for her to ever even consider him as a source of happiness. They were just two strangers passing in the day, each to their own ends and requirements.

Though he was more than aware of their opposing goals and lifestyles, he couldn't help but admit that there was something in the way she looked at him that made him want to get to know her just a bit better. But it could have had something to do with the fact that she looked a little like the woman who had broken his heart.

There was a twitch at the corners of her cerulean blue eyes that made him wonder what had happened to her to make her look so angry, and at the same time, he wanted to be the one to fix her. That being said, he had more than enough broken pieces in his and his family's life—so much so, that he was having one hell of a time trying to bring the pieces together into some semblance of a manageable and functional organization.

The Shadow team, his family's private military contracting company, had taken a hit ever since they had grouped up underneath STEALTH and the Martin family…though that was through no fault of the Martins. It was just that ever since AJ and his siblings had formed the Shadow team, they had been taking one hit after another after another, and he couldn't help but feel like the rival contracting group, Rockwood, was at the heart of it all.

Ever since Conflux, a company they had been hired to help keep secure a few months back, had fallen under attack by Rockwood, the Shadow team had been having regular run-ins with them. Months ago, Rockwood had lost out on a major contract, to manufacture machines and parts for the US government, to Conflux. That had pit the two companies against each other in an all-out cyberwar, complete with corporate spies and counterspies.

After the STEALTH team had exposed the group for illicit dealings, they promised revenge. Now, anytime something bad happened within a hundred-mile radius of one of their contractors, AJ constantly found himself looking for the Rockwood operative who had pulled the trigger.

Even now, with the rogue bear, he couldn't help but wonder if somehow they were involved in its sudden appearance at the ranch. Sure, he understood bears came and went, but this one seemed hell-bent on keeping AJ from doing his normal job—a job that required a lot of brain space and even more concentration.

The game warden was walking around the snow-covered meadow and occasionally crouching down as she studied the area. Truth be told, she wasn't a bad-looking woman. He liked her long blond hair pulled into a ponytail at the base of her neck. He could imagine her letting it fall loose around her shoulders after she slipped out of her brown uniform.

The top two buttons of her shirt were unbuttoned, which meant she was probably not as high and tight as many of the women he knew in law enforcement—women who had had to fit in with the men around them and the only way to do that was to make themselves as asexual and untouchable as possible. Though, not all were of that way of thinking. He'd also met a few women who aimed to control the men they worked with through physical manipulation; the woman in front of him didn't seem like that kind, either.

If anything, Amber seemed like the kind of woman who just didn't notice. She lived in her own world, probably one in which she spent copious amounts of time in her truck, driving around from one fishing access to another. There were likely interesting moments in her job, and even more curious investigations into poaching and missing persons, but by and large her job seemed far simpler than his as head of the STEALTH Shadow team—he envied her that.

"Find the bear yet?" he called out the window after her, knowing full well he was being a smart-ass and was probably going to piss her off.

She glowered at him as he got out and started to walk toward her. "Yeah, it's standing right behind you."

She said something else that he couldn't quite hear, but he was sure was something to the effect that she hoped it really was…and that it was a second away from mauling him while she watched and took pictures to show her friends.

Yeah, she was definitely the highlight of all the crap that was happening. If anything, it was nice to be around someone who didn't resent him for his job and only resented him for his presence—he could work with that, maybe even make her realize he was not as big a pain in the ass as she appeared to believe. Then again, that would be a long shot. He couldn't remember the last person who didn't think of him as a pain in the ass.

"Seriously, though," he began. "The bear has been frequenting this area. I'm surprised you are having to search for bear sign."

"Oh, no," she chuckled. "I'm finding sign." She pointed in the direction of a large black pile of scat to her left. "If anything, I'm actually wondering what it has been feeding on." She turned her back to him, hunching over as she made her way deeper into the timber that stood around them like black, mossy ghosts.

He followed behind, looking deeper into the trees. The hairs on the back of his neck and down his arms prickled. God, he hated that feeling.

Running his hand over the back of his neck, he tried to get control of himself. There was nothing and no one around; it was just his imagination getting the better of him. Just because the bear had been frequenting the area didn't mean that he hadn't just as easily decided to move along. It was just the nature of his job getting to him, making him look for threats everywhere.

His world was filled with secrets—none greater than

the fact he hated being alone. If anyone looked from the outside, they would have probably assumed he was the kind who relished the freedom that came with being a single man in power. With all of his siblings shacking up and getting married, he had come to realize that work didn't have to be everything and threats didn't have to exist everywhere. But he'd become so used to the constant motion and requirements of his job, he wasn't sure how he could make time in his schedule for anything else.

"You coming?" She looked back at him, making him realize he had somehow fallen behind her thanks to his bevy of thoughts. She started to turn back, but suddenly stopped. "What in the hell?" She darted into the shadows cast by the shrouded trees.

He hurried to catch up, skirting around the skeletal branches that reached out to him like hands. One caught him across the cheek, just hard enough to sting but hopefully not deep enough to draw blood.

Running his finger over his cheek, he glanced down at his hands. There was nothing on his fingers, but on the snow below were dark speckles of blood. He grabbed for his cheek, but it wasn't wet or sticky like he had expected.

"AJ!" Amber's eyes were wide and she motioned wildly for him to come to her. "AJ, look at this." She pointed to the ground.

He carefully stepped over the blood by the tips of his boots—telling himself it was nothing—as he went to her.

There, lying next to a downed tree that had turned gray with age and weather, was a long yellowish bone. Drawing closer, he sucked in a breath. Near the ground, covered by part of the dead log, was a mass of flesh. It was stringy and loose where it must have gone through the teeth of the bear, who'd scavenged and left it looking like pieces of floss.

He didn't want to disturb the remains, but he picked up a stick and pushed back a bit of the cold, stiff flesh. Flipping it up, he found a hand. A woman's... On the middle finger of the right hand was a sapphire ring—one that he knew all too well.

He'd spent hours poring over the design and how the white gold was meant to swirl around the three sapphires, each one steadily darker and a deeper blue than the one before.

Sinking to his knees, he stared at the ring as he hoped he was wrong. Yet, there was no denying it—it was the engagement ring he'd given to his ex. It was a ring she had never returned, but instead had worn to meet her death.

Chapter Three

Death was a constant in her line of work. Amber had started to wonder if she was even some sort of grim reaper, one who carried a Glock instead of a scythe. It was an unfortunate side of her job, spent out in nature, that she regularly had to face the downside of living—dying.

It sucked, there was no other word to describe it, but at the end of the day she had to look at death as just another soul passing through this plane and moving to the next.

All of that being said, it wasn't every day that she had to face the death of a person, or at least human remains. Without a team to come in here and take inventory of the scene, it would be hard to say just how long the person, whose hand they had found, had been down. It had been cold now for a spell, which kept decomp to a minimum. Over a winter, remains could appear as fresh as if the animal had died a matter of days before.

She stared down at the partially chewed-on hand. There were tooth marks at the wrist where the bear had gnawed away at the bones and fascia. The animal had probably held down the hand like a dog chewing a bone, working it sideways in an attempt to get the high-fat and nutritious marrow. There was a bit of dirt between each of the fingers and the fingertips had turned a dark shade of purple. The nails were longer than hers, but the beds looked as though they had started to shrink with cold and time, pulling back from the nails and making them appear longer than they had when the person had been alive.

She didn't want to touch the hand or disturb the scene. They would have to call in the sheriff's office on this one. She let out an embittered laugh at the thought.

"Amber, you okay?"

She jerked as she looked up and remembered that she wasn't alone. "Yeah, sorry."

She hadn't noticed until now, but the man's face—which had been pinkened by the cold—was now lacking color. "Are you okay?"

He looked away from her, turning so she couldn't see his face. "I'm fine, but what were you laughing about?"

"I didn't mean to laugh. I'm around death a lot, and it just never gets easier."

At that, he swiped a hand over his nose and turned back. "That… That is something I *totally* understand. Death is…it's always hard to face." The way he spoke made it clear there was something to his admission— more than simply met the eye.

It made her wonder exactly who this man was. He hadn't really told her much about what he did here and what he had given her had been ambiguous.

"You around death a lot, too?" she asked, trying not to raise her eyebrows and give away her leading question. "What kind of *club* are you in, exactly?"

AJ ran his hand around the back of his neck and peered up at the sky. "We are security consultants."

That didn't really answer her question and it irked her. "Seriously? What in the hell is that supposed to mean?" She tried to stop the annoyance from entering her voice, but it was too late so she rolled with it, crossing her arms over her chest as she instinctively stuck out her hip and cocked a brow.

"Ha," he said, "I should have known that wouldn't satisfy you."

There he went, intensifying her annoyance. They'd just found a body on his property and he seemed determined to be evasive. She didn't suspect him for a minute—the look on his face moments ago said he was just as shocked as she was, but now wasn't the time to play coy with what was going on here. "Answer."

He gave her a smirk that was entirely too sexy for her liking. Especially when she was playing good cop and trying to get answers that he wasn't keen on giving. "That smile may get you a million miles with some women, but regardless of what you think, it's not going to work on me. I'm not like most women."

"And that is exactly what most women say," he countered.

That was strike three. He was outta here. She turned away from him, starting toward her running truck, not waiting for him, or for him to realize that she wasn't here to play some stupid simpering game that he could control with a cloying smile.

She didn't slow down even when she heard the crunch of his footfalls moving fast from behind, like he was jogging to catch up to her.

"Amber, wait," he called after her.

He could be as sorry as he wanted. He'd been an ass and there was nothing he could say or do to make her think anything else about him. He'd burned their amicable bridge. Now he was a pain in her ass, nothing more...even if she had thought he was kind of cute, in a bad-boy way.

Don't give him an inch.

"Amber..." He said her name again, this time with a softness that nearly made her stop.

Instead, she slowed down and let him catch up to her side. "What?"

"I'm sorry. I'm an ass."

He could say that again. "I didn't mean to say that. I'm not that kind of guy."

"Now, that is what every guy who is *that kind of guy* says," she said, knowing it was against her better judgment to lower herself to his level, but at the same time unable to find the restraint to stop herself.

He stepped in front of her and when she looked up at him, and into his blue eyes, her breath caught in her throat and for a moment she almost forgot how to breathe. How could someone who made her so—so *pissed* one second, make her swoon the next?

Yep, I need to get away from this man as fast as humanly possible.

"Amber, I didn't mean to be an ass—it's just that all of this—" he waved in the direction of the remains "—is more than I expected."

She took a much-needed breath. "All I was asking was that you tell me a little more about yourself. You wanted to be vague."

He raised his hands, like the action was some kind of gesture of peace, but she noted that he was missing half of the middle finger on his left hand. She tried not to stare at the nub, but found her gaze drawn to the missing digit.

"It's okay, you can look at it. It got shot off during a mission." He gave her a sad smile.

She reached over and pushed down his hands. "I don't need to look at your finger."

"You want to know what a security consultant does?" He paused. "We sacrifice our bodies and souls to whomever is the highest bidder. Usually, we are on the good guy's side. Yet, even when we are fighting for what we see as justifiable reasons, we find ourselves having to make some hard choices. Choices that no one should ever have to make."

A sickening knot formed in her stomach. "If that is the kind of life you've led, why—" she motioned in the direction of the lone hand they'd found in the woods "—why would you have any problem when it came to that kind of thing? You made it sound like you didn't care about death, but your face… It said something different."

"I don't know what you mean, but that hand back there… We will deal with it. Right now, I want you to know that I am genuinely sorry for being a jerk. I had no right to treat you like I did. I know you have a job to do, but when regular people start asking questions, I get a little on-edge."

Did he mean that when people started asking questions, his life was on the line?

Given the brief amount of time she had interacted with this man, she couldn't imagine she was reading him right, but at the same time there was no denying the inflection of his words or the way his features seemed to harden when he wanted to close her out. Just now, she could see the flicker of the muscle at the edge of his jaw.

This once, she would cut him a break.

Chapter Four

AJ didn't know why he didn't tell her that he recognized the ring.

Hell, just because it looked like the one he had specially designed, it didn't mean that it was actually unique. Even if it was, it didn't mean that his ex-fiancée, Tammy, hadn't pawned it off after they had broken up. He damn well would have after their tough breakup.

He flipped up the neck of his jacket as he stood in the cold, waiting for the sheriff's deputy to arrive. It had been at least forty-five minutes since Amber had called them. Over the last few years, his family had required officer assistance on the ranch; unfortunately, he had grown used to waiting for them.

But with this incident cutting so close to him, the forty-five minutes felt more like forty-five hours.

He was tempted to walk over to where they found the hand, but he resisted the urge. Part of him wanted to take a picture of it, and look more closely at the ring just to negate any possibility that it was actually the one he thought it was. Yet, he didn't want to draw any scrutiny if, in fact, it did turn out to be the ring he had purchased. If it was, this hand had to belong to Tammy. His stomach turned to knots.

It couldn't be her...

Amber sighed, glancing down at her watch.

"If you have somewhere to be, you don't have to wait around here with me," he said. "I'm sure that whether you are here to escort law enforcement to the hand or not, the result will be the same." As soon as he was done speaking, he wished he hadn't opened his mouth. "I mean, don't get me wrong, but I bet you have better things to do then sit around here."

He wasn't sure he had made the situation any better, especially thanks to the sour look on her face.

"Yeah, I'm not going anywhere." She leaned up against her truck, crossing her arms over her chest.

He had seen her do that a couple of times now when talking to him. It made him wonder if there was any chance whatsoever of them moving past antagonizing one another. He really needed a friend right now, and there was something about her that wasn't too bad. If they just met at a bar, or at some kind of social gathering, he probably would have even thought she was datable.

He'd much rather take things slow with women, get to know them and love them for who they were rather than just jumping straight into bed. Sex was easy, but having a real relationship that meant something was damn near impossible.

Relationships, whether they were friendship or romantic, took far more effort than any facet of his job as the leader for STEALTH Shadow team. Just the relationships with his siblings took more out of him than he wanted to give, but for them he would make exceptions. They drove him nuts, but they were his people, his *tribe*. Regardless of what the world threw at them, they would always be a single unit. That, in and of it-self, was worth whatever emotional turmoil it created.

Relationships built around sex didn't last. He'd learned his lesson when it came to that one, thanks to Tammy. They'd had incredible passion, but when they weren't having sex, they were fighting and things eventually fizzled out. Unfortunately, once again, she had found her way back into his life. Even if that hand wasn't hers, it was like she was a ghost who was constantly haunting him. He would never be free of her.

"You know, *you* don't have to stick around." Amber looked at him as she spoke.

There was something about the darkness in her eyes, or maybe it was the tone of her voice, but he wanted to take her hands in his and tell her it was all going to be okay.

What is wrong with me? He felt like a hot-mess dumpster fire, out of control of his emotions...especially when it came to women.

Maybe it was best if he did leave. He could call Zoey Martin, head of STEALTH, and have her come out and deal with all this, but if he did, he was sure he would hear about it. She had a million commitments—which was exactly why she had hired him and his family as a secondary team and why he needed to be the leader she expected. He pulled out his phone and sent a quick text to her, letting her know what they had found on the ranch. She couldn't be kept in the dark about this, or she would be pissed.

"You don't think the bear is going to come back to-night, do you?" he asked, sidestepping Amber having basically asked him to leave.

"There is only another hour or two of daylight. If

the bear is going to come back, I bet it will be closer to dusk. They are diurnal, but they do most of their moving around at night in order to avoid people. That being said, you mentioned that you have seen this bear during the day?" she asked.

He nodded. "Yeah, my sister told me she had seen it by our barn a few days ago. We have a lot of deer, whitetails mostly, up by the house. It was early morning—the bear may have been taking a look for easy prey before moving to the woods to sleep for the day." He shrugged.

"You're probably right. They don't like a lot of activity. More solitary creatures." She dropped her arms to her sides. "By the way, how many siblings do you have?"

Finally, he was getting somewhere with her. Inch by inch, maybe they would become friends, but only time would tell. "I'm one of six kids. Our parents passed away a few years ago in a car accident and we took over the family business before it was bought and moved under the STEALTH umbrella."

He wasn't sure why he had said that, but a softness returned to her features, and he was glad he had opened up.

"Do all of your siblings live here on the ranch?" She seemed genuinely interested.

"Most of them do. Every one of my siblings works for the team, though. Recently, my sister Kendra moved back to Montana to be with her fiancé. She's an attorney and he's a bounty hunter—interesting stuff."

She looked a bit surprised. "So all of your family members are badasses?" She smiled, and as she did, there was the sparkle in her eyes that made them appear even bluer than before.

Yeah, a man could definitely be moved by a smile and a look like that. She was beautiful.

"Yeah, everybody but me." He sent her a half smile, but it was weighed down with his concern for Tammy. "I'm just an average dude, with a badass job." He forced a chuckle. "But come on now, you're pretty interesting yourself. You have to admit not everyone spends their days worrying about being attacked by a grizzly bear."

"We are not going to be attacked by a grizzly bear," she said with a chuff, like such an idea was unfathomable, even though there was evidence that the bear had made lunch of another person.

"True, *you* are probably more likely to attack," he teased.

She sent him a quelling look.

"Ouch," he said.

Her cheeks darkened with a blush.

He grinned. He couldn't help but enjoy the way that blush brightened her cheeks and made her look more delicate. "It's fine. I'm teasing you. I'm just glad you decided you can finally like me."

She pulled back, giving him an appraising look. "Who said I liked you?" There was a playful edge to her voice.

"There are only two reasons for you to use your verbal claws on me. One, I'm a jerk and I deserve it. Which, I guess, could be the case." He laughed. "Or, what I assume is going on here, maybe you kind of like me." He wasn't sure why he'd said it, and unease swept through him. Considering what had forced them together in this situation, the last thing he should be doing was flirting.

But he couldn't help it. It had been a hellish day and she was distracting him.

She looked totally affronted by the idea and the accusation, and she opened her mouth to speak but before she could, there was the crunch of gravel in the distance, and they looked over to see a four-wheeler careening toward them.

Son of a...

The vehicle came to a skidding stop behind the warden's pickup, and a woman stepped off and slipped the helmet from her head. Zoey Martin's black-and-blue hair was longer than it normally was and she had a large ring in her nose today.

She looked from Amber to him, seeming to sense the awkwardness between them, and smirked. "What in the hell is happening out here?"

"Nice to see you, too," he said. "Zoey, this is Amber Daniels, the game warden we called to get this bear situation under control."

"Charmed," Zoey clipped. "So how exactly does a game warden and my employee come up with a hand when they are out looking for a bear?"

Amber shot him a look, like she was disappointed in him for having let the cat out of the bag.

Zoey walked past them, in the direction of their footprints in the snow. "Where is this hand?"

"Out there, at your three o'clock," he said, motioning her ahead. He waited with Amber for a moment, until Zoey was out of earshot. "Hey," he whispered, "I'm sorry about her. She has zero tact. Her world is blood and war. Be patient with her."

Amber opened and closed her mouth, but instead of saying anything, she simply nodded. She followed Zoey, unsteady as she stepped into the uneven and crunching snow.

He had finally started to gain ground with Amber, and now he was losing it all over again.

Hell, maybe it was a good thing.

After being with Tammy, who had hated him so much, he shouldn't be thinking about getting involved with any woman.

Just as he started to follow Amber, there was the sound of another car approaching. He turned as a deputy pulled up in a Chevy Tahoe. They hadn't been running lights, and he was glad. They didn't need to draw scrutiny from their neighbors or passersby. Sure, they were a ways from the road and public areas, but that didn't mean crap out here.

Zoey whistled at them. "Tell him to meet us over here," she called, sounding annoyed at the dog and pony show that this was already starting to become.

"You got it, boss." He didn't normally call her "boss," but it felt right with Amber there with them.

Yeah, he needed to get over his need to posture for that woman.

The deputy turned on his interior light and he could see the dark-haired guy talking on his handset. No doubt, he was letting Dispatch know his location and his objective. That was how he ran his team, and police were much like the Shadow team.

AJ slowly made his way over to the guy's rig and waited for him to get off his radio and open his door. The deputy stepped out and AJ recognized him as Deputy Terrell, a guy he had spoken to, though infrequently, when he'd been to the ranch in the past. "How's it going,

Terrell?" he asked, making sure to give his voice as friendly an air as possible.

"Things are going all right. Can't complain." The man stepped out and put his hands in his utility belt, instinctively framing his junk like it was some primal display of dominance.

"Well, we certainly appreciate you coming here and helping us out. Just sorry it has to be under these kinds of conditions. Ya know?" He tried to throw the guy a proverbial win in the game AJ didn't want to play.

The deputy nodded. "I read you all found what you think are human remains out here? You got any idea how they got here?" The guy moved his hands up and latched his thumbs under the edges of his bulletproof vest.

"We called in the game warden—Amber," AJ said, motioning in her direction, "to help us with a rogue griz we have on the property. It's been roaming around looking for food. Looks like it was down here munching on a body."

The deputy drew back slightly. "Oh, damn. Bear and a body. You definitely got your hands full with all the things happening out here at the ranch. You guys are always busy."

Damn it. The guy definitely had a long memory and that wouldn't do them any favors when it came to these remains and the investigation that would likely ensue— his family definitely had a reputation when it came to causing upheaval in the community.

"We do try to keep things to a low roar, but you can't control everything on a place like this. Just too much land to cover and people to keep track of," he said, though he didn't mean any of it. "The hand is over there. Zoey wanted to take a peek before you arrived."

He turned from the deputy and started leading him over to the remains. He didn't really want to be a part of this investigation, but if he was going to be in for a penny, he was going to be in for a pound. Whether he liked it or not, he had been on scene when the hand had been located.

The deputy started toward Zoey and Amber. "Hey, you guys, you want to take a step back from there? Let's try not to contaminate our scene any more than necessary."

Amber nodded and waited for Zoey as she turned away from the hand in the snow. Zoey looked straight at AJ and glared. Had she recognized the ring?

No.

There was no way Zoey would know that ring or whom it had belonged to. He hadn't been engaged to Tammy at the time his family's company had moved under STEALTH. That had happened later. Then again, Zoey was the queen of information gathering. That woman knew everything and didn't let a damn thing slide. No doubt, she had done her due diligence and done all kinds of digging into each and every one of the Spade siblings' lives. She wasn't one to miss things.

But he wasn't about to say anything to her out here, or in front of law enforcement. His best defense now would be a strong offense, regardless of the fact that he had done nothing wrong. But when it came to the murder of a woman, it was definitely the love interest or former love interest that was the first one to go on the suspects list. Not to mention the fact that, if this was Tammy, her remains were now on their ranch.

He was so screwed. If he was lead detective on this investigation, it would take him ten hours max to get a positive identification on the remains. From there, it would only be a few more hours before the police would be looking right at him.

It was crazy how fast a person could get tracked down in the electronic age.

He could very well be arrested before the end of tomorrow.

Yeah, there was no way he could allow that to happen. He needed time to find out if these really were Tammy's remains, and if they were, he needed to come up with one hell of an alibi in order to clear his name.

As much as he wanted to keep on the right side of law enforcement, he had to buy himself more time before they started poking around the ranch and collecting evidence. At the very least, he needed to talk to his sister Kendra, who was also the family attorney. She would have all the answers and tell him exactly what he needed to do.

"Hey, Terrell?" he called after the deputy, who turned and faced him.

"What's up?" Terrell asked, almost side by side with Zoey and Amber.

"I'm sure that Zoey, the owner of the ranch, will be on board with me on this. Our lawyer can get a bit salty when not kept in the loop when it comes to law enforcement getting involved with our family's business," he said, giving Zoey a pointed look. "As such, I think it would be best if we put a pin in this for a bit. I'm going to need you to get a search warrant before you take one more step toward those remains."

Zoey frowned, but then her face went blank.

Amber looked shocked. "AJ…"

"I'm sorry, but I think until we talk to our attorney and get things cleared from a business level on our side, it is best if you both, Amber and Terrell, don't do anything more until you get a warrant."

Amber turned away and started to walk to her truck, not looking back at him as she strode away.

He tried to ignore the ache in his chest, but just like that, there was no doubt that any chance he had with Amber had just gone out the window.

Chapter Five

Amber shouldn't have been hurt, but she couldn't help the way she felt when it came to AJ. He was everything she both loved and hated when it came to men. He was the embodiment of desire and lust, secrets and truth, loneliness and company. And damn if he wasn't the sexiest man she'd ever met.

Not that she could officially say that he was sexy—that would be unprofessional and stupid. Sure, she had made a lot of stupid decisions in the past when it came to dating the wrong men, but that was when she had been young and dumb…and she'd made sure to keep them out of her parents' line of sight. When she turned thirty, she'd promised herself that those days were behind her; and if a man came into her life, their relationship was going to be healthy from the very beginning or it wasn't going to happen.

She didn't have the time or the patience to deal with any kind of toxic behavior in her private life. Especially when the toxicity came in the form of a man whom she had no business desiring, and who had literally kicked her off her investigation an hour before.

Yes, she definitely didn't like him. Not even a little bit.

Everything about him screamed that she should run, and yet here she stood on the road at the center of the ranch, waiting on a search warrant with the police officer so she could remain near him. Well, not *him* exactly.

"I appreciate you sticking around," Deputy Terrell said, breaking the silence as he stood beside his car, a spotting scope aimed at the area so they could make sure the scene was in no way being tampered with while they waited for the warrant. "I would like to get the trap sorted out for the bear. Last thing my team needs, while they are poring through this, is to run headlong into a hungry bear."

"Yeah. It's no problem." The sun was starting to set and if she'd had her way, she would have already had the trap dropped and baited. "With food sources around, that bear isn't going to go too far. Once you get the warrant, I'll just get the trap set and I'll get out of your hair."

Terrell frowned. "Actually, we have a lot of officers out right now, and I could use an extra hand securing the scene. I mean, if you're not too busy."

As a game warden, she was a sworn officer with statewide law-enforcement authority. But she knew how police officers saw them—most of the time they simply assumed that game wardens were people who couldn't make the cut, or couldn't deal with the politics of working in their police department. That wasn't the case for her. She had no desire to be a deputy, but she did enjoy helping them out. Knowing how he would perceive her, however, she had to play it cool and not sound too eager.

"Yeah, it's been a long day, but I have no problem sticking around for a few more hours if you need me. I know how it is working with a skeleton crew. We only have sixteen game wardens in the entire state of Montana. We're running at half staff."

"It shouldn't be too much longer to get on the scene. The detective on this has already heard back from the county attorney, so all I need now is the approval from the judge. We'll be back on this investigation in no time, and from there we'll just be waiting for the detective to arrive."

Zoey and AJ had disappeared back to the main house, no doubt coming up with a game plan of how to handle the situation. She didn't envy them for having to go through this. By now they were probably regretting their decision in having a game warden show up at the ranch at all.

If Zoey was the kind of woman Amber thought she was, she was probably chewing AJ's ass right now and telling him a thousand things he should have done instead of calling her in. Though Amber shouldn't have felt bad for bringing this drama to their doorstep, she did. In no way was this her doing, but she still felt responsible for all of the complications that were about to rain down.

She hated that she had all these feelings. This was work, he was work, and this was all nothing more. To treat it as anything other than that was just setting herself up for hurt and failure, neither of which she enjoyed. Besides, it wasn't like he was even that great, anyway. AJ had been nothing but a pain in her ass since the moment she'd arrived here. Why call in the police and then send them away? What had changed?

The deputy's phone pinged. "Looks like we got it. Detective Baker is asking that we give them five minutes before we go down and completely rope off the scene."

"Why would he ask for something like that? Doesn't he want us to get started?"

Terrell looked at her like she had lost her mind. "Do you have any clue who this family is? Who they run with? Or what they do?"

The way he asked the questions made her wonder if she was the last person in the entire state to understand who AJ Spade and his family were, and then she thought about the conversation she'd had with AJ earlier. He made it sound like they were not a family that was well-known in the area, nor did they wish to be, and yet, it seemed as though they had one hell of a reputation—one that had inspired the police to give them some sort of professional courtesy.

"No," she said, pinching her lips and shaking her head. "Is there something I need to know before I head back out there? I don't want to walk into the line of fire without a clue."

"So the company your buddy there works for…" He nudged his chin in the direction of the ranch house. She wanted to tell him that in no way was AJ her friend, but she held off. "They are a world leader in private military contracting. When you think of black ops and assassins, those are the guys."

Her stomach dropped. Of course, she would be attracted to the most dangerous dude possible. Why couldn't she just be attracted to an accountant type her parents would adore? They would love nothing more than to see her happy and with a safe man, especially after all the grief their family had gone through.

"Well, I guess I know why you didn't want me to

leave you out here alone." She audibly groaned. "All that being said, I don't quite understand why the detective would want us to wait."

"Detective Baker is a good dude, and he has worked with this family in the past. I don't know all the ins and outs, but they definitely have adequate respect for one another."

"But waiting to investigate an unwitnessed death…"

There came that look again from Terrell. "The remains being out here is odd and probably not just random. Yet, they may not have anything to do with them. I've come to learn that this family is on a lot of people's hit lists. And I'm not just talking about single individuals, but entire countries who want them dead."

A knot formed in her stomach. Just who were the Spades? There were definitely people who didn't like her for the job she was hired to do, but she had never gotten an impression that any wished her dead. She couldn't even begin to imagine how that must have affected AJ and his team. The only things that had ever really wanted Amber dead had been a protective cow moose with her calf, and the bear who had taken a swipe.

The door to the ranch house opened and at least ten people came walking out. No one appeared to be armed, but if she had to guess, thanks to the no-nonsense looks on their faces, they were all carrying.

Suddenly, this was starting to feel all too much like the Old-West shoot-out at the O.K. Corral. One false move and guns would be blazing. Few, if any, would be left standing.

If things went in that direction, she doubted she and Terrell would make it off this ranch.

A cold chill moved down her spine. This was what she got for wanting to stop a grizzly from getting killed.

Last to come out of the door were Zoey and AJ. It surprised her, but AJ looked calm. Maybe she had gotten it all wrong in assuming that Zoey would be upset with him. Or maybe this was all just an act in order to make her and Terrell feel completely out of their element. If that was the case, they didn't need to try so hard.

From behind her, she could hear car tires crunching on the gravel as a vehicle made its way toward them. Hopefully it was the detective, and he'd come with backup.

A black Suburban pulled to a stop next to Terrell's car. Stepping out was a stout man, with frosted tips on his dark hair. He had a serious look on his face and he said something to the deputy she couldn't quite hear.

Zoey Martin made her way out toward their caravan, like she was coming to parley. Everything about this felt like a battle, but Amber couldn't quite pinpoint why. This family had nothing to hide, and AJ had nothing to hide…right? There was no reason for a standoff.

"Detective Baker, how the hell are you?" Zoey said once she'd approached, throwing her arms up jovially in the air. Her hair blew slightly in the wind as she came over and wrapped her arms around the detective.

Detective Baker was all smiles as he looked at her. "What in the hell is up with this needing-a-search-warrant crap?" Detective Baker leaned back from their embrace and took her by the shoulders. "I was just sitting down for dinner. If you needed something, you should have just called. This is ridiculous."

Zoey looked to Amber and the deputy before glancing back to Baker. "You know as well as I do that sometimes we have to dot the i's and cross the t's, and you know…all the things." She stepped out of Baker's grip. "With so much going on, we just have to make sure that we make our lawyers happy. You know how it is." She chuckled, but as far as Amber was concerned there was nothing funny about the situation.

Ninety seconds ago, everyone had seemed ready to draw down and shoot anyone who got in their line of sight.

"Damn, don't I know how you feel. Lawyers are nothing but a pain in the ass." Baker reached behind his back and pulled out a set of papers, then handed them over to Zoey. "Here, these are for your lawyers, and I'm sure for mine as well."

"Much appreciated," Zoey said, taking the papers and putting them in her back pocket without even looking. "Now, let's get your team back there and get things going. We really have no intention of making this investigation any harder than necessary. We want to get to the bottom of this just as much as you do."

Detective Baker gave her a pointed look that made Amber wonder what they had just exchanged nonverbally.

Amber's gaze moved to AJ, and she found that he was staring at her. For a second, their eyes locked and then he quickly glanced away. What was it about this family that they wanted to only communicate with glances and they couldn't just talk like normal people?

But, of course, assassins wouldn't be that kind.

Assassins. The word rattled through her.

This morning, a team of black-ops assassins would have been the last thing she would've thought she would be dealing with. If asked, she wasn't sure she would have wanted to take this call again. AJ was a beautiful man with a dangerous job, which was one hell of a good reason to stay as far away as possible.

Suddenly, she missed driving aimlessly around in her pickup truck looking for illegal operations in the woods. She would take a team of hillbillies any day over a family of black-ops members and their bosses. Before this thing with him went any further and she got any more confused, she needed to handle her business with Terrell and the bear, and then get off this ranch.

She moved toward the others, but AJ came toward her with a smile. "I was thinking I'd come help you set that bear trap. We still need to get that situation under control."

Before she even realized what she was doing, she jerked away from him. Though she wasn't sure if she was right or not, she had a feeling that she was safer with the bear.

Confusion swept across his face at her sudden reaction.

But that smile he'd given a moment before… She didn't trust that, either. What was he playing at? "What is going on with you?" She studied him for a long moment, watching as his smile faded.

"Huh? What do you mean?" He motioned for her to walk with him toward her truck.

"The last time I spoke to you, you were telling us to leave."

"Yes, but did you leave?" He gave her a side look as he walked to the driver's door and opened it up for her. "No, you didn't," he responded for her. "Just as I knew you wouldn't."

"I could have left," she countered, getting into the pickup and turning on the engine while she waited for him to get in on the passenger side.

"You could have, but that's not like you," he said as he got in.

She turned to him and put up her hand, stopping him. "You know, you seem to have a constant issue with assuming you know more about me than you do. You have no idea who I am."

He gave her a cute, albeit somewhat dismissive, smile. "Amber Daniels. You're thirty years old. No children. You've never been married. You have a bachelor's degree in wildlife biology from MSU. Your favorite color is green. Your eyes are blue. And your parents think you're perfect. You never give them any problems."

"Wait... What the hell? You talked to my parents?" She dropped her hands onto the steering wheel. The rest of the people AJ had come out with were getting into trucks and following the detective and the deputy as they made their way down the road and toward the remains.

She wasn't going to put this truck in Drive until she was sure she wanted him at her side. This man, this infuriating, terrifying and impressive man, was constantly throwing her for a loop. She didn't like it.

"Strictly speaking, I never spoke with your parents, but my brother Mike did." He pointed at the stocky man with dark hair in the passenger side of the nearest pickup. "I gotta say, what we managed to pull about you in just a matter of hours was impressive. You've done a lot of good things in your time as sergeant." He motioned after the taillights that were starting to disappear into the darkness as Mike and the rest of his team made their way into the encroaching darkness. "We should probably catch up."

Right now, the only place she was tempted to take this truck was anywhere that didn't involve this invasive family. "I don't know who you think you are, but you and your team shouldn't be contacting my parents without my consent or knowledge."

As she thought about her mom, who was in her early seventies, she got instantly furious. The last thing her parents needed was some nosy jerk calling them and making them worry about her. They had more than enough going on in their lives that they didn't need to fuss over Amber's welfare.

This guy knew every button to push when it came to making her angry.

"I can see this is upsetting for you, but that wasn't my intention. It really was meant to be a compliment," he added. "There're very few people who are actually *good* in this world, and I have to say I think you are one of them."

"Clearly, you are *not* one of the good ones," she countered, anger marring her tone.

He chuckled, as if he was enjoying her frustration. "You are going to regret saying that to me later, you and I both know. So in an effort to save you an apology… It's accepted already and we can move on from this." He grinned at her. "Besides, I'm sure that by now you did a little digging and you know exactly who I am and what our team does. I'm proud of the work that we do, by the way."

She wanted to bite at him again, but he was probably right about feeling bad, and she would regret going for the jugular. "How did you know I wouldn't leave? And why do you feel the need to dig into me? Between the two of us…"

His smile widened and she felt the gravitational pull of it, so she put the truck in gear and started down the dirt road after the rest of the convoy.

"I like to know who I'm working with. I've learned the hard way that sometimes it's the ones we care for who have the power to hurt us the most."

It was quiet as they drove to where everyone had parked. She wanted to dislike him, but couldn't find a real reason when he had been so complimentary of her. On the other hand, she was going to need to talk to her parents about not giving strangers personal information about their family. At least it sounded like they had avoided the topic of her brother.

"Hey," AJ said, "for what it's worth, I'm sorry about shutting you guys down. I admit I got a little freaked out with the hand and stuff. A lot of people depend on me to make good choices, and sometimes it can be overwhelming. My asking you to stop wasn't personal."

Before she had a chance to respond, he jumped out of the pickup and started after his teams.

With him went her chances of trying to dislike him.

Assassin or not, he was a good guy with a lot on his plate. There were definitely things going on in his life that she didn't understand, nor would she probably ever understand, but she could tell he was doing the best he could.

His opening up to her had to be hard for him and yet he was still talking. It said so much about how he felt about her; and against her better judgment, she was flattered he had chosen to open up. She doubted he spoke to many people with the level of honesty that he had just bestowed upon her.

She walked out into the meadow. Before everything had gone haywire, she had found a location that would have made a perfect spot for her to drop the trap. However, she would need to move away from the location a bit, so if they were working around the area, she wouldn't draw a bear. They didn't like a lot of activity, but the bait had the potential to override their fear. They didn't need an investigator having a run-in with a hungry griz.

She walked over to the working team and approached AJ. "I'm going to drop the trap." She motioned to the back of her pickup where the trap sat. "I'll put it down a couple draws over, check in with Terrell and then head out."

"You mind if I help you?" he asked, surprising her.

She nodded and they walked back to the pickup. She made her way down the road until she couldn't see the officers or their cars anymore. She found a spot up a ravine between two large pines and a new growth stand that would act as a natural corral and push the bear into the trap instead of going around. It would work well if the bear wasn't savvy. If it had been caught before, or tagged, it would be another story.

They didn't talk and AJ just went to work as if he had done this kind of thing before. He waved her back as she reversed into position to lower the trap.

It only took a few minutes to release the winch and let the culvert trap drop into place. She had thrown in a roadkill carcass, and after opening the trap, she made her way inside and quickly hung it up. It had been dead for a while and the smell, even in the cold, was something she was wondering if she would be able to get out of her hair in one wash. Bears were notorious scavengers and often took on the fetid odor of the carrion in which they had been feasting. There was little doubt that it was the scent of the remains that had likely brought the bear to the property. Although, bears were also known for killing the weak.

Had that been the victim—the weak?

Coming out of the trap, she glanced back at her handiwork as she took off her work gloves and slapped them against her leg. AJ stood beside her. "Good work, warden."

She smiled. "This isn't my first rodeo."

"I can tell," he said as they got back into the pickup and rolled toward the squad. "I don't even know why you let me help you. It was clear you didn't need me. You just rolled right in and started dropping it down without an issue."

"I wanted you to think you were being helpful." She inadvertently fluttered her eyelashes as she smiled. *What in the hell? I have stink on my hands and I'm flirting?*

AJ laughed, his breath coming out as a long cloud. "Yes, I definitely need to feel helpful. It's what keeps me going."

She smiled, soaking up his laughter. He really was a sexy man. It was just unfortunate that this would likely be the last time she would see him.

She stopped behind what was steadily turning into a parking lot in the woods. "Speaking of going—" she nudged her chin in the direction of law enforcement and his team "—I'm going to get outta here. It's a long ride home and I have to work tomorrow so I guess this is goodbye." She tried to keep the sadness out of her voice, but she could hear it fleck her tone. Hopefully, he couldn't hear it.

"You're from Superior, right?" AJ asked, opening the passenger door of the pickup and stepping out.

She was sure he had probably already memorized her address as well. As much as she should have been annoyed, she did find it a little endearing. "Yep, it's about a two-and-a-half-hour drive from here. If I hurry home, I will get maybe five hours of sleep before I have to be back at it in the morning." She took another look in the direction of the trap. "As far as this trap goes, I would recommend that no one comes near this area. Let the bear come to us. If you see that the bear has been captured, don't be afraid to give me a call." She started to reach for her card. "Wait, you don't need my number, do you?"

"You are correct." He laughed. "Which number would you like me to call you on, your business or private line?"

AJ probably even knew her shoe size. "Either is fine."

He closed the door to her pickup.

She didn't want to say goodbye. For a moment, she didn't move. She wasn't sure why. There was nothing more she needed to do here, yet something made her want to stay.

"Hey, wait," AJ said, knocking on the window of her pickup.

She rolled down her window. "Yeah?" A police car passed by her on the small dirt road. "It looks like you guys are going to have a long night."

AJ nodded. "Yeah, but Detective Baker just asked

that everyone from my team go back to the house and leave them so they could work."

"Even Zoey?" she asked, surprised.

"He did ask Zoey to leave, but I'm sure you can imagine how well that went. She will play nice, but there is zero chance that she is going to miss out on this kind of thing on her property." He paused. "As it is, do you mind giving me a ride back to the house? I'd appreciate it."

She could have been reading the situation wrong, but she had a feeling he didn't want to say goodbye, either. Or maybe, it was just that he really did want a ride back to the house and it had nothing to do with the words that would or wouldn't be said.

"Sure, hop in." She tried to cover her smile as he smacked the window and then jogged around to his side of the truck.

He got in and slammed the truck door behind himself, then sent a text before throwing his phone on the dashboard and turning to her. "Where are you supposed to be in the morning?"

"As the sergeant, I don't necessarily have to be anywhere, but I need to be rolling in on the clock by six a.m. to get my hours in. Plus, I think it's a good example for my team if I'm up and rolling when they arrive on the clock."

"But it's not you going to an office?"

She shook her head. "I just clock in on my laptop and then send off reports of my activities for the day to my lieutenant—he can be a bit of a ballbuster." She tapped on the computer between them. In many ways, her vehicle was just like any law-enforcement vehicle in its setup. She even ran red-and-blues.

"If that's the case, I don't think you should leave the ranch tonight." His arm twitched as though he was thinking about reaching over and taking her hand, but she didn't move, and he didn't, either.

As much as she wanted to take him up on it—skipping the long commute tonight and tomorrow morning was tempting—it wasn't a good idea. She shook her head.

"Before you say no, hear me out. If I hadn't requested the search warrant, you would've set that trap and been on your way hours ago rather than been held up at the ranch all day. I'm just being reasonable. I mean, it doesn't make sense to drive that far and then have to come back in the morning or whatever." He seemed to be stumbling on his words. Like he wasn't used to apologizing and making it up to people.

The thought that he was making an exception for her made some of her reticence in liking him disappear.

She chewed on her bottom lip at the thought of staying at his home overnight. Her body clenched with want.

"What do you think?" he continued, pulling her out of her thoughts. "We have plenty of extra cabins. You can have one completely to yourself." He pointed in the direction of a set of row houses that ran behind the main ranch house and to the west of the barn. "There is one that has a huge rain showerhead."

"Where do you live?" she asked, trying her best not to think about him taking a shower with her in their private cabin.

"I live in one of the row houses. There are a few private cabins on the edges of the ranch's property, too. They aren't as nice, though…"

Despite her mind telling her to stay away from AJ,

she could feel the weariness of the long day slip through her. The promise of sleep was too appealing. "I... Yeah. If you don't mind... Sure."

His smile widened, causing her body to suddenly wake up. "Turn here."

Suddenly too aware of the small space they shared in the cab, her hands threatened to shake if she let go of the steering wheel as she followed his directions and stopped at the house second from the end. It was a log cabin, with a green galvanized steel roof and cute green shutters. It looked as though it had been recently built, the logs still the beautiful rich tawny browns of fresh oil, not the gray that crept in with hours of drying sun.

It was a cute place, a far cry from her 1914 cottage house, complete with knob and tube wiring and a leaking toilet that refilled every thirty minutes or so. Sadly, the sound of water running was one of the few comforts in her place. The rest of the night was filled with the sound of wind against the thin glass of the windows, and various creaks and rattles as the ground settled beneath the foundation.

She parked and he moved to get out. "I'm just two doors down. If you need anything, whatever it is—ice, beer... Whatever. I'm here."

Just like that, any desire to actually get some sleep and then catch the bear drifted from her mind. Every thought was quickly replaced by those of AJ, and exactly how he would feel between her thighs.

Chapter Six

He didn't often find he needed to drink, but tonight was one of those rare nights. After grabbing a beer from his fridge and flipping the lid into the trash, he walked out to the back porch of his cabin. His hair was still damp from his shower, but the air felt good on his skin. It was a cold night, but he wasn't sure if he wanted to get a campfire going or just go back inside.

He took a long drink of his beer and stared out at the cloudless night. There was a crescent moon and from where he stood, he could make out the riverlike Milky Way. To the north, there were wisps of reds and greens as the aurora borealis danced in the sky.

The lights were on in Amber's cabin, and he was tempted to go over and knock on her door and make her come outside to see the ballet of colors, but he stopped himself. Though he wanted nothing more than to show her nature's beauty, he couldn't. She wasn't going to stick around here for any real amount of time. He was already far too attracted to her for his own liking. Besides, he needed to get answers about the hand and Tammy.

If he had been smarter, he would have found another place to stay tonight—somewhere that wouldn't have been a quick walk to her bedroom. He only had so much willpower.

He could see Amber walk into the bedroom and move toward the bed. She pulled the Velcro from her Kevlar vest. Though he knew he should look away, he watched as she lifted it over her head.

There had been no doubt she was beautiful and had a great body before she had taken off her vest, but now, seeing her with just her uniform on…she was breathtaking. Her ass was in perfect proportion to her breasts and he wasn't sure, if he had been in the room with her, which he would have wanted to put his hands on first. She reached down and unbuttoned her brown shirt.

His mouth watered as he turned his back to her window and tried to stare at the northern lights. As majestic as they were, they didn't have the same pull as the beauty of nature behind him.

Before he had a chance to take a second drink from his beer, his phone pinged. It was a message from Zoey. The words were simple, but he hated everything that they implied: We need to talk.

That message never meant anything good. The last time he had gotten that exact text was from Tammy. What followed was her breaking off the engagement. He liked to tell himself that the only triggers he had were on his guns, but reading that text message, he knew that wasn't true. Or maybe, it was just the day and everything that had happened that was making him more sensitive than usual.

What's up? he texted back.

In true Zoey style, she answered instantly. My office. 5 mins.

She was never one to mince words.

He made his way back inside, taking one more glance in Amber's direction, but her lights had been turned off. At the very least, he wasn't going to have to worry about his willpower anymore.

By the time he was walking into Zoey's office at the far end of the main house, his stomach had started to turn sour. It hadn't been a long walk, but it felt like his legs were made of lead as he stopped at the door and knocked.

He could only imagine the number of things that she would want to chew him out for now. Zoey had definitely gone to town on him about the hand and having to call in his sister Kendra, the family attorney, while they waited for the warrant. Kendra would have lost her mind if he hadn't paused everything to get her input. They didn't need any kind of additional legal issues, and hopefully by putting a pin in the recovery of the remains and the required investigation that would ensue, he and Kendra could head off any potential problems. Plus, it would give him time to come to terms with possibly losing Tammy. She had been such a big part of his life and if these remains did belong to her, he would want answers. Had she been mauled by a bear, or murdered and dumped on the ranch?

No matter how she had died, though, this couldn't all just be about him—he had his family, and their jobs and futures, to consider.

He had already screwed up. He hadn't mentioned the possibility of the ring being Tammy's or anything else. He should have, but the more and more he thought about the hand and the ring, the less likely it was that it was hers.

Even if it was, there were no documents pointing to

it having come from him. He had been careful to keep his private life private, even when it came to engagements and purchases.

He loved to live in a world of cash. Someone would really have to do some legwork when it came to connecting the ring back to him. Though, if it was Tammy's hand…

There was nothing good that would come from him swirling the drain on this. He hadn't done anything wrong. Besides, the detective was a friend of the family. That would go a long way in clearing his name of any possible suspicion…or so he hoped.

The door opened. Zoey frowned at him. "Come on." She motioned for him to come inside.

He did as ordered, and she scowled outside behind him before closing the door and turning back.

Her office was filled with computer screens, a few running stock numbers and what looked like code. Others were filled with pictures—some he recognized as security clients and others as potential threats. There were always people who wanted them dead, but he both loved and hated that their lives were hanging in the balance. Neutralizing them, the people who intended on bringing harm to their clients or to the family and STEALTH, was one of the best parts of his job.

"Where's your friend?" she asked.

"Huh? Amber?" he asked.

Zoey nodded.

"Oh, I put her up in a cabin. Number eight. Hope that's okay with you."

She nodded. "Yeah, I thought you might." Her voice was unemotional and no matter how long he looked at her, it didn't seem like she was going to give away whether or not she thought his action was a good or bad thing.

"Is that why you called me here?" He ran his hand over his chin, rubbing his stubble. He needed to shave.

It was funny how the mind wandered when it was under a certain level of stress. Though he was sure he wasn't going to get fired—Zoey really did trust and like him—he still didn't like walking into her office without the faintest clue as to why she would call a late meeting.

"What you do with her is on you. That ship—" she waved in the general direction of the police "—has already sailed. We are in on the investigation whether or not we want, now we're just going to have to wait it out. Besides, she seems nice enough. Trustworthy."

A wave of relief washed over him. "Weren't you going to stay out there? Help them out? Or did something happen?"

"Baker made it clear I wasn't to approach the scene, but if it hadn't been for the phone call I received, he could have taken those instructions and stuffed them where the sun doesn't shine."

"I should have told you earlier, but—"

"We've got a problem—besides the remains on the ranch," she said, talking over him.

He nearly bit his tongue. "Where? With whom?" His heart started to thump hard in his chest. *God, I love these moments.*

Zoey pointed toward a computer screen, where there was a mug shot of a man and a bio next to it.

The man had dark brown, midlength hair. Dark eyes. His nose was slightly larger than average. He wasn't smiling in the picture. AJ didn't recognize the man and walked over to the screen, tapping on the bio. The guy was twenty-five, an avid hiker, loved to ski, came from money. His name, Luca Fellini, besides sounding Italian, didn't ring any bells.

"Who is he?" AJ asked.

"Luca Fellini is the son of Frank Fellini."

He shook his head. Nothing.

"Frank is the Italian foreign minister of trade."

"Oh," AJ said. That meant one thing for sure—the guy was going to bring them trouble. Either they were going to fight for him, or against him, but it was going to get dirty.

"An operator working in Rome was sleeping with Luca," Zoey said, giving him an evil smile that spoke of the lengths operatives would go in order to get a job done. "It's amazing what too much wine, a beautiful woman and a little ecstasy can do when you need a man to spill his secrets."

He chuckled, but something about the heady mix made his mind drift to Amber before he pulled himself back to center.

"What did our man Luca say?"

"Do you remember Conflux?"

"Uh, yeah." He laughed.

That was one company he couldn't forget. His brothers Troy and Mike had nearly died working for them a couple of years ago. Conflux was a military engineering company that machined parts for the US government and the different branches of the armed forces. They were worth multimillions and, as such, were an open target for corporate spies. It was one of STEALTH's best clients—there was always guaranteed work.

"And their enemy, Rockwood?"

He nodded. Rockwood had gotten caught sending

spies into the belly of the Conflux beast. Their spying had cost them millions, and exposed the fact they were running illicit contracts with foreign nations. They were treasonous bastards.

Bastards who had threatened to take down his family and STEALTH when their team had exposed them, leaving the organization in shreds and in a lot of trouble with the US government.

"What about them?" he growled.

"Since then, we have been running surveillance on the group. We knew these rats would stick their heads back up. It took a while after they took such a big hit, but some of their handiwork is starting to show back up on the dark web."

"And?" The hair rose on the back of his neck.

"Luca, our boy, was talking about his father. The foreign minister. Apparently, he has been buying and selling American military secrets."

"Is the operative running Luca one of ours?" he asked.

"No. She was with the CIA. Unfortunately, she was taken out by Frank when he learned about her relationship with his son."

AJ shuddered. "Those ruthless bastards. I'm sorry to hear about her."

Zoey gave a thin smile. "She didn't go out without a fight. Plus, she is a goddamned hero for her work. She is going to save thousands, if not hundreds of thousands, of servicemen's lives in making the military aware of the data breach. CIA is already looking into it."

He nodded. "So how does this involve us?"

"Luca let it slip that his father was the leader of Rockwood before we took it down. He is trying to resurrect the organization, using it to buy and sell state secrets. According to Luca, his father's number-one mission is to destroy STEALTH. They've put a bounty on our heads."

He would have laughed, but this company had last paid a spy fourteen million dollars to supply them with machining secrets. It made him sick to think about how much they would put out to take down an entire contracting operation like theirs.

"The good news is that they don't know much about STEALTH besides it being a company…except, somehow, they knew the name Spade."

His chest suddenly tightened.

"I need some air," he said as he walked out of Zoey's office. The scent of electronics and dust permeated his senses and clawed at him.

He gulped the night air and looked up at the red lights curling like a whip in the sky.

His family. His entire *family* was in the crosshairs.

They had all been careful in making sure they hadn't left digital trails any more than necessary, but in the social-media age, where facial and voice-recognition software was traded like playing cards on the dark web, they were as good as dead.

That was…*if* they were found.

Kendra had recently been involved in a social-media tit-for-tat deal with a crooked senator and it had blown up, but that was in Missoula. She was now living on the ranch with her fiancé, but according to social media and the web, she was currently residing in New York City.

He did a mental checklist of all the ways their location could be outed as he walked back toward his cabin.

They hadn't been named in any court documents;

only false company names had been used. As for anything else…he couldn't think of a way they could be, or had been, exposed.

He was so lost in thought that it wasn't until he was walking in his front door that he even spared a thought for the griz. If it wanted him tonight, it could have had him.

He took off his jacket and threw it over the couch. His beer was sitting on the counter where he had left it. Little beads of condensation were slipping down the brown bottle and the top of the label had started to lift. He was tempted to pick off the paper, like some weird tick, but instead he grabbed the bottle and emptied it with a long drink.

He should have known that between bears, exes and a being so close to a woman he could never have…well, this day was not going to get any better. He just hadn't expected it to fall so dramatically far from grace.

Life had one hell of a way of getting ridiculously complicated in the blink of an eye.

That was all without even taking into consideration their normal everyday running of the teams.

He sighed and pitched the glass bottle into the trash.

Looking in, it had landed next to a cork from a wine bottle. His thoughts moved to Luca and the dead operative.

Too much wine… Zoey's words echoed in his mind.

He didn't even drink wine. Hell, he didn't recall having a bottle in the place. When it came to groceries, he kept the cabin pretty sparse.

Ever so carefully, he reached around behind his back and touched the flesh-warmed grip of his Glock.

He hadn't locked his door when he'd left, but out

here there wasn't much of a need. No one got the sneak on this place—at least, no human. There were security systems wired throughout the entire area of the houses, exits and entrances to the ranch.

"Hello?" he called, trying his damnedest not to draw his weapon.

"Yeah…hey, it's just me. I'm out on the back porch."

He recognized Amber's voice and he dropped his hand from his gun. He tried to calm his racing pulse as he slowly walked into his bedroom.

Amber had her arm under her head and a glass of wine in her other hand. She was leaning back in a patio chair, covered with his wool Pendleton blanket, complete with a blue-and-orange geometric pattern. Her blond hair was loose and cascading down and over her shoulders, and ending in curls over the edge of the blanket.

Her nearly *naked* shoulders.

She was so beautiful.

Breathtaking.

Oh, for all that was good in this world. He thanked every single one of his lucky stars as he stared at her and smiled.

He reached up and loosened the top button of his shirt—it seemed to be choking him.

Her skin was so pale, so soft-looking. She was the color of milk and there was a freckle at the top of her left shoulder that begged for his kiss.

"AJ…"

Even the way she spoke his name was creamy and smooth, beckoning for him and the night of fantasies he wanted to fulfill with her.

"Is *this* okay?" She did a tiny motion toward her body

with her wineglass. "I know I shouldn't have just bor-rowed your blanket, but it's cold out here."

He didn't want to point out that she was only wear-ing a tank top, as her being here was more than okay. It was what he had been thinking about, though not *ex-actly*, all damn day.

He sat on the chair closest to her, looking at her. "You said you wanted to talk. What's on your mind?"

"You told me if I needed anything, to come talk to you. Did you mean that?" she asked, giving him one of the sexiest looks he had ever seen.

"Absolutely," he said, reaching out and putting his hand gently on the blanket over her knee. "Is every-thing okay?"

She gave a slight nod. "Yes, I just…" She sighed. "I want you to know that I appreciate you and your team letting me crash here. It's nice." She waved at her sur-roundings, but her gaze moved to his hand on her.

"You can stay here as long as you need," he said, sending her a gentle smile. Though he was aware that he wasn't offering her a place completely unselfishly, he liked having her here.

"I live alone, sometimes it's pretty quiet. All of the action that happens here, it's a bit refreshing. Though," she said, looking away, "I have to think that a lot of what is happening now with the human remains is directly tied to you and your decision to push everyone back."

"I told you, that was for legal reasons. Nothing more. I thought my asking you here would help prove my in-tentions were honorable." He frowned. Until he knew for sure the ring on that hand was the one he'd given Tammy… "Don't be offended, but you seem to have a hard time trusting." Not that he could blame her, especially when she had found herself at the literal center of a den of trained killers, but he wasn't about to point that out—this was about her.

"First, I work in a governmental job," she said. "They can be cutthroat."

"Yes, but that's not what I'm sensing here. It's almost as if you were hurt a long time ago."

She stared down at her fingertips as she stretched her hands wide. "My brother died quite a while ago, and it was incredibly hard on my family. In the end, we learned who our real friends were and who the people in our lives were who wanted to tear us down." She paused. "It turns out that there are far more people out there who want to judge you in silence than help."

"I'm so sorry to hear about your brother, Amber." He wasn't sure what else to say, but he loved having her feel safe to open up to him. He liked getting to know more about her and to learn why she worked the way she did.

"It's okay. Like I said, it was a long time ago."

"Time doesn't really matter when it comes to losing the people who you really love. Loss is loss—it changes a person forever."

"Oh, that is one lesson I know all too well." She balled her hands into fists.

There was a glistening in her eyes that made him wonder if she was going to cry. That had been the last thing he'd wanted. "Amber," he said, lifting her chin so he could meet her gaze directly, "I think you are an amazing woman. I know how hard it is to trust, but believe me when I say that I never want to make you hurt." As he took her lips with his, she drew in a breath that was almost like the gasp that came when two bodies melded into one. His body responded, instantly hard-

ened by the gentle touch of her lips against his, mixed
with her sexy sound.

Her hand moved up into his hair and she gripped it,
just a little roughly, and pulled him harder against her
lips. A moan escaped him as she nipped at his bottom
lip, gently grazing his skin and beckoning the predator
within him to come out and play.

He wanted to kiss her until she couldn't breathe, to
reach down and feel the river between her thighs and
to taste all that was her. If she let him, he would love
to take her to the brink and then some.

"AJ, would you hold me?" she asked, but before the
words had even fully left her, he pulled her into his
arms.

There was the steady beating of her heart and the
warmth of her breath on his skin. It had been so long
since he had held a woman like this. A part of him
wanted to take this so much further, to let themselves
fall into the darkness of the night and let the shadows
bring them reprieve from the stark illumination that
came with the light of their truths; but ignoring reality
didn't keep it from reappearing in the morning.

She leaned back slightly and pressed her lips against
his. Their breaths mingled, mixing into a heady storm
of want and fear. She broke their kiss, gently pushing
him away. "I have to go."

Her words lashed against his soul. "I get it." He stood
up, moving back from her. "I'm sorry for kissing you."

"There are a lot of things you could be sorry for, but
kissing me isn't one of them." She smiled up at him as
she slipped out of the chair and moved toward the door
to leave. "If our situation was different, tonight would
be far from over."

Chapter Seven

That was one hell of a night. Amber had not opened herself up to a man like that in a long time, but not an ounce of her regretted her decision. AJ was beyond anything she'd expected. They had definitely taken things to another level. She had wanted to take things further, but was glad that things had ended where they had.

She'd felt silly for asking him to just hold her, but he hadn't hesitated for a moment. He had just pulled her into his arms, and held her tight.

Recalling the sound of his heartbeat made her smile. In theory, it would've been nice to hear it again, but that wasn't what was going to happen. Something like that wouldn't be good for either one of them.

As soon as she got the bear, she was done here. He knew that just as well as she did.

Yeah, they could call each other and text and do all the cutesy things that people in relationships did, but they were both so busy it would never work.

He had been gone for nearly an hour last night. Though she had seen him go into the ranch house, she didn't know what had been going on; for all she knew, he'd been ordering hits on people. She laughed at the thought as she laced up her boots.

The deputy had told her what they did for a living and he had vaguely explained it as well, but last night AJ definitely didn't seem like the kind of guy who was an assassin. Not hardly. He was sweet and giving. If asked, she'd honestly have to say that he was one of the best kissers she had experienced. She could only imagine how good he would be when they actually had sex. Maybe that was reason enough not to go there. If they did, she wasn't sure that she could leave it at a one-night stand.

After getting ready for the day in her cabin and making herself a steaming cup of coffee, she went outside and got into her truck. AJ's lights were still off and it didn't look like he was up yet, surprisingly.

He didn't seem like the type who would sleep in, but he had put in some time on her.

She smiled wildly at the thought.

Yes, keeping this to a one-time thing was already going to be a challenge.

Hopefully the bear trap was sprung and she could spend the rest of the day figuring out the logistics in getting the biologists and her team out here to help her relocate the animal.

Thinking about that… She needed to do a little digging. Part of her was tempted to sit out in her rig and work. If she waited, she might get to see AJ when he came out to go to work, but then again, she didn't want to risk falling back into his arms. She had already self-rescued from those arms once. If she fell back in, work wouldn't be getting done—at least not the kind that got her paid.

As it was, his lights weren't even on. She had a few minutes to get some work done before hitting the road.

She popped open her laptop and signed in to work. If she had to guess, there would be phone calls all day.

At least hunting season was over—that would limit the number of random calls that would come in from people wanting to report trespassing and the like. However, there were a few poaching calls that her deputies would need to continue digging into in order to solve and prosecute.

She pulled up her email. There were forty sitting in there from yesterday and twenty-three from just today. She had been thinking she would beat everyone to their proverbial desks this morning. Nothing appeared as if it needed her immediate attention, so she turned her focus to what she was looking for—collared grizzly-bear locations.

The locations were exact, but sometimes the data was slow to upload, with approximately a three-day lag. Sometimes, if a bear was in certain areas, the data signal wouldn't even be attainable, but hopefully she could get a general idea.

Last year, they'd had a bear, Lingenpolter, that had been caught in a culvert trap—like the one they had set last night—and had been relocated more than two hundred miles to the north, near Glacier Park. In less than two months, the bear traveled more than five hundred miles in a zigzag pattern and had last pinged farther south than where they had originally caught him. It was incredible just how far and wide a male could travel.

If the bear on the ranch was a male, it very well may have been traveling through when it found food and holed up. If it was female, or a sow with cubs—which there hadn't been any evidence of—it would be another story entirely. She could very well den up near the ranch and move in to the territory. Meaning, the Spades and the Martins would be dealing with her for years to come.

Amber pulled up the latest report of GPS readouts of collared bears. The information was from last week, and if she added three days to that… She pulled together a general geofence for the area.

There were four known possibilities—three females and a male.

Those were just the ones that had been caught and collared. If the reported sightings were to be believed, more than a dozen grizzly bears could have been the one that was visiting the ranch.

Based on the probabilities, she had to assume it was a female.

She clicked on bear number 832. It was, approximately, a twenty-nine-year-old sow griz who had originally been captured and tagged in a drainage twenty miles to the east. The girl had been chomping on a farmer's chickens, then hit the garbage inside a neighbor's garage, which led to her capture and tagging. They had moved her north, but like Lingenpolter, she had eventually picked her way back to the general area. Her epic adventure wasn't as much of a zigzag as the boar's, but she had steadily come back to what she no doubt thought of as home.

Amber couldn't blame the bear, but if that was the one that they were dealing with—one that had been somewhat habituated to people and the food sources they provided and was now back looking for more— it could prove fatal for the sow. They had to have a somewhat rigid policy; a habituated bear was a dangerous one.

If this was the bear seen out here, it was very likely that the woman whose hand they'd found had fallen victim to a bad bear.

Amber was torn. She wanted to hope that the bear hadn't killed the woman, but had only scavenged, given the alternative—both for the woman and the bear.

There was already enough of a target on grizzly bears; much of the public wanted to pull them off the endangered-species list and start to allow for an active hunting season on the predators. A woman being killed would definitely draw more strength to the case.

From a conservation perspective, predators needed to be controlled or it would lead to massive swings in predators and prey. She'd rather it be steady instead of bears overloading the balance and turning to unhealthy practices that left her holding the scale.

There was a knock on the driver-side door of her truck and she jerked back from her computer. AJ was standing outside her window, holding two cups of coffee from Starbucks.

"Oh, hey," she said, rolling down her window. She was both excited and embarrassed at seeing him.

AJ smiled at her. He was nearly irresistible when he gave her that look. "Sorry to surprise you—that wasn't my intention." He handed her the venti cup. "It's just a regular latte with sweetener, I didn't know what you liked."

"That was really thoughtful of you." She took the coffee and pulled the stopper from the cup, then took a long sip. The coffee wasn't very hot. "Is there even a Starbucks around here?"

He shrugged. "Not really, but there are a few in the city. I ran in there about an hour ago. After you left I couldn't really sleep..." There was a tug of sadness in his voice.

Or maybe she was just hearing things. If he was upset with her, he wouldn't have been bringing her coffee—a coffee that had taken almost an hour to get. He really was a good man.

Before she could allow herself to think about the likeable parts of him, she needed to focus. Here came the awkwardness.

She sighed. "About last night—"

He shook his head and from the pinched look on his face, he wanted her to stop.

Good. We have an understanding.

She smiled with relief and she could feel her body relax.

"You going up to check the trap? If you are, I'll come along and show you around the ranch a little. Maybe we can track the bear a bit more and see where it's been going."

He stood quietly by her window for a moment, sipping on his coffee. She squirmed slightly, but really... what did it hurt if he was by her side today? If they were in the truck, working, there wouldn't really be much time for any type of shenanigans to happen.

Besides, they had an unspoken *understanding.*

"I'd be happy to have you along." She did enjoy his company.

He gave her a quick nod and made his way around to the passenger seat. "I talked to Zoey this morning. There's a sheriff's deputy keeping an eye on the scene. They tried to stay out of the way of your trap, and inside their car all night. I expect that the full investigation team will probably be here in the next couple of hours to go over the entire area."

"Yeah, I don't expect that anybody wanted to rush around in the woods last night with just a skeleton crew when there's a grizzly around. I certainly didn't advise it."

"Is there a chance we can put more traps out?" he asked.

"We have one more trap that's available, but it's in Kalispell. If we don't get a hit on this trap, we can start thinking about it." She paused. "It's my hope, though, that this bear just moved on and isn't a continuing problem."

He grimaced slightly, like he didn't totally agree with her, but instead of thinking too much about his reaction, she turned back to the road.

"Baker and his team canvased a small area and collected the hand last night. They didn't find any other remains. They dropped the hand off at the medical examiner's office already. According to Zoey, they were going to pull some fingerprints." The pinched expression on his face seemed to intensify as he spoke.

"That's good. At least we can get an ID on the remains. I always like bringing closure to families. Even if they learn their loved ones are dead, it is better than living with the agony of not knowing what has happened to someone you care about." Her thoughts moved to her brother.

He cocked his head, studying her. "You say that like you've been through something like that."

It hadn't been her intention to open up this can of worms with him, or with anyone. "What happened in the past doesn't matter. There is only moving forward."

"Mmm-hmm," he said, not sounding satisfied in her dismissal of the subject. "Do you like being a game warden?"

She was grateful he was changing the subject as she slowly made her way toward the trap. "It can be rewarding, but challenging," she said, smiling.

"I bet it's a really fun job."

"It certainly can be. Some people think we are more like law enforcement than anything, but I like to look at our profession like we are conservators of the natural resources. We protect Montana for generations to come."

He nodded, but she could tell from the way he was staring in the direction of the location of the remains that his mind was somewhere else. Of course, he would've been more concerned with the comings and goings of the ranch instead of their little interlude. No wonder he hadn't wanted to talk about it this morning. She was as much relieved as she was slightly hurt.

She shouldn't have been hurt, though, since this was exactly what she wanted. Ambivalence.

"You have any idea when the crime lab will be done with their tests?" she asked. AJ didn't look away from the window and merely shrugged.

She had a sense he'd been hiding something since yesterday, but she wasn't sure it was appropriate to ask or not. She didn't want him to be offended, but her curiosity was getting the better of her. "Is there any way you would know who the hand belonged to?" AJ tensed. She could tell he was making an effort to not look at her.

"Odd, Detective Baker asked me the same question last night." He paused, looking away from her. "Just know everything that has been happening in the last twenty-four hours is way outside my comfort zone."

Everything?

If he thought the kiss, being held by him, was inside of her comfort zone, well, he had another think coming.

On the other hand, maybe he was just focused on work and not on their growing feelings toward one another. Or maybe he meant exactly what he'd said, but in a *good* way—like he wasn't the kind of guy who expected or had experienced brief interludes.

Was it his way of saying that he wanted more?

No. She took a breath and tried to pull herself back to the moment. *I'm overthinking this. It's just this, riding in a truck, nothing more.*

As they made it to the trap, she stopped the truck and put it in Park. From where they sat, she could see that the gate was still open and it hadn't been tripped. No bear.

Farther down the road was a cruiser. In the front was a deputy, his head tilted back in sleep. She chuckled at the sight, but she didn't begrudge the guy. She'd never taken a nap out in the woods when she had been on duty, but it would have been easy when a person was on their own in the peaceful timber.

Unfortunately, if this guy was caught sleeping on duty, it could very well spell the end of his career—the politics in law enforcement and in being a game warden could be brutal and unforgiving. "Should we wake him up?" she asked, sending AJ a malicious grin.

"It would be the thoughtful thing," he said with a chuckle. "If I caught one of my team members doing this, they would be in deep."

With her lights off, she drove up to the cruiser and let her truck roll into the front bumper of the guy's car. The deputy woke with a start, grabbing the wheel like he thought he had fallen asleep while driving. He stared out at them for a long second before seemingly coming to his senses and realizing what he had just been caught doing and by whom. A guilty smile erupted over his features.

She laughed as she backed up her pickup and then stopped by the guy and rolled down her window. "Hey," she said, a smile on her lips.

"Morning," the deputy said, looking from her to AJ like he was hoping against hope that neither of them was from his department. "You caught me studying there."

"Yeah, we noticed." She chuckled. "How long have you been sitting out here?"

The guy looked down at his watch. "They had me roll out here about six hours ago. It was overtime for me, so... You know how it goes."

The guy was definitely embarrassed. In an attempt to mollify his embarrassment and guilt, and any underlying concern for his job and reputation, she had to throw him a bone. "Definitely. As for studying, we didn't see anything." She winked.

AJ tipped his fingers in the man's direction, reiterating her statement.

The guy perked up. "Sounds like this is a really interesting case. Baker told me a bit about it. You guys helping with the search today?"

That hadn't exactly been her plan.

"I'm not sure if we are. We have a bear to locate," AJ said, but he rubbed awkwardly at the back of his neck. "You know what area they covered last night?"

He had said he'd talked this through with Zoey this morning, so she was surprised he was asking the deputy questions. Yet, maybe he was verifying the information or hoping for more.

"They just worked the direct area last night. Inside the tape there," the deputy said, pointing at the yellow tape that was tied up in a makeshift square around the area where they had located the hand. "Any sign of your griz?"

She shook her head. She wasn't exactly sure what AJ had up his sleeve, but she had a feeling part of him was struggling with what had happened last night...just like she was. She quelled the urge to be annoyed as she tried to be vague and relaxed.

AJ seemed to have noticed the shift in her demeanor and he reached over and gently touched the tips of his fingers to her leg, silently reassuring her without drawing attention from the deputy. "I'm thinking we are going to go up the hill a ways, see if we can find any more signs. Let us know when the incident commander or detective arrives and maybe we can link up."

The deputy gave them a stiff nod. "Will do, and let me know if you find anything. I'll be here until they arrive."

They pulled away from the deputy and she made sure to close her window before speaking. Opening her mouth, she tried to think of the exact right words to navigate this, but none came. She wanted to reprimand him for including her in his offer, but she wasn't actually upset and it would only push him away. Though, that would be better in some ways. It would make her internal struggle that much easier to ignore.

Chapter Eight

Amber was trying to be cool as she kept driving along the bumpy road, but every thought she had was about AJ kissing her. If she was this caught up with merely a kiss, maybe it was good she'd left before they could have taken things any further.

"I pulled some information about the bears that are known to be traveling in the area," she said, finally deciding to avoid anything but their immediate needs. "I'm thinking if we can find the place where it came through your fence line, we might be able to get a hair sample and run the DNA. If it is one of the bears on file, we can at least get a better idea of what we are dealing with—if this bear is going to be more of a problem or not."

AJ nodded. "We have sensors on our fences. I can have Zoey send me a GPS pin of any recent activity." He pulled out his phone and sent a quick text.

She was used to tech, but this was extra cool; though, it reminded her of just how out of her element she really was with this family and this man.

He pointed ahead. "Up here, the road is going to split and then there will be a cattle guard and gate." He clicked away on his phone, looking over a map.

"How many acres do you guys have here?"

He shrugged. "Thousands. I don't know exactly. Zoey doesn't really talk about it a whole lot. It seems huge, though." He pointed at the mountain to their left. "This all abuts public land, though, so it makes it feel infinitely bigger." He turned to her, looking up from his phone for a second. "And, hey, I'm glad you agreed to let me come along today."

She shook her head and waved him off as if the thought hadn't already crossed her mind. "It's no big deal. The nice part about my job is that I have a lot of flexibility as long as I keep my superiors happy. Besides, we need to make sure you and your teams are safe. I have to admit—" she smiled "—it is intriguing to be working with a death investigation. Normally, I just report the bodies and go. It's interesting to get to be involved in the whole process." She hadn't known that was exactly how she felt until the words rolled out of her, and in them she found her truth.

He nodded and turned back to his phone. "I'm glad to hear that you aren't just out here for me."

There went any good feelings that she was starting to have about working with him. *Poof. Gone.*

With it went some of the awkwardness she was feeling with him. *Good. Work, it was.*

"You have a job, same as I do. We are both just trying to do the best for our employers and the communities that rely on us." She pulled to a stop at the gate. There was a lock with a number code.

His face fell slightly, but he turned away from her as he got out of the truck and unlocked the gate. The cattle guard rattled as she drove over it and waited for him to close the gate and lock it behind them.

"The pin Zoey sent me, the one she thinks might be where the bear has been moving through, is just another mile or so up the road." He seemed to have let their earlier point go and she was all too happy about it.

There was silence between them until he motioned for her to pull over. "The fence is this way," he said, motioning toward the west.

The snow was thick and heavy, the kind that fell on warmer days, and it crunched and squeaked under her feet as they started to descend into the timber.

Her mind wandered to the Inuit. They had more than fifty words for snow. No doubt, there would be one for this kind, one that would stick around and get covered with the light, powdery snow of brutal winter days, all while acting like a blanket for the world beneath. Protector and base…permanently impermanent. She didn't know all the words, but the term *matsaaruti* came to mind. It was the type of snow that would freeze to their sled runners when they were mushing.

She kicked at the snow, harder than she'd intended, and it flew up, with a few of the pieces smacking AJ in the back.

He turned and stared at her. "What was that?" he asked, giving her a playful look.

"I… I didn't mean…" Instead of continuing and admitting she hadn't meant to hit him, she reached down and made a snowball. She pitched it at him, hitting him in the middle of the chest.

"What the…?" he said with a laugh. He grabbed some snow and chucked it in her direction. It stuck to her coat.

She laughed as she walked up beside him, brushing the remnants of snow from her jacket before reaching

over and brushing the wet bits of snow from his back.
The muscles on his back were hard and tense as she
touched them and she quickly dropped her hand.

As they started to walk again, with her by his side,
she was struck by how badly she wanted him to reach
over and hold her hand.

They walked for ten minutes or so. There were little
birds that looked like shrikes flitting from tree to tree,
and as the sun worked its way up in the sky, there was
the occasional creak of a branch and a thump of snow
as it slipped from its hold and hit the ground.

Every day in the woods was a damn good day. She
didn't get to spend nearly the amount of time hiking as
she would have liked.

In the distance, she spotted a barbed-wire fence. The
fence posts were still the tawny color of freshly treated
wood.

"Zoey said an animal triggered the system in this
stretch. Could be fifty feet or so from this point—it's
not super exact." He motioned toward the fence.

She nodded, not wanting to tell him that this was far
more exact than anything she had done to this effect
in the past. Usually, if she was trying to collect hair
samples, she would end up walking for miles trying to
find the place where the animal may or may not have
come through a fence. More often than not, she came
up empty-handed. It turned out having him come along
was a good thing.

"I bet you work poaching cases a lot," he began as
they walked up the fence line, looking for a place that
would be bent or pushed down by a bear moving over
the wire.

She wasn't sure why he brought it up or what made

him think about it, but she nodded. "Yep, right now we have a case where we think a guy killed ten deer and three elk. Left the animals, took the antlers."

"Oh, that kind of thing pisses me off. People do know they can just *buy* antlers, right?"

"No kidding, but to some of these people it's not really about the acquisition of a food source or even really about the antlers, instead it is an act of rebellion. It is a way for them to act out against the government. You know, 'no one controls them' kind of mentality."

"I can only imagine," he said with an annoyed grumble. "How do you even catch them?"

"Nowadays, it's a lot easier than in the past. Just a couple years ago, though, someone shot a bear and took its paws and gallbladder before leaving the rest. Fortunately for us, where they had stepped out of their truck and shot, they had dropped an ATM receipt. Made it pretty easy to track them down." She smiled victoriously.

"Damn." He chuckled. "That's almost as good as them literally leaving you a business card."

"Actually, it made freezing their assets that much easier." She smiled. "Turned out they had been dealing in exotic animals and parts on the black market. That one felt damned good to take down."

"That is awesome. I know the feeling you are talking about, when you get to do the right things for the right reasons and end up making a difference. Feels *damned* good." He stopped walking, but she moved ahead.

She looked down the fence line. A couple of posts from where she was, she caught sight of a bent top wire. Stuffed into several barbs were what looked like tufts of brown fur. She rushed up to the spot. Sure enough, it was hair. Better, it was the coarse, kinky hair of a bear, not the more straight, hollow kind of the herbivores in the area.

They had just struck gold.

"AJ, look!" she called back to him excitedly.

Instead of hurrying to her side as she expected, he was staring down at his phone.

"AJ?" she asked, worried. "Is everything okay?"

He didn't look up; instead, it was like he hadn't even heard her speaking.

"AJ?" she called, this time a little bit louder.

Finally, he glanced up, his face hard and his eyes a bit unfocused, his mind elsewhere. "Huh? Yeah?"

"Is everything okay?" she asked again.

Her question seemed to pull him back to the moment. "Yeah," he said, slightly shaking his head. "I'm fine. It's all good. What did you find?"

She pointed at the top wire. "We found it. We found hair. We are hopefully going to get answers."

He huffed, saying something just under his breath. She wasn't entirely sure, but she could have sworn he'd said, "At least one of us will."

Chapter Nine

AJ wasn't exactly thrilled as they made their way back to the ranch house. He had really been hoping that they wouldn't find anything up there on the hill. If anything, he had been counting on them being out there in the woods all day, searching for something that they would never find but would keep them away from people and the intrigue that was swirling around the place.

The thought of being around a death investigation that was likely tied to Tammy threatened to break his heart. If they learned it was her, he wasn't sure that he could keep his composure. Besides, he had Rockwood's threat looming heavily over their heads and both that and the field trip gave him something else to concentrate on besides that ache in his chest.

Now, thanks to the text from Baker, he was even more leery to head back. According to the detective, he was hoping to meet with AJ this afternoon. Apparently, though he was taking the lead on the case, he wasn't on the ranch but was having his team run the search patterns instead. Which meant one of two things—either he had gotten a positive ID on the victim, and had tracked the ring and was now looking to question him about his role in it being found on the ranch, or the detective just didn't want to have a part in the actual digging through snow and ice in hopes of finding more remains. AJ hoped for the latter.

"Where do we need to run the hair?" he asked, turning to Amber.

She took off her hat and threw it on the dashboard. She let out her ponytail, her hair falling over her shoulders…reminding him all too much of kissing her last night, holding her.

His body jerked to life, but he tried to control the response. He had done very well in pretending like nothing had gone on last night.

It was fine. He didn't want a real relationship. She was a good woman and she made him laugh, but that wasn't going to be enough. Just like Tammy, Amber would want compromises from him and his life that he couldn't make—not as team leader and not as the man he was. He was all in on this life. A heart couldn't have love for a woman and the kind of work he did.

His thoughts moved to his siblings and the Martins. They had found love and relationships, proving him a bit wrong, but they weren't working in the same role that he found himself in. Sure, Zoey was married, but the work had to be taxing on both her husband and her kiddo.

If he went back to working directly in the field and had to take on a more active trigger-pulling role instead of just overseeing the operation, he didn't want to have a woman or family back at home to worry about him. It wasn't fair.

He had been the man coming to the door to tell a wife her husband had died far too many times and he never wanted anyone else to have to bear that duty for him.

Yes, arm's length or farther was even better.

"The lab for the hair is in Missoula, at the university." She smiled over at him, and it made his heart both shift and ache in his chest. "It shouldn't take too long for me to get the answer."

He nodded. "Then what?"

"Based on the bear, we go from there. If it's not a problem bear, we will continue to try and trap. I'm thinking about moving the trap closer to where we found the hair, but just because we found hair there doesn't mean it will move through that exact area again."

"What if it is a trouble bear?"

She pinched her lips. "Then we may have to make a harder choice than just trapping and relocating. We may need to take down the bear and do a necropsy to find if it was ingesting the person whose hand we found."

"It's a woman, by the way." He tapped on his phone.

"Was that the text you got up there? Confirmation of some kind? I didn't want to ask, but you seemed really bothered."

"Baker wants a meeting later," he said with a grumble. "I can only imagine what he wants to chat about."

She gave him a side-eye. "He just wants to talk to you, or with your whole crew?"

From the sounds of things, she had the same gut reaction to a detective asking for a meeting as he did. That didn't bode well.

"Just me."

She gave him a long look, reading him, and he hated every second of it. "Is there something you should tell me, AJ? Something I don't know?"

He wanted to tell her about the ring, about Tammy, about everything, but in doing so...after last night. *Gah*.

AJ ran his hands over his face—he didn't know

where to start. "This is turning into more than I ever expected or bargained for. Thank goodness Baker is a friend."

"What does that mean?" She slowed down the truck, but she pulled past the ranch house and headed toward Missoula.

This was going to be a long drive to the city.

"It's a long story." He gave a long exhale. "I was engaged before. A couple years or so ago."

Amber shifted in her seat and he noticed her gripping the steering wheel incrementally tighter. "Oh?"

She didn't lead him. He appreciated she wasn't pushing him to tell her more than he was ready to in this moment, but at the same time, he wished she would give him a clue as to how much she wanted to know.

"Yes, I was engaged to a woman from New Jersey. She was a total city girl."

Amber started to laugh. "You?" She looked down at his boots and Wranglers. "Did she have a thing for cowboys or something? How did you get hooked up with her?"

"First, we haven't always lived on this ranch. My family's company was bought out by STEALTH, and we moved here to be a part of their group. We haven't really been here that long."

"Now, that—you not being here long—I did know. Where are you originally from?"

He answered with a tired smile. "Contracting kids are a bit like military kids—home is where your family is, it's not a place."

"That's not a bad way to live," she said, but there wasn't conviction in her voice.

"Yes, I loved it. I lived in Belgium and Africa, just

about the A to Z of countries. I don't even think I could name them all." He stopped from going too deeply into his history. That would lead to thinking about the shadows in his mind where all the dark thoughts and deeds lingered like ghosts. "I met her when I was twenty-five and we dated long-distance for a while. Then she hinted it was time."

"Time for what?"

"You know. Get married or break up." He shrugged.

"You do know that an ultimatum never leads to anything good, especially if we are talking about marriage."

"Ha," he said, "don't I know that."

"But you still asked her to marry you?"

He ran his hand over his face again. "There were a lot of things changing in my life at that point. Company's future was up in the air and everyone's jobs depended on me. Getting engaged was the easiest choice. Though, I didn't really ask her."

"You *didn't ask her*?" She furrowed her brow. "How does one get engaged without someone asking them the question?"

He let out a gut-deep laugh. "We were walking through a little town with a jeweler and she walked in. I followed her. We ended up designing a ring for her. A few months later, she picked it up from the place and she just never took it off of her ring finger."

"Did you guys talk about being engaged?" Amber asked, as they rolled down the highway toward the city.

"She did. I guess I didn't say anything. So pretty soon it was just a thing. We started planning the wedding and the honeymoon. Unfortunately, my schedule never really allowed for time off. Not then. She didn't like it. She didn't support who I was or what I wanted." He ran his hand over his throat as if just the mere thought of those days threatened to suffocate him.

Amber sighed.

He paused. "Sorry. I didn't mean to talk about her like that." They'd been so young, and neither of them could be blamed for knowing what they wanted...or didn't want. "Clearly, though, it didn't work out between us. It wasn't a pretty breakup. Then I moved to Montana. She tried to talk to me a few times after we broke things off, but no. Just *no*."

Amber glanced at him after a moment. "Have you talked to her lately?"

He tried to think of the last time he had actually responded to one of her calls or texts. "She texted me a few months ago, but I didn't respond. I know she tried to contact Kendra, but my sister would have none of it. I think there were four-letter words exchanged."

He was glad to see a flicker of satisfaction flash over Amber's face. "Did your family not really like her?"

"Meh," he said with a shrug. "They were fine with it—they didn't really want me to get married to her. Yet, they are my family so they went along with the idea. They always support my decisions when it comes to my personal life, but that doesn't mean that they go along with my plans warmly."

"I can see that being a problem with them," she said, tapping her fingers on the wheel. "The united front, like what they presented the detective and I with, can be a bit intimidating."

"Oh." He chuckled. "That wasn't anything. We can be far more unapproachable when we need to be."

She smiled at that admission, but there seemed to be a look of disapproval there, too. "Tammy didn't fit," he continued. "She said she understood what we did, accepted it, but when the rubber hit the road and she was asked to accommodate, it didn't work. That sealed the deal when it came to my family disliking her."

"I definitely understand what having an unconventional job can do to a person's personal life…or, in my case, lack thereof. Long-term relationships are too much work, so sometimes it's easier to ward off *all* relationships."

He wanted to reach over, take her hand and tell her that what he really wanted was a woman just like her—independent, strong, smart, beautiful, soft and a touch brutal when life required it.

Admitting all of that to her would only make it harder when it came to the kiss he was trying to forget. It had been nice, but that was where things needed to stop. To ask for anything more from her or from their situation was only opening the door to pain and not possibilities. He'd learned to be skeptical of love, all thanks to Tammy.

"Right now, I don't know about having a woman in my life." He wasn't sure if he should rip off the Band-Aid or gently tug at the edges when it came to the topic of their situation. "I guess I'm a little gun-shy about jumping into anything. You can see how well it worked for me last time." He laughed nervously.

She sighed and nodded. "I have had some of the same issues in relationships. Not imposed engagements, but significant others that wanted more than I could give. Being in the jobs we are in, I think it's impossible to find someone who *gets it*. I'm going to be gone sometimes. Especially during the hunting season, and I can't say that I've had a relationship that has stood that test.

A man wants a woman who can be there in the night—every night."

"Exactly."

"I can't even imagine what it would be like with both people having jobs like ours," she said, looking over at him. "We probably wouldn't even end up seeing each other in the day, let alone the nights."

How did that adage go…? Death by a thousand paper cuts. Yeah, that may have been preferable right now. He shouldn't have been feeling or thinking about any of these things when all they needed to do was find a bear, and then she would move on to the next call…and disappear from his life.

Thankfully, before they could go any deeper into their nonplausible relationship, they pulled up to the Skaggs Building at the university.

"Do you want to run the hair samples in with me? It may take a few minutes. I'm going to try and see if they can push things through a little quicker than normal, given the circumstances."

AJ's phone pinged in his hand. "Nah, it's okay. You go do your thing. I'll wait out here for you and answer some emails." He lifted his phone for her to see, just as the phone's screen lit up with another message. "It's definitely going to be a workday."

"I get it," she said. "I'll leave the keys in, so you start the truck and keep warm if you like. I'll be as quick as I can, but give me fifteen or so."

He nodded. "Take your time."

She grabbed her hat and put it on, then grabbed her bag and got out. She gave him a little wave as she turned and started to walk toward the large brown building at the edge of the parking lot.

He couldn't help but watch her army green pants stretch over her ass as she walked away. It was hardly the first time he had stared at her ass today, but it was magnetic. She was so sexy. His mouth watered as his thoughts slipped back to last night and how her body had felt in his arms. Hell, she had even tasted perfect.

There was the vibration of his phone, pulling him back just as she stepped behind a line of cars and out of view.

He should have gone with her, but he really did have a list of things to handle this morning. None more pressing than hoping that Baker didn't have anything on him, at least not yet.

Clicking on the screen, he opened up his messenger. Kendra had started texting an hour ago. As their attorney, she needed the truth, and he had made sure to tell her about his seeing the ring and assuming it was Tammy's. She hadn't given away a single spark of emotion at the news. He appreciated that about her—she was all business when she needed to be, and he could trust her to keep things at a professional level. As for everyone else knowing his secret…he had to keep it close to the vest. Even Kendra agreed.

He clicked on her picture. It was a long text, but she reiterated that he wasn't to answer any condemning questions without her present. He knew the game, but it was nice to have a sister who always had his back, legally.

He was going to return her text, but before he had the chance, his phone rang. "Hello?"

"You won't believe it." Kendra sounded breathless, like she had been running.

"What? What's going on?"

"I did a little digging. Tammy had been staying in Missoula. She had a hotel room at the Red Lion."

"Oh…" His stomach dropped, landing somewhere near his boots on the dirty floor mat of the pickup. Tammy had been in Missoula. That meant…the hand could have very well been hers. Kendra, no doubt, knew that just as well as he did. He hated being so unsure of everything, but prepared for the worst-case scenario. For once it would be nice to have some clearly defined answers.

"Are you around this morning?"

"At the ranch? No. I'm in the city with Amber."

"I'm not saying you should meddle in a police investigation, but ideally I would love a peek at the footage from the hotel."

"I don't think it's a great idea if I go anywhere near Tammy's last known location."

"I'm aware," Kendra said, sounding slightly annoyed, "but it would be damned nice to know if she is still standing or not. I don't want you to walk into your meeting with Baker tonight without us knowing exactly what he is going to bring to the table…at least as far as findings."

"You know what I say about going into anything blind," he said, his voice low.

Kendra huffed. "Unless we find out what Tammy had going on…yeah, we are both going to be as good as dead."

Chapter Ten

Amber gave the tech at the lab one last wave before making her way back to her truck, where AJ was waiting—hopefully, that was. Though he had opened up to her about his ex—whom she still wasn't sure why he had brought up—she couldn't help feeling like their growing closer wasn't the best idea. To reveal everything about herself would only draw focus on how different they really were. He was a worldly man with the power to effect wars around the globe while she spent most of her days traveling around the state helping animals.

When he figured out how far apart they were, he would pull away and she would be left in the tailings of his affection. As such, she couldn't open up anymore.

Acknowledging the rationality of her thoughts, she couldn't help the grin that erupted over her features when she spotted AJ talking on his phone, waiting for her.

He had finally opened up to her about his life, and, of course, it was just when they had gotten to the university. How did that kind of thing always seem to happen? Did men just wait for the most inopportune moment to speak their minds, or did it just seem like it was too late, because there was never enough time to ask all the questions that were swirling through her mind? It had to be the latter.

In this case, though, she wasn't sure what she should or shouldn't ask. AJ was a man with secrets, some of which she wasn't sure she wanted to know.

He looked up and their eyes connected. Dipping his head in acknowledgment, he sent her an exhausted smile. Hopefully the tired look in his eyes wasn't there because of her. He had said it was a workday. She knew all too well what that could entail in her world; she couldn't even begin to imagine what all that would mean for a man whose profession and employees spanned the globe.

She slowed down, politely waiting for him to end his phone call before making her way to the truck.

There was a strain in his face, but his eyes widened as he watched her get in. Regardless of what she was feeling and they were saying—or not saying—he liked her. She could sense it in the way he looked at her and the way his body moved toward her when she settled into her seat. There was definitely a pull of some kind between them.

In fact, that was exactly how it had felt when he had been kissing her. She could definitely go for feeling his tongue on hers again.

She clenched her thighs together, tight, as she tried to make the blood rush back up to her brain because clearly, she wasn't thinking with the right part of her body. Work first.

"How'd it go in there?" AJ asked, motioning toward the Skaggs Building.

"It was fine. They said they could get us the test results pretty quick. Less than seventy-two hours."

He nodded like he was thoroughly impressed. "I had no idea they could move it through that fast."

"The tech said their lab could do it in seventy-two. It just depends on what all they have in the system."

"That is pretty amazing." He scratched at his freshly shaven chin for a moment, like he was thinking. "Do you need to take any other calls today?"

She shook her head. "Nope. I need to put up some signs and work through some cases and get statements, but there is nothing that is pressing."

"Could you drop me back at the ranch? I don't expect you to put up with me all day." His words were clearly meant to show that he was being thoughtful, but there was an air to them that made her question if he was just trying to get rid of her. Which was ridiculous, since he'd offered to shadow her today. Had she said something? Or maybe not enough when he'd spoken about his ex…

She kept her tone neutral in an attempt not to sound hurt as she said, "Yeah, I can run you back."

He didn't respond as she started the truck. He was still looking at his phone, like he had been earlier.

"Everything okay?" she asked.

He sighed, glancing up at her. "Not really… I'm stuck. I don't know what to do here."

His admission caught her off guard. The man, the team leader and boss, was letting her in to a moment when *he* didn't know what to do. She was flattered but she tried to play it cool. "What's going on?"

He scrunched his eyes shut and reached up and scratched under the brim of his white cowboy hat. "So, I just got a call."

"Oh?" She sat back in her seat, watching for cars

behind them, but not going anywhere for a minute. "What's up?"

"It was Kendra. You know Tammy? My ex?"

"Kendra is the attorney, right?"

"Yeah."

"Why would she call you about your ex?" And then it hit her. Tammy hadn't just randomly come up in their conversation. Suddenly, the ring on the hand they'd found flashed into her mind. It wasn't that he was trying to deepen their relationship, he was telling her secrets… Secrets that his family was involved in and helping to conceal. "AJ, whose hand was that on the ranch?"

His face turned white. "To be honest, I don't know." There was a long, drawn-out silence. She didn't dare speak. "It is a woman's hand. Like I said."

"But?" She tried not to spit out the word, but there was no stopping.

"The ring on that hand… I've tried to tell myself it wasn't Tammy's, but… That ring… It's probably her engagement ring."

Chapter Eleven

Just like that. His secret was out and now Amber would be out, too. It was too bad. They'd only just met, and yet something about her had calmed him. Both last night and again today, despite his world feeling like it was starting to fall around him, her presence had been a comfort.

They were silent for the next fifteen minutes as she sat in the truck next to him, unmoving except for the occasional slow blinking of her eyes and her steady breathing.

This was purgatory.

Finally, she turned to him, their gazes meeting. "I think it's best if I take you back to your ranch."

His stomach, somewhere already on the truck's mat, sank even lower. "I'm sorry, Amber." There was a quake in his voice. "I should have told you right away, but I was hoping that ring wasn't the same one. I still am."

"You knew the moment you saw it. You chose to keep the secret from me." She was deadly calm as she spoke, and it was more terrifying than if she had been screaming. When he didn't respond, she continued in that tone. "Everything you have done since you met me has been calculated, and—"

"Whoa. No. That's absolutely not true. I just…"

"It's okay. You don't owe me anything. You don't owe me an explanation now, either. You did what you did, and I can guess why. I don't need tired excuses or justifications." She made her way out onto the road.

"Amber… Please, don't," he begged. "I'm so sorry."

She lifted her hand, beckoning him to stop.

There was no doubt in his mind that if he didn't take this chance, riding with her back to the ranch, that he wouldn't get another to make up for what he had done. She was right, though. He had made the choice to keep her in the dark.

"I know you say you understand why I did what I did, but just know… I didn't want it to be her hand out there." He sucked in a long breath before continuing. "And I promise, on my mother's grave, that I didn't have anything to do with it being on our property. I'm still hoping it's not her hand. Yet, the fact that Detective Baker wants to talk to me… I'm thinking that it's probably her…that they've got a positive ID. It's eating me up."

Amber cringed at his words. "You swear… You absolutely *promise* that you didn't have a thing to do with hurting her?"

He nodded and put his hand over his heart in sincerity. "Amber, I promise."

Her shoulders relaxed and she slowed the truck down. "When was the last time you talked to her, really?"

He shrugged. "Like I told you before, months ago. She had texted and called, but I didn't respond."

"But she has your phone number?"

"She does. Tammy and I ended on a crappy note, but

that doesn't mean I hated her or that I wished anything but the best for her."

Amber pursed her lips. If anything, she seemed torn. That, he could understand. He reached over and put out his hand, palm up, offering himself to her. "Amber, I wasn't using you. I wasn't keeping you in the dark on purpose. I just… I was *stupid*."

She hesitated for a moment, but then reached over and took his hand. "Please, promise me one thing…" she said, begging him with a look. "No more secrets."

He tensed. "Amber, my world is all secrets, but I will promise that I will not keep anything from you that you need to know."

She frowned, clearly not loving his answer, but she eventually nodded. "I get it, but I can't do *this*—" she motioned to each of them "—if we can't be open. Well, *open-ish*. I know that your work requires certain amounts of limitations, but when it comes to here and our lives, I need to know everything about this case. And so you are aware, I wasn't judging you, AJ." Amber looked at him with a pleading expression.

"You absolutely were judging, Amber." He squeezed her hand like he was trying to make it okay. "And it's understandable that you would judge. I've done a lot of things I'm not proud of in my life. Yet, if we try to date, I'll never do anything to hurt you."

She gave him a gentle smile, like she heard the well-intentioned promise, one he couldn't keep. "Let me think about this—*us*."

He slipped his hand from hers. He wanted to tell her she could trust him. And that he really would do nothing to hurt her, and yet he knew from his many experiences on the battlefield when a battle was lost. He had been stupid for even thinking that he should approach the topic of being together. She could do better than a man like him. Besides, now she knew more about him than just about anyone, and he couldn't blame her for not wanting to be a part of any of it. If someone came at him with what he was trying to sell her, he would've run. In fact, he was surprised she was even still in the truck.

"And, hey, maybe it's better if we just don't do this, but… Yeah." He stared out the window, consumed by the awkwardness between them. Maybe this was part of the reason he didn't do relationships. He definitely wasn't good at talking about them.

"Did your sister say anything else about Tammy?" Amber asked, dispelling some of the awkward tension between them and changing the subject.

"She said that Tammy had been staying at the Red Lion."

"We could go see if she's there," Amber said, motioning in the direction of the hotel.

"I don't think it's a good idea for me to be seen anywhere close to Tammy's last known location. You know the detective would have a field day with that."

Amber's features tightened. "You know, if things go squirrely, the detective and his team are going to be watching that security footage at the hotel pretty closely." Amber tapped on the steering wheel, but she turned in the direction of the hotel downtown. "Then again, if it's not her out there in the woods, we'll have an answer whether she's alive if we go over there and knock on the door and she opens it."

He hadn't thought of it that way. If they were making this all into something it wasn't, they would look like fools. They needed to do a little recon—if nothing else, it would give them some peace of mind.

"Plus, thinking about this from the detective's point of view... As far as you telling me the truth about the ring, I think it's going to be helpful. Clearly, you're willing to work with law enforcement so it's not like you're concealing things. That being said, you definitely should tell the detective about the ring when you meet with him. He's probably going to ask you questions as to why you didn't give him the information earlier. So be prepared."

"If he starts asking any condemning questions, Kendra already made it clear that I'm to call her for representation."

"I have to say, from a law-enforcement standpoint, I hate when people lawyer up," Amber said. "However, from a civilian perspective, you're so lucky to have a lawyer as a sister, do you know that?"

"Oh, I'm more than aware. She has saved our asses for the last couple years now." He sighed. Brick buildings passed by as they made their way downtown. "My sister was actually shot once. She was the victim of domestic violence. Now she has started to make it her mission to help women who are in situations like where she once found herself. I'm really proud of her."

"As you should be. That is amazing." Amber shook her head slightly, like she was in disbelief.

"What?" he asked.

She stopped and let a man cross the street in front of them. "Is there anyone in your family who isn't just amazingly accomplished?" She laughed. "Seriously, the more you talk about them, the more intimidated I become."

"You weren't intimidated just by the fact that we were contractors?" he asked, with a laugh.

"Oh, for sure. I guess, though, knowing you were a contractor was fine, so long as your weapons weren't pointed at me."

He was strangely comforted. There were women who liked being with men who were in different areas of special operations and special forces, but finding women who were into what many looked at as mercenaries, or spies, was a little bit more of a challenge. Again, it came down to the unpredictable lifestyle. She seemed to understand that, though, and it only made him want her more. However, her being resistant to the idea of a relationship really was good for both of them.

She pulled to a stop a block down from the Red Lion, but within view of their parking lot.

"The SUV right there," he said pointing at a white Pathfinder. "That's her car."

Though he had known Tammy could be creeping back into his world, until now, he had been keeping some irrational hope that it was nothing more than his own imagination. Yet, seeing her car with the dent just above the left rear-wheel quarter panel, where Tammy had backed into a pole on their third date, and the scratch where she had opened the back into a trailer hitch… It brought everything she had been and all of the old feelings he'd packed away back into the light. Damn, if he didn't want to run away.

Chapter Twelve

Detective Baker could hardly be called intimidating. It wasn't that the man wasn't capable—AJ was damn sure that if he needed to be, the guy could make a grown-ass man piss himself, but for the most part, he just seemed nonchalant. Everything about him, from the way he leaned back in his chair and threw his arm over the one next to him when he laughed, to the way he seemed to constantly wear a low-grade smile, was almost *inviting*. That fact might have been what disarmed people and made the man good at his job.

"So, you think the ring may have belonged to your ex-fiancée?" Baker asked, his peg tooth shimmering thanks to the pendant lights hanging over the island in AJ's little cabin.

AJ liked how Baker carefully picked his words. They weren't incriminating or accusatory, just a statement of what may or may not have been the case.

"Yeah," AJ said, glancing at Amber, who was casually sitting beside Baker on one of the barstools.

Baker looked over at Amber and tapped his fingers on the top of the empty chair next to him. "And he told you about this ring this morning, without you prompting?"

Amber nodded.

There was a pregnant pause, as if Baker was trying to make heads or tails of the information they had given him.

"What kind of relationship did you and Tammy have?" Baker asked.

AJ thought for a long moment, but all he could think about was the moment they had said goodbye in person for the last time. It had been in Louisiana, while he had been overseeing contractors. She had come down to visit him and the entire weekend had been nothing but a hellacious fight. "Our relationship unraveled from the inside. I wasn't there when she needed me, and I couldn't be upset for her feeling that way."

"Were there a lot of hurt feelings…? Hers or yours?" Baker asked, but his body language shifted slightly, and he leaned in, tenting his fingers in front of him like he was listening intently and genuinely concerned.

AJ knew that game entirely too well; he had taken his fair share of interrogation courses over the years, too. No matter what Baker came at him with, though, he felt comfortable in the knowledge that he had nothing to hide…at least when it came to his personal life.

"She initiated the breakup and seemed to move on with her life. That was two or three years ago." He looked over at Amber. "I also told her, Amber, all about this," he said, motioning to her with a smile before looking back at Baker. "I am happy to be an open book when it comes to everything to do with Tammy."

"Then why did you not tell me about the ring last night? Why did you wait?" Baker asked.

"Like I said, I was hoping I was wrong." He put his palms down on the island, the stone cold against his hot skin. He wanted to tell Baker that he also felt the need to protect STEALTH first, to follow the chain of command there in order to protect secrets that went back generations and crossed oceans. Everything happening here had the potential to open a veritable Pandora's box of issues. He had to be careful. "Hell, I may actually be wrong. I hope I am, but then I was told about Tammy being here in town, I knew the odds were stacked in favor of it being Tammy's ring."

"Did you see her while she was here in town?" Baker asked.

AJ shrugged. "Like I said, I only just found out she was here. After that, Amber and I ran over to the hotel and I did see her car."

"But you never saw Tammy today or any other time in the last few weeks?" Baker continued.

Amber's eyes were wide and she opened her mouth to speak, as though she wanted to say something in AJ's defense. He gave her a tiny shake of the head. He appreciated that she wanted to help him, but this was something he was going to have to handle.

"I have had nothing to do with her. She reached out a few times over the years since we broke up, but I didn't talk to her. You are welcome to look over my phone records, if you like."

Baker nodded. "I appreciate that."

"I've been really up front with you. Now I hope you're willing to be up front with me as well," AJ said, staring down Baker. "You called this meeting today. What were you hoping to learn? Or, was there something you wanted to tell me?"

The detective had a guilty smile. "You know, you and I make pretty damned good friends. I can see we speak the same language."

"You mean that we don't blow smoke?" AJ asked with a laugh. "You got that right. I've been at my game, and you've been at yours, for long enough that we don't have to dance around subjects."

Baker tilted back his head with a laugh, and the action made his paunch jiggle. He definitely had the body type of a detective. For a moment, AJ wondered if the gut was a requirement of the job, or if it just naturally came with the gig over time. As much as he judged the guy, he definitely understood how a person's job could both physically and emotionally change them.

"So, are you going to tell me why you called this meeting?"

Baker turned to Amber. "Miss Daniels, I appreciate you being here for this, but I would like to talk to AJ alone for a minute, if you wouldn't mind?" he asked, but there wasn't really a question as much as there was an order.

"Absolutely, I'll be outside." Amber got up from her seat, and as she moved AJ noticed the sweat around her vest.

She must have been feeling as nervous as him. It made him wonder why. He had been as honest with her as possible. Knowing what she did about him, it seemed like she should have been reassured that he would make it out of this line of questioning without too much of a problem. Maybe she saw something in him or in his demeanor that set off alarm bells, and if she saw it... then Baker definitely would.

He pinched the inside of his palm as he tried to control himself and his desire to start explaining all the ways he was innocent. Honest people reacted to interrogation in a variety of ways, but the most common was indignation, and another was candor. While he could act indignant that Baker was calling his life and actions into question, he would never sell outrage. He could understand why Baker was asking the questions he was, so pretending anything else would come off as false.

Amber put her hand on his shoulder and gave it a reassuring squeeze before walking out of the cabin. The door clicked shut behind her.

Baker watched behind him before turning back. "Amber is a great woman, good warden, but I don't want you not to be able to tell me something just because you are uncomfortable."

That was a damn good reason for him to ask her to step out, not to mention the fact he had made sure to validate her job performance.

No. I can't keep going down this maniacal tunnel of overthinking.

This was a terrible habit, but then it had saved his ass just as many times as it had been a hindrance.

"Like I said, here to help. Whatever you need to do to get what you need, I am happy to acquiesce." He put his hands up in supplication, a simple gesture but a powerful one.

"Much appreciated." Baker tapped his fingers together. "I actually came here because of a phone call I received."

AJ nodded, but all the questions rolled through his mind and forced him to pinch the skin of his palm harder. Instead of speaking up, he allowed Baker to run the show.

"Do you know if Tammy had a child or children?"

AJ felt the blood rush from his face. "No. None that I know of…why?"

"We did a search of Tammy's hotel room today. Apparently, your ex… Tammy had a child. A boy named Charlie. He is two years old. And, you were named as the boy's father on a notecard we found."

A stiff breeze could have knocked him over. He had a son. A boy he'd never known existed. He'd not even considered being a father before. Not really.

Wait—if they searched Tammy's hotel room in the first place, did that mean the cops had ID'd the hand?

He couldn't think straight.

Was he a father?

Holy crap…

He did the quick math in his head. If the baby was two, it was definitely possible that he could have been the boy's father, but he doubted Tammy wouldn't have told him. They hadn't hated each other that much, bad breakup aside.

In fact, he and Tammy had talked about having children on a few occasions, but their talks always dissipated once they started really delving into what the needs of a child would entail—who would be responsible for feeding and caring for the newborn baby around the clock? When they'd been together, he was gone more than he was home and all the burden had fallen on her. He hadn't blamed her for not wanting a family with him, and yet…

"Yeah, I don't think that can be true." AJ ran his hand over his face as if he could wipe away all the possibilities with the action. "You guys haven't found out anything about the remains, have you? Did you even find any more remains or was the hand the only part?"

"Slow down. Let's deal with one thing at a time." Baker stood up and walked to the sink. He grabbed a glass out of his cupboard and poured a glass of water, then handed it over to AJ. "Here, take a drink. I can tell this came as quite a shock for you."

AJ nodded in appreciation as he took the glass and took a long drink. Tammy had damn well never said a word about a kid. If she had, he would have done the right thing. He would have taken the kid into his life, been a father in every way that Tammy would have allowed him to be. Hell, he would have loved to have had a kid.

"So, back to my original line of questions, AJ. Did you and Tammy have an antagonistic relationship? One where she would have wanted to keep the existence of a child secret from you?"

He stiffened. "She didn't like the work my family does, and she knew I wouldn't be around a lot." AJ's voice threatened to give out as all the reasons he wouldn't have made a good father came rushing to the forefront of his mind.

Maybe she had just thought he wasn't up to the task.

That hurt more than learning about the boy.

"*Is* the child really mine?" He choked on the words as he spoke.

"To be clear, we are just trying to get as much information as possible." Baker sat back down in his chair, but there was an apologetic look upon his wide face. "As such, I wanted to talk to you before we pull out all the stops to find the child to see if you might possibly know where he would be located."

"I didn't even know I had a kid. How would I know where to find him?" AJ asked. "It's just…none of this makes any sense."

For the first time since their conversation had started, Baker didn't seem capable of looking him in the eye.

"What aren't you telling me?" AJ asked.

Baker jerked, his eyebrows rose and he looked slightly thrown that he had been caught in his attempt to suppress information. "You didn't have anything to do with Tammy's hand being found on your ranch, did you? Maybe so you could gain custody of your child without a long, drawn-out legal battle that could possibly put your family in the public eye?"

"What in the actual hell? Are you kidding me? What a load of…" He struggled to keep his temper under control. "This," he said, motioning between them, "is the first time I'm hearing about a kid. Mine, or otherwise." He pursed his lips, then let out his breath in an attempt to regain composure, when all he wanted to do was find out who would ever say such a thing about him. "And you are absolutely crazy if you think I'd intentionally hurt a woman I loved. We may not be together anymore, but that doesn't mean I just stopped caring about her."

Baker nodded. "From what I know about you and your family, I don't doubt what you are telling me. I'm satisfied that you didn't know about this boy or his mother. As for the hand…" The man looked down at his own as hands he opened and closed them into loose fists. "I had our forensics team pull the fingerprints."

There was that feeling again, the sensation of all the blood rushing from his body and pooling on the floor. In a moment of being irrational, he wondered if he stood up and walked away if he would actually leave bloody footprints in his wake.

"Was it her?" His question was simple, but those words held every hope and fear in his entire being.

"Unfortunately, it appears as though the hand *did* belong to her. We can't say for certain, but we believe she is likely deceased."

Just like that, what remained of his quaking resolve gave way and he dropped to his knees. It was one hell of a feeling to have his life unravel.

Chapter Thirteen

There had been very few times Amber could recall when she had heard a man sob. One was when her brother had passed away, and she had been there to hold her father's hand when the nurses shared the news. Her father had gone to pieces in a way that she had never before witnessed and never wanted to see again.

From inside the cabin, she could hear a noise like that of her father's and it made her heart threaten to shatter. She walked to the door and held the knob, not sure if she should go in and take care of AJ in his moment of need, or stay outside and be here for him in the moment of his choosing.

If he was anything like her stoic father, he would never want her to see him broken. AJ had shown her how strong he was from the moment she had first met him out in the timber. If she ran to him now, he would be just as likely to shirk from her touch as he was to fall into it.

She could only imagine what Baker had said to him behind these closed doors to make him fall to pieces like this, but she wanted to punch her fellow officer in the nose for hurting AJ.

Without realizing it, she had been gripping the handle so hard that her hand was shaking.

She couldn't do this. She couldn't stand out here in the cold when AJ so clearly needed her. Yet, if she went in there and took him in her arms like she wanted to, the nature of their relationship would definitely come into question. She had come here to do a job and was already too close to the man she had been working with—that kind of thing was taboo. Until now, she hadn't feared losing her job over it, but if she made it obvious, she very well could find herself in the HR office at the regional headquarters by the end of the week.

Still, that wasn't reason enough to stop her from going to him.

Without giving it another thought, she opened the door. Baker was standing beside AJ; his hand was on his shoulder, and when she walked in, Baker looked up. There was a pained expression on his face.

"What happened?"

"The hand...is Tammy's," AJ said, looking up at her. He ran the back of his hand under his nose, which was running. There were tear streaks on his cheeks and the sight of him in such a state pulled at her heartstrings.

She nearly snarled at the detective. "Go grab him a Kleenex." She pointed in the direction of the bathroom.

The detective opened his mouth like he was going to argue, but after looking at her, he seemed to think better of it before doing as she said.

She moved to AJ's side. "Just because they gave us a positive ID on the hand, it doesn't mean she's dead."

"You and I both know she is dead." AJ pulled in a deep breath like he could regain his composure in a single inhale.

She put her hands on his shoulders and stared into his eyes. "You are going to be okay. No matter what happens, I'm here for you. We've got this."

"There might be a kid out there... *My kid*." He choked on the words and tears started to well in his eyes. "Baker asked if I had anything to do with Tammy's possible death for custody reasons."

A chill skittered through her. *A child?* A *child* he hadn't thought to tell her about...who might be missing. Her fingers trembled as she pushed away a tear that had broken through his resolve. Her heart broke for him, but she didn't know what to say. There was nothing in anyone's life that could prepare a person for a moment like this. Not only had he just lost a woman who had once meant a great deal to him, but he might have also just lost a son.

A son he hadn't mentioned to her. Had he been lying to her and stringing her along this whole time?

She tried to tell herself he wouldn't do that to her, that he hadn't been using her and this was all just a misunderstanding, but she struggled.

She started to step away from him, but before she could, he reached up and held her in place.

"I didn't know I had a son. I had no idea. I still don't even know if it's true."

From behind her, Baker cleared his throat. "He is telling you the truth."

Turning to the detective, she couldn't help the sneer that registered on her lips. "Did you look into the allegations before you just hit him with this?" she snapped.

"As much as I could," Baker said, giving her a look of understanding and pity.

She hated that look. He had no right to completely

overturn AJ's life in such a way without a positive ID. She was absolutely furious, and every word came out like a spent round, each narrowly missing her intended target as Baker never seemed to waiver. "You need to get out there, do the legwork. How dare you come here and break him like this?"

"Miss Daniels… Amber." Baker said her name like it was an apology. "I didn't come here to hurt him, or anyone for that matter. It is just an unfortunate part of my job that sometimes I have to be the bearer of some damn hard truths and even harder allegations." He didn't move any closer to her.

She appreciated that the man could tell that he was almost within striking range and knew to keep his distance. She wasn't sure that she could completely control her rage, no matter how much she understood that he wasn't the person she should be targeting and she was here as a guest out of professional courtesy. He was only the messenger and as much as she hated this, he was doing his job and asking the required questions to keep the public and the ranch safe.

No one had to like them, least of all *her*.

Just like that, she was pulled back to reality and it hit her harder than she could have expected. This wasn't her battle. No matter how much she cared about AJ, he could have been lying to everyone. He could have been playing her right now and she could have been acting like a fool for a man who was using her.

Yet, everything in her gut told her that this was real. That AJ was a broken man and not just putting on an act for her and Baker's benefit.

She pulled herself back from AJ. At the very least, she needed to talk to Baker alone. As much as she hated this, she and Baker were on the same team. "We need a word." She pushed past Baker as she motioned for him to follow her outside.

As he stepped outside, she slammed the door behind them. She walked out into the falling night to the middle of the road that led to the different cabins. Spinning around, she came face-to-face with the barrel-chested man. "Why didn't you notify me of your findings? I thought I was a part of this investigation."

The battle-hardened detective looked her in the eyes. "You are, but we both know that your capacity for this is limited. I know you are angry and you feel that I was working behind your back. But you need to be objective." He gave her arms a light, reassuring squeeze. "This situation is outside of your job requirements. I can tell that you and AJ Spade are something more than work colleagues, and I'd be remiss if I didn't tell you what a terrible idea I think that is. Yet, I don't think it's going to matter to you. Not with you looking at me like you are."

Some of the anger seemed to seep out of her as the man's words struck her like a fist to the gut. Amber wasn't sure what had made her think that confronting the detective was a good idea, but she felt like a mama bear going straight to rage and attack when it came to protecting her cubs. AJ definitely wasn't her cub, yet she couldn't help the instinct to protect him…even from a bear who was professionally far larger and more powerful than herself.

At least Baker was kind in his rebuff of her charge. However, just because he'd spoken to her like this, it didn't assuage her anger, at least not completely.

"You… This… You should have told me," she said,

trying to gain control over her words as feebly as she could gain control over her feelings. "I was the first officer on the case, after all." And how dare he blindside AJ with this information? They could've broken it to him together.

Baker cupped her shoulder like he must have done every time he delivered bad news and the motion reminded her of her father the day her brother died. She hated the feeling and the memories it sparked.

"I couldn't tell you, or anyone else, until I went in there and got a good read on him. I needed to know he wasn't the one pulling the strings here."

She exhaled, hard. "And? What did you get?" Every cell of her being silently prayed that Baker had come to the same conclusions about AJ and his integrity as she had.

Baker's brow furrowed, as though he was trying to attempt to reconcile his thoughts and his feelings. "I think AJ is a good man. He tries to do the right thing and his heart is in the right place. Yet, that doesn't mean he isn't guilty of wrongdoing here, Amber."

Until now, she hadn't realized she was crying, but hot tears rolled down her cheeks like the punches she wanted to throw. She shook her head, as if she could shake away the truth of what he'd just said.

"Don't misunderstand me." Baker gripped her hand, hard. "I don't think AJ killed Tammy. My gut is saying he isn't behind this. He wouldn't be stupid enough to leave a trail."

"Did he know about the boy?" she asked.

Baker shook his head. "There's no way. I think what really broke him was when I told him about the note Tammy had left behind, saying he was the father. He had no idea that Charlie existed—and as for the allegations that he might have killed her. *Never.*"

She exhaled and her grip loosened on the detective.

"Amber, as a fellow law enforcement officer, I'm asking you to help out on this case. We need to find out if this boy is dead or alive. If not, AJ may see jail time for this."

From behind Detective Baker, AJ walked outside. Up the road, by the main house, there was the sound of truck engine revving to life.

Dollars to donuts, AJ had called Zoey. He could see her through the front window the closer the vehicle got. Hell, his whole entire family was probably already in the know…and they were all coming to his side, ready to find the missing child.

It was one hell of a family and team that would come to the aid of their brother and teammate like this when he needed them all the most. She would give almost anything to be a part of a world like this—a world in which a family stood together.

The truck pulled to a stop beside them and Zoey came out with two other men that Amber recognized as Mike and Troy, AJ's brothers.

"What in the hell is going on?" Zoey charged toward the detective. "Did you talk to Kendra?" Zoey looked over at AJ, who was standing on the edge of the porch, a stunned expression on his face. "AJ, did you call Kendra?"

He nodded.

"Good," Zoey said, turning back to Baker. "You're a friend of ours, yes?"

Baker nodded, and for the first time since she had known the man, he looked slightly afraid.

"I don't want you to do a damned thing, or call a single person, until we get more info about this boy. Do you understand?" Zoey stared down the detective like he was a disobedient child and not the only person who stood between AJ being arrested or being cleared of any wrongdoing.

Baker nodded. "You know I have a job to do here, too."

Amber stepped back from Baker and let Zoey move closer. "And what do you think that job is, right now?" Zoey growled. "Tammy is dead."

"Is she?" Baker asked, sounding like he had just found a little store of bravery.

"Only you would know that, Baker, but we all know that this now needs to be treated like a possible crime scene."

Baker nodded. "Yes."

"We won't stand in your way. We want to get to the bottom of Tammy's *possible death*. We are going to work with you, and do everything—and I mean *everything*—to get answers. Yes?" Zoey asked, leading him to the answers by his nose.

Baker nodded.

"Give us twenty-four hours to get to the bottom of this, and then you can have this all back. Do we have a deal?"

"Zoey, you know I can't do that," Baker said.

"Why can't you? First, we don't even know if she is alive or dead. Seems like there is no actual crime to speak of—that being said, you can keep your men out here on the ranch, but I want you to go inactive for the time." When Baker started shaking his head, she gave him an imploring look. "Please. You know we have the team and resources to do this, and if this boy is one of ours—" she glanced at AJ "—then we're not going to sit back and do nothing. We can help you. Whatever we find, we will give you. All I'm asking is that you get out of the way and let us do what we do best. In return, everyone will get the answers they need…and justice will be done."

Chapter Fourteen

AJ knew all too well how quickly a life could change— a car accident, a diagnosis, a proposal or even a phone call. He had been on the end of far too many life-changing moments, both receiving and giving. Yet they all paled in comparison to the secret the detective had shared—AJ was likely a father.

Not only had he been thrust into a new life, a new definition of himself, but he was also forced to face the fact that his baby was also at risk. In his wildest imaginings, he would have never gotten to this point. This was worse than a nightmare—at least in nightmares, a person could wake up.

Until now, he hadn't hated Tammy. He had moments when he'd disliked her, and he had been relieved that she was no longer a part of his life, but now a sense of loathing filled him. This secret—or rather, this *lie*— didn't just affect her, or even himself. Her not telling him about the child had also hurt the baby.

He thought of all of his nieces and nephews, now more than five of them, who would have loved to meet Charlie and incorporate him into their life here on the ranch. Tammy had denied him that. She'd denied his entire family the chance to meet one of their own.

"AJ?" Amber asked, her voice gentle and supplicating, as though she could sense the war within him and feared catching a stray round.

"Hmm?" Words failed him.

Since she had come to his rescue with the detective, he had been barely able to speak. Thankfully, she seemed to understand that he had reverted back to a guttural, instinctive language—it was the dialect of a pain so severe it could only be called transformative agony.

"Zoey wants to talk to you in her office. Do you think you are up to going in there?"

He hated that he had been brought to his knees, but nothing in his life had prepared him for a moment like this—a moment that went far beyond betrayal.

Amber held out her hand and he put his fingers in hers. He stood up from the couch. The fire in the fireplace was crackling and it was emitting tongues of light that lashed over the floor like they were reaching for him and wanting to consume what little was left.

He couldn't give in to his pain. He couldn't. It had been more than half a day now. Sleep had been impossible, but luckily Amber had drifted into a slumber in his arms and had gotten some rest. Even in what could have been a peaceful moment, all he had found himself thinking about was all the nights he had lost in his son's life, nights when the baby had been down with a cold or an ear infection. Nights when he should have been holding him in his arms.

He followed Amber blindly, thinking only of how he was going to get to his son.

He swallowed back the lump in his throat that seemed to rise every time he thought about making it to the toddler, only to find out it was too late.

Amber knocked on the office door, and they made their way inside. The room hadn't really changed much since he had been in it the other day, and yet he felt as though he was in another world. Even the pictures on the screens seemed to take on a different, more ominous feel.

Zoey looked at him and then pulled out a chair and motioned for him to sit down, like he was some kind of invalid. His boss wasn't the kind to feel sorry for anyone, and she certainly wasn't the kind to take it easy on a person, so the look of pity on her face when she glanced at him threatened to shred what little resolve he had left.

Damn it. He wasn't this man.

He didn't get dropped to his knees like this.

Still, here he was.

"Amber told me about the notecard. I tried to get a copy of it from Baker, but it's a no-go for right now as this is a possible criminal investigation. Regardless, it's going to be okay," Zoey said as he took a seat.

Amber moved beside him like she was guarding him against any further pain—if only she could have. If only life took pity on those it inhabited, but it was a cruel master. Still, he appreciated it. Once again, she was proving to be a comfort to him when he needed it most.

"Find anything?" he asked, his voice hoarse and raspy.

Zoey sent him an odd, kind smile that didn't seem to fit her face. No one was being themselves and it was all because of him. He hated this.

He cleared his throat. It had been a long night and he had given himself to the feelings that coursed through him—now he needed to keep moving forward. It was the time for work.

"We managed to find a record of Charlie." Zoey motioned toward the computer screen at the center of her work area. There, on the screen, was a picture of a baby. It looked as though it had been pulled from a hospital's birth announcement page. "His birthday is April twenty-seventh. There was no paternity test and no father named on the birth certificate, but from what we know, he could definitely be yours."

He stared at the boy's chubby cheeks. The blond baby was sucking on his fist and gazing up with unfocused blue eyes. AJ never thought newborn babies were cute, but this little one was different than most he had seen. He was plump and round instead of the nearly translucent hairy creatures that cried any time he was near.

He also never thought newborn babies looked like one parent or the other, but as he looked at the infant, he could make out the almond-shaped eyes that often went hand in hand with the people of his family.

There was no question. This little being was his. AJ could just feel it…and just like he could feel the boy's life force, or whatever it was that he intrinsically picked up on, he also already loved him.

"Charlie," he said, putting his hands on the edge of the computer screen as though he could reach through the screen and touch the baby's soft skin.

"Charles Alexander Reynolds," Zoey said, touching his arm gently as she said his given first name. "You and Tammy may have had your problems, but she gave him your first name as his middle one."

Amber smiled over at him. "Your name is Alexander?"

He nodded as he dropped his hand from the screen

and turned toward her. "Yeah, Alexander James. My family has just always called me AJ." He looked back at the baby on the screen. "I know this is crazy, Zoey, but would you mind printing me that picture?"

She sat down at her computer and a second later, there was the sound of a printer.

Amber slipped her hand into his and gave it a squeeze. "Are you okay?" she asked, putting her head against his shoulder.

"I will be, when we find him." He reached up and gave her a gentle hug.

Zoey grabbed the picture from the printer and handed it to him.

Taking it, he stared down at the little cherubic face. This was his baby, and in a way, this was the first time he was actually touching him. Emotions pooled within him and tears welled in his eyes, threatening to spill once again.

He hated that he cried. It absolutely floored him that within hours he had gone from a man who could unleash hell on his enemies to a man weeping over a baby.

Thankfully, Amber didn't seem to judge him poorly. She really was too good for him.

"We are going to age him up, and then run a facial-recognition program and see if we can pull anything about his location online. From there, we are going to go through all of Tammy's information and contact what few family members she has left. So far, we've found her social-media locations and run a geofence based on her phone's last known locations." Zoey picked up a piece of paper from the desk by her keyboard. "We came up with these coordinates."

There was a series of numbers on the paper she handed him.

"Her phone went dark four days ago. I'm thinking that gives us a window of a few days for when she went missing."

"Do you have any indication that Charlie was with her at that time?" His mind went to the predator that had set this all into motion. If Tammy had been killed by the griz…

A bear would usually go after the more vulnerable prey. A two-year-old would definitely not put up a fight.

The thought made him sick to his stomach.

Amber squeezed his arm and took the piece of paper with the coordinates. "We will look into these, but first we need to go out and check on our trap."

He pulled his arm out of her grasp. Though he shouldn't have been irritated that a bear would take precedence, he couldn't help his irritation. "Who cares about the damned bear?" He shouldn't have been rubbed wrong by her words but he couldn't help it. "Screw the bear. I have a kid to worry about."

She stepped back from him and her face fell, along with her shoulders. "I… Why don't you just stay here? I can run out there and then you can use this time to help Zoey." She flashed a look at Zoey.

He had hurt her. "Amber…" He groaned. "I'm sorry. I didn't mean it like that. I just…"

She shook her head as she peered at the floor. "You're fine. The bear is my job, anyway."

He reached for her, but she gently pulled away.

As she turned away, he thought he saw pain in her expression. He was such an ass. She had come here to help him and his family, and now he was sniping at her.

From the second she had stepped foot on the ranch, all she'd done had been for him. He'd had no right to lose his patience with her, even if he was struggling.

Zoey tipped her head in Amber's direction and motioned for him to go after her, but he shook his head. He needed to be here, in the office, where the magic happened in finding his son. As though Zoey could read his thoughts, she mouthed, *It's fine. Go.*

He shook his head. He wanted to be with Amber—that wasn't a question—but somewhere out there was a little boy who might need him even more.

Walking over, Zoey pushed him toward the door leading outside. "Amber, wait!" she called after her.

Amber stopped as she made her way to her pickup. "You coming?" she asked Zoey.

She shook her head. "AJ is. He'll be right out."

"Damn it, Zoey," he whispered so only she could hear. "I need to help find Charlie."

"You aren't going to be able to do anything in this office that I can't. Plus, I have our whole tech crew working from around the world. Just go apologize and try to clear your head out there. If you don't, you will regret it."

There were a million moments he regretted in his life, but he was glad that his boss was helping him from regretting this one. Amber was special; there was no denying that. No matter what he did here, though, he couldn't help the nagging feeling in his gut that he was doing the wrong thing and making the wrong choice.

Zoey pushed him outside. "We've got this. Trust your team. Just go look into the pins and let me know if you find anything. In the meantime, know that there is no stone that our team will leave unturned."

Though he wanted to find peace in Zoey's words, he found only confusion. She had no right to turn him away when it came to his role in finding his son, but then she was his boss—so she did.

He exhaled, his breath making a cloud of visible emotions in the cold night. Every bit of that mist was a demon that he was fighting. Unfortunately, no matter how much he tried, he would never be done fighting within himself.

Amber was waiting for him inside the truck when he got in. She was silent as she put the truck in Drive and they bumped down the snowy road, which was now so well-traveled that there were deep ruts filled with icy potholes that were shattered and left jagged by tires.

"I am sorry about losing my temper back there," he said. "That's not like me." *But nothing about this situation is normal.*

Amber sent him a soft smile. "I know you're going through a lot. I can only imagine all of the things you must be thinking and feeling." She hesitated for a moment before she continued. "And I realize that you don't need me bringing any more stress to your life. So as soon as we are done, I think I should head out."

That was the last thing he wanted. He wanted her to stand by his side and tell him everything was going to be okay, and that they were going to find his son and the boy would be healthy and safe. It was unexplainable, but he felt letting her go from the ranch would be letting her go from his life, and he wasn't ready to say goodbye just yet.

Surprisingly, as they drove to the area where they had set the bear trap, it appeared that no one else was in the area. Detective Baker had pulled out his entire team. The man really must have had the utmost faith that he was innocent. AJ appreciated it.

Baker really did have his back. It felt good knowing that the detective was a man of his word. Now he just hoped that they didn't let him down.

In the distance, in the trees, the bear trap was obscured in the shadows. From where they had parked, he couldn't tell whether or not the trap had been sprung, but from the tense look on Amber's face, he grew concerned.

She turned off the pickup and stepped out, but as she did, he noticed her putting her hand to her sidearm, instinctually. He followed suit, reaching down to his ankle holster, and pulled out his Glock, before stepping out of the truck.

"Is everything okay?" he asked, moving to her side.

She nudged her chin in the direction of the trap. "Houston, I think we have a bear."

He'd never been one to be afraid of wild animals, but the thought of walking up on a bear seemed like it was against his better judgment. "Do we need to call in your team?"

"If this is the collared bear we are after, we're going to have to make some phone calls. We need to find out if it is your bear first, then we can work on getting it released in a different location. That is, if it's not a *known* nuisance bear."

"You okay releasing this bear if it had something to do with Tammy's death?"

Amber stopped moving, and looked him dead in the eyes. "Without knowing the circumstances of Tammy's potential death, this is going to be tough." Her hand dropped from her gun, and she seemed to have taken pause. "We have two options. We can euthanize the bear, and do an analysis of its stomach contents... But even that wouldn't tell us if the bear was responsible in her death or if it was merely scavenging. Or, we can simply treat the bear like a nontroublesome animal and relocate it."

The answer seemed obvious to him. There was no sense in euthanizing a bear that may or may not have had some impact on Tammy's death. If the bear was simply doing what bears do, and scavenging on the remains, it didn't seem right to penalize the animal.

"Before we make any choices," Amber said, "let's just get up there and make sure we even have a bear inside."

The trees around them whined and moaned as they slowly made their way to the steel culvert trap. The world around them was eerily quiet, and even though they were walking in the tracks left by her truck, their shoes squeaked on the cold snow. This morning's temperatures were brutally cold.

It was a little bit of a surprise that with this level of cold, a bear would have been out of its den. He'd always been taught as a kid that bears hibernated. As such, he would've thought they were sleeping nonstop through the winter.

"Is it normal for bears to be this quiet, when they're trapped?" His breath made the familiar white cloud in the air as he spoke.

She shook her head. "Did I show you my scar, the one on my leg?"

"No. What happened?"

"A few months ago, I was helping my team do research with a grizzly bear. The big boar was so strong that he was capable of actually bending some of the steel bars. That was unbeknownst to me, until I was standing in front of the trap, and he reached through and managed to get a hold of my leg with his paw. Bears are a lot stronger and faster than anyone realizes, until they are on top of you."

She lifted up the leg of her pants, and there were four dark purple claw marks.

"Damn, that's one hell of a war wound. You should be showing that one off."

"I always kinda hide it. While it's a great bar story, it seems counterintuitive to tell anyone about an injury from a bear when I should know what I'm doing." She laughed as she spoke. "Though, I guess bringing that up right now, that's a bad idea, too."

He chuckled. For the first time since yesterday, he realized he had actually laughed. With it came a sense of relief. "I have no doubt about your professionalism or your abilities when it comes to handling wildlife."

She shot him a look. "Oh, I've been questioning it plenty, even without you doing so."

"Why would you do that?" he asked.

"Really?" The way she said it made it sound like he was missing something completely obvious, but he wasn't sure what she was implying. "It was not a great idea for me to kiss you." A faint blush rose in her cheeks.

Until now, he wouldn't have thought it possible, but it made her more beautiful. She quickly looked away and moved down the leg of her pants, covering her scar.

"We are both adults, there was nothing ethically questionable about kissing." He followed as she started to walk again. "As team leader, I wouldn't condemn one of my team members if they had been in a position like we are."

"You don't really expect me to believe that, do you?"

"Yeah, I do. I absolutely would not reprimand one of my team members. Not for a relationship. Now, if it somehow impacted their judgment, or affected their work, that would be different. But this thing with us…"

"You can't say that it's not affecting my job." She sounded at odds with herself.

"The only way this has affected your job is positively. At least, as far as I can tell. You're here on the ranch, you've been doing your job to the best of your ability—if anything, you've been more accessible. If I was your boss, I wouldn't even blink."

"I know you're trying to make me feel better, but you aren't going to sell me on this." She let out a resigned sigh.

This woman was so stubborn. Even when he made a sound argument, she was never going to let him change her opinion. He liked that about her—even if he wished he could make her see things from his perspective in order to keep her from feeling any undue pain.

There were no sounds coming from within the trap as they grew closer. Amber frowned. "Sometimes these things spring and we get nothing," she said, sounding slightly annoyed.

As they got nearer, though, on the snow leading up to the cage, there were the unmistakable tracks made by a grizzly's paw.

Stepping around the trap so he could look inside, there, lying behind the steel bars, he saw an enormous, motionless brown bear. Even from where he stood, he could tell the animal was dead.

Chapter Fifteen

Amber stared at the bear's remains. This was the last thing she had expected to find and the sight made her heart break. She loved all animals, yet this was a part of her job. Souls passed by her, the grim reaper.

Now it was up to her to find out how the bear had died…and why.

It seemed strange to her that this bear had made it all the way into the steel trap if it had been sick or injured. The griz couldn't have been inside long enough to have died of exertion or stress, either. In all of her days, this was the first time this kind of thing had ever happened.

Just to make sure the animal was deceased, she poked a stick through the steel bars and prodded the bear. It didn't move and there was no steady rise and fall of its chest. Its paws were stiff, nearly frozen from the cold.

"What do you think happened?" AJ asked. He looked at her with wide eyes, confused.

She shrugged. "No one was out here last night, were they?"

AJ shook his head. "I don't think so."

Amber hated the idea that someone on the ranch had

something to do with this, and until they looked over the bear, she didn't want to jump to any conclusions.

She moved to the winch, which ran the lift for the gate, and pushed the button, then the steel trap door slowly lifted with a shrill whine of metal on metal.

Part of her expected the bear to jump up and charge at her as she stepped back. Yet, it remained motionless. The scar on her leg throbbed as she stepped closer to the bear, as though her body was reacting to the old trauma and warning her to stay back.

Kneeling down, her hands were shaking as she reached in and touched the bear. It was cool to the touch and definitely not going anywhere. Its head was resting just below the bait and if she hadn't been sure otherwise, it could appear to be just taking a winter slumber.

She touched the bear's back paw. It was enormous in comparison to the size of her hand. The claws alone were longer than her fingers. The power this animal had, what it conveyed, and the role it played in nature were incredible. Feeling an ethereal pull, she said a silent thank-you to the animal in honor of its life.

"Amber? Are you okay?" AJ asked.

She looked over her shoulder at him. "Yeah, I always give honor to animals when they have passed."

"That's really cool. I do the same when I have to, but it's been a long time," he said. He stepped up beside her, closed his eyes and did the same.

Moving deeper into the trap, now that she was sure she wasn't in immediate danger, she pulled back the bear's lip. The animal's teeth were short and the right canine was worn down completely to the gums. Touching the animal, she could feel its ribs.

"Is there anything in there, in the trap, that you

know…belonged to Charlie?" AJ asked, his voice barely above a whisper.

She looked over her shoulder at him. "No. And from everything I've seen so far, I don't feel like this bear had any contact with him," she lied, trying to reassure the stressed man but aware that there was no way she could be sure without further analysis.

AJ nodded, seeming to find peace in her answer.

She glanced back at the bear. The animal was in poor body condition, especially considering how late it was in the season. Its fur was the same tawny brown of the hair they'd found wedged into the barbed wire on the fence, but until they got the DNA results, she couldn't be 100-percent certain this was the only bear they were dealing with.

"Do you want to grab me my bag out of the pickup? The one in the back seat. It has all my supplies in it for taking samples."

AJ nodded. "Yeah, do you need anything else?"

"Grab my phone. I'm going to need to get some pictures as well." She could hear his footfalls as he made his way out toward the pickup.

It was nice having another set of hands around when she was working. Normally, when she first arrived at a location she was on her own until the bear team got there to do their work before releasing an animal. As it was, with this being a deceased animal, it was all going to be on her shoulders. Unfortunately, as this bear was likely involved with Tammy's case, it meant that she was going to have to take it to the university.

She peeled back the front of the animal's lip. Inside was a tattoo. It was number 832, the female who had been feasting on chickens years back and had been relocated north. At twenty-nine, the griz was considered an anomaly for a wild bear. Normally they died well before the age of twenty-five and most before they were even a year old.

On the lips, around the tattoo and along the gums was an odd red rash. Its edges had started to turn black, almost necrotic. Yet, it didn't make sense. The bear hadn't been down long enough for any sort of decomp to start. She had to have been sick.

Amber ran her hand down the bear's torso, feeling for any sort of bullet wound or trauma, but found nothing but a thin bony figure. Even its hair wasn't as thick or oily and heavy as she normally saw in bears this time of year.

Without a doubt, this girl had been incredibly sick.

The bait had been taken down and some of it had been eaten. There was a sense of peace in knowing the animal had feasted before it had lost its battle against nature.

Many times, if humans were attacked by a bear, it was a bear in this physically deteriorated state, or one with cubs they were attempting to protect. In this case, it seemed possible that Tammy might have just been in the wrong place at the wrong time—

AJ came back as she stared down at the bear and he handed her the phone. She snapped a few pictures, then with AJ's help, they turned over the bear and she took some of the other side. Amber pulled back the lips and got some pictures of the animal's teeth and the black marks on the gums. Even the tongue had some of the blackness. It was so strange, and it made her wonder if the bear had come in contact with some kind of toxin.

A few years back, a herd of elk had mysteriously

died a few hundred miles from where they stood. After a long battery of tests, they had found out that because of a lack of food, the elk had resorted to feeding off lichens and mosses on a rock outcrop. The lichens had ended up being poisonous and the entire herd had perished. Perhaps something like that had happened here.

"What is going on with its mouth?" AJ asked, pointing at it.

She shrugged. "I don't know. I can't say I've ever seen anything like that before."

"Huh," he said, tapping his fingers on the steel of the trap. "You know what that reminds me of?"

She looked back at him, unsure of where he was going to go with his statement.

He had a serious expression. "You know… Tammy's hand had that same weird blackness. Do you think they could have been related?"

"I can't imagine how, but without running tests I don't know." She shrugged as she tried to remember exactly what the hand had looked like—instantly she was brought back to the purple fingertips. "I mean… I thought the hand was just frostbitten, but I'd have to look at it closer. Even then, I'm not a medical examiner." With the elk, it took a good month to get the results back from all the labs they drew on.

There was a sound of a car approaching in the distance. "I hope you don't mind. I called my crew in case we needed more hands loading or unloading."

She smiled. "You and your family and friends make one hell of a team. You are a lucky man to have such an incredible support system." As she spoke, it hit her how alone she normally was, and it made her miss her brother more than ever. She would give anything to have him back. So much had been taken from their family when he had died.

"I really am a lucky man, but everything I have has taken a long time and a lot of work to accumulate—even the relationships with my family sometimes take a lot."

He had opened up, and everything she'd learned about him just made her more drawn to him. But after spending time with him and his family she wasn't entirely sure how well she would fit. This team was nearly seamless; they communicated and they adapted for one another. She wasn't even sure she would know where to start when it came to becoming a part of this team.

Not that what she and AJ had going could really be considered a team… Though, at the same time, that was exactly what it was. They were working together.

Going into her bag, she pulled out a set of nitrile gloves, tweezers and her sample collection kits. Moving around the bear, she carefully took hair, a tooth and tissue. Wrapping up with her collections, she looked up to realize that AJ and his two brothers were standing outside the culvert trap and watching her.

"That is seriously cool," Mike said, motioning toward the bear. "Can I touch it?" As he spoke, he looked a bit like a kid the night before his birthday party—all hope and smiles.

"Come on up," she said, motioning for him to step inside and check out the animal.

She explained the body state and showed him the lips, as she had done with AJ. Both of his brothers took turns checking it out. After a few minutes, her legs started to cramp and she made her way out of the trap.

Stretching, she stood beside AJ. "Thanks for that,"

he said, motioning to his brothers. "They love this kind of thing."

She nodded and for a second it felt like she'd known AJ for years.

Everything with AJ was confusing, though also not. It was simple. She loved to be around him. It was easy to talk to him and open up and tell him what she was thinking about things and why; and she couldn't say that she had ever had friends or romantic interests before where things had flowed so naturally.

Maybe it was that they were just cut from the same cloth. Or maybe they had just formed some empathic bond because of everything they had both been forced to face from the moment they had first met. There was definitely something to the idea of trauma bonding people. And yet, that wasn't what it felt like when she was close to him. When she was near him, she wanted to touch him and to hear him speak. It was simple, and it wasn't. She was afraid, and yet it was a *yearning*.

It was those feelings that actually scared her the most. She could put up with a lot and had seen many things that other people wouldn't and couldn't emotionally handle, but feeling safe and wanting to be near a man was where she apparently drew a line in the sand. It was almost funny in its absurdity.

"Hey, Amber," Troy said from inside the trap, his voice echoing off the steel and amplifying the sound. "If you want, Mike and I can run the animal to the lab for you."

She pulled off her gloves and shoved them into her pack with the samples she had taken for her work. "Actually, I was going to run it down to the university and their lab. They are doing the DNA testing, and—" She paused. "However, if you guys are offering, it would save me a drive. I could just let them know you're coming."

She wasn't exactly sure why she had given the go-ahead on this. Normally, she didn't mind all the windshield time. Admittedly, it probably had something to do with the oh-so-handsome man at her side. If she ran back into the city with the bear, those were hours that she wouldn't be able to help him. They still needed to check out the coordinates that Zoey had listed for them.

Sure, AJ was capable of going through GPS coordinates and running to the locations, but she didn't like the idea of him going to them alone. Even that was silly. He was literally a trained killer and she was worried about him. She huffed. If they ever actually had a real relationship, one that didn't leave her with ethical and moral conundrums, she doubted that she would ever stop worrying about him…regardless of his training.

"Are you sure you guys are okay with that? I know you are working your butts off with Zoey." *And the search for Charlie.* But she didn't dare say the last bit aloud.

"We're waiting on some phone calls and emails," Mike said, giving Troy a questioning glance.

Troy nodded. "Yep. We've got this. Why don't you guys just go ahead."

"I'll let the lab know you two are coming," she confirmed. "I'm sure they can meet you outside the Skaggs Building and get you all set up. Normally they have me pull into the underground area so anyone passing by doesn't get upset."

Troy nodded. "Got it. Shouldn't take us too long. Do you think you're going to need the trap set up again?"

"No. I think this is our girl." From here, she would just need to find out if this bear was Tammy's killer, but that was going to take some time and she was glad she wasn't the one who was going to have to get her hands dirty in finding out by doing the necropsy.

AJ stared at the bear and she was forced to wonder if he was thinking the same things she was, and facing the same questions. "Are you okay, AJ?"

He jerked slightly as if she had pulled him out of some kind of daze. "Yeah, I'm sure I'll be fine. I'm just…" He waved his hands and appeared to struggle to find exactly the right word to explain the chaos that was likely happening inside his head and his heart.

"I'm sure you're exhausted." She grabbed her bag, then looped her arm through his and led him slowly back toward her truck. "Let's go check on these locations to see if we can find anything. Then you need to take a break. Hell, if you want, you can sleep while I drive. Fair?"

"I couldn't sleep now, not even if I tried. We need to find my son." He sent her a tired smile. "Amber, I hope you know how much your help means to me."

She laughed, dismissing his compliment gently. "That is just your exhaustion talking. Clearly, you're not at the top of your game." As she spoke, she found her feelings and her words at odds. She loved that he had expressed his gratitude and saw her in the manner in which she hoped he would—as a resource and a steady presence in his life, while being a person who wholeheartedly wanted the best for him—whether or not that meant she was going to have a place in his life.

For now, all they had was hope.

Chapter Sixteen

There were few other times he could remember feeling this exhausted. Once, while he had been going through his early training, his instructors had kept him and his class up for four days straight. By the end of the fourth day, he had started to hallucinate and he felt outside of his body. While that exhausted, the instructors had had them running and pushing their bodies past the point he thought he was physically able to continue.

It was during those weeks and months of work and training that he had found out exactly how tough he was. And yet, a little boy and a new friend were having the power to weaken him.

AJ didn't know exactly what it was in Amber that he saw; there were so many things that she was doing for him. Better, her actions and her words were matching. She wasn't just throwing him empty promises and pity. Instead she was knee-deep in the mire that was his life and the mystery that it was revolving around.

She really was an amazing woman. To make it all worse, at least when it came to his heart and his ever-growing feelings about her, she didn't want a relationship with him.

Add a child to the mix, and there was zero chance

that she was going to change her mind. He didn't blame her for her choice before the news, and now he was glad she had chosen as she had. Regardless, it wasn't like he could have made a relationship work. Not now, not with so much on his plate and hanging in the balance.

He was just damn lucky he hadn't been arrested—they had probable cause, not to mention his withholding information.

His phone pinged with a message from Troy. They had loaded the bear into the back of one of the trucks from the ranch and were just about to head out to the lab.

He'd been thinking a lot about the bear, too. He had really assumed that the bear had been sleeping when they had first come upon her, but it hadn't taken long to prove otherwise. Though he felt bad for the loss, all he had been able to think about was what this animal—this enormous ball of fur, teeth and claws—could have possibly meant for Tammy in her last moments.

From the way Amber had spoken, it was very likely that the animal had been behind his ex-fiancée's demise. Whether it had or it hadn't, he was still left with the nagging question of where Charlie was.

While the feeling in his gut couldn't tell him exactly what had happened to Tammy, there was no question about how it felt when it came to Charlie being his child. There was just some inexplicable link. Charlie was *his*.

He closed his eyes for a moment, blocking out the moon as it reflected off the snow and into the truck as Amber followed the robotic voice of their navigation system. According to the GPS coordinates and the nav system, they were heading to the Kootenai Falls Trailhead and parking area.

From the information he had so far gleaned from Zoey, Tammy's phone had pinged at that location for nearly a day. He wasn't sure what they were going to find. From the location alone, he could assume that Tammy had merely gone to the area to hike and perhaps camp. Nothing out of the ordinary, except for the fact it had been cold for the last two weeks—and according to the time line it would have only been in the low teens the night she had been at the trailhead.

Yet, it was something. It was a starting point in the search for Charlie.

That was…if Charlie was still alive.

He blanched at the thought.

The trailhead was not far from the ranch, and as they pulled into the parking area, he noted that if a person had a high-end spotting scope, it was possible to watch the entrance of the ranch's property.

Strange.

Amber was working on her phone as he got out and made his way around the trailhead. Based on the tracks, several cars had come and gone over the last few days, but there was no one in the parking lot. From the trailhead, there was a broken path in the snow, even one track that looked as though it had been made by a snowshoe. Everything about the area, except the view of the ranch's turnoff from the highway and entrance, seemed painfully routine.

As he came back to the truck, Amber looked up at him as he got in and buckled. "Did you find anything interesting?"

He shook his head, trying to ignore the feeling of failure that was creeping through his gut. This had been a waste of time. They were no closer to answers and no closer to finding Charlie.

"I have been looking over the maps and punching in the coordinates that Zoey gave us." Amber looked at her phone so he could see the pins that she had created on her mapping app. "Did you notice that every point is pretty close to the ranch?"

"Can I see your phone for a second?"

Without a moment of hesitation, she handed him her phone. He scrolled through the pins. There were a few other hiking trails that Tammy had stopped at. And two of the pins were just locations along logging roads, adjacent to the ranch and on US Forest Service land.

For someone from Montana, spending a couple weeks cruising around on logging roads and public land wasn't that unusual in the fall. That time of year, people spent a great deal of time hunting and exploring the woods.

"Zoey said these pins are from the last two or three weeks, but I wonder how long Tammy had been in Montana. I'll need to ask Zoey if she pulled any other info from the hotel." It wasn't a question, so much as a statement. It was this continued lack of information that was driving him bonkers. However, there was a lot of legwork to do, and not a lot of time to do it.

"Yeah," Amber said, like she could read his mind. "I would be happy just to know why she was here. I would've thought she would've tried to contact you quite a bit more, if her being here had something to do with you or your family. Yet, you said she was relatively quiet."

He picked up his phone and flipped through his call log, searching until he pulled up Tammy's call records.

"Yeah, according to this, her last call to me was three months ago. She didn't even leave a message."

His thoughts moved to Tammy's phone. Cell-phone records, at least for the company that she had been using, were only available for thirty days. That was, unless a law-enforcement agency filed for the company to retain records. As far as tracking her through those, it would be a challenge. They might be able to see whom she had been calling, but he was sure Zoey was already working on that angle.

Though Zoey could do quite a bit on the computer, especially along with their tech teams, they were limited by the resources available to them from cellular data. However, as he was pondering ways to track Tammy, his thoughts moved to her credit cards and banking information.

He texted Zoey, asking her if she had found Tammy's banking information yet. Almost instantly, Zoey texted him back with an encrypted attached file. He couldn't help but smile. He really did have one hell of a team. If getting answers to this mystery was half as easy as getting answers from Zoey, they'd have Charlie in no time.

If he is alive.

Just as quickly as he thought it, he tried to strike the naysaying from his mind.

There was no sense in assuming the worst. In this case, it would only slow them down. He had to hope that Charlie was alive, and plan for the rescue. It went against his normal mantra of "hope for the best and prepare for the worst," but since the moment of learning about Charlie's existence, the worst thing he could imagine was never meeting the boy.

For that, there was no preparing.

He opened up the document that Zoey had sent, skimming through the credit-card purchases that Tammy had made for the last year. According to the statements, nine months ago she had accumulated a significant amount of debt. One month, she had owed more than 124,000 dollars on one of her cards.

What the hell?

When they had been together, she had made a point of never having any major debt. He couldn't imagine how she had gotten herself in this position. If she had needed money for Charlie, or to survive, she should've known that he would be there for her. He'd made that clear, even before he knew about Charlie.

He'd not had many relationships and Tammy knew that, and she also knew where he stood when it came to her. Why hadn't she come to him? Why hadn't she asked for help?

She didn't tell you about Charlie. If she hadn't told him about his child, then, of course, she wasn't going to tell him about any sort of financial difficulty she was having. Perhaps there were secrets about her that kept her from wanting to reach out to him. Though she had been vetted by his family before he'd started dating her, her life after him was a bit of an unknown. Clearly, she had gotten herself in trouble.

The thought broke his heart. He had only ever wanted the best for her.

"Are you okay?" Amber asked.

It was equally unsettling and amazing how Amber always seemed to pick up on his struggles. "I'll be fine, it's just challenging to see anyone you care about struggling…or having struggled." He scanned down to the next month of financial records. She hadn't used her credit card for months.

"What did Tammy do for work?" Amber asked.

"She was a corporate marketing manager. She flipped from job to job when she was younger. Last time I spoke with her she was working for Brontë Group. They are a company that work with international trade."

Amber frowned. "Did your work ever overlap with hers?"

He wasn't sure where she was going with that, but he could assume. "When we got engaged, she considered moving out here and at that time she gave up her job. She was a bit of a trust-fund kid, so she had a stable enough income that along with my income, she didn't have to work."

Looking over her financial records, it didn't appear as though she had gone back to work since they had broken up. And perhaps that was how she'd gotten into the situation she had. It surprised him that her parents hadn't taken a more active role in her finances, either. Which made him wonder if she had not told them about the baby.

If she had, her parents were old-school and probably would have pushed her to reconcile with him and pursue marriage. Perhaps that was what she had been running from. Maybe she knew that they weren't destined to be together, and she hadn't wanted to burden him with the responsibilities and requirements the child would bring to his life.

There were so many assumptions that could be made, and conjectures, but unless by some miracle he found Tammy alive, which didn't seem likely, the chance for any sort of hope for any real answers was gone.

He glanced over at Amber—she looked worn-out. "I'm so sorry about all of this. I can't imagine how you are feeling having to deal with my past and all the drama that seems to be circulating through my life. I'd like to tell you that it's normally different, and though the upheavals that I deal with don't generally come from my private life, it would be a lie to say that I am not constantly inundated by needs."

Amber reached over, taking his hand. "I can't say that I've ever had a bear case quite like this one, but I'm glad I got to help."

He appreciated that she wasn't focusing on his apology, but it couldn't be ignored even though he wanted to do nothing more than kiss her. "It's just, with everything, I don't want you getting in over your head. I know all of this goes way beyond your usual job."

She leaned across the console, her Kevlar vest rubbing hard against the computer that rested between them, making a scraping sound. She didn't seem to notice. Instead, she reached up and pressed her palm to his face and rubbed her thumb against the stubble on his cheek. "You don't need to worry about me. What you need to worry about right now is your son. Charlie needs you." She gently kissed him, stealing his breath for a moment. Having her lips against his was the only moment of peace he'd had since learning about Charlie. He wanted to hold her there, but when she pulled back, he let her go. She cleared her throat. "Now, let's go check the next GPS location."

She picked up her phone, as he struggled to find the right words. He was so grateful to have her these last few days. She was so good to him. So understanding and kind. There was a comfort in the knowledge that regardless of what happened next, they would go through it together. He could ask for nothing more.

"Hey," Amber said, frowning at him. "Did you know that there is an old, abandoned gold mine near the ranch?"

He shook his head. "How do you know that?"

She pointed back to her app. "I use the USFS mapping database, which includes geological studies. Plus, one of my friends is the lead archaeologist for the state, and he sends me points when he and his teams are working at different locations. They worked on one of the encampments associated with this mine a few years ago."

AJ smirked. "And here I thought I had cool friends. Gotta say having a friend who is an archaeologist is pretty neat."

"I don't know, running with people who travel all over the world and overthrow governments is pretty amazing. That being said, I think you'd really like my friends. Maybe someday I'll get to introduce you to them."

"I'm down for that, whenever you'd like." He loved the thought of being incorporated into her life in a more substantial way. It was funny, but he could almost imagine a life with her, walking into places and having her on his arm. He would love to show her off as his girlfriend.

Amber's smile widened. "Let's find Charlie first." She turned back to her phone. "As for the mine, I don't know how big it was, or what kind of yield it delivered. From what I have here—" she tapped on her phone "—the claim was originally filed in 1890, not long after Montana became a state. Mining at that time was really interesting. There were several methods that people used, but in this area and through this formation toward Butte, the most common method for extracting minerals from ore was through a method called leach mining."

AJ enjoyed listening to her, though he didn't really know why or how any of this information would help them. At this point, though, he was willing to delve into anything, if it led to answers.

"I've heard of leach mining. It's where they use cyanide, arsenic and other heavy metals to get gold and copper out of minerals. Right?" he asked.

"Something like that, yes." She nodded. "Companies still do leach mining now, though it is more regulated and the environmental effects, arguably, aren't as catastrophic as they were in the earlier days of mining."

She shot him a curious smile.

"What?" he asked, confused by what could have possibly made her so animated.

"I just had an idea," she said. She drew her phone to her chest as if she was trying to control herself. "You know what one of the major signs of long-term contact with arsenic is?"

He shook his head.

"Arsenic is a poison and it's been used for years as a pesticide, but when people historically working with the poison were around it for long periods of time, they would build up somewhat of a tolerance. However, they would develop rashes, odd pigmentation and dark black discoloration on their hands and feet. People can get what are called Mees' lines in their fingernails."

His thoughts jumped to Tammy's hand. Her palm had been splotchy and blackened, and her nail beds had taken on a purple-and-green hue. He couldn't recall seeing white lines on her fingernails, but he was sure it wouldn't take anything to get a picture of the remains and look.

"If there is a mine on the ranch, a leach mine with high levels of toxins, and if Tammy was there for an extended period of time—like *months*—it would explain her hand." Amber's eyes widened. "It also would explain the bear. If it had been in that cave, denning or living… Oh, my God, AJ, it all makes sense."

Chapter Seventeen

It was macabre, but Amber was thrilled at the lead they'd just got. Sure, it may well not be the answer, but it was the best theory she had come up with for the bear and the series of events that had led them to finding Tammy's remains.

She drove fast, bumping down the logging road and heading back to the ranch.

"Every point Zoey gave us has views of the ranch. Tammy was definitely scoping us out." AJ sounded a bit breathless as they hit another pothole in the road.

Amber wasn't sure if he agreed with her idea about the arsenic poisoning, but it wouldn't be hard to prove now that they had the bear's remains.

"Did your brothers get the bear to the university yet?" she asked.

He tapped on his phone. "Mike said they dropped her off about thirty minutes ago."

Amber pulled over and sent off a quick text to the lab tech she had been working with: Test stomach contents and hair for arsenic poisoning.

The woman sent her a thumbs-up in response. It was such a simple response that it almost annoyed Amber, but then she reminded herself the woman most likely had her hands full as she prepped the necropsy. She literally held the possible answers in her hands.

"One of the telltale signs of arsenic poisoning is also anorexia," AJ said, staring at his phone. "According to the CDC, it also greatly affects the neurological system."

"We need to get video from the hotel and see if there is any footage showing Tammy. Maybe we can get a better read on her physical and neurological status from the video." Amber couldn't help the wave of hope filling her that they were close to finding answers. Yet, she tried to remain calm. They still had to find Charlie.

AJ was working away feverishly on his phone; she could see he was texting Zoey and his brothers in a group chat. "Zoey is on it. I'm sure we can get the video soon, but I think she is going to have to go through Detective Baker."

"That's good, then he can let the medical examiner know to test for arsenic on Tammy's hand as well." She tapped her fingers on her steering wheel and smiled.

He was so incredible to her, and she loved his ability to talk to her and communicate as he did. It had been a long time since she had felt so at home with someone's presence. There was no denying that there was something between them, even if it was something that she couldn't act on.

He went back to his phone as she careened down the road, thinking about the samples she had taken from the bear. If need be, she could possibly do her own testing. She had always enjoyed that kind of work, but hopefully the lab would take care of everything.

As they approached the ranch, she could see there were a number of trucks missing. It appeared as though

AJ's teams were on the move. It didn't take long before they were rumbling over the cattle guard near the area in which they had first gotten the hairs from the bear.

So much had happened in so little time. It was unbelievable to think that just a few days ago, AJ hadn't been a part of her life and this assignment was nothing more than an annoyance.

In all of her wildest imaginings, she would have never thought she would have found herself here.

"Zoey let Baker know about the bear. He seemed pretty relieved, apparently. He also is sending her the video footage from the hotel. Should be here in the next hour or two." He looked down at his watch. "It's getting late, but I want to keep looking for Charlie. I don't want him to possibly be spending another night alone."

"Yeah," Amber said, thinking about the boy possibly out in the winter night by himself, but she couldn't bear the thought and she stamped it down.

"Let's swing over to the old miner's cabin and see if we can get inside. It's the only place I can think of that a toddler would have holed up on the ranch and gone unnoticed."

They drove to the belly of the ranch, where the old miner's cabin stood. In the dark, it seemed far more ominous than she remembered it, with its looping webs of horsehair moss chinking and abyssal windows.

They crunched through a layer of snow as they got out of the truck and made their way up to the cabin. AJ shone his flashlight inside as they neared the windows, but from even where she stood, she could see that the place was deserted. She opened the door but was met with only the sounds of scurrying mice. Though it was unlikely, the inside of the cabin seemed colder as the air bit at the insides of her nostrils and seemed to freeze in her lungs.

It was odd, but in finding it cold, empty and undisturbed—so far as she could tell in the dark—Amber found comfort. If the little boy had been inside, the chances he would have still been alive were dismal.

When she looked over at AJ, she could see the exhaustion on his face. The poor man probably hadn't really slept in days. Though he was tough, everything was taking a toll. "You need a break. For now, there's nothing more we can do for Charlie," she said, turning back toward the truck and leading him by the hand. "Don't worry, we will come up with something. We just need to keep digging for ideas."

He smiled, but even that looked like it had taken a strain. "I'm sure you're right."

It was a quick ride back to the ranch, but she kept glancing over at him. It hurt her to see him so road-worn, but damn if she didn't know how he was feeling. If only she could make him feel better and take some of the pain and pressure from him. She parked in front of his house. He got out and walked around to her side, opening her door for her.

"Why, thank you," she said, and he answered with an acknowledging nod.

"Of course," he said, motioning her toward his place.

He opened the door for her and held it for her as she passed by. There was something in the way they moved together that made her feel as if they were stepping into the relationship that they had both been avoiding—well, she had, more than him. Yet, she had picked this place and this moment; she was making choices that didn't align with what she was telling herself she should do, but what her heart pointed her toward.

"Do you want a drink or something?" She smiled over her shoulder at him as she walked toward his kitchen.

"I was going to say you are welcome to make yourself at home, but I can see that won't be a problem," he teased. "I'd definitely take some water." He touched her shoulder as he stepped beside her and reached up into the cupboard by the sink and grabbed a glass. He poured water into a glass and handed it to her, then did the same for himself before sitting down at the island.

He took a long drink and then ran his hands over his face, as though he could wipe away his exhaustion and disappointment in not locating Charlie.

"Why don't you go sit on the couch?" She motioned toward the overstuffed leather couch that sat in front of the fireplace a few feet from them. "I will put together a little something for us."

"You don't need to do that," he said. "You're my guest."

"Don't worry, you just go and rest. Let me take care of you for a little bit."

"I appreciate that, Amber. I got the next meal." He smiled and stood up, then, almost instinctively, he gave her a soft kiss to her cheek in thanks. He stumbled slightly as he walked toward the couch and then sat down. He turned on the television to a news channel—it seemed like it was all out of habit and she couldn't help but smile at how well they just fit together.

This could be their life. After having nearly every meal by herself in the woods or inside her truck for the last few years, it was inexplicably comforting to have this moment with a man she cared about. It was funny how the little things in life could mean more than any over-the-top expression of affection. If anything, it was the simple things and these types of moments that built a life and reaffirmed love.

She walked to the refrigerator and peeked inside. The contents were pretty sparse, with just a pack of turkey lunch meat, bread and sliced cheese. She smiled as she took out the items and put together sandwiches for them.

Walking over, she went to hand him his plate, but his eyes were closed and she could tell from his steady, quiet breaths that he had fallen asleep.

Oh, he is so handsome, she thought, looking at his sweet face, finally relaxed in the comforting hands of sleep.

He needed this. Quietly, she put down his sandwich, walked to his room and grabbed his blanket. Bringing it out, she gently placed it over him.

It had been years since she had taken care of anyone like this, and it pulled at her in ways she didn't think possible. Something about it reminded of when she had taken care of her parents after William had died and it equally warmed and broke her heart. She hadn't talked to her parents since Thanksgiving, so she really needed to give them a call.

She made quick work of her sandwich and then turned to her phone. She started to press in a number, but then she didn't want to disturb AJ. Instead, she went to her email and started to sift through all the work issues that were piling up. Apparently, there was a herd of elk on a nearby ranch that was causing havoc on the rancher's hay. The rancher wanted permission to haze the animals away, but she always hated giving the go-ahead on that kind of thing—it opened up a can of worms when it came to the legalities and the humane treatment of animals.

After more than an hour of responding to the most pressing emails, she decided to call it a night.

She stood up and moved to AJ, then gently sat down beside him. She moved a stray piece of his hair out of the middle of his forehead as he slept. His eyelids fluttered at the sensation and he opened his eyes slightly and glanced over at her. He smiled, reached up and touched her face. He leaned over and took her lips with his.

The action was so unexpected and sweet that she melted under his touch, forgetting about the emails and the work that needed their attention. Instead, she leaned into his kiss, beckoning his tongue with her own as they nipped and played.

His kiss turned deeper and his hand moved down from her face, and he pulled her into his lap. From where she sat, she could feel him grow harder beneath her.

Without warning, he swept her up into his arms. She threw her arms around his neck as he carried her into the bedroom and gently laid her on the bed.

She pulled open his shirt and he slipped out of his pants in almost a single motion.

He moved onto the bed beside her. She reached up and started to unbutton her shirt, finding herself entranced by the heat of the moment after the drama of the day. Everything had been so stressful, so full of emotions, that this felt light—a needed moment of reprieve.

Not saying a word, he gently nudged her hands away

and unbuttoned the top two buttons before pulling the shirt up and over her head.

He kissed her lips as he unclasped her bra and slipped the straps from her shoulders. The cool air hit her nipples and made her gasp in his mouth. She could feel him smile at the sound, but he didn't break their kiss.

This man... This incredible man...

His hand slipped down to her pants and he made quick work of the button and zipper before pushing them down. She wiggled and grabbed the ankles of her pants with her toes as she pulled them off, all without stopping their kiss. She never wanted to stop kissing him.

He moved down between her knees and kissed the insides of her thighs as he lay down. He lifted her legs, putting them over his shoulders as his kisses worked to her center. She quaked under the gentle pulse of his tongue, the strokes and flicks.

It... This... Him...

He traced her lips with his fingers and he gently pressed inside, humming as he penetrated her. She moaned, the sound coming from deep within her, and echoing the primal urge she felt building. His tongue was like the beat of a drum, echoing the tempo of her heart and the rasping calls of her breath.

This. Dance. Oh...

"Amber..." He moaned her name against her and it made her breath come faster.

Her body moved with him, rising and falling in cadence with his mouth.

"AJ..." she replied as she reached the point of no return and the tempo of his touch brought her to the end.

He tried to move against her, kissing away the wetness he had created, but she pushed his head away, unable to bear even the gentlest of his touches.

"Come here," she ordered, nearly breathless.

He moved to kiss her as he eased his body up hers, but she reached down and took his chin and looked him in the eyes. "I want you to kiss me," she said.

There was a sparkle in his eyes as he answered her with a devilish smile. His kiss was hard against her lips, just like the rest of him.

She licked his lips, pulling her flavor from him like she was the sweetest of lollipops.

"Amber," he said, moaning into her mouth as her body started to pulse again and hunger for more.

She reached down, wetting her hand and moving to him, and started to stroke. He was so hard.

Hard for me.

Working his length, he grew impossibly harder in her hand and she slowed. She couldn't spend another night with him without feeling him inside. She stopped as she looked up at him. "AJ..."

His eyes were narrowed with lust and longing as he looked upon her. "Yes?" he asked, pressing against her, showing her exactly where he also wanted to go.

"Grab a condom," she said.

He moved quickly, going to his nightstand and pulling one out.

Before he had a chance to rip it open, she took it from him. "This is my job."

After ripping open the package, she took out the condom and slipped it over him, careful to not play too much so he could last inside of her. She needed to feel him. All of him. For as long as she could. She needed to remember every second of this.

He moaned as she moved him between her thighs and eased him inside of her, lifting her hips to meet his body with hers. She gripped the sheets as he slipped out slightly and then moved deep into her, filling her to the point of sweet pain. He was so big.

This man was perfect.

He stretched and pressed into her like nothing else she had ever felt before. As he moved, he hit a spot inside of her that made her fear that she would be the one who couldn't last. She had to wait, to take him to the place he had already taken her.

She'd always thought the G-spot was a myth until now. There was something.

"Right there," she moaned, grabbing his hips and guiding his thrusts into her. "Right… There."

He made a sound, like a growl, as he took her again and again, following her body's moves and the movement of her hands.

"Amber, it's okay… I can tell—"

Before he could finish speaking, she felt her body give way.

She cried out, giving everything she was to him and for him in a way she had never given before. He followed, making the ecstasy even more exquisite as they gave themselves together. In this moment, there was only this…and only them.

Chapter Eighteen

AJ had forgotten how good it felt to wake up next to someone he cared for after a long night of lovemaking. There were few feelings in the world that could compare to the utter, blissful exhaustion that came with melding souls. That was the only way he could adequately describe what they had done.

She was his and he was hers.

There wasn't much that he could pull together for breakfast, but he had made sure to make her some fresh coffee and just about when the coffeepot was full, he made out the sound of her getting dressed from inside their room.

Their room. He smiled at the thought.

It may have been a little premature, but after what had happened between them last night, it seemed like they were both finally on the same page in really giving this relationship a chance. He loved the idea as much as he cared about Amber. While he wasn't in a hurry to take things too fast or jump into marriage, he was glad that they could finally start acting naturally on their feelings and see where they would go together.

He hummed as he poured a to-go mug for her, making sure to add a little bit of powdered creamer and some sugar. He wasn't sure exactly how she took her coffee, but just like everything else about her, he couldn't wait to learn.

Tapping on the door, he said, "I come bearing gifts."

She opened the bedroom door and gave him a kiss on the cheek as he handed her the coffee. "Thank you, honey," she said, and it was so natural that it was like they did this kind of thing every day.

He slapped her ass as she sauntered by him, ready and dressed for the day.

"So..." she said, taking a sip of her coffee and looking over the rim at him.

Damn. I am the luckiest man alive.

"So?" he asked.

"Should we talk about what happened?"

He wouldn't have been more surprised if he'd woken up in another country. He knew he shouldn't compare Amber to anyone in his past, but he'd never been with a woman who was just nonchalant about their sex life, or wanted to just casually talk about what did or didn't happen behind closed doors.

He had a feeling that maybe he was a little behind the times, or maybe it was just that he was inexperienced when it came to that kind of thing, but he liked that this would be how it was going to be between them. He liked candor and openness when it came to someone he trusted and brought into his life. That kind of honesty would be what would make their lives together.

"I'm just grateful. I have wanted to have you in my bed almost from the moment I set eyes on you. I'm honored that you would share your body with me." He leaned in and gave her a kiss on her head.

She looked up at him and took another drink of her

coffee, taking in what he had said. "Babe, I knew you were an incredible man, but every second I spend with you it becomes more and more obvious that you are out of my league." She giggled.

"More like the other way around," he said, pouring himself a coffee and turning back to her. "You know, though, what may make our relationship strong is the fact that we both think we are getting someone outside our coverage area."

She snorted so hard that a little dribble of coffee dripped from her nose and she hurried to wipe it away. "What was that?" she asked between choking laughs.

"It's dumb, just a football reference. I was just trying to say that I love that we both think the other is too good for us. It means we are a perfect fit."

"Just as long as you don't expect me to be perfect, we will do fine." She smiled.

"I don't want a perfect person—it would be entirely too much pressure to keep pace with." He paused. "Plus, I've learned that the greatest times in life and in relationships come in moments when everything goes wrong. Those are the moments when you get to see a person for who they really are, not the version they want you to see."

"Yes," she said, pointing at him in agreement. "You get to see the authentic self."

"You have definitely seen me at my worst over the last few days, and for that I'm sorry. I wish you could see me at the top of my game."

She shook her head. "If this is your worst, then I think I would have been far too nervous to talk to you at the top of your game. You're the hottest man I've ever dated."

"We are dating?" He sent her a cute side-glance. "Does that mean I can start calling you my girlfriend?"

She beckoned him over to her with the wiggle of her finger. He did as she ordered, but then she motioned to have him come even closer so she could whisper in his ear. "You are mine."

"Then girlfriend it is, or would you prefer mistress?" He gave her a playful kiss as her fingernails pressed into the skin on his chest.

Her phone buzzed on the counter next to them, pulling him from his reverie of all that was Amber. She picked it up with a sigh, like she hated that she had to give up this moment just as much as he did.

His fingertips found the place on his chest where she had marked him, almost in exactly the same spot she had just a few hours ago, when they had been in bed together. He loved the idea of being marked by her— he really was hers.

He walked into the bedroom then tidied up and made the bed while she handled whomever it was that was on the other end of the phone. After ten minutes or so, he came out, and she was thumbing the edge of her coffee mug, staring at what little was left in the cup.

"Yes. Got it. Thanks for calling," she said, but then set the phone back down. Her face was impassive as she looked up at him.

"Everything okay?" he asked.

"That was the lab. The DNA tests came back. The bear we had in our trap was the same that had crossed your fence."

"Good, that's at least one less thing we have to worry about. We didn't need a multitude of predatory animals rolling through the ranch."

Her face tightened. "They also got the arsenic results—they came back positive. They said the animal had most likely been ingesting the toxin for a long period of time because it was also found in the hair as well as the stomach contents."

"Was that all they found, you know...in the stomach?"

She tapped the coffee cup like she was answering him in Morse code. "The animal had ingested human remains. It will be another day to see if they can get adequate DNA from the samples they took, but they believe it is likely Tammy."

He sat down on the chair next to her. He wasn't exactly surprised, but the news still wasn't easy to hear. There was no longer any doubt about this being Tammy. He had shared so much of his life with her, so many memories, and a renewed sense of grief washed over him.

For a moment, he wondered if there was anything he could have done to change the outcome, or prevent her death. If only he had called her, or reached out. Yet, there was no way that he could have known what was going to happen to her or her life. "Was there any evidence as to how she died in the contents?"

She shook her head. "It will take a bit to get that info, but I did get enough information to know that my feeling was right—there was no evidence of the bear having eaten a child. The bones ingested were that of a full-grown adult."

It felt strange to be relieved over the results of the stomach contents of a bear, but nonetheless he was, as the odds of Charlie being alive had just gotten significantly higher. Now he just had to find him.

He was filled with a renewed energy. Charlie was out there somewhere, alive. The one thing he was damn good at was locating those who were nearly impossible to track down.

"Can you please let Zoey know about the findings?" he asked, pointing toward her phone.

She nodded, then picked up her phone and sent off a series of texts and emails.

It was great having Amber around. He could get used to this. In fact, if he had his way, he would. However, Charlie first.

"AJ, come over here." She was staring intently at her phone. "I don't know if it will lead to anything, but I just did some digging and found out that there's a mine shaft near the homesteader's cabin. It connects in with a ton of other shafts, but according to the data I got, the shafts collapsed sometime in the past."

He walked over and looked at the screen with her. She'd pulled up the maps on her phone of the geological data of the area.

According to it, the mine shaft had once connected in with a trail of other shafts, one of which originated on forest service land a few miles up from the ranch. Amber pulled up the coordinates—coordinates that were strikingly close to those Zoey had given them. Either Tammy's remains had to have been brought by the bear onto the ranch, or she had to have gotten in another way...or someone had dumped her body.

Yet, if someone had disposed of her body, they wouldn't have done it on the ranch unless they wanted to set up the Spades and Martins to get in trouble for the murder.

Then again, if someone had stepped foot onto the ranch, everyone would have had to have known. Plus, it didn't explain everything. There were so many facets to this, making it as intriguing as it was infuriating.

He frowned—they needed to start by confirming the most likely connections. "So, you think those were the shafts where the bear and Tammy might have gotten into the arsenic?"

"Oh, yeah, totally. Short of a bear eating loads of bait with ant poison…it seems like the likely choice. I mean, if there is a water source down there, the bear might have been drinking from it daily. Thus, why it would be losing weight and having all the health issues it was—all added to the fact it was getting up there in age."

"That doesn't explain Tammy being there, though."

"I already thought about that. If Tammy was trying to get onto the ranch, it would be damned hard to get in and out without being noticed. Best alternative would be these tunnels."

She had a point, but he was still struggling to make sense of everything. "Why would she want to be on the ranch, though?"

His stomach dropped as he thought about what Zoey had told him about the Fellinis trying to recreate Rockwood and the bounty Frank Fellini had out on them. With everything that had happened the last few days, he hadn't been able to focus much on that threat, but maybe he should've been. "Son of a…"

"What?" Amber asked.

"We—STEALTH—have a lot of enemies. Zoey told me there are some high-powered individuals who are on the hunt to take us down."

"And you think Tammy had something to do with that?"

AJ shrugged. "It's the only thing I can think of that

would make sense here—if she was working for them and trying to get information about us."

"But what does this have to do with Charlie?"

"Again, we are going to have to do some digging, but I'm going with Occam's razor here—the simplest answer is probably the right one. And there are a few things that motivate people better than anything else— love, hate and money." He put his cup in the sink, tipping out the rest of the coffee. "She loved me once, hates me now and had found herself ass-deep in debt."

"If she was in debt, I'm sure you're right. She was probably desperate to take care of Charlie. And if she hated you, it definitely makes sense why she wouldn't call and ask for help." There was a sadness in Amber's voice.

"The worst part of all of this, is that she had to have known that I would've supported them. All I can think is that she didn't trust me with Charlie." His thoughts moved to last night, and sharing his bed with Amber. Would she figure out that he wasn't a man worth being a father or husband, as well? He wouldn't blame her if she did. They hadn't known each other long enough for her to really hate him yet, but maybe that would come.

He couldn't go through that kind of heartbreak again, and he definitely couldn't risk losing his heart. Yet, he couldn't help but feel like it was too late to make different choices. He was in too deep with Amber.

Amber put her hand on his lower back and looked up at him. "I can see you are really upset, and I don't blame you. We are going to find Charlie. When we do, you're going to have a chance of being the father you want to be."

"But what if Tammy was right?" He felt his chest

tighten. "I mean, what if I'm not meant to be a father? What if I'm no good at it?"

Amber chuckled. "You do see the irony in this, don't you?"

He frowned, not following exactly what she was thinking. "What do you mean?"

"Here's a woman who was afraid of letting you be a father because of who you are and what you do, and yet she was the one who may well have been the biggest threat to your son. I'm sure she was being the best mom she could be, and doing what she had to for them to survive—and for that, she's commendable. Yet, she was putting him in situations that were probably questionable at best. I mean look, she left him somewhere to go on a hunt for you, and left you no way to find the boy."

"Maybe she didn't want me to find him. Or it could have been due to the cognitive impairment because of the arsenic. It's possible she just wasn't all there toward the end." He shrugged.

"AJ, it's also possible that we were initially right with assuming the marks on her hands were merely frostbite."

It was just so much easier to hope Tammy had been in an altered state when making her decisions. At least if that was the case, he wouldn't have to feel so bad about himself, and make assumptions about what she thought of him as a person. However, in the end, it didn't really matter what she had thought of him. What was done was done.

There was no point in revisiting the pain of the past.

He picked up his phone and texted Zoey, filling her in about their thoughts on Tammy and her motivations, and that he wanted to head down into the mine. He hated that all of this that was happening at the ranch was his doing. He was one hell of an ineffectual leader if he couldn't even keep his personal life from affecting his entire team.

Thinking about his being a father, if he did find Charlie—no, *when* he found Charlie—he would need to be the father that the boy deserved. And while his parents had been able to raise him and his siblings in this black ops world, it had definitely left a mark. Not only that, but this work had also cost his parents everything. He couldn't risk leaving the child an orphan just like his parents had left him and his siblings. Yet he knew of no other world.

Tammy was probably right—he would be a terrible father and she'd had every right to keep the boy from him. Maybe he was wrong even trying to find him. She wouldn't have left Charlie in a position where he would've been compromised, but any number of things could have changed in her life, since he'd last seen her, that would have resulted in her making this kind of decision. Clearly, things had.

His phone buzzed; Zoey had texted. He opened it up. It read: Be careful in the mine, but yeah, see what Tammy was into. Still waiting on video from Baker. Stay close.

He raised his phone for Amber to see. "We have our marching orders."

Amber nodded. Walking toward the door, he grabbed her jacket and helped her slip it on. He grabbed his keys, motioning toward his truck, then walked her to her door and helped her inside. It was strange, but before Zoey had texted, they had been so talkative with one another, but now… Nothing.

"Are you okay?" he asked. "I know this is a lot. I didn't mean to overwhelm you back there."

Amber blinked a few times like she was trying to shake off some kind of daze. "Nah, you didn't overwhelm me, but did I ever tell you *how* my brother died?"

He shook his head, but he had a sense that today was exceptionally difficult for her. She was such a courageous woman.

"I don't talk about it much, but the reason I became a game warden was because of him. William and I were best friends growing up. You know that two-kids syndrome, where the kids become besties out of necessity. We were both good students, and he was three years older than me, so when I had problems or issues, he would help me with my homework. We were each other's everything."

"Is that why you acted like you did when you found out my team had contacted your parents?" AJ was filled with guilt. Here he had been so wrapped up in his own life and drama that he never stopped to think that everything they were doing was affecting her in a personal way.

She nodded. "My parents will never get over his death. So, I try to bring nothing negative to their life. I want to be the easy child. I never want them to worry about me."

"I'm sorry, Amber," he said. He wasn't sure whether or not he should ask what had happened to her brother, but before he had the chance, she continued.

"When he left to go to college, he went to school in Bozeman. It wasn't far from where we grew up, but it definitely provided him with some much-needed independence. And one day he was out skiing, and it was a day a lot like today, and he ended up falling in a tree well. They didn't find him until two months later. There's nothing worse than not knowing what happened to a loved one. So, I understand how you're feeling."

"Why didn't you tell me this before?" he asked.

"You already had enough going on. It happened ten years ago. There's no going back and changing it. And when you're going through something like this, the last thing you need, especially when you're in the thick of it, is someone telling you about a death in their family. He was actually the one that was going to school to be a wildlife biologist. I followed in his footsteps, in his memory."

He wanted to be mad at her, for keeping this a secret from him. However, he could understand her line of thinking. "That's amazing that you did that for him and your family." He paused, thinking about his own crew. "You know, one of my biggest fears is to lose someone I love."

Her eyes welled with tears, but she rapidly blinked them away. "I can understand why you'd never want to experience anything like it. It has a way of ripping a family apart—it changes everything."

"That I can believe. The Martins lost a sister. They still talk about her—she died in the line of duty. I know they still struggle." He reached over, took her hand and gave it a kiss. "I know things will be hard sometimes. Yet, if we're going to be together, remember—no secrets. Okay?"

She gave him a simple smile. "I'll try. Just know that today, going into the places that may or may not have been where your ex died, it brings up a lot of weird stuff for me. I thought I'd be fine. And… I will be. Just be patient."

"I promise to always try and be patient. No matter what is going on."

He held her hand as Amber pointed him in the right direction of the mine-shaft entrance near the home-steader cabin. Before this week, he hadn't spent a great deal of time out in the woods on the property, but now that he was, he had to admit it was a beautiful place.

"According to my map," Amber said, pointing at her phone, "the mine shaft was located about fifty yards from the cabin." She stepped out of his pickup and started walking to the west of the cabin.

He followed behind her, just trying to catch up. She kicked away the snow on the ground as she moved around the area.

Not far from where he stood, there was an odd shape in the snow. It was probably nothing but he moved closer to check it out. Scratching away the snow, he discovered a large hole. It had to be the entrance to the mine shaft. "Amber," he called, "I found it."

He cleared away more of the snow, and she looked at him with an excited smile. "You did it." She threw her arms around his neck, like they had just found the answer to all their questions. And yet, as she held him, and he held her, he couldn't help but feel that their search had only just begun.

Chapter Nineteen

There was the sound of dripping water coming from deep inside the belly of the earth as they made their way down into the tunnels. Amber was behind him, but AJ doubted that she would let him take the lead for long.

The light on his phone reflected off the icy walls and mirrored down the shaft, making it less ominous than he would have expected. The shaft was about eight feet wide in most places, as though it had been constructed for a donkey loaded down with ore to pull a cart in and out of the mine. If he sat still long enough, he wondered if he could hear the echoes of the bygone era and the animals that made it all possible.

If they hadn't been down there looking for evidence of Charlie, he might have almost thought being in the mine was pretty damn cool. As kids, he and his brothers would have gone gangbusters in a place like this, playing army and shoot-'em-up games while giving their parents a reprieve from their constant mischief.

The thought made him smile. It also reminded him of Amber's brother and the loss that must have been so hard on her and her family. No wonder she hadn't wanted to talk about it, but now she definitely made a lot more sense to him. She wasn't independent because she wanted to be, she was that way out of necessity.

He'd seen what happened to families after a loss of a child. It was difficult for everyone, and parents found themselves guilt-ridden and lost. Parenting of other children either became the primary focus to the point of being overbearing and repressive, or, in their sadness, they lost sight of the remaining child or children.

Either way, Amber had been dealt a tough hand.

If he had his way, she would never find herself hurt like that again. He would do anything to keep her safe and protected.

She stepped beside him like she could tell that he was thinking about her and she slipped her hand into his.

He loved that she would just take what she needed from him, but he should have known that she would have liked to hold his hand. Giving her fingers a little squeeze, he asked, "Are you doing okay?"

She nodded. "Caves are definitely not my kind of thing. I prefer knowing there is sky over my head." She moved closer to him as they continued to walk. "Did you know that Montana has more than seven hundred earthquakes a year?" She glanced up at the earthen ceiling above them.

"It's going to be okay," he said, but as he did, he couldn't help but be reminded that these tunnels had caved in and not that long ago he had heard about a sinkhole in a school playground when a mine shaft gave way.

He tried to start walking faster, but gently, so to not draw any unnecessary alarm.

It would all be okay. The ground was frozen.

Then there was the sound of another drip.

He wasn't sure how the ground above them could be frozen and there was still water dripping, but it did nothing to comfort him.

After walking for another ten minutes or so, he was tempted to turn around. This place was admittedly dangerous, and they were already aware it was full of toxic chemicals. Add on the danger of being caved in on... Yeah, they needed to get out of here.

"AJ," Amber said, stopping. "Look."

There, on the ground at their feet, was a large tuft of griz hair. It was matted together with dried blood and as he crouched down to get a better look, he saw the hair had the roots still intact.

The floor of the cave was covered in dirt and gravel, and ahead of them a few feet was a rock, about the size of a man's fist, covered in blood and more bear hair.

"Do you think...?" He paused, looking up at Amber as the reality of the scene started to soak into his senses.

He stood up and took a long series of breaths.

Amber put her hand on his back. "AJ, it's okay. You're okay."

Nodding, he couldn't pull his gaze off the rock that was covered in blood. At least Tammy had fought back. She probably used the cobble to hit at the bear while it was attacking. His thoughts twisted to what her last moments must have been like, the bear coming at her, starved and half-mad in the underbelly of the earth. He couldn't imagine much more hellish of a scenario. There was no way she could have made it out of this alive. Their suspicions had been right—she was dead.

He caught himself wishing that she'd had a swift end, but looking at the rock, he knew that wasn't likely the case.

"Oh, baby," Amber said, reaching up and wiping away a tear that had slipped from him without him even being aware.

"Sorry, I swear I'm not the kind of guy who loses his crap like this…" He rubbed the base of his palm against his forehead as if he could strike the emotions from him. Yet, no amount of rubbing would erase the scene before them.

"AJ, it's okay. I know your relationship wasn't perfect with her, but you loved her. Seeing this has to be so hard for you." She leaned against him. "I'm just glad that I'm here to help you through this, but if I could, I would take this pain away and do this for you."

"But you hate caves," he said, trying to joke.

"Not going to lie, I hate them even more now, but that doesn't change the fact that there isn't a thing that I wouldn't do for you. You deserve to be loved and cared for, and I don't know if you are aware, but your pain is my pain. Seeing you hurt like this, hurts me."

Her words both warmed him and yanked at his heart. He stepped to face her and pulled her into his arms. "I hope you know I feel exactly the same way about you. We will get through this. It's hard and it hurts, but at least this way we know exactly what caused Tammy's death. I don't have to wonder anymore."

Amber hugged him tight, pressing her face against his chest.

Nothing with Amber was ever going to be very easy…except having feelings toward her. That was the easiest thing that had ever come to him in his life.

She stepped out of his arms and put her hand back in his. "Let's keep looking—maybe we can find the rest of Tammy's remains."

His stomach sank as he was pulled back to the reality of their situation. Yes, they needed to get out of this hell.

She moved the light of her phone back and forth as they pressed deeper into the cave. They walked slowly, passing by several bear tracks where the animal must have scratched at the dirt, or possibly where it had been running.

He couldn't imagine what Tammy had been doing down here. It was dark and foreboding, and apparently home to a top apex predator. It was hard telling what else could have been found here, and she had never been the kind he would have expected to just adventure into a place like this.

Hiking around a bend in the cave, they came to a large cavern. Flashing his light in the direction of the walls, he spotted a number of man-size metal cases. Amber shot him a look and they walked over toward them.

The one nearest him was latched closed. There wasn't any dust accumulated on the top. On the side of the boxes were a series of barcodes and labels. He leaned in and read what appeared to be a shipping label—addressed to Tammy Reynolds at the Red Lion hotel.

For a second, his mind went to a dark place. At times in the past, he'd heard of troops running into traps like these, and when they moved the box or opened them, they had been blown up. Had Tammy set up a bomb for him or his family?

No.

These are just boxes.

Under the ranch.

Where she was trespassing and possibly spying.

He tried to think of something else that was inside

the boxes, but his mind kept circling around the idea of this being a bomb.

He glanced around the cavern. On the other side of the cave were more boxes. They were of varying sizes, but most were so large that he wondered how she had gotten them down here. There was no way she could have carried them in. He hadn't seen a cart or any tire tracks, but looking around the room, there were several tunnels that ran into this room. It was possible this was the main hub within the mine.

Amber let go of his hand and walked across the cave, her footfalls making a crunching sound on the gravel and dirt. He turned back, thinking about the boxes. Taking a few steps, he noticed a brown purse sitting on the ground behind one of the smaller boxes.

He picked it up and sat it gingerly on top of the blue, metal box next to him. He zipped it open—inside was a wallet and cell phone.

He pulled out the wallet. Tucked inside of it was Tammy's driver's license and a number of different debit and credit cards.

The cell phone was off, but he pressed the button and it lit up, but as it started it died.

Jackpot.

Chapter Twenty

It took far less time to hike out of the mine than it had going in. Aside from the cell phone, AJ was careful to leave everything in its place for Baker, and had chosen not to open the metal boxes. It was one hell of a comfort to know that with what they had just found everyone would be cleared of any possible wrongdoing.

Well, except for Tammy, but her mistakes had cost her desperately.

Getting in the pickup, he took out his charger and plugged in Tammy's phone.

Amber stood outside the truck. Her cell had been buzzing from the moment they had stepped into the light. From the tight look on her features as she pressed her phone to her ear, she wasn't pleased.

She motioned at him that she would be a minute, then turned her back and walked out toward the timberline.

He texted Zoey about the phone. As usual, she was quick to answer and told him to bring it up to the office. AJ tried to give Amber her privacy, but as she paced, he wondered what was upsetting her.

Ten minutes later, Amber walked back and got into the pickup. There was a tired look in her eyes.

"Everything okay?" he asked.

"I don't want to talk about it." She stared out the window of the pickup. "I need to get back, though."

He nodded, putting the truck in gear and heading back toward the main house. He couldn't imagine what had just transpired, but his gut was telling him it had something to do with him.

He opened his mouth to speak several times, but each time her body tensed and he shut up.

Everything had been going so well between them, and now she was basically giving him the silent treatment. It didn't make sense, but maybe she was just working through something and trying to figure out a way to tell him about it.

He wasn't sure how to get her to talk, but when he was in one of those moods, or had a firestorm at work, sometimes he just had to work things through in his mind before he could talk to others.

Regardless, it was a long drive back.

Zoey stood outside the office when they pulled up to the house and she had a huge smile on her face as she waved.

He picked up Tammy's cell. The thing was girlie, complete with a flower-encrusted case with a rose gold phone inside. It said it was half-charged, but it would at least be enough to get it to turn on. Unplugging it, he got out of the pickup.

Before he could close the door, Amber turned toward him. "I need to run back to my cabin and grab my things."

"What's going on?" He leaned against the truck door.

Amber gave a tired sigh. "You don't need to worry about my stuff. Just go and take care of the phone."

He was burning to get the phone to Zoey, but he also didn't want to fail Amber.

"Go," she said, but there was a touch of annoyance in her tone.

"Okay," he said, not wanting to upset her further. "Are you leaving the ranch or coming back when you're done at the cabin?"

She chuffed. "I don't know yet, AJ. All I know is that if I don't do what I need to do, my job is going to be on the line."

"If you need me, I'll be right here." AJ pointed toward the house. "Go ahead and take my pickup down to the cabin if you want." He tossed her the keys.

She grabbed them. "Yeah, thanks. I'll leave it parked down there."

He stared at her, wanting to ask but not wanting to pry as she scooted over into the driver's seat. He closed the driver's door and gave her a quick wave. She drove off, not looking back.

He made his way to Zoey, and she was frowning. "What is going on there?"

He looked in the direction of the truck, afraid that if Zoey watched him, she would see how confused he was. "She said she needed to run down to the cabin."

Luckily, as he turned back to Zoey, she just shrugged and didn't seem concerned about what was or wasn't going on between him and Amber. "Do you have the phone?" she asked, extending her hand and motioning for him to hand it over.

He gave it to her. "It's half-charged, but the screen was working."

"Great. That will make this all a hell of a lot easier." She turned on the phone as they walked inside.

Going to her computer, she hooked it up and set to work on her keyboard.

"Did you call Baker?" he asked, watching as she typed away as she worked to unlock the phone.

She nodded. "He was definitely curious about what was in the boxes down there. And he said to make sure to tell you he was glad you didn't disturb the scene."

He dipped his head in acknowledgment. "I'm just glad we got some answers."

Zoey tapped on the phone. "Hopefully this will help us find out why she was on the property and maybe it can even lead us in the direction of Charlie."

Hope wasn't even the tip of the iceberg of how badly he wanted and needed those answers. "So, your tech teams haven't had any sightings of him?"

"Lots of possibilities and I've been working through them. The problem is that at two years old, there is a lot of the same-shaped faces. We get a lot of false hits. Slow work."

"What about Tammy's credit cards and all that?"

"Again, we are working on it, but so far we've not had any luck." Zoey looked over at him and pushed her blue hair out of her eyes. "You know there isn't a damned thing I will stop at when it comes to protecting kids."

He was filled with the strange sensation of gratitude, but also disappointment at the lack of progress.

Patience.

"Why don't you jump on that computer, there?" she said, pointing at a laptop on the corner of her desk. "It should be on the page you need."

He sat down in an extra rolling chair and pressed a key, and the screen turned on. He was met with the image of a chubby-faced, blond boy who was sucking his thumb as he looked up from his stroller. The photo was slightly grainy, like it had been taken from a distance. If this was the quality of the images they were working with as they looked for Charlie, what she had said made sense. This was an uphill battle.

As he tried to decide whether or not the boy was Charlie, he couldn't help but admit that he didn't really know the face he was looking for. Aside from the picture that Zoey had printed off for him, he had never actually seen his son. Though he had nearly memorized the almond-shaped blue eyes and his toothy smile, he wasn't completely sure he would be able to identify him.

The realization broke his heart.

He flipped through a series of pictures of children, picking each apart. Some were definitely not Charlie, but there were a few that he pinned to look at again. According to the information provided, one he wasn't sure of was located in Abilene, Texas, and the other was in Southampton, England.

It killed him that his child could have been anywhere in the world.

Zoey cleared her throat. "AJ, you need to come look at this."

He rolled over to her. She held up the home screen of Tammy's phone. She clicked on messages and pulled up a text from an unnamed number.

The text read: Ms. Reynolds, I need an update.

It was followed with another: Update, Ms. Reynolds.

Chills slipped down his spine as Zoey looked up at him.

"I ran the phone number," she said. "Of course, it came back as unknown, but I dug. It was going through a spoofing app—an app not frequently used, but downloaded to a phone located in Montana."

"Whose phone?" he asked.

Zoey shook her head. "I haven't gotten that far yet. Running it through the system now, may take a little bit. All I managed to pull was a digital signature on the device. I'm going to have to pull some strings to get the owner's info."

"Do you have any clue if this contract they are talking about is that bounty on STEALTH?" he asked.

"If I had to bet, I'd say it is." Zoey tapped on the keyboard. "Tammy had deleted all the other texts in the conversation, but I think I can probably get them back with a little more time and some elbow grease."

As she spoke, a text popped up on Tammy's phone: Charlie depends on you.

"I'm going to kill them," AJ said, not even waiting to think what it would take or who it was that had his boy. It didn't matter. He would find them, and when he did, he would have blood on his hands.

Chapter Twenty-One

Amber's phone rang again just as she was stuffing the last bits of her clothing into her go bag and zipping it up. She'd had enough of her lieutenant, and that was without this third phone call. Apparently, using governmental maps to find and access the privately held mines had been a breach of protocol—a policy she hadn't known and wasn't aware of, but had gotten her in trouble nonetheless.

She should have known that the mineral rights and the mining claim were not a part of the Widow Maker Ranch and the STEALTH complex, but it hadn't occurred to her—in their search for answers—that this kind of thing would have caused a problem. Rather, she had seen a need and fulfilled the need. Now it was her neck that would be taking the axe.

If only she hadn't clocked in to the computer for the day, they would have not had grounds for dismissal. She wasn't sure exactly how, or if they were going to fire her for trespassing on private property without consent for search or a search warrant, but this was far outside her normal working parameters. Still, she had definitely screwed up.

Her bosses had every right to be upset with her, but

since she had been a game warden, it was the first major screwup on her record. In fact, normally she went above and beyond the call of duty.

And here she had been thinking that she would be getting an "atta girl" for her work on the bear and discovering the truth of the attack and Tammy's resulting death.

She picked up the phone, telling herself to stay strong as she answered. "Hello, Lieutenant King. I'm just heading out now. I'll be at your office within an hour or so."

"It's fine, Sergeant Daniels. You don't need to come down to the regional offices. We have decided to put you on administrative leave, pending a thorough investigation by the regulatory board. As you know, Daniels, this is going to be a tough one to make it out of. If I were you, I'd be brushing up on my résumé. In the meantime, you need to return all state-issued gear within the next day or two."

She swallowed back the lump that had started to form in her throat. "Sir, I'm sorry for any perceived mistakes or breaching protocol. It was not my intention."

"Stop right there, Daniels. Ignorance is not a defense."

"What does it hurt that we were inside the mine?" she countered, not waiting for him to continue his tirade.

There was a pause on the other end of the line. "The mine owners have ties that run deep. They made a call and the higher-ups had to do what they felt was required. Rest assured that thanks to you, others' heads are going to roll. If anything criminal comes from what you found, you may have very well just caused us a lot of headaches."

Of course, that's what they're worried about—legal headaches...

Her stomach ached with guilt and embarrassment. Not only was this misstep going to cost her the job that meant so much to her, but she was also going to have to tell the STEALTH team what had transpired. Her guilt and mistakes were going to be public knowledge on a grand scale.

That was all to say nothing about the effect it would play on her private life. AJ would be supportive, but it would affect everything between them. In fact, if it wasn't for him and the blinding effects her feelings for him had on her, she wouldn't have found herself in this position.

Though logically she was aware that she shouldn't, and couldn't, really be upset with him for her stepping into the wrong, she found she was still angry with him. He had to have known that his family didn't retain the mineral rights to the area, and therefore they couldn't legally access the mine shafts beneath. If he didn't, there had been enough time for him to check in with Zoey to see if there would be any conflict.

"Amber?" her boss asked, sounding as though he had been waiting for an answer to a question she hadn't heard.

"What was that?" she asked, anger lashing within her like a loose live wire.

"I will be awaiting the return of your things to the headquarters no later than five tomorrow evening. Does that work for you?"

No. It didn't work for her. None of this worked for her, but she didn't have a real choice.

"Fine." She cleared her throat. "Please set aside some

time for me tomorrow morning. I'm going to need to speak to you in private regarding all of this."

There was a pause; he probably wanted to tell her there was no use. That he wasn't the one pulling the strings on this, but he remained quiet. Finally, he said, "I really do appreciate all that you do, Amber. If it was up to me, we would be sweeping this under the rug. Your heart was in the right place and good things came from your work. Unfortunately, this is coming from the top down."

As hard as she had worked in this job and regardless of all the advancements she had made and animals and people she had helped, it disgusted her that when push came to shove, all that mattered was politics. Right there was the problem with every governmental job. There was no real loyalty—there couldn't be, because everyone was just a cog in a machine that would limp along with or without a person.

"Yep, got it. I'll see you tomorrow," she said, hanging up her phone. Though she knew she was mishandling this, she couldn't help the rage and bitterness that filled her.

She would be the first to admit she had screwed up, but in doing what she had done, she had only helped... and stepped on toes. Even though everyone close to this understood and would have probably done the same damn thing, in the end, it wouldn't really matter. She was fired.

She grabbed her go bag, then went outside and threw it in the back seat of the pickup. She was going to have to run back to her place and take out everything that belonged to her before she left for headquarters tomorrow. On top of that, she wasn't even sure how she would get home after she returned the rig. She could ask AJ, but at the thought the live wire within her sparked.

No, he had gotten her into this mess.

That left her with asking her mother.

Great.

She would have to tell them what happened, if that was the case. There was no way she would want to go into detail about her life. They would make a huge deal about what had happened and want to know everything—and she wasn't sure that she wanted to tell them about AJ.

If she did, first, she would have to get over being pissed at him for this, but on top of that it would also imply a depth in their relationship that she had started to feel, but she wasn't sure he reciprocated.

She should have never been so quick to trust him. Getting close to AJ had been against her better judgment, but she had allowed her heart to lead. She was definitely a fool when it came to men, and this was one man who was damn good at making her feel like the most special woman in the world.

She stepped on the gas pedal, a little too hard for what the conditions allowed, and the back end of the pickup fishtailed as she roared out of her parking spot and got onto the main ranch road.

She was tempted to keep going and roar out of this ranch and never look back, as she thought about the mine. There were too many questions for her to just ignore them, and she parked in front of the main office. She had to talk to Zoey.

She got out of the truck, and tapped on the door of the office. She was met with the sound of AJ's voice. "Yeah, we're here."

His voice made her stomach clench and she was tempted to turn around, but she wasn't one to run when things got tough.

She opened the door and made her way inside. Zoey was sitting behind her computer, typing away. She barely looked up as Amber came inside.

AJ's face erupted into a wide, genuine smile, but as quickly as it showed up, it disappeared and was replaced by a deep look of pain. It hit her that they had no idea what had just happened in her life, and as angry and hurt as she was, she wanted to lash out and tell them everything.

She glanced at the laptop that was open next to her. On the screen was the picture of a little boy who looked similar to the picture she had seen of Charlie. She could tell that she had missed something in their search for the boy.

"What happened to him?" she asked, staring at the pained expression on AJ's face.

As mad and confused by everything as she was, she couldn't stop herself from worrying about him.

"Charlie is with the people who put out the bounty on us," AJ said, his voice cracking. "They are going to kill him. They think Tammy reneged on her deal with them."

The blood rushed from her face and her body turned cold. They couldn't hurt the baby. Charlie was innocent. They had to get him to safety, now. "What was the deal?"

"That, we don't quite know." Zoey turned to face her. "I'm working on trying to dig up all of Tammy's deleted messages to find out, but it's possible I won't be able to find them. The person she was talking to was using an app called TextZap. It is a spoofing app. Once things are gone, I'm thinking they are gone, unless I can hack into the provider's network and pull up the last thirty days of information. Even then, we may not get what we need."

"Have you tried texting the people back?"

Zoey grumbled, sounding annoyed. "I considered it, but only as a last resort."

"Just do it." Amber smiled as she felt some of her anger toward them dissipate. "Here, hand me the phone."

Zoey disconnected the device from her computer and handed it over. "What are you going to say?"

"I'm going to ask them when and where they want to meet for the handoff."

"Handoff of what?" AJ asked.

Amber shrugged. "I have no idea, but they clearly are waiting on something and they still think Tammy is alive. For the moment, we need to take advantage of their ignorance. At the very least, we have a chance to know where Charlie will be and when we can find him."

"A lot of things can go wrong with that plan," Zoey countered.

"Yeah," Amber conceded, "but it's better than inaction."

AJ nodded. "Damn, do I know that. It's gonna be a hell of a lot easier to pivot while moving than while rooted."

Amber smiled over at him, thankful that he seemed on her side with this, though she hadn't really expected him to be any other way—not when it came to Charlie. If they didn't get their hands on Charlie, all they had been working for, all they had done and all the sacrifices they had made would be in vain.

If they got Charlie, at least she would have lost her job for a reason.

She tapped on the phone's screen, sending off the text.

Her heart was pounding as she looked up at AJ and Zoey. "Now we wait."

Zoey sighed, but Amber couldn't decide if it was out of anger or just her being resigned to the fact that their moves were limited.

She put down the phone on the desk next to her.

Zoey took the phone and tapped on the screen, reading the text. She seemed satisfied by the simple words: I'm ready. Where and when?

They didn't have to wait long. The phone buzzed with a reply: One hour.

A second text hit the phone—a GPS coordinate.

Though things were still in the air, and there was a chance everything could go wrong, they were a step closer to saving a life and Amber couldn't help but feel a little excitement. However, it was met with resistance as she thought about what had just happened back at the cabin.

"Zoey," she asked, not sure how she would breach the subject with them without actually letting what happened to her career slip.

"Yeah?" Zoey was punching in the GPS coordinates as they spoke.

"Does your family own the mineral rights to the ranch?" Amber asked, trying not to give it any sort of inflection that would raise an eyebrow.

It didn't work.

As she glanced over at AJ, he was studying her. "Why would you ask that?"

She shrugged, thinking about the moment when he had made her promise that she wouldn't keep any secrets from him. "I was just wondering."

He looked perturbed, like he knew she was trying to avoid any kind of real answer, and she was forced to look away.

"Zoey?" she asked, hoping to relieve some of the pressure.

"I think we do, but I'd have to look."

She nibbled at her bottom lip as she considered what to say. "I think you guys may have a problem. From what I've managed to learn in the last little bit, there is another company that owns the mining and mineral rights to the mine that sits partially under this ranch."

"What?" Zoey stopped typing and looked up at her. "That's not possible."

"If you look up mining claims, we could figure it out in a matter of minutes. The mine was once called the J-Bar-P claim." She walked over to Zoey's computer as she turned to face the screen.

Zoey tapped away, pulling up mining claims and plat maps within a matter of minutes.

AJ stepped beside her, putting his hand on her shoulder. She loved the feeling of his touch, even if there were so many mixed emotions that came with being so close to him.

"Are you freaking kidding me?" Zoey said, slapping the desk hard with her hand. "How did you find out?" She glared over at her. "How did they get away with this?" She jabbed a finger at the screen.

"Who owns it?" AJ asked, leaning in toward the

screen trying to make sense of what Zoey was raging over.

"J-Bar-P is in a holding company, but there are direct ties—albeit, not legally binding ones—to the Fellini family." Zoey spat out the name. "I knew they probably knew where we were located by now, but this is complete and utter nonsense."

Zoey closed her eyes and ran her hands over her face. "We need to get off this ranch. If that mine belongs to the Fellinis, then we are in incredible danger."

Chapter Twenty-Two

AJ's stomach hurt. He had been conditioned to withstand incredible amounts of pressure and still be suited to lead, but that was before the ranch was in danger and his son's life was on the line.

Everything had just become so real…and they had just had the rug pulled out from under their feet.

Their location had been exposed and there was a bounty on their heads. There was no way they could come back to this ranch in Montana. The bastards had taken his home, his freedom and his child.

They would pay…and he would give his last breath to get his boy to safety.

It had been hard grabbing all of his things and hitting the road as soon as they had learned that Fellini had gained access to them. Zoey had taken a sledge to the computer's hard drives, making sure to leave nothing behind when their enemies descended…and they would most certainly descend.

Baker was standing beside Amber and they were talking as he glanced over at the detective's Suburban. Baker had been unusually stoic when they had told him about everything. Yet, the detective had made sure to make it clear that they were welcome to pool resources and improvise as required, in order to get Charlie.

Troy and Mike were standing with a few of their contractors. They were wearing snow-based camo and waiting for orders from him, but before he could take action, he had to take care of a few last-minute things. They were definitely down to crunch time and if they didn't move into their positions quickly, their trap would fail.

Baker's phone rang and the man answered. Amber excused herself and made her way over to him and Zoey. "What did Baker have to say?"

Amber pinched her lips. "He has unmarked police cars in both directions coming and going from this road. A mile out from the meeting point, they have guys with Stop Sticks ready to deploy, if necessary."

"Good," AJ said, turning to Mike and giving him a nod.

Mike tipped his head and turned back to his men. They were going to take the high points, readying their rifles from a variety of points in the event a firefight broke out.

"Baker also recommended that I put on some clothes he brought. They found some of Tammy's things in the hotel room, and he thinks I can pull off her look. It might give us a few more minutes to exchange Charlie."

Goddamn, AJ loved when things started to come together in a way that was advantageous to his team and their goals.

"Great." AJ smiled.

Zoey was working on her phone. She hadn't smiled since the moment their cover had been blown, but he could understand why.

"Did you find anything?" he asked.

Zoey shook her head. "No, but I have arranged for travel for us as soon as we can hit the runway." She glanced at Amber and then to AJ, silently questioning whether or not Amber should be coming along.

He didn't know what to say or how to react, so instead he pretended not to have seen the silent gesture. Amber wasn't looking at them; instead, she was turned toward Baker, who was stepping out of his truck.

He wanted to bring Amber to wherever they were going to end up once this handoff with Charlie was over and they had to be on the move to escape the Fellini threat, but it seemed wrong to ask her to run away with him. Besides, she had her own job and her own life to take into consideration.

No matter what had happened between them, she would never want to give up everything for him—including her brother's legacy and a world she had built for her family. And he couldn't ask that of her. He cared about her too much.

Baker sauntered toward them carrying a gym bag. "Here you go." He handed Amber the bag. Taking it, she headed toward the bushes to change and Baker turned to him. "So, my bomb team just called. They have been working down in that mine. Those boxes you found… looks like they are full of C-4 explosives. Whoever they belong to better be ready for federal prison."

"Holy crap," Zoey said, finally looking up from her phone.

"You can say that again," Baker said, nodding. "You guys are damned lucky Amber uncovered this place. Though, it sounds like her job is a goner."

"What?" AJ coughed out. "What are you talking

about?" He looked in the direction in which Amber had disappeared.

"Yeah, the higher-ups are pretty upset with her. Apparently, she didn't get the appropriate warrants. Your girl is going to be out." Baker paused. "I asked her for her help on this case and she did uncover one hell of a massive bomb and saved a helluva lot of lives. In an attempt to help, I made some calls to help her out, but minds are made up."

Why hadn't she told him that she'd been fired? Had that been why she had been acting off ever since she had run down to her cabin?

She didn't have to be embarrassed about losing her job, or anything else.

"She deserves a damned award, not to get canned," AJ growled. "We were sitting ducks down there and we didn't have a clue. We owe her our lives."

"I can't argue any different. I think it's a load of bull-pucky, too." Baker sighed.

Zoey didn't look back up from her phone and her fingers were nearly a blur as she typed. "Don't worry, I'm on it now. Let's just say that her bosses are going to get the ass-chewing of a lifetime from ranks and people they didn't even know existed. They won't walk right for weeks."

AJ was equally relieved and oddly sad. For a half second, he and Amber had the chance to make things work. It was selfish of him to even imagine, but if she didn't have a job, she could join their team and hit the road with them. She was so goal-oriented and dedicated to her work that she would be a tremendous asset when it came to operating the company.

Baker's phone buzzed. He tapped on the screen.

"Looks like my spotters just located Fellini. He is driving a white Silverado north. They are thinking he will be at the meeting point in ten minutes. You guys need to get into position."

Amber came walking out of the bushes. He did a double take at her wearing Tammy's tight blue jeans and a button-up white collared shirt with turquoise buttons and a heavy wool jacket. She had a cowboy hat on and her hair was down. She looked entirely too much like the Tammy he had known, the one who could dress up for a honky-tonk on Saturday night and wear the same clothes to work on Monday.

Though, if truth be told, Amber did a hell of a lot better filling out every curve of those jeans. His mouth watered just looking at her.

She was pulling at the collar of the shirt as she made her way over to them. "Well, everything fit, but this coat is tight as hell." She looked over at him and gave a little laugh.

"Tight can be a good thing. It looks good on you," he teased.

Zoey turned and started walking back toward her ranch pickup.

"Are you okay with staying back?" Amber lifted the bottom of the white shirt so he could see that she was carrying a gun. "I won't be going in there unarmed."

"I'm not worried about how you will carry yourself if this all hits the fan. I'm just hoping that we can get you and Charlie out of there without an incident."

Amber pursed her lips as she looked at him. "We both know things aren't going to go well here. I don't have anything that they are hoping to get—I don't know what update they were after."

"I'm sure it had to do with the massive bomb that they had Tammy plant under the ranch."

Amber's eyes widened. "The what?"

"Oh, you heard me. Those boxes we found were full of explosives." He let out a stressed little chuckle. "I'm glad I didn't go ahead and open them while we were down there. Who knew finding a woman's purse would be the one thing that probably saved our lives? Well... that, and you. Baker told us you got fired."

"Not fired," she said, her cheeks turning red as she wiggled her finger. "I was put on administrative leave. Totally different."

He smiled. "Well, regardless... I know what you did for me...for *my family*," he said, barely managing to get the words out. The realization of all she'd done for him—what she was still doing—threatened to overwhelm him.

She squeezed his hand gently. "I know how much they mean to you. And now, I expect to do everything I can to bring your son safely into your arms as well." He knew she meant it, and it made her that much more special to him. "If I lose my job because of what I've chosen to do, then so be it. At least I left on my own terms and all while being a good person." She was a good person...and he loved her for it. The truth of that hit him as she continued, "If the government or the lawmakers don't like it, well... I will deal with that when the time comes—"

Without thinking, he pulled her into his arms and kissed her lips, knocking off her hat.

He didn't care.

Their lips melded hard and hungry against each other, no more reservations or withholding. He was hers. "Amber," he said, pressing his forehead against hers, "I love you. I can't tell you enough."

"I love you, too. No matter what happens out here today, know that I am doing this on my own accord. I want to do the right thing. I couldn't save my brother, I couldn't fix my family, but I can stop yours from being destroyed." She kissed his lips gently. "And when this is all over, I want to stay with you."

He put his hands on her face and looked deeply into her eyes. They were full of love, love he was sure was mirrored by his own. "You absolutely will, Amber. You will be my wife."

Chapter Twenty-Three

Five minutes later, Amber was standing at the meeting point. She'd driven Tammy's Pathfinder to the hand-off, watching the little spinning picture of sunsets that hung from the rearview mirror nearly the whole time. Tammy had loved her son, there was no denying that, but she couldn't understand how the woman had gotten herself into such a bad position.

She pulled down the cowboy hat low on her forehead, slipping on a pair of sunglasses for just a little extra disguise. Amber doubted that Luca Fellini would be foolish enough not to recognize the fraud she was, but her safety wasn't what was paramount.

Besides, if things went wrong, she had the comfort of knowing that at any one time, there were at least four guns pointed directly at their enemy's center mass. One false move and the bastard would be going down.

He definitely deserved it. Anyone who wanted to hurt a child deserved the most painful of deaths.

A white Silverado pulled up across the parking area off the little trailhead in the middle of the woods. The truck's engine echoed in the stillness of the snowy trees and mountains around her.

Her heart thrashed in her chest and the world seemed

to slow to the point that out of the corner of her eye she watched a single snowflake spin and drift down to the ground. It was a strange thing that happened to the human mind when facing incredible stress.

She was one decision and one misstep from death, yet she wasn't afraid, was only at attention.

A dark-haired man stepped out of the pickup, a man she recognized from the pictures AJ had shown her as Luca Fellini. He was wearing a large coat that was still crisp and bright black, like it had just come off the rack of one of the sporting-goods stores in the city.

"Ms. Reynolds?" the man asked, his words rolling from him with an Italian accent.

"Where's Charlie?" she asked, trying to keep from speaking any more than necessary.

Luca smiled, his actions so far off from what she expected that she wanted to smack the look off his face. Then she remembered who she was supposed to be and whom Tammy had been working for.

"He did very well. Loves his pasta and gravy." Luca walked to the door behind the driver's seat and opened it. "Don't worry about his dirty face, he's been eating on the way to see his mama." The way he said the word tore at her heart.

This boy's mother had died. In a moment, the boy would know that she was a fraud. There would be no faking it for much longer.

There were the sounds of Luca unclipping Charlie's car seat. The little boy was talking and giggling in a language she recognized was English, but she couldn't make out the words. Her heart pounded in her chest.

He lifted the boy out, holding him so that Charlie faced away as he walked toward her. The little one turned and peeked a glance back at her before burying his face in Luca's neck. It made her wonder how long it had been since Charlie had been with his mother, that instead of holding out his arms to her, he would be shy. Or did the toddler know already that she wasn't his mother?

"Did you do as I asked?" Luca patted Charlie's back like he was the boy's father.

Amber nodded.

He stared at her for a long moment, studying her and not moving any closer. "So, you armed the bomb?" he asked. "You followed my instructions to the letter, I hope?"

She nodded.

"What did the wire harnesses look like?" he asked, but his body language was closed off and he started to turn his feet away from her, like he was thinking about running.

She could tell her game was coming to an end. "Give me Charlie." She stuck out her hands.

The boy snuggled in tighter to Luca.

"I'm not giving this boy to a stranger. There's no way." Luca turned around and started toward his truck.

"Wait, stop!" she called after him, running around him to get to the pickup before the man could disappear with Charlie.

She pressed her back against the truck. "You won't leave here with that boy."

Luca laughed at her, and for the first time since she'd met him, he sounded malicious. "You can go to hell. Whoever you are."

She reached under her shirt and drew her Glock. She put it down by her side, just showing him she meant business without endangering the baby. "I'm Amber Daniels, I work with STEALTH, the group you hired Tammy to destroy."

"Is that what you think was going on here?" Luca's gaze dropped to her gun. "You thought I wanted to kill you and your friends, Ms. Daniels?"

She didn't quite know how to respond. "All I know is that I'm going to need to take Charlie to his father. I don't want anyone to get hurt. Not you, not me and not that baby," she said, motioning toward Charlie. "As it is, right now there are people all over in these woods who would be happy to pull the trigger and end whatever pathetic life you think you have."

"Ms. Daniels, I can see how you would make such assumptions…if you were not aware of the deal Ms. Reynolds and I had made." Luca motioned to her gun. "If you were aware, you wouldn't have that gun. Instead, you would be thanking me. I'm saving you and your friends' lives, not taking them. I've already had more than my fill of blood and guts in the name of my father."

"What does this have to do with your father?"

"Fathers have a way of forcing a son's hand, but it is up to the son to choose the direction." Luca smiled as Charlie wiggled in his arms. "My father is not a good man. He killed my fiancée, an operative with the CIA, when he found out I had fallen in love. As a result, I promised myself I would take away his greatest love— the hate he held for the STEALTH organization. Your group has been his greatest passion for several years."

"By bombing us?" she countered.

"I had no intention of killing you. If I had wanted to, I could have merely told my father about your location and this would have been taken care of long ago.

As it was, I was going to wait until things were ready and then have Tammy go to her former lover. He would have been given a choice—a choice I know AJ would have taken. Now, I hope he still will."

"AJ will never let you blow up the ranch."

"Tammy and I knew there would be no easy way of talking your teams into giving up this life—we had to act a bit, we had to convince you this was the best way to move forward." There was almost a pleading tone in his voice, or perhaps it was an air of pain. "Think about it—we could stage your deaths. In essence, I was giving you all a card to start over. You can stay in the business and change your identity or you can all go your separate ways."

She felt a lump rise in her throat as she thought about AJ being free from the burden of his position. Yet, it was everything to him. AJ *was* STEALTH.

"Why did you kidnap Charlie?"

"I did no such thing," he said, aghast. "Ms. Reynolds had me watch the boy."

"This doesn't add up. How, if you weren't forcing her, did Tammy—Ms. Reynolds—come to work for you?"

"She knew the bounty that was out on the Spades' and STEALTH's heads. You may not believe this, but she still loves AJ. They weren't meant for each other, but she felt bad for not telling him about Charlie. I think she was using this good deed as a way to clear herself of any guilt about keeping the boy away. She didn't want Charlie taking up the family business… In fact, I think making sure the whole thing goes up in smoke is like her way of ensuring that her boy gets a future of his own."

Amber didn't know what to believe, or what to do. Yet, from the way Luca spoke and his body language, she didn't believe that he was lying. This was a man on a mission, a man who wanted to protect the boy who was in his arms.

"You sent a text about Charlie—you said his life depended on this meeting. You can't tell me—"

Luca shook his head. "I know you find this hard to believe, but you are seeing this all out of context. Charlie's life is in danger, but not from me. Rather, my father will stop at nothing to bring your team to their knees. If he found out about AJ's son, he would most definitely go after the boy. While we were quietly readying everything, there was no safer spot for Charlie in the world than with me. The last place my father would ever think to look."

Amber's head was spinning with all this. But she raised her hand up into the air, signaling to her teams.

"What are you doing?" Luca asked.

"I'm letting my team know that they aren't to shoot. Don't give me a reason to change my mind."

Luca smiled. "I'm glad I've convinced you."

"All you've done for now is convinced me that you have useful information and aren't worth killing...*yet*." Amber put the gun back into its holster, satisfied that she was no longer in danger. She gave the safe signal to the teams. "Give me Charlie and it will prove to me that you are telling me the truth."

Luca gave the boy a kiss to the top of his head, whispering something in Italian in the little boy's ear. "It's okay, Charlie." He lifted the boy from his hip and sat him down on the ground, taking him by the hand.

They walked toward her and he placed the little boy's winter-chilled fingers in her hand.

The boy looked up at her and sent her a toothy smile.

These Spade boys had one hell of a way of making a girl fall in love at first sight.

Epilogue

AJ sat on the beach, reading the article on his phone about a mysterious explosion at a ranch in Montana. Thirty people had been killed and it was rumored that they were an antigovernment group of some sort.

The public outcry, thanks to their little lie, had been minimal. No one cared about outliers and extremists, unless they were in their faces. As it was, the ranch had been made ready for winter and cloaked for satellites.

According to Zoey, the uppity ups in the government were happy to play along with their ruse. Everything had gone surprisingly well thanks to Luca's plan. It had taken quite a bit of convincing on his part to prove his intentions were legitimate and, though his methods were unique, in the end even Zoey had come around to his line of thinking and had helped plan their out.

It was amazing what a person could do with a little technology and all the right friends. Blowing up a back corner of the ranch had been hard, but necessary to signal to their enemies that they were gone. Making them all virtually disappear had taken slightly more work—faking death certificates and recreating identities—but it had all been worth it in the end. Each and every one of the Spades and Martins and their families were free.

It was a hell of a feeling to not be on hit lists around the globe.

He glanced down the beach, where Zoey and her husband, Eli, were on boogie boards with their oldest child. Even from here, AJ could make out the bump of the baby that was now growing in her belly.

His thoughts moved to Tammy. He had missed so much with her, not seeing this stage of her pregnancy with Charlie, or even being there for his first steps. Thankfully, he and Amber—now officially retired, thanks to Kendra's very fine legal and negotiation skills—were making it up in true Spade fashion by showing the boy everything the world had to offer.

Admittedly, part of his desire to spoil his son was out of the guilt he would forever feel for Tammy's sacrifice. Though he would never agree with what she had done or be okay with her concealing the baby from him, in the end she had gotten what she had most wanted for their son—a stable home, one out of the line of fire and far from the world of black ops.

Tammy's autopsy had been taxing, due to the state of her remains, but the pathologists had reported that they hadn't found any arsenic in the tissues of her hand or other remains. The news had come as somewhat of a relief as he was glad she had been saved the ravages of poisoning—a poison had still played a role, though tangentially, in her death.

Her funeral had been brief, but respectful. It had been a beautiful service, and Charlie had played on the grass near the area where she had been laid to rest. Luca, as well as everyone from the Spade and Martin families, had shown up to pay their respects.

In a way, it hadn't felt like a funeral for only Tammy; rather, it felt like a dirge marking the ending of an era.

He took a long drink of his beer and let the sun soak into his skin as he stared out at the sparkling water.

"You okay?" Amber asked from beside him on the beach.

He smiled over at her. "Absolutely," he said, taking her hand in his and smiling brightly.

"Retirement is agreeing with you, baby. I don't think I've ever seen you look so relaxed." She brushed a bit of sand from her leg as she smiled.

"It's a tough gig when the hardest choices I have to make in a day are how we're going to keep Charlie busy, what we are going to have for dinner and then how I'm going to make love to you at night." He lifted her hand and gave it a quick kiss, then sent her a devilish smile.

Amber giggled. "Well, I can't wait to see what you have in store for me tonight."

Charlie stood up with his little yellow plastic shovel and toddled over to them from the mound of sand he had created on the beach. "Look what I built," he said, his words still that muddled sound of a toddler.

Amber smiled over at him. "What is it, buddy?"

"It's a dragon, Mama," Charlie said, standing up and putting his arms out. He zoomed around flapping his arms like they were giant wings, completely unaware of what he had done to his father and Amber.

AJ looked over at her. Amber's eyes were wide with excitement and there were tears starting to form. "He's never called you that before, has he?"

She shook her head. "You heard it, too?"

He leaned over and kissed her gently, brushing a hair

off her tanned face. He turned the diamond engagement ring on her finger. "I guess it's official."

"What is, honey?" she asked, looking into his eyes and smiling brightly.

AJ gave her one more kiss to her forehead. "We have Charlie's blessing. We are a family—now and forever."

* * * * *

COMING SOON!

We really hope you enjoyed reading this book. If you're looking for more romance, be sure to head to the shops when new books are available on

Thursday 13th October

To see which titles are coming soon, please visit
millsandboon.co.uk/nextmonth

MILLS & BOON

MILLS & BOON

THE HEART OF ROMANCE

A ROMANCE FOR EVERY READER

MODERN

Prepare to be swept off your feet by sophisticated, sexy and seductive heroes, in some of the world's most glamourous and romantic locations, where power and passion collide.

HISTORICAL

Escape with historical heroes from time gone by. Whether your passion is for wicked Regency Rakes, muscled Vikings or rugged Highlanders, awaken the romance of the past.

MEDICAL

Set your pulse racing with dedicated, delectable doctors in the high-pressure world of medicine, where emotions run high and passion, comfort and love are the best medicine.

True Love

Celebrate true love with tender stories of heartfelt romance, from the rush of falling in love to the joy a new baby can bring, and a focus on the emotional heart of a relationship.

Desire

Indulge in secrets and scandal, intense drama and plenty of sizzling hot action with powerful and passionate heroes who have it all: wealth, status, good looks…everything but the right woman.

HEROES

Experience all the excitement of a gripping thriller, with an intense romance at its heart. Resourceful, true-to-life women and strong, fearless men face danger and desire - a killer combination!

To see which titles are coming soon, please visit

millsandboon.co.uk/nextmonth

LET'S TALK
Romance

For exclusive extracts, competitions
and special offers, find us online:

- facebook.com/millsandboon
- @MillsandBoon
- @MillsandBoonUK

Get in touch on 01413 063232

For all the latest titles coming soon, visit
millsandboon.co.uk/nextmonth

MILLS & BOON
A ROMANCE FOR EVERY READER

- **FREE** delivery direct to your door

- **EXCLUSIVE** offers every month

- **SAVE** up to 25% on pre-paid subscriptions

SUBSCRIBE AND SAVE

millsandboon.co.uk/Subscribe

WANT EVEN MORE

ROMANCE?

SUBSCRIBE AND SAVE TODAY!

'Mills & Boon books, the perfect way to escape for an hour or so.'

MISS W. DYER

'Excellent service, promptly delivered and very good subscription choices.'

MISS A. PEARSON

'You get fantastic special offers and the chance to get books before they hit the shops.'

MRS V. HALL

Visit millsandboon.co.uk/Subscribe and save on brand new books.

JOIN THE
MILLS & BOON
BOOKCLUB

* **FREE** delivery direct to your door

* **EXCLUSIVE** offers every month

* **EXCITING** rewards programme

50% OFF
YOUR FIRST
PARCEL

Join today at
Millsandboon.co.uk/Bookclub

JOIN US ON SOCIAL MEDIA!

Stay up to date with our latest releases, author news and gossip, special offers and discounts, and all the behind-the-scenes action from Mills & Boon...

 @millsandboon

 @millsandboonuk

 facebook.com/millsandboon

 @millsandboonuk

It might just be true love...

GET YOUR ROMANCE FIX!

Get the latest romance news, exclusive author interviews, story extracts and much more!

blog.millsandboon.co.uk

MILLS & BOON
Desire

Indulge in secrets and scandal, intense drama and plenty of sizzling hot action with powerful and passionate heroes who have it all: wealth, status, good looks…everything but the right woman.

Four Desire stories published every month, find them all at:

millsandboon.co.uk

MILLS & BOON

MODERN

Power and Passion

Prepare to be swept off your feet by sophisticated, sexy and seductive heroes, in some of the world's most glamourous and romantic locations, where power and passion collide.

ght Modern stories published every month, find them all at:

millsandboon.co.uk/Modern

MILLS & BOON
MEDICAL
Pulse-Racing Passion

Set your pulse racing with dedicated, delectable doctors in the high-pressure world of medicine, where emotions run high and passion, comfort and love are the best medicine.

Eight Medical stories published every month, find them all at

millsandboon.co.uk

MILLS & BOON
True Love
Romance from the Heart

Celebrate true love with tender stories of heartfelt romance, from the rush of falling in love to the joy a new baby can bring, and a focus on the emotional heart of a relationship.

Four True Love stories published every month, find them all at:

millsandboon.co.uk/TrueLove